CRASH
A Novel

Patrick C. Marks

Markarian Publishing / Snowfall Press
Phoenix, AZ

Crash
A Novel
Copyright © 2018 / 2020 by Patrick C. Marks

All Rights Reserved

Cover art by Ron Zeilinger: Painting by Mark "Pappy" Monroe

Printed in the United States of America

Special Thanks

Special thanks to Ron Zeilinger for cover design and artwork. Thanks to Mark "Pappy" Monroe for the cover art oil painting. Thank you to my editor, Jody MacArthur and the team at Snowfall Press. Thank you, Joy Gallagher, for revision reading and Dale Phillips for formatting and many helpful suggestions. Special thanks to Josiah Marks for helping me get over a particularly nasty bout with "writer's block."

Dedication:
To my wife Melissa Marks
and to my children:
Patrick "Josiah", James, Jillian, Nathan and Emily

Who each have given me more
Than I can ever give back

Other Books by Patrick C. Marks

Nonfiction:
Someone's Making a Monkey Out of You
Understanding Evolution and Creation

Fiction:
Legend (A Novel)

One

This is bad...and I swear it isn't my fault - no matter what Misty thinks! I was just getting on my feet - that's all! I didn't trip anybody. Even Misty should know I have to get on my feet every fifteen minutes or so.

She *should* know that...right?

I mean, if I don't stand up every so often I won't be able to feel my toes for half an hour because of my back brace – so how is it my fault if the flight attendant is a twelve-fingered klutz? I was just standing behind her in the aisle. I didn't trip her. She goes and dumps a cup of coffee onto Misty's bodyguard and blames me. I didn't dump it on him – she did!

It's stupid times a million too. I never even touched her.

Now Misty is tossing daggers at me with her eyes, the flight attendant has a look on her face that could kill puppies, and I'm sulking back to my seat in the back of the plane while half the other passengers stare at the back of my head.

This is bad...feels worse...and there's nothing I can do about it.

I'm not very comfortable on airplanes anyway because of my back brace, but it doesn't help that my parents were killed in a plane crash a year and a half ago either. This whole situation just keeps getting better and better.

The back brace I wear is called a "Boston." It's basically a body cast made of thick, white plastic that extends from my hips to just below my shoulder blades so sitting down in it is like shoving the edge of a kitchen cutting-board into my upper thighs with all my weight. And I get to live with it until my spine quits growing, somewhere supposedly around the magic age of eighteen – that is, if I can survive for another four months. In the meantime, I've got a spine shaped like a big question mark and I also have the distinction of being the only high school senior at St. Mark's Preparatory Academy in Seattle, Washington who can't bend over to tie his own shoes!

I nearly toss myself into my seat. As always, I sit in the back of the plane, next to the aisle. Fortunately, there isn't anyone next to me, so I can sort of lean over at a stiff forty-five-degree angle and look out the window. I still feel like everyone is looking at me. It's like invisible lasers are searing off the hair on the top of my head, but I can't get any lower in the seat. Guess I'll have to endure the lasers.

I hear the flight attendant apologizing to Misty's bodyguard and I'm thinking, *this is not what I had in mind.* I've been trying to come up with some way to talk to Misty since I joined the jazz band. I thought since we just won the tournament in Anchorage, Misty might be a little less frosty my direction. After all, I'm the guitarist, we just got a superior rating and even Mr. Towns told the band my "contribution" made the difference. I always thought she was sort of off limits because she's the governor's daughter...but what about now that a flight attendant is blaming me for baptizing her bodyguard in java? I'm not getting to first base with her today, man...I'm not even getting into the same stadium now.

Misty Woods isn't just a little bit beautiful – she's a LOT beautiful. 5' 5", long dark hair, blue eyes that shine like fire and ice. Her skin is slightly brown, almost like a tan, but it's her natural color. I don't know if she's Spanish or what, but she doesn't need to visit a tanning booth. Her eyes flash when she looks at you...well, she never really looks at me, but I've seen her eyes – blue and deep like a drop off in a Caribbean reef. And she has a body I can't even think about without getting short of breath. Good luck seeing any more of her now!

And it doesn't help feeling guilty about the whole "thinking about her body" thing either! Not right now anyway...after all, I do

2

remember my parents were Christian missionaries and thinking about human female body parts was sort of frowned upon. If my parents knew what sort of things cross my mind when I think about...better stop there...

Since my Dad was a bush pilot for Remote Tribes Air, I grew up between Africa, Alaska and New Guinea following his insane flight assignments around the world. So, I basically lived in whatever church was at the local airstrip and my Mom homeschooled me in every mission station we were based at - up until the crash. They were seriously committed.

And I believe the whole thing too. For myself...I believe there's a real God, I believe there are real rules...so I believe I really think about naked girls way too much. But what can I say? I'm seventeen...and I'm male.

It's no fun being me.

I try not to think about the whole mess again. Misty...going to St. Mark's...I don't think I'm ever going to get past the crash. Of course, maybe I shouldn't. You know? How do you get over losing your Mom and Dad in a day?

I shift in my seat again. Despite feeling like a peeping Tom, I can't help looking over the seat back toward Misty. The flight attendant tries to mop up the coffee on the bodyguard's shirt. Misty tries to help, and I think her bodyguard is way too young and pretty to be a Secret Service agent. He looks more like a Nordstrom's mannequin with a gun. Misty's dad is the Governor of Washington State...and the Vice-Presidential nominee on a ticket everyone expects will blow like a hurricane into the White House on election day three weeks from now. So, she gets a personal assistant who just happens to be trained to kill.

I don't know who I'm kidding. Misty is so far out of my league she may as well live on Mars. I didn't grow up in her circle, that's for sure - far from it. One day I'm in a mobile home trailer in Papua, New Guinea doing a homeschool assignment while Mom and Dad are flying supplies. Next thing I know I'm in my Uncle's mansion on Lake Washington in Seattle, my Uncle enrolls me at St. Mark's, I have to wear a tie to school, I feel like life smacked me upside the head like getting hit by a train and I'm wondering what the smell happened.

What the smell?

Yeah…my dad's corny way of being a Christian and still being able to drop a phrase when he wanted. He loved creative "Christian cuss words."

I miss them so much…It's like I'm wandering around in an ugly black and white photo that's out of focus. Life has not been going my way and today is no exception. I just tried to get a conversation going with a drop dead beautiful girl only to end up crawling back to my seat like a scolded puppy.

The flight attendant isn't getting anywhere with the bodyguard's shirt. She looks sort of pale. I guess dumping coffee on a Secret Service agent is a bad plan. Misty gets up and tries to help a little more.

"I'm so sorry Todd," she says. "I can't believe Kyle did that…"

I just want to scream. I didn't do anything…I was just standing behind the flight attendant. I didn't touch her. And "Todd". What's with the name? Mr. Mannequin's got a preppy name. I seriously don't like him now.

The flight attendant sort of scoops "Todd the Mannequin" to his feet. He gets up kind of reluctantly and steps into the aisle.

"I think you might want to go to the lavatory and…I don't know…sort of wring this out," she says.

Todd doesn't say anything. He's obviously too mad to even form a sentence. He sort of storms down the aisle toward the back of the plane and I see his gun under his sport jacket for a second. He sets his jaw and glares at me on his way past.

"I'm sorry man," I say. "I didn't do anything. I wasn't even near her."

He doesn't answer. He just prowls past me to the back lavatory, flings open the door, steps inside and slams the door shut behind him. The flight attendant pushes her cart to the back. She doesn't look at me either. I swear half the passengers on the plane crane their necks to look back at what's happening. I feel my face flush red and I just want to cower down below the seat back in front of me…but I can't. Unless I lean over sideways, the stupid Boston keeps me seated up as straight as a wooden post, so everyone can stare at me. And I can only lean over at an angle for so long before I'm in real pain, meaning I'm literally forced to sit up straight.

I decide it's in my best interest to look out the window again.

It's going to be a while before I'm able to get out of here. The flight from Anchorage, Alaska to Seattle, Washington is three hours and twenty-five minutes from gear up to touchdown. I know this because I looked it up before we left Seattle last week. Yeah…I look up those sorts of things…because *I'm a moron* – just ask anyone. Try asking Misty, I'm sure she will agree!

But I'm willing to bet how I learned to play guitar is a lot more exciting than how Misty learned to play clarinet. She probably learned to play in a junior high classroom or maybe had a private teacher. I learned my first chord in a mud hut in Liberia, West Africa. I learned to play barre chords in a mobile home trailer in Papua, New Guinea, and an Inuit native taught me how to play major six and minor seventh chords sitting in front of a tin roofed shed in the snow in Sunny Cove, Alaska. That's a long way from Misty's junior high band class.

My Dad was a commercial airline pilot when he met my Mom, but together they gave up their airline careers when I was nine, so they could fly missionaries and supplies into some of the most God-forsaken places on earth. And it wasn't just a big change for me either! My Dad had to switch from jumbo jets getting serviced by an army of mechanics to puddle jumpers he had to know how to fix himself. I remember sitting on a stool under the front engine cowling handing him wrenches like a nurse assisting in surgery.

Out in the sticks, guitars are a big deal because you can't just pull out your piano and drum set for a church service – you can; however, pack a guitar to pretty much anywhere. Over the years various guitar guys took time out to teach the pilot's kid a few chords. I pretty much cut my teeth on an acoustic guitar and I could read music better than I could read English by the time I was eleven. But St. Mark's doesn't have a church music team, so I joined the jazz band. I'm glad I did because at least being in the band put me in the same room as Misty, only I don't particularly like jazz. I know not being fond of jazz is a musical sin, but I'm more into rock. You know...Classic Zeppelin, U2, 80's hair bands, that sort of thing. I made the mistake of saying something like that where our band teacher Mr. Towns overheard me, and I nearly got tossed out of the jazz band. But I'm actually pretty good at jazz guitar, so he couldn't get rid of me without hurting St. Mark's competitive edge.

I look up the aisle toward Misty. She sits in the aisle seat, three rows ahead of me watching something on a portable DVD player. I can see her left leg peering out from beneath her skirt. She wears skintight black leggings - it's pretty cold in Alaska in October and...man, those tights are killing me. It's like she painted her calves with black chalk. The DVD player in her lap pulls her skirt up a bit over her knee too and that just makes it worse.

I shake my head like a dog trying to fling off water. It doesn't help.

The whole female obsession thing is truly annoying. It's sort of like having an itch you know you can't scratch. If you scratch, you'll bleed and the itch will just come back anyway. Only it shouldn't itch at all in the first place. It's not like I haven't seen every inch of the female form. It's not a mystery! I mean, in Papua, women routinely walk around without anything on from the waist up. In Africa, it wasn't unusual to see young girls and even young teens wandering around stark naked, so I shouldn't be so freaked out.

But I am freaked out. I can't seem to get it under control either. I mean, I've seen it all, but I can't quit thinking about it. It's just...there's something about a girl's shape that makes me feel...I don't know...almost like feeling hungry.

Just telling myself that I'm seventeen and it's all natural, and whatever, doesn't really help. It's almost like there's two of me. My one self is all in control, but my other self wants to flex like a body builder and throw big rocks around or something.

I hate being me sometimes.

6

What's worse is my Mom told me that once a girl hits her teenage years she is very much aware whenever a guy is looking too long. So, Misty KNOWS...it's like she has "boy radar" and her anti-aircraft missiles are locked onto my forehead.

Some girls, I've noticed, are like Misty - sort of disgusted when they know you're looking. But other girls, like Sean McFarlen who plays alto sax in the jazz band – she's a total flirt. If she knows you're looking, she'll flex, or flaunt, and sometimes it's so obvious she may as well be in front of a camera. Either way, as a male in this game, I'm the ball, the girls are the goal line and someone else is kicking.

I look Misty's direction again. Just beyond her, a dark-haired man who was seated toward the front of the plane has stood up. I guess he wants to use the lavatory at the front, but the other flight attendant blocks his way. I don't know why he can't figure out that he has to trudge all the way to the back until she's done "beveraging" everybody. Maybe I'll get lucky and everybody will turn to look at Mr. Doofus instead of me. I want to shout, *like she's gonna move dude!*

But he doesn't turn around and head for the back of the plane.

Instead, he grabs a can of soda from the flight attendant's cart. In one savage motion he swings the can in his fist like a club. His swing connects with the flight attendant's face sending a blast of blood from her broken nose onto her white blouse. She lets out a shriek that would wake the dead, but the blow is so powerful she is knocked completely off her feet.

This...is really Bad...

Two

Someone screams, and half a dozen people partially stand up from their seats in shock or twist sideways to get a better look. Immediately, there is a flurry of sudden movements. A man in a long-sleeved white shirt nearly leaps out of his seat, but instead of rushing to tackle the man who attacked the flight attendant, he slides past him and jogs toward the closed cockpit door. Soda Can Man does nothing to stop him, doesn't even flinch when Mr. White Shirt strides past him. They're obviously working together.

I'm feeling some serious panic. I'm not sure how you're supposed to feel when your plane gets hijacked, never had the pleasure before, but for a split second, I'm afraid Misty might see how I feel. I don't know why I care what anyone thinks of me, not now, but for some insane reason, I'm afraid everybody is looking at me like I'm the only coward in the cabin. I'm afraid the words, "nearly having a stroke from terror", are going to flash up like a neon text message on my forehead any second. I'm sure everyone can hear me hyperventilating.

The wounded flight attendant is collapsed on the aisle floor. I can see one of her knees sticking up. Soda Can Man brandishes his can over her like a club. He crouches, eyes filled with hate darting back and forth, his hand shaking slightly as if he's expecting the entire cabin of passengers to rush him at any second. He's obviously wound up so tight; if someone lets off a loud belch, he might have a massive heart attack. I can only hope…

"Everyone sit down and shut up or I'll crush her skull!" he shouts.

His voice is pitched, like someone more scared than angry. He has a heavy accent too. I've been all over the world, but I can't place the sound. Behind him, I see Mr. White Shirt doing something to the cockpit door. Everyone is swinging his or her head back and forth, trying to figure out what Soda Can Man is going to do and what Mr. White Shirt is doing at the cockpit door.

In one of the seats in front of me, and across from where I sit, another man wearing a tan sports jacket calmly stands up. I figure Soda Can Man is going to start playing "Smash the pumpkin" on the attendant's face if someone tries to interfere. But again, Soda Can Man doesn't react to the man in the tan sports jacket. Instead, Mr. Tan Jacket almost casually strolls toward the back of the plane as if nothing is happening. Soda Can Man says nothing too, so I have to assume Mr. Tan Jacket is in on the plan. Aren't we all just happy campers?

Behind me, I hear my flight attendant take in a sharp breath. I turn my head, expecting to see her being strangled by the man in the tan sports jacket. Instead, I see her calmly hand him another soda can from the beverage cart. If he's going to smash her face in, why is she handing him the club?

This is insane. I don't know what's going on, but it's bad. Real bad! And what if this isn't a hijacking? What if it's a suicide mission? Take over the plane, drive it face-first into the Seattle Space Needle like a jet-engine pile driver ramming a monstrous spike into the earth. Kill the Governor's daughter, all her friends, and half of downtown Seattle in a blazing orange fireball.

What if?

Well…if that is the plan…I'll be dead and then I won't feel like a pinhead anymore, daring myself to ask Misty out and knowing I'll only get humiliated if I try. I won't spend almost every night trying to choke back yet another fit of tears and anger to keep myself from crying myself to sleep. I won't miss Mom and Dad anymore or wonder what would have happened if they had come home that day instead of dying. That might not be so bad. All I've ever believed is that heaven is on the other side of my last breath – and that's where we might be headed right now.

Not that bad! Right?

Despite my upbringing, I think of the nastiest cuss word I can come up with and let it loose. My heart hammers in my chest and I wonder if everyone can hear it. My tongue feels like a metal file rasping back and forth over the soft part of my gums. I never knew facing death was so grossly terrifying. I wonder if this is how Mom or Dad felt. How long did they have between when they knew the engine failed and the crash? Did she think of me? I hope they weren't this scared.

No one moves for a moment. A thickset man seated in the middle of the plane stands up. He's a big guy and it's obvious he's royally ticked off. He points his finger at the man with the soda can.

"Put it down or it's your skull that's gonna get crushed!" he shouts. Soda Can Man doesn't even twitch.

Suddenly, Stan Warwick, a trombone player in my jazz band, also stands up. I've always thought that Stan was a real toad. I mean, he plays on the lacrosse team, so he struts around the band room like he's the athletic department's gift to the band nerds. With him, it's as if the rest of us are too lame to catch a ball with a little net on a pole! That's lame if you ask me.

But nobody asks me.

Another guy gets up, but I don't recognize him. Something's happening now. I'm thinking 9-11. The people on the one plane that went down, they rushed the terrorists. They didn't wait to get smashed into the White House, and it looks like the same thing is happening now. I feel a real, ice-cold chill run up my spine. If this is going down 9-11-style, it's going to be a screaming fit of flailing bodies dropping out of the sky in about five minutes. That picture scares the earwax out of me, but I don't want to let anyone think Stan Warwick is the only guy in the band with any brass. I set my feet on the floor and get ready to join the charge. Maybe my back brace will come in handy – sort of like a suit of armor.

"I said sit down!" Soda Can Man shouts. He lifts the can over the poor woman's head. "Sit down...now!"

The thickset man puts one foot into the aisle. Soda Can Man swoops down and drags the attendant up to his chest by her neck. He still holds the soda can but his arm locks around the attendant's neck. She's still dazed, but it's obvious Soda Can Man is cutting off her air. Her face already flushes.

"Everyone sit still and you won't get hurt. We are taking over this plane," Soda Can Man says.

The attendant's nose is smashed beyond recognition. Her eyes are dazed, and I can see the whites as if she is on the edge of consciousness. A trickle of blood drips from her chin onto Soda Can Man's arm around her neck. If he doesn't give her some air in about five seconds, she's going to die.

Stan looks over at the thickset man as if he needs reassurance. Two slow seconds drag by until the finger-pointing man spits out a curse and slumps back into his seat. Stan hesitates, but I can see his ears flush red even from the back of the plane. I'm betting he feels like an idiot, but he doesn't want to look like a coward either. Soda Can Man looks at him. The moment their eyes connect, Stan sits down in a rush.

I look behind me and I can't believe what I'm seeing. My flight attendant has wedged the beverage cart against the lavatory door, blocking Todd in, and she's helping Mr. Tan Jacket do something with a soda can. Whatever they're doing must be taking longer than they want it to take because I see her hands shake as she pours the liquid from one can into another. Mr. Tan Jacket's hands are wagging up and down as if he's saying, *come on, come on, come on!*

This can't be happening. My flight attendant is in on it. The plane is being hijacked, and the only guy with a gun on board is trapped in the lavatory. I see the bathroom door snap open, but the door opens inward and Mr. Tan Jacket lunges forward, crushing Todd against the door. With his free hand, Mr. Tan Jacket tosses the contents of the soda can that he and the flight attendant had just been toying with into the lavatory. From inside, Todd screams, and I smell burning flesh, even from three rows ahead.

Todd launches his body at the lavatory door. Mr. Tan Jacket leans in with his shoulder, holding him inside. Todd's arm thrusts out of the gap between the lavatory door and the bulkhead, flapping it around like the neck of a decapitated goose. Todd lunges again with a strangled, gurgling cry and Mr. Tan Jacket is thrown backward. Todd tries to get out of the lavatory, flounders over the beverage cart while clawing at his face. It looks like he's covered in some sort of acid. His face is red and blistered and there's blood pouring from his eyes. Mr. Tan Jacket regains his footing and tackles him. There's a brief struggle, but Todd is in no real condition to defend himself. He makes some effort with one hand to push Mr. Tan Jacket away and it's a useless move. The terrorist leans back and then drives his elbow down onto Todd's neck, knocking him senseless instantly.

Mr. Tan Jacket bends over and fishes Todd's firearm and the extra clip out from underneath his coat. He stands up with a look of confidence and triumph on his face. Expertly, he pulls back the gun's slide, checking the load. He clicks it back into place as he turns to face the cabin. Everyone is shouting at once. Half a dozen people are trying to hide under the seats and another half a dozen are trying to crawl over the seats in panic. I'm frozen in place, not even five feet from an insane terrorist holding a gun.

"Silence!" Mr. Tan Jacket shouts. "We are taking over this plane. If you do not do exactly what we tell you, you will die. Unless you think I am bluffing…"

Mr. Tan Jacket turns his weapon and takes aim at my flight attendant. Her face register's shock and betrayal in the one horrific second it takes for Mr. Tan Jacket to pull the trigger. The explosion is so loud, I jump up, nearly smashing my head on the overhead bin. The flight attendant's blood and brains are splattered on the bulkhead behind her. Her body crumples into a bloody heap. Several girls scream. One girl is nearly hyperventilating in screaming sobs.

"We have control of this plane," Mr. Tan Jacket continues.

Mr. Tan Jacket shouts something in a foreign language. Mr. White Shirt, still working on the cockpit door, answers. Soda Can Man nods his head and drags his hostage closer to the cockpit, still brandishing the soda can like a club, daring anyone to interfere. Soda Can Man is obviously guarding whatever the man at the cockpit door is doing.

Todd moans feebly from somewhere down at Mr. Tan Jacket's knee. The terrorist hesitates, keeping his eyes fixed on the passengers. I see him glance down at Todd as if deciding whether the wounded man is worth using another bullet. I guess Todd isn't worth a bullet. Mr. Tan Jacket takes the gun by the barrel and viciously hacks the butt of the gun into the back of Todd's skull. Someone screams again, and I cringe back. Even from three rows away, I can see that Todd's skull is crushed.

My face feels stretched, like my eyes are so wide open they must look the size of dinner plates because I'm scared out of my ever-loving mind. I take breaths in, one at a time, in huge bursts, and I can feel my face getting hot. I can't seem to tear my eyes away from what's left of the flight attendant's brain, streaking down the bulkhead like some sort of modern art painted by Satan. I feel my lunch about to come up, so I force myself to look away toward the front of the cabin.

I look closer at what the man at the cockpit door is doing. He smears some sort of gel onto the door lock from a tiny tube. He has what looks like a pocket CD player in his hand but he's pressing the end of the ear bud cord into the gel. It must be some sort of plastic explosive. He looks up from his work and shouts something toward Mr. Tan Jacket.

Mr. Tan Jacket confidently strides forward, holding the gun with both hands. He doesn't look at me, but I cower back all the same. When he gets in front of Soda Can Man, he whispers something to him and squeezes past. Soda Can Man literally tosses the flight attendant into a seat, still holding the can as if it's a live grenade. Mr. Tan Jacket examines the door, nods confidently, and says something to Mr. White Shirt. He steps back from the cockpit door. There is a small workspace for the flight attendants, almost like a closet, just behind the cockpit door, opposite from the front exit to the plane. This space is divided from the rest of the cabin by a half wall. It's probably built that way, so the flight attendants can get to their "coffee, tea and me" stuff without being seen, at least by people seated on the right side of the plane. Mr. Tan Jacket scoots past this area and leans with his back against the workspace wall. He puts the gun at the ready and braces his feet, his eyes sweeping the cabin. There are two women, both chaperons for the band, seated in the front aisle just inches from Mr. Tan Jacket's knees. I know one of them is Mrs. Carlyle, but I can't remember the other lady's name. Both of them cower back into their seats, trying to melt into the fabric.

The man holding the portable CD player turns his head away from the door and presses a button. There's a bright flash and a booming crack. White smoke drifts like fairy dust from the door, nearly filling the aisle. Mr. White Shirt drops the portable CD player, grabs the cockpit door, and wrenches it open. Mr. Tan Jacket whips around the attendant workspace wall with the gun in both hands like a cop. He snarls something at Mr. White Shirt in whatever awful language he speaks. Mr. White Shirt snakes behind him, reaches over with one hand, and grabs Mrs. Carlyle by the hair. She shrieks and throws both hands up, but Mr. White Shirt just yanks her forward. She slams into the cabin floor on both knees, screaming her head off.

"Show me your hands!" Mr. Tan Jacket shouts at the pilots.

Mr. White Shirt drags Mrs. Carlyle with him back to the front exit door. Soda Can Man backs away but his eyes never leave the passengers. He must be the lookout, only I'm not so sure his soda can is going to be much of a weapon. Still, nobody tries to rush the terrorists, so long as one of them has a gun pointed at the pilot's head. Mr. Tan Jacket takes another step until his arms and the gun are right in the cockpit. I can see the pilot and co-pilot looking over their shoulders.

"Hands...put your hands up!" Mr. Tan Jacket shouts again. "Try and move the yoke and I'll kill her!"

14

Mr. Tan Jacket suddenly swings the gun around and puts it directly into Mrs. Carlyle's temple. Mr. White Shirt still holds her firmly by the roots of her hair. She screams repeatedly, hysterically trying to pull away.

Neither pilot moves. Mr. Tan Jacket reaches across himself and grabs a second handful of Mrs. Carlyle's hair. He pulls her head higher, pressing the barrel of the gun into her temple.

"Put up your hands or I blow her head off!" he shouts.

His voice has gone from commanding and in control to a shrill bark. No one can doubt from the sound of that voice that he will kill her, and kill the pilots, and kill us all.

Both pilots comply. Mr. Tan Jacket glances back at Mrs. Carlyle, then back at the pilots.

"Pilot – get up first. Co-pilot, keep your hands where I can see them."

The pilot extracts himself from the seat and stumbles into the cabin. Mr. White Shirt lets go of Mrs. Carlyle and pounces on the pilot from behind. They both fall to the floor. Mr. White Shirt uses a cord of some kind to tie the pilot's hands behind his back. It looks like another ear bud cord. He drags the pilot to his feet and shoves him into an empty seat at the front.

"Now you!" shouts Mr. Tan Jacket at the co-pilot. "Slowly!"

The co-pilot carefully complies, eyes fixed on Mrs. Carlyle, still sobbing uncontrollably with Mr. Tan Jacket's gun fixed firmly onto her temple.

Soda Can Man kicks behind the co-pilot's knees. He drops to the floor, throwing his hands in front of him to break his fall. Mr. White Shirt drops down onto the co-pilot's lower back with his knee and I can hear the co-pilot groan in pain as Mr. White Shirt begins tying his hands up as well.

Mr. Tan Jacket keeps the gun firmly pressed against Mrs. Carlyle's temple. He turns his head and glares at the rest of the cabin.

"We have control of the plane," he says again. "We will not hesitate to kill you...but you do not have to die. There is a cargo on the plane we will get. We will land, then negotiate to release you.

15

Stay in your seats and be silent, and you will live. Try anything and you will die."

Mr. Tan Jacket lets go of Mrs. Carlyle. He mumbles something to Soda Can Man, hands him the gun, then steps past him into the cockpit. I can see him get into the pilot's seat.

Misty looks back my direction and I catch her eye. Her makeup is smeared from tears. She is obviously terrified, but she isn't looking at me. She's looking past me at the body of the man who was supposed to have protected her. Her face crumples into a fresh wave of sobs and she turns away.

"Give us your cell phones," Soda Can Man says. "Put them in this bag...quickly."

He walks down the aisle, holding a gym bag open. I see an older lady toss her phone into the bag. Across from her, a middle-aged man puts his phone into the bag, but the lady next to him is clawing through her purse.

"The phone!" he yells. "Quickly!"

He reaches for the woman's purse, tears it out of her hands, and pours the contents into the aisle. He kneels and gets the cell phone. I see that both Soda Can Man and Mr. White Shirt at the front are distracted for a second, so I slip forward into the row behind Misty. I lean forward toward her seat and I try to whisper.

"Misty?"

She jumps with a fright and looks back at me. I can see her shock that I'm seated right behind her.

"What are you doing? You're going to get us killed."

"They're not going to kill us...they..."

"Shut up!"

I look forward. Soda Can Man has moved forward and is nearly on top of us. Everyone is moving quickly to give up his or her phone. I can see that the terrorist's gym bag is getting a little heavy.

I feel the plane begin to descend. Someone begins to sob loudly. Someone in the middle of the plane is gasping for air.

"We're crashing..." someone yells.

16

"We are not going to crash!" Mr. White Shirt yells. "Shut up and get your phones! If we were going to crash, why would we care about your stupid phones? Just shut up and put them in the bag."

Soda Can Man has reached our position. I don't have a phone, but Misty throws hers into the bag. Next to her, Misty's best friend, Angela, hands over her phone. I remember Angela because she's a good trumpet player, which is sort of rare. Most girls I know play saxophone or clarinet. Angela's the only girl in the horn section.

"You...give me your phone," he says to me.

"I don't have one."

I put up my hands to show I don't have anything hidden. Since I'm wearing the standard St. Mark's uniform and tie I obviously don't have any place to put a phone except my pants pockets. Remembering this, I reach down and quickly inside-out my pockets, both jacket and pants, to prove my point.

Soda Can Man seems satisfied. He moves on. Across from my new seat is a young couple in their twenties. They look like business professionals. I see a pretty expensive phone disappear into the bag.

The last three rows of the plane are empty. Soda Can Man turns and begins to head back toward the front of the plane. He stops next to Misty's seat. He looks down at her and nods his head.

"You...get up and come with me," he says to Misty.

I feel a spike of adrenaline in my gut. Misty is the Governor's daughter, the man most likely to be elected the next Vice President of the United States in less than a month. Are these guys hijacking a plane just to get to her?

Misty doesn't move. Angela starts to cry.

"I said, get up!"

The terrorist grabs a handful of Misty's beautiful black hair and pulls. She screams, and I just react. I don't know what I'm thinking, but I just stand up and scream at the guy.

"Let her go!"

The terrorist is so shocked he lets go of Misty. In a second, I see him change his mind. He swings his fist at my stomach - but that's a bad plan because I'm wearing a piece of thick plastic and aluminum

17

under my shirt. When his hand hits the brace, he yanks it back with a shocked yell. I am knocked back into my seat but otherwise unharmed.

I'm willing to bet Soda Can Man has a broken hand, or at least, it will be seriously swollen. On a normal day, I would laugh, only the situation is anything but funny.

"Get up!" he shouts at me. His eyes are wide and crazy. "Take off the shirt! Take it off! Now!"

I stand up slowly and unbutton my shirt. I pull the shirt out of my pants where I had it tucked in and open it. Everyone can see the plastic and aluminum back brace. The terrorist stares at my abdomen, and I can't help cracking a little smile.

Soda Can Man drops the gym bag. He swings his uninjured hand, open palmed, at my face and slaps me so hard I see bright sparkles in my eyes. The pain is stunning. I fall back into the seat. The sting on my face is so intense I can barely breathe. My skin burns like someone poured boiling water on my cheek. I'm trying to catch my breath, but I can't seem to get any oxygen. I can feel blood pouring out of my nose.

The terrorist retrieves the gym bag.

"I said, get up!" he yells at Misty.

Misty gets to her feet, and I can see she is shaking like a leaf in the wind. She looks back at me, but this time, her expression has changed.

This time she looks grateful.

Three

I try to keep the tears from coming, but I can't stop them. I feel ashamed of them, so I try to imagine they're flowing simply because I was slapped so hard.

Yeah… it's just a natural reaction – that's all! Right?

My cheek throbs and burns like a trillion burning mites are boring into my skin and I can't hide from the truth - the tears are more than the sting on my face. The truth is I feel helpless and stupid for standing up and shouting at a terrorist who could have killed Misty just because I ticked him off and he can still kill her while I sit cock-eyed in the corner of a seat with tears boiling over onto my red cheek. It was a stupid move – plain and simple!

The last time I gave into tears was after my parents' funeral. At first, I managed to get through the entire service without shedding a tear and I'm not certain why I was able to hold them back so long. I did feel a real catch in my throat when the honor guard did the rifle salute. I even caught my breath when the staff sergeant handed me the folded flag. But I didn't shed a tear, not in front of so many people, and certainly not in front of a Marine Staff Sergeant. There was just something so shocking about the whole thing, it almost didn't seem real. After the service, when I was finally alone, that's when I let the tears loose.

I loved my mom and dad. Most of the teenagers I rub shoulders with everyday have exactly nothing good to say about their parents. But they aren't orphans either. It's ironic, too, since my classmates are from the richest families in western Washington State. Their parents have showered them with everything from St. Mark's, the brightest preparatory education money can buy, to new cars and designer uniforms. Yet, they still endlessly text complaints about their parents to each other on phones their parents bought.

It's hard not to despise them, but I suppose they can't help their situation any more than I can help mine. After all, none of us asked to be born. We just woke up one day and found ourselves saying "Mommy" and "Daddy" to a couple of strangers we suddenly realized had been feeding us and peering into our cribs for years. Would any of us have picked the parents we found ourselves with? I've met so many people all over the world who would gladly trade places with me or any of the other kids on this plane – but they didn't ask to be born either. The one thing I've learned so far, is that everybody finds something to carp and moan about, no matter where they are in life. It's really all about what you're familiar with. Prep school and country club dinners at Thanksgiving are all Misty and her classmates have ever known. If I'm honest with myself, I know most of these kids are decent, not even spoiled really. They just have a limited point-of-view.

I wedge myself into the seat next to the window and look out. I don't want anyone to see me wipe the tears out of my eyes. Outside, I can't see anything except clouds. It will be sunset soon so every few moments a shaft of light penetrates the mist and hits me right in the eye. We're still descending, but I can't tell if we're over the water or land. A sudden, slight bump rattles the plane, and someone yelps nervously.

I look at the two terrorists near the cockpit door. Mr. White Shirt still has the gun. He whispers something to Soda Can Man, but his eyes never leave the cabin. I can see the back of Misty's head. I can't figure out why, but for some reason, they've seated her next to the emergency exit on the opposite side of the plane from where I sit, and she doesn't look at me. Just thinking about her causes another wave of adrenaline and fear to crawl across my chest. What if this isn't a suicide mission? What if the cargo Mr. Tan Jacket said was on board is Misty? Newspaper headlines across the nation are already almost handing her dad and his running mate the election. The hijacking and kidnapping of the soon-to-be Vice President's daughter might

20

give the terrorists some serious leverage, but it isn't going to sway the election. In fact, if Misty is the hostage they want, the sympathy vote alone will probably guarantee Governor Woods and Senator James will win. Trying to sway the election doesn't make sense. After all, everyone knows Woods and James are not going to be soft on terrorists if they win.

I try to calm myself. I figure they can't be planning to use the plane like a 9-11 airplane bomb either. That doesn't make any sense. We're on a flight from Anchorage, Alaska to Seattle, Washington so there's nothing to the west except the Pacific Ocean, and nothing to the east except the wild part of western British Columbia - about a million square miles of nearly uninhabited forests and mountains. If they are planning to use the plane like a flying bomb, they might only take out the 68 of us on board, and maybe a grizzly bear or two, if they are lucky. It's not even a full flight. I wondered about this when we left Anchorage. I mean, it is a Tuesday, but someone must have pulled some strings because 90% of the people on this flight are members of the jazz band. Seems obvious Governor Woods wasn't above making a phone call or two to keep his daughter's flight from being full.

Confiscating our phones only makes sense if they really are planning to land somewhere and negotiate for something they want. But where? Vancouver, B.C. in Canada is the nearest major airport I know of, and I don't think there's an airport that can handle this kind of aircraft in Victoria - but I don't know that for sure. Maybe there's an airport in Victoria, but why would they want to land in either Victoria or Vancouver?

So, where are they taking us? And why are we descending? Trying to get below radar coverage? That's not very practical. Hijacking the plane mid-way into the flight, they must know the Canadian Air Force will be swarming into the air before they get within five hundred miles of Vancouver or Seattle. I know enough about a Boeing 737 to know you need a pretty decent runway to get one on the ground. The dirt runways my dad used to land on are not going to do the trick either.

21

My dad was a great pilot. After he served in the Marines, he used the G.I. Bill and worked his way up to commercial airline pilot. But after he joined Remote Tribes, he learned to land almost any plane, almost anywhere. Half the time, the airplanes he flew were held together as much with faith and duct tape, as anything else. He even flew floatplanes. I remember one little bay we worked out of in Alaska that was so small, he had to touch down, spin the aircraft around and gun the engine to keep from running into the other side of the bay.

Dad could land this bird. I know he could...if he were here. He would know what to do in this situation, too. He wouldn't have come out of the cockpit cowering like a ten-year-old, that's for sure. I can just imagine what he would have done. Dad was a former Marine and he told me time after time after time that there's no such thing as an ex-Marine. *Once a Marine, always a Marine,* he would say. And every Marine was trained to do whatever it takes to get the job done. He wouldn't have crawled out of the cockpit with his hands in the air. Not my dad.

Just thinking about him gives me a little hope for a second. But just for a second...because he's not here. And he's never going to be "here" ever again either. Neither is Mom. My little flash of hope evaporates so fast I don't have time to stop an actual shuddering sob from coming out of my mouth. I cower down a little lower in my seat as tears well up so heavy again, I feel like I'm carrying lead weights on my eyes.

I guess it doesn't make sense to hold back my feelings. Besides, if I'm honest, I know I can't hold back. Not today. That slap took more out of me than a layer of skin off my cheek. It threw me back, back to knowing I'm alone and afraid and ashamed all at once. I'm back to wanting to grab someone, maybe someone like Stan, who struts around acting all Mr. Man and looking at me as if I'm a ten-year-old pretending to be in high school. He doesn't know! He doesn't know who I am, and he doesn't care, and I hate that. I hate feeling like everyone is somehow disgusted with me. Like I'm forever surrounded by people, but never connected, never wanted, and never heard. I want to shake Stan and scream in his face. I want to vent everything on his stuck-up little smirk until he feels like I feel. Until he knows!

But I can't...

So, there's nothing to do now except to feel it. All I can do is cower in my seat and wait to either get vaporized on impact or endure one terror after another until the Navy Seals storm the plane and kill half of us before they can gut Mr. Tan Jacket. For some reason, maybe it's the slap, or maybe it's just connecting my situation with my parents' last seconds on earth; for whatever reason, the memories come back like a tidal wave.

Mom and Dad's plane went down in a sudden storm over a jungle in New Guinea. What they could find of their bodies is buried in a cemetery in Bellingham, Washington. Their graves are on a hill surrounded by beautiful fir trees. I remember it was a cold day when we put them in the ground. Broken clouds, like the ghosts of tumbleweeds, spilled across the sky, throwing shafts of sunlight this way and that. I kept looking up at the sky, away from the honor guard, away from the caskets. My dad would have been proud. The Marines, like polished statues of ancient heroes come to life, stood over him to honor his memory. When I could force myself to look, I remember thinking they were so beautiful. You're not supposed to think of Marines as beautiful. They're warriors and guardians and...family. But to me...that day...they were beautiful. So beautiful, I had to keep looking away because I could hardly take it in. I already suspected by then that my back brace would keep me from being a Marine. So, watching them, I couldn't help but know in a way so deep, it felt like cutting a gash in my chest, that I will never wear that uniform. I can never honor my Dad the way the guard could. I'm a Marine in my heart, but no one can really know what that feels like...except me alone.

I remember wandering through the graveyard after the funeral. The other people there just sort of faded into the background and let me wander away. I guess they knew I needed to be alone. At the bottom of the hill, I found a grave marker made of weathered, white marble. The date of death on it was 1864. That's when the tears began to flow. I cried for my dad and mom, because I couldn't read the name on the marker, just the date. The name was so faded I couldn't make it out. I couldn't even see the date of birth.

That's when it hit me. That poor little white marker was all that was left of an entire life. I know that right now, here on this airplane, that marker still sits there, quiet and alone, slightly tilted and nearly invisible because of encroaching trees and underbrush, at the edge of the cemetery. It's nothing but a faded white piece of stone. No flowers, no memory, no one to care or grieve. One entire lifetime faded into nothing. I wondered who was buried there. The name was faded, so I couldn't tell if it was a man or a woman. 1864. I decided it was a soldier, a gallant hero who gave his life in the Civil War to set the slaves free.

But I couldn't know. And no one cared anymore. A man born the same day my Civil War soldier died would have died himself from old age fifty years before I was born. I wondered how long someone came there to mourn for him. How long was he remembered? How long before no one came, before the wind and the snow and the rain tore his name away? I suppose there's probably a record of the gravesite in the cemetery records. But even if I could find a name, anyone who would care died long before.

So, I cried. I cried for that little white marker, as much as I cried for my parents. I cried to think that my dad and mom's memory was going to be forgotten before long – just like my Civil War veteran…if that's even who it was under there. I cried, knowing that I would go on with my life and gradually think of them fewer and fewer times, until they became just as faded a memory as that white marker, even to me, their only child. I had a crazy thought that every time I came to visit my parents I would bring a rose to put on that lonely white marker. I felt like it was something I had to do.

Then, I remember feeling a fierce anger take over from my tears. I remember thinking about how I wanted my life to matter. I wanted something more than a faded stone where no one can read my name. But now, I sit on this plane and stare out the window at the clouds and wonder if I'm going to die in an hour. I wonder if all I'll ever be is another marker next to my parents.

I hear one of the terrorists say something in whatever gibberish of a language they're using. Someone starts walking toward the back. I scoot sideways a little, so I can just see over the top of the seatback in front of me. My right leg is going numb from sitting cockeyed against the window of the plane anyway. I quickly wipe the tears from my eyes, but no one looks at me. It's Mr. White Shirt prowling down the aisle. He has left the gun with Soda Can Man. He glares at me, so I look quickly down at my shins, but he doesn't stop to do or say anything to me. He just keeps going. After a second, I look up again.

Mr. White shirt grabs hold of Todd's limp arm. He pulls and drags Todd's body into the flight attendant workstation at the back of the plane behind the lavatories. Todd's body makes a hollow, thumping sound that reminds me of slapping a steak onto a cutting board. The idea makes me wince. Mr. White Shirt returns and takes hold of the flight attendant's arm. He starts dragging her to the back as well. As soon as he pulls on her body, I see a flash of what's left of her skull. It looks like a head of cauliflower covered in ketchup. Her head flops unnaturally sideways, exposing what's left of her brain. Someone behind me gasps and I feel my lunch coming up once again. This time, I can't hold it back.

I retch harshly onto the cabin floor at my feet. Whatever I had for lunch is chunky soup now. The sight and the smell make me nauseated again, so I throw up a second, then a third time until there's nothing left except a thin, gray water coming out of my mouth. When I'm done yakking up my lower intestines, I push back to the window to get away from the mess I left on the floor. I would love to get out of the seat, but after what happened, I would rather endure whiffs of vomit perfume than stir up one of the terrorists again. Unfortunately, just tossing my lunch can't get the sight of the flight attendant's head out of my mind.

She looked so shocked and betrayed in that one, split second before Mr. Tan Jacket blew her skull apart. I was only five feet away. I saw the look in her eye, her last thought flashing across her face and

I wonder what they said or did to get her to cooperate in the first place. In that last second, did she regret her deal? Or was it just one split second of surprise and fear? No time for regret. I wonder if it was all about money. People will do insane things for money.

My dad gave up a lot of money when he walked away from commercial aviation, but he did that because he wanted to invest his life into something that was more valuable than making money. He used to tell me this when I complained about some of the places where we ended up setting up our home. He became a missionary pilot, he said, because he believed he could make a greater difference for people by bringing Bibles, and supplies for on-site missionaries than he could by delivering business travelers to major airports. Standing by that little white stone, I remember thinking I wanted to do the same thing. Not the flying part - the making a difference part.

I really believe in God. I don't believe in Him because my parents were missionaries. I don't believe in Him because I grew up going to church either. I believe in Him, because I believe. My own choice, my own decision! Sitting here, waiting to find out if I'm going to die today, pushes me to think about what I believe and why I believe it. I guess my parents' funeral really clinched it for me, too. That day was like coming up to a "T" in the road. I could have turned left, given up on God, given up on everything. But I turned right. It wasn't an easy decision either, and it didn't make me feel better right away. It was sort of like starting to move at a crawl rather than accelerating to eighty miles an hour in three seconds. Standing over their graves, I didn't quit believing in God, but I didn't get all "religious" either. I grew up with religious people. I've seen them dance and wave flags and even roll on the floor. I'm not like that, but just because some people are doesn't mean I believe any less.

Really believing in God, I mean, way past just reciting Sunday school stuff, started out slow for me because I remember being so angry. It's been like having a smoldering piece of charcoal in my chest, smoking and sizzling every day since they died. The day of the funeral, that fire threated to rise up inside me and lead me to scream at everything and everyone. I wanted everyone to know my dad and

26

mom made a difference. I wanted everyone to know I was going to make difference.

But I didn't shout anything that day at the funeral. I just stood there in the fading sunlight and cried. I looked up at the trees, and I could barely see them through the blur in my eyes. I remember wondering where God was that day. I remember deciding I was going to believe God existed whether He liked it or not! I felt strange and cold, deciding to believe that He existed even if it felt like somehow God didn't know that I existed...or at least, He knew I was breathing but He had much better things to do than worry about my feelings. That's probably a scary thing to say about God.

But it's how I felt...

My Uncle Jack and Aunt Helen took me in after the funeral. It was all in my parents' will. Uncle Jack is nearly five years older than Dad, but they had been great friends growing up, so Dad and Mom made him my guardian. Uncle Jack is a partner in a business law firm and probably makes more money than the Queen of England. I would like to say I was excited to live in their six thousand square foot house on Lake Washington, but I have yet to feel very good about it. I don't resent my uncle or my aunt or anything. They're sweet people and they really do try to help me. They're never mean to me, but I do hear them whisper in the hallways when they think I'm not paying attention, and I know they're whispering about me. I know they're worried.

My uncle James "Jack" Miller and his wife, Helen, are not actually biologically related to me, which is obvious to anyone who looks, since Uncle Jack is African and I'm as a white as bleached all-purpose flour. I get a kick out of people giving us funny looks when he introduces me as his nephew. But he really is my uncle in so many ways beyond genetics and birth parents. I grew up seeing Uncle Jack all the time. I was the ring bearer at his wedding when I was about four.

My dad and mom had a rough childhood, which is probably what drew them together. Dad's drug-addicted mother abandoned him when he was three. He grew up in a group home and Jack was

27

his best friend. Jack was a lot older than my Dad so when Dad showed up, so little and scared, Jack took him under his wing. They grew up together, did Boy Scouts together, and when Jack joined the Marines, my Dad had to follow. Uncle Jack and my dad were the kind of friends that would literally die for each other. There was never any question that Uncle Jack was family.

Uncle Jack married late in life and Aunt Helen is considerably younger. As a result, my cousins are way younger than me. Uncle Jack and Aunt Helen have three adorable little girls named Deanna, Darla and Denise, aged five, seven and ten. The girls seem to think I've moved in just so I can play "monster" with them and chase them down the hallways every day after school. I'm not unhappy chasing the kids, and I don't hate living in the Miller's house, but I can't relate to their life. I can't really connect with the girls either, no matter how many shrieks I get out of them, chasing them through the house. They're just so young. They don't really understand yet what happened to my parents - their Uncle Kevin and Aunt Melissa. They don't really understand why someone who looks so different is living in their house, either. But for them, I'm their best friend, and I think that maybe I can be for them what Uncle Jack was for my dad.

My uncle and aunt come from a different planet than the one I've been living on. After eight years in the Marines, Uncle Jack went to law school. He did exceptionally well, worked a hundred hours a week, and ended up a partner in one of the largest law firms in the Pacific Northwest. He's done nothing except make money hand over fist ever since. I guess growing up in the group home gave him a drive to never live without because Uncle Jack lives well, and he's determined to make sure his family has the best. When we were on the mission field, Uncle Jack was one of our biggest supporters. Every Thanksgiving, we would get a full Thanksgiving feast sent to us, no matter where on earth we were hiding out at the time. I love my uncle, I really do, but the truth is, I just feel so alone all the time.

Sometimes, I go to my room and sit with the light off and just stare into the darkness. I don't even think about anything. I just sit in the dark and stare, sometimes for hours. I don't know why I do that.

You would think I would play a video game or read or something, but I just sit there. I'm willing to bet the psychiatrist Aunt Helen set me up with could write a new book about my staring habit, but I haven't told him about it. I don't really tell him much of anything. I only show up in his office because Aunt Helen wants me to go. I'm not mad at my aunt, so I show up, sit in the doctor's fluffy chair, and talk about Misty, or homework, or what college I'm thinking about attending. I don't talk about sitting in the dark, and I never talk to him about the crash. Believe me, he tries to get me to "open up" about it, but it's not going to happen.

Mr. White Shirt is done dragging bodies into the back of the plane. He makes his way slowly back up the aisle. I hear Angela sobbing quietly in the seat in front of me. I sit up and lean forward so my face presses against the crack between the seats in front of me. I can feel the smooth seat fabric stick to my face.

"It's gonna be okay," I say. "It's gonna be alright."

I don't know why I say this to her. Angela is nearly as indifferent to me as Misty. We're not friends, not at all. But I've been thinking about my dad and mom, and I just need to try and comfort someone if I can't comfort myself.

"They wouldn't take our phones if they weren't going to try and ransom us, you know? It's gonna be okay."

I can't see anything except the back of her head, but her sobbing seems to subside a little. I lean back and look again toward the front of the plane. Mr. White Shirt takes the gun from Soda Can Man and turns to keep an eye on the cabin. Soda Can Man disappears for a minute into the flight attendant's workstation. When he comes out, he's nursing his hand in a small plastic container filled with ice. A grim satisfaction fills me with sudden warmth. I hope he's broken every bone in his hand. My back brace has finally achieved some good purpose rather than just torturing me for the last three-and-a-half years.

A middle-aged lady near the center of the plane raises her hand, trembling slightly. She sits next to a boy about eleven years old and a man in his late thirties. They're obviously a family unit. Mr. White

29

Shirt looks directly at her. He still points the gun at the floor of the cabin, but I can hear a collective intake of nervous breath. He shifts the gun and nods his head at her.

"What do you want?" he asks. Everyone in front of the lady almost involuntarily turns to look back.

"Can we…can we use the bathroom?…Please…"

Soda Can Man whispers something, Mr. White Shirt glances over his shoulder and shrugs. Soda Can Man turns, shakes the water off of his hand, and looks back at the lady.

"One at a time", he says. "Let's go."

"It's my son", she says.

"Then let him up here. Hurry up."

The woman's son doesn't move. He seems rooted into his chair.

"He's scared," she says. "If you'll let me come with…"

"He comes alone or he can wet his pants. Make up your mind."

The lady tries to comfort the boy with a whisper, but it takes his father to make him stand up. His mother shakes her head, purses her lips against tears, but she clings to her husband's arm and lets the boy go. He steps over his mother's legs into the aisle. I can see that he's terrified, but somehow, he walks to the front. The terrorist steps aside and waves at the boy to get into the lavatory. At the last moment, the boy trips or somehow gets tangled in his own nervous legs. Either way, he falls.

Nearly everyone in the cabin gasps. Mr. White Shirt reaches out automatically and catches the boy before he hits the floor. The terrorist simply helps the boy get back to his feet and almost gently guides him to the lavatory door. I can feel the tension in the air, but Mr. White Shirt just looks back at everyone in the cabin with a small half-smile. It's almost as if he's trying to say: *What kind of a monster do you think I am? This is just business.*

It is in this moment I'm suddenly confident - every single person on this plane is going to die! I don't think helping the boy to his feet is anything more than an empty gesture. I can see it in his eyes. He's playing a nice game to keep everyone calm, but there's something behind his expression. I don't think they're going to intentionally crash the plane, but they have no intention of letting any of us survive.

I'm certain of it.

Four

We're descending and banking to the east. I feel the pitch of the airplane turn nose-down and slightly to my left. Outside the window, I see more and more of the sunset as we begin to break below the cloud ceiling. Every few seconds, a lower cloud blocks my view and then gives way to brilliant sunshine. As I watch the sun sink into the Pacific, I suddenly realize the air conditioner valve in the console above my head is open and pointed at my face. The cool air makes my eyes feel dry, so I reach up and turn it off.

Funny. For all I know our descent is going to be right into the side of a mountain at four hundred miles an hour and because my eyes are dry, I turn off an air valve. You would think I might be more concerned with dying than with dry eyes. So why did I even notice? I guess you don't realize how much you really want to live until you're really facing the end. I've spent the last year-and-a-half feeling sick to my stomach because I lived, and my parents died. I've spent many nights unable to fall asleep thinking about it, hoping that when I finally dozed off, I wouldn't wake up again. For a long time, that was what I hoped would happen, and the idea of drifting off to heaven in my sleep was almost comforting. The shrink my aunt makes me visit calls it "survivor's guilt".

I rub my face and try to massage some moisture back into my eyes. It feels like tiny rocks are scratching my eyeballs, so I open and shut them a few times until they feel normal again. I look back out the window. Around me, the plane is unnaturally quiet. I feel the tension in the air. Fear, like a ghostly vapor, creeps through the air, chilling my lungs, and, suddenly – I want to live. I thought dying would be so much better than living with the pain in my heart. It's been a lot like living with a growing, burning tumor in my chest. I've felt on the edge of sobbing almost every day, but I never open up about it to anyone – not to my family, certainly not to the shrink, not to anyone.

And that's why I don't have any friends at St. Marks. It's not because they're all stuck-up and rich. It's because I've been slinking through the hallways projecting a giant "leave me alone" force field. I've convinced myself that no one likes me, so I've been treating everyone as if, well, as if they don't like me. And guess what? Everyone has gotten the message. If I keep treating everyone like an enemy, they're going to be enemies. The truth is, I haven't given anybody a chance. But if I live through this, I've got a change to make.

Living through this isn't guaranteed, no matter how much I suddenly want to live. Looking out the window as we descend, I know we're still a long way from any sort of population center. When we lived in Alaska, we often flew back to Seattle for family gatherings with Uncle Jack. I pretty much know every turn on the route. Whenever we flew down from Alaska, my dad would sort of narrate the trip, telling me about the radar markers the pilot could expect in the Queen Charlottes and then over Vancouver Island. East of the flight route, he said, there was nothing except nearly uninhabited forest and mountains. There are a few isolated fishing harbors and logging or mining camps, but not much else. Dad used to tell me a man could get lost out there and probably wander for twenty years before seeing any sign of civilization. Alaska was like that too, tens of thousands of square miles of cold and wet and mud, alive with bears and mosquitos. Dad used to joke that the mosquitoes in Alaska were big enough to carry off small children.

The plane banks to the left, steeper and more insistent, as if we're turning away from a cliff face. We're turning more directly toward the wilderness of western British Columbia, Canada. At this speed, we will be over the coast in minutes. I cannot imagine what the terrorists are thinking. There are no cities in the wild and no airports, but we continue to descend. I look out the window at the wing of the plane. Having grown up with a pilot for a father, I have some idea what it takes to land and take off in an airplane, so I look to see if the flaps are being deployed. They aren't, and the engines seem to be humming along at the same rate they've been burning since we reached our cruising altitude.

In Alaska, Dad flew a Cessna 206H floatplane. It's not a large plane, but large enough to intimidate the average wanna-be pilot. He started teaching me to fly when I was about fourteen. If he had a local run, he would often put me in the co-pilot seat, but all of that was cut short when I was sixteen and he died. I learned a lot about flying before the crash, except afterwards I haven't been able to even look into a cockpit. I don't really want to think about flying now, but I can't help wondering what in the world these idiots in control of the plane are thinking.

Obviously, Mr. Tan Jacket is a trained pilot because the turn we just made was smooth and practiced. Banking left or right in a plane isn't as easy as turning the "steering wheel". In fact, most people don't even realize that the "steering wheel" in an airplane cockpit isn't even called a steering wheel – it's called a yoke, doofus! Actors on TV make it look like all you have to do is jump in the pilot's seat and steer it like a car. What a joke! The first time I tried to bank an airplane, I lost several hundred feet of altitude and we probably would have done a full barrel roll, if my dad hadn't been there to take control. Banking is a combination of holding back the yoke, so you don't lose altitude, pushing the right or the left rudder pedal, depending on which way you want to go and turning the control wheel. Too much rudder and you'll over-correct. Too much yoke and you'll ascend and stall. Not enough and you'll dive. Too much control wheel and you'll flip over. Of course, in a plane like this, the autopilot can turn the plane. It's possible Mr. Tan Jacket simply punched in the coordinates and the computer turned the plane automatically. If he did, that means he knows exactly where we're going.

Dad and Mom left the commercial aviation business right about the time I turned nine years old. We spent a year in San Diego, in training. Dad had pretty much every license to fly known to man and a lot of hours in commercial airliners but flying for missionaries was a different animal. Most of the work was all about dropping onto the kinds of runways most sane people would fear on a good day. Not only that, he had to take Bible classes because they expected him to be a missionary, as much as a pilot. I can't figure that part out because I don't remember Dad ever having to preach or conduct any kind of church service. He just flew in, dropped off whatever the locals had ordered, and flew back out again. I could be wrong about that since I spent most of my time being home-schooled by mom in whatever living quarters we were given at the time.

Our first assignment was in Cameroon, West Africa. I turned eleven by the time we got there. It was hot in Cameroon, and dusty, but the people were amazing. I've never seen people so happy to be utterly dirt-poor. It's like they honestly didn't know how miserable they really were. The women were always singing, and there was a smile on pretty much everyone's face. I suppose they figured there was no sense being unhappy since there was no way they could change anything. But I was unhappy all the time, and I had no right to be unhappy. I grew up in the States; I never went without a meal, I was healthy as a horse, and I wasn't destined to live out my life scratching out a living in the blood-red dirt of West Africa. Eventually, I would get to go back to America, back to McDonald's and paved roads and I was just too short-sighted to see it at the time.

I started seeing things differently, very gradually. I held onto my resentment about no video games or TV for quite a while, no matter how much my parents lectured me about how spoiled I was. It was a slow process to get me to see that life wasn't all about my personal entertainment. I think the beginning of my change-of-heart started in the marketplace. I remember how strange it was going to the market in Cameroon because everything was divided into tiny Ziploc baggies or paper envelopes. In America, you buy a box of cereal; in Cameroon, you buy a Ziploc baggie of cereal with just enough for one person and one meal. Every day, the locals would buy exactly enough to eat for one day. There were few refrigerators where we were out in the sticks, and even fewer freezers. Meat was a rare treat, and since you couldn't be exactly sure what kind of meat it was, or how long it had been sitting in the sun, or how exactly it came into your kitchen, we often went for weeks without any meat. So, my dad pointed out that the market really showed how the people of Cameroon were honest about life. He said, *It's really one day at a time, son. No one gets out of this life alive and no one knows how many days you're going to get, either. So, put a smile on your face, because you're alive today.*

For the last year-and-a-half, I'd forgotten that lesson. I wonder what he would say about my feelings over the last eighteen months? Why did I give myself permission to wish I were dead? How could I secretly puff myself up about how much more life experience I've had than everybody else at St. Marks because I've had the stupid good luck of having lived in two different third world countries and, at the same time, forget what I learned there?

I was sullen for a long time when we first got to Africa, but the African kids didn't seem to care. Most of them had no idea what a video game was, so they didn't know what I was so upset about. But they had a soccer ball and that's all they needed. I was only eleven and didn't speak French at all, but that didn't stop them from pulling me into their soccer games. I'm not sure they understood the rules of the game either since it was more or less full-tackle soccer, sort of like a mix between the NFL and hockey on a soccer field, minus a hockey stick or beautiful cheerleaders. I learned a fair number of interesting soccer words in French too, the colorful sort of words you don't repeat around your mother. I found out later their idea of French was a long way from Paris too so, what few sentences I mastered, were only useful in Cameroon. It took a few months to pry me out of feeling sorry for myself, but eventually, I became a team captain. We played for hours in the red dust, kicking a ball that was so patched up, it was an old-fashioned miracle it held any air in it at all.

We stayed in Cameroon for almost a year and ten months or so, if I remember correctly. Our next assignment was in Sunny Cove, Alaska. I think we were given that assignment because it was sort of close to our home in Seattle. We stayed in Alaska for two years and then went to New Guinea. It was only about three weeks into our time in New Guinea before the crash. I didn't even have time in New Guinea to get over the basic culture shock before I was standing at my parents' funeral back in Washington State. I don't have many memories of New Guinea, but I do remember the pigs. There were pigs everywhere and they seemed to be a sort of currency, like a squealing savings account. For whatever reason, pigs are a big deal in New Guinea. In fact, I witnessed women nursing pigs at their breasts instead of kids. That sort of thing sticks in your mind, believe me, but I think I'm blocking out my other memories of New Guinea because of the crash.

I look out the window again. I can see the coast like a dark smudge of smoke in the near-distance. I look up at the front of the plane and see the kid who went to the bathroom making his way back to his seat between his parents. Mr. White Shirt ignores him, but his eyes do not waver from the cabin. I can hear a few people whimpering but it seems strangely quiet. After all, there's nothing to do but wait…and think…and remember. I look over at Misty, but she is nearly invisible from where I'm seated.

Somewhere close to the front of the plane, I see another hand go up. It's a younger guy with strawberry-blond hair and a red goatee. I remember passing him when I boarded the plane. He's a pretty big guy, and I wonder how silly it must feel for him to raise his hand to ask permission to take a squirt. Mr. White Shirt says something to Soda Can Man, who snorts derisively, and looks over at the strawberry-blond man with contempt written all over his face. It's like, *so the big boy has to go potty. Everybody say, "Oh, that's so cute."* Reminds me of the few times I've had to go into the locker room when the football players were gearing up. I'm the band dweeb with a back brace; it's about as non-manly as it is possible to be, and they were not shy with their grins and grunts. It was like parading a housecat in front of a pack of wolves.

"You need to go?" he asks. No one can miss the snide tone in his voice.

37

"Yeah, I gotta take a leak. Is that gonna work?" he says.

"What is your name?" asks the terrorist.

"Sam", the man answers.

"Okay, Sam", the terrorist says. "But I think you need to be quick."

Sam doesn't answer. He carefully gets to his feet and steps into the aisle. He's a big man, maybe six inches taller than Mr. White Shirt. Soda Can Man gets up and turns to face him. Mr. White Shirt steps to the side and the flush on his face betrays his thoughts. He wasn't expecting Sam to be a giant. The guy's big enough to crush a linebacker. I'll bet Mr. White Shirt is wondering how many bullets it's going to take to bring him down. How many more football crushers are going to need to flush their beverage service down the toilet before somebody tries to rush the terrorists?

Sam moves toward the front. Maybe Sam's thinking the same way I'm thinking, because there's something about the way he moves that makes me hold my breath. There's a steadiness to his pace that makes me think he can handle himself in a fight. I'm not the only one who thinks so, either. Soda Can Man takes a step back and Mr. White Shirt readies the gun to fire if he feels threatened. I get a grim satisfaction at Mr. White Shirt's reaction. I've had plenty of fantasies about smacking a few football players into choking on their opinion of me. Sam closes the gap down the aisle and I hold my breath, but he simply steps into the lavatory. Everyone takes a deep breath with me. Even Soda Can Man relaxes a bit.

Mr. White Shirt leans back against the bulkhead. He carefully watches the lavatory. After about two minutes, Sam opens the lavatory door and steps out. I can make out the blush on his face all the way from my position at the back of the plane. Everyone stares at him, expecting something. Sam looks down at the aisle and begins to make his way back to his seat. I can almost hear everyone let out a slow breath. Mr. White Shirt shifts his eyes to Soda Can Man. He says something I can't hear. Soda Can Man flashes a nasty smile and rolls his eyes. I can only imagine what they're saying.

Bullies. They're all the same. It doesn't matter what language they speak or what country they come from, either. I thought I left them behind when we left the States, but I ran into them again. My dad tried to help me understand them. He said bullies are forever trying to belittle anyone they see as weaker because, deep down in their self-centered little hearts, they're all alone with how pathetic they really are, and they can't afford for anyone to see the truth. They will cause you to bleed to cover up their own fear. They know they're just as weak and vulnerable as everyone else, and their greatest fear is someone will find out. So, they belittle and taunt and laugh. They're also eternal, from every culture and every time period. Dad tried to teach me that, so I wouldn't feel the sting of their taunts, only it didn't work. Just knowing they were really scared little kittens in their hearts didn't take away the ugly feeling I got when they made fun of me because I was the only white kid they had ever seen, or when I couldn't keep up on the soccer field. It's not helping now, either. My current hope is that Sam will take these particular bullies and stomp on their skulls.

But he doesn't.

As Sam steps past the second row of seats, a skinny man I had not noticed before, leaps to his feet and rushes Mr. White Shirt. Sam sees the movement out of the corner of his eye. He seems to duck involuntarily down into the aisle.

Soda Can Man shouts. Mr. White Shirt swivels his head, but the skinny man full-body tackles him before he can react. Instantly, half a dozen people toward the front of the plane start shouting. Sam sees what is happening. He hesitates for a moment. Soda Can Man tries to grab the skinny man, but Sam throws himself forward, driving Soda Can Man back against the bulkhead. Mr. White Shirt is on the floor, covered by the skinny man. I expect to hear the gun go off any second. Soda Can Man shouts at the top of his lungs. Sam pulls back and drives a wicked right fist into Soda Can Man's stomach. This could be over in the next ten seconds. I leap to my feet to get a better view.

39

From the open cockpit door, I hear Mr. Tan Jacket shouting something. I hear someone in the front row shout, "Let's go!" I see three more men get to their feet. They are going to try to overwhelm the terrorists. Everybody's ready to be a hero now!

Mr. Tan Jacket begins to frantically shout over his shoulder.

"Shoot them, shoot them!" he screams.

Sam throws another punch at Soda Can Man. He wilts like a punctured tire. I see him frantically punch at Sam's head, but he screams and yanks back his hand. Score one more for my back brace! He must have really hurt his hand when he punched me. I can't help yelling like a football fan at a playoff game.

The skinny man smothers Mr. White Shirt, pinning the gun against his chest. If Mr. White Shirt pulls the trigger, he's likely to shoot himself. The skinny man takes a fistful of Mr. White Shirt's hair, slams his head against the cabin floor, and I hear the terrorist scream again. This is a savage fight to the death and there are no rules.

Suddenly, the cabin floor beneath my feet gives way. The whole plane lurches suddenly downward and then pulls up. Gravity seems to go from zero to three times normal in two seconds. Everyone seems to scream in panic at once. I fall headlong over the seat in front of me, nearly into Angela's lap. I slam into the seat head first, my neck twisting painfully to my left. My forehead digs into the rough fabric as if an invisible giant is trying to crush me. The plane swings wildly and my feet swing to my right. I crumple onto the floor between the seats. The front of the back-brace drives into my throat like a fist to the throat. I cough and hack, trying to get a breath. Mr. Tan Jacket is screaming.

"I'll kill us all! I'll crash the plane! Get back, get back, or we'll all die!"

"Oh my God, oh my God!" I hear someone plead.

My heart races. I feel my stomach rising into my throat but it's as empty as a moist paper sack. I heave up nothing but air, over and over again, as the plane falls like a stone. It seems like a thousand voices are wailing all at once, bodies seem to flail all around me. My

40

feet are tangled in Angela's lap. She pushes me away from her as if I'm an unclean thing and then begins to kick me. She is completely crazy. I try to wiggle out of the space between Angela's seat and the seat back in front of her, but a horrific pull of gravity glues me to the floor. My arms seem to weigh a thousand pounds. I begin to crawl into the aisle, right under Angela's stomping feet. I get a heel in the eye and I know I'll have a shiner tomorrow. Angela suddenly pulls her knees all the way up to her chest, wraps her arms around her legs, and moans over and over with a harsh sort of croak.

There's a loud bang. Mr. White Shirt has pulled the trigger. Somehow, I manage to pull myself up to my knees. I turn my head toward the front of the plane. Sam continues to wrestle with Soda Can Man and the skinny man rolls into my view. His neck is limp and dead. I can smell the acid-like scent of gunpowder and Mr. White Shirt shouts something in his language. Suddenly, the plane begins to level out and the unnatural pull of heavy gravity lessens.

Mr. White Shirt pulls himself to his feet. Four men still stand up at their seats, ready to join the rush, but Mr. White Shirt aims the gun back at them.

"Sit down...NOW!" he shouts. No one moves. "I said, sit down!"

Mr. White Shirt takes a step toward Sam and Soda Can Man both writhing on the floor. He puts the barrel of the gun into Sam's temple, so he stops struggling and goes limp.

"Sit down! Put on the seat belts! Get back!" he screams.

No one moves. Mr. White Shirt pulls the trigger and I see Sam's brains splatter on the lavatory door. Someone begins to scream hysterically, and I hear a man's voice spit out a nasty cuss word over and over like a pagan death chant. Sam's body crumples to the floor on top of Soda Can Man. The echo of the shot makes my ears ring. Mr. White Shirt lurches forward. He grabs a dark-haired girl in the second row and pulls her to her feet. She howls and claws at his arm, but he puts the barrel of the gun to her temple. She appears to faint, and I recognize her. It's Judy Torren, an alto sax player from my band. She's only a freshman.

"Get back! Sit down or I kill her next!" he shouts again.

There is a pause, a split-second break in the craziness as if everyone is deciding what to do. Slowly, the men sink to their seats. I scoot backwards and slide quickly into my original seat near the back where my greatcoat is still wadded up in the corner of the window seat.

"Put the seat belts on!" Mr. White Shirt yells.

I frantically reach for the seat belt. The terrorist isn't looking at me, but I don't think that matters. Judy is going to die in about three seconds if everyone doesn't calm down.

I'm gasping for air. I can see Sam's body on the floor. A pool of red puddles around his head. The skinny man's hair is almost touching Sam's blood, and I feel my stomach clinch for round three of the "vomit comet". I tear my eyes away from the bodies and cower back in the seat. Without really knowing why, I throw my hand over my mouth as if I'm desperately trying to keep my terror from exploding out of my mouth.

"Oh God, oh God, oh God…please let us live! Please let us live!"

It takes me second to recognize my own voice…

Five

Mr. White Shirt has the gun smashed into Judy's temple. I can see the whites of her eyes even from the back of the plane. She is obviously unconscious and limp. Mr. White Shirt wildly scans the cabin for any possible threat. Behind him, Soda Can Man gets to his feet. His hair is disheveled, and I can see his left eye is black and puffy. At least Sam gave the scumbag a shiner before he died.

I can't get the image of Sam's body and the pool of blood out of my mind. It's like seeing a bright light and shutting your eyes. When you shut your eyes, you see an after- glow, a greenish, yellow image of the light that seems burned onto the inside of your eyelids. Sam's blood is like that in my mind. Every time I shut my eyes, I can see it glowing hot, but green and yellow instead of red, swirling around like the northern lights I used to see in Alaska on summer nights. It's an awful fascination. I turn to look back at the front, resisting the urge to look down at the bodies.

Four people are dead. It's like a horrific game of "Musical Chairs". Every time the music stops, somebody pops! They're picking us off one by one. I don't know how many bullets are in the gun, but I seem to remember Mr. Tan Jacket got Todd's spare clip when he pulled the gun off the body. You would think I might know something about guns, having lived within spitting distance of the tundra, but the irony is I've never actually gone hunting in my life. Fishing and even camping in homemade shelters - sure, but never hunting. So, I don't know anything about the gun. He can't have enough to kill everybody on the plane though. Still, it's enough to keep everyone wondering if the next time the music stops, it will be their turn to pop. And nobody seems to be in any rush to find out, either.

Mr. Tan Jacket shouts something from the cockpit and Mr. White Shirt responds. I don't know what language they're screeching in, but I can sift out the stress in their voices. It's like a dark harmony lurking underneath a melody. Mr. White Shirt slowly relaxes his grip on Judy, but he drags her back toward the bulkhead. He steps over the skinny man's body. Stepping back once more, he suddenly releases Judy and nearly tosses her toward the front seat. The pilot and the co-pilot are seated there, but their hands are tied behind their backs. Judy falls into the pilot's lap. Her head slides to her right and she nearly flops over onto the skinny man's body on the floor, but Mrs. Carlyle, in the seat across from the pilot, instinctively reaches over and grabs her shoulder. The pilot begins to wiggle into the middle seat as Mrs. Carlyle leans across, holding Judy's weight. The man sitting behind the pilot leans forward and with Mrs. Carlyle's help, they pull Judy into a seated position. Her body is still limp, but the pilot leans his shoulder over. They put Judy's head on the pilot's shoulder and sit back into their seats.

I recognize the man behind the pilot suddenly. It's Mr. Towns, our band director. I didn't notice him at first because he looks like he's aged twenty years since he got on the plane. His hair is frizzed out, his tie is torn nearly off, and his shirt looks stained by something that looks suspiciously like dried vomit. I guess I'm not the only one who lost his lunch.

Mr. Tan Jacket says something in whatever language they are speaking. Soda Can Man rubs the side of his head and nods. He turns to the cabin.

"Everyone, put on your seat belts," he says calmly. "We are going to land soon. Put your seat belts on and lean forward. I don't want to see any faces. Do it now."

Leaning forward? Those are crash-landing positions! But not a suicide crash - the kind of crash-landing you're hoping to survive. Unless they're just trying to get everyone under control before they plow us into a building, ordering us into crash-landing positions only makes sense if they're going to try and set us down. But if they just want control before we all die, why not just throw us into a dive and

44

be done with it? Why the crash positions unless they're really trying to land? But where? There can't be any airports anywhere near our position.

And leaning forward isn't much of an option for me. I've got a piece of plastic tied to my mid-section, held in place with three strips of industrial-grade Velcro, but I figure this is not the time to argue. I reach down and loosen my belt. If I spread my legs, I can at least lean forward enough to hide my face from view. I think about trying to get the brace off, but I don't think there's any time.

Angela leans forward so completely, she looks like she's bent in half. I can hear her sobbing, but as I look her direction, I can also see out the window. I'm startled to see a mountain floating past us. We are awfully low, and I can't imagine where we are or what the terrorists intend to do. I try and peek out the window without raising my head above the seat in front of me, and I'm startled by what I see. We are passing a huge mountain peak. It's so close I feel like I could reach out and scrape my hand on the rocks. And the plane is still descending.

The plane slightly shudders, there's a shooshing sound, and I realize Mr. Tan Jacket must have lowered the flaps. The engine noise changes as he lowers power. I only have about twenty hours as a pilot-in-command with my dad in the co-pilot seat, but I've brought a Cessna in enough times to know what it takes to land. My Dad used to say that a landing is a controlled crash. I can feel the plane slipping right, then left, as Mr. Tan Jacket corrects his angle of descent.

This is insane. I can feel my heart racing. There's no way on earth they can get this thing on the ground safely. Even the world's best pilot isn't going to take a 737 onto an empty dirt field without breaking the thing in half. A single serious bump and the entire plane will explode. It's simply not possible.

In a panic, I bring my head up. Both Soda Can Man and the terrorist are seated in the forward jump seats, normally occupied by the cabin flight attendants during take-off and landing. Both lean forward, braced for impact.

45

I swear under my breath and Angela turns her head to look at me. I can see she is terrified and crying. I look out the window again but raise my head a little higher to try and make out where we are. I can see trees and then...water.

We're landing in a lake.

Of course! That's it! It's a nearly perfect runway – if it's a calm day. My dad used to rave about the "miracle on the Hudson" landing all the time. He told me all about it, how an Airbus taking off from La Guardia in New York made an emergency landing in the Hudson River – and everyone lived to tell the tale! He used to talk about the pilot, Captain "Sully," like he was a superhero. And he told me why too. That landing, he said, was epic. About ten million things could have gone wrong, but Sully brought her in safely.

Dad had a huge respect for Captain Sully because Dad flew float planes most of our time in Alaska. It was hard enough to get a floatplane down safely, especially on a choppy day. I've landed on the water a hundred times with him. Of course, the beauty of a water landing is having a long runway, and in the north, there are lakes in the wild that are miles long. But a Boeing 737 isn't designed to land in the water. My dad's plane had pontoons and even then, it could be rough. Dad was impressed with the Hudson landing because Sully's Airbus was traveling at nearly 150 miles per hour. It could have potentially cartwheeled into a hundred flaming pieces if it had caught the waves at just the wrong angle. But right now, even if the water is perfectly smooth, a 737 has two engines hanging from the wings just like the Airbus and that's like having two shovels dropping down under the wings. The "miracle flight" had one engine instantly torn off and huge holes gouged into the fuselage by the force of hitting the water. It was a true miracle the plane's back wasn't broken by the impact. My dad used to go on and on about what an awesome pilot Sully was to get that Airbus down safely. He must have told me fifty times about how many things could have gone wrong. And now I'm living it – but I'm willing to bet Mr. Tan Jacket is nowhere near as good a pilot as Captain Sully.

On a normal landing, a good pilot can take advantage of something my dad called "ground effect." I remember having some trouble with ground effect when my dad was teaching me to fly. When you get close to the runway, the wind coming down off the wings can hit the ground and swirl back upwards, creating a sort of pillow or cushion. It gives you a strange sense of floating, and, if you're not careful, you can cut power and slam hard into the runway. I did that on my first landing and we bounced twice. My dad told me how ground effect can fool a pilot into thinking he's ready to "flare" for touchdown when in fact, he's still a fair distance over the runway.

I have no idea if Mr. Tan Jacket is a good pilot. For all I know, he flew for Taliban Airways for a dozen years, or like me he's only had twenty hours in a Cessna, or just played around with a computer training program for a 737 that was little better than an advanced video game. Landing on water and not flipping end over end into a million tiny pieces is going to require slowing to the lowest possible speed before letting the plane touch down. Too high, and he will slam us into the water. At over a hundred miles per hour, hitting the water will be like flying into a brick wall. Too low, and the engines will catch the surface of the water before he can flare the nose up, and we'll spin around like we're in a tornado. If he's any good at all, he can conceivably get us down to about 110 knots before we hit - but 110 is still awfully fast.

I've heard the flight attendant's little speech about "what to do in the event of a water evacuation" a thousand times and I've never really paid any attention. Honestly, who does? Flight attendants go on about sticking the seat belt tongue into the buckle as if everyone on board is a complete ignoramus, while normal people are already in their seatbelts trying to get their headphones on. And besides, if we're really going to crash, what's the point of a seatbelt? I mean, seriously! Does it help with identifying bodies if what's left of my charcoaled corpse is still strapped to a seat? And up until today, I never gave much thought to a "water landing" either. My dad told me that hitting the water at over a hundred miles per hour is like launching a steak with a grenade launcher against a concrete wall.

And besides all that, if we're landing on a lake and we somehow survive the impact, we're going to have about two minutes to get out before the plane begins to sink. Flying an airliner is like flying a brick attached to a rocket engine. If the engine quits, we're going to drop like a sack of lead so, without landing gear and a runway underneath us, we're going to sink to the bottom in minutes. And since a landing is just a controlled crash anyway, trying to land on anything other than a real runway is like trying to jump off a running horse onto the hood of a Porsche that's traveling faster than a cheetah. Any way you look at it, without a miracle, we're totally muffed.

I hear the engine whine slow again. The plane drops a little more. I look at Angela again. She's so scared, I can almost read her thoughts. I look away from her out the window again, but I can't see anything. We must be well out from the shore of the lake.

I feel the plane vibrate harshly. A sudden chorus of whimpers and cries fill the cabin. The sound of the engines seems louder than I ever remember on any landing. Maybe it's because my ears are on overload, or my senses are frayed like a shredded electric cord. The smell of sweat and vomit and blood mixes with the shuddering whine of the engines and I'm losing control. I hear a loud, savage cry come out of my own mouth. I want God Himself to hear me, but I don't know what to say. Out of nowhere, I remember the old nursery prayer: *Now I lay me down to sleep, I pray the Lord my soul to keep*…but that just doesn't seem right. I grit my teeth and wish to the Lord Himself that I could just hold someone's hand. I just need a human connection, an anchor, something to keep me from completely going off the deep end.

"Oh God," I cry over and over. "Please let us live. I believe, I believe…I believe you've washed away my sins. I believe I'm going to heaven…"

I feel the plane pitch slightly up and I recognize "the flare." I grit my teeth.

The plane slams into the water. My head snaps forward into the seat back in front of me. I taste the nasty saltiness of blood from my nose. The brace digs mercilessly into my thighs. The sound of the

48

plane sliding over the surface of the water is so loud I can barely hear the shouting around me. Several overhead bins pop open. Luggage spills out onto the aisle and the cabin lights go out. The shearing sound of the water is as loud as a freight train running at full speed. The plane pitches up and to my right. It's going to flip!

"Lord, please!" I yell at the top of my voice. "Don't let us go over! Don't let us go over!"

Every muscle in my body tenses. I grip the armrest so hard I can feel my finger-nails puncture the fabric. Angela screams, and I hear a wrenching sound of metal being torn apart. The plane shudders so harshly I'm surprised it doesn't crack open like a boiled egg but then it falls back to my left. The impact with the water is so sharp, most of the air flashes out of my lungs in one huge whoosh. My body is thrown toward the bulkhead. There's a popping sound, then silence.

Somehow, by some incredible miracle, we're not dead.

Emergency lights flash on. I lift my head and cough on the blood flowing from my nose. I suck in air in quick, short gulps. Another passenger's head pops up in front of me and I'm so surprised, I flinch back. It's Danny Edgecomb, a freshman alto sax player. His eyes are wild, like a hunted beast, and he's making a throbbing sort of whine in his throat. He looks away from me, and I wonder if my eyes don't look the same.

"We're still alive," I say aloud. "We're still...Oh my...Thank you, Jesus!"

Light streams in from the windows on both sides of the aisle, but the main cabin lights are out. Most of the overhead bins have popped open. Luggage is strewn everywhere. In the front, Mr. White Shirt gets to his feet. He still has the gun, ready to fire, but the look on his face is anything except confident. He seems just as surprised as I am that we're still in one piece. He says something to Soda Can Man and suddenly, they hug, patting each other on the back. Passengers begin to stir, and several people stand.

"No one move!" Mr. White Shirt shouts.

Soda Can Man stumbles to the front cabin door and opens it. The light streaming in is so bright compared to the dim interior that I blink several times. I smell the cool and the wet from the lake outside. Soda Can Man fiddles with something and I guess he must have pulled the emergency slide lever, because I hear the whooshing sound as it fills with air. From the cockpit, Mr. Tan Jacket appears. He is visibly pale. Even from a distance, I can see the landing was as terrifying for him as it was for us. Obviously, Mr. Tan Jacket is no Captain Sully, but we are currently alive. He surveys the cabin and smiles.

"If you do exactly what we tell you," he says, "you will live. We will open the emergency door over the wing. Do not move until we tell you to move."

Mr. Tan Jacket shuffles down the aisle, stepping over luggage. The skinny man and Sam's body must have shifted during the landing. I can't see them on the floor, but it's pretty dark except for the pale light coming in from outside and the emergency lights on the cabin floor.

Mr. Tan Jacket gets to the middle of the plane where Misty is seated. He steps in front of her and opens the emergency exit door over the wing. He activates the emergency slide and then turns back to look at the cabin.

"Everyone, do as I tell you!" he shouts. "Reach under your seat and get the life jacket you will find there. Put it on. Do this now!"

Misty hasn't moved. Mr. Tan Jacket kneels in front of her and reaches under her seat. She flinches and almost throws her legs into the aisle to get away from his pawing hand. But he just smiles, loosens the life jacket, and hands it to her.

I can hear a sucking wet sound, like a wet paintbrush getting slapped on a wall, and I can't place the sound for a second. Then I get it. Water is seeping into the cabin from somewhere. I look down and see nearly a half an inch of water has already seeped into the plane. The water jolts me back into the situation. I reach to unbuckle my seatbelt and spend five seconds fighting to get it loose since it has somehow gotten twisted in the lower part of my shirt. I finally rip it off, slide forward, turn around, and reach for the life jacket under my seat. The water seeping in makes me think about the cold so I quickly unwad my great coat, slip it on and button it up. The life jacket isn't anything to get terribly excited about, just a thin piece of yellow plastic, but I slip it over my head and snap the belt buckle around my waist anyway.

"Everyone in front of me, get out through the front!" Mr. Tan Jacket shouts. "Everyone else, get out over the wing. Don't take anything with you. Get onto the slide – it will float like a raft."

Mr. Tan Jacket grabs Misty's arm and pulls her to her feet. He nearly drags her out the door over the wing.

This whole thing has been all about her, that's obvious to me now. She's the daughter of the next Vice President of the United States and a master terrorist has her in his grip!

I get up and step into the aisle, a little shaky on my feet. Then I look at Angela and she's still bent forward clutching herself with her arms. Her face is so white I think she's going to be sick.

"Come on, Ang. Come on."

But she doesn't move. She just sort of whimpers and stares at me. I can tell she can't actually see me. It's almost as if her eyes are shut off from the inside even though her eyelids are not shut. I know what that feels like, so I know she literally can't move; she doesn't even know what's going on around her. I look wildly around, not sure what to do or who to ask for help. Passengers have already filled the aisle, streaming toward the front. Surprisingly, no one is shoving or screaming. They're just sort of shuffling forward just as they would if we were de-planing in Seattle. After all the screaming, four dead passengers and landing in a half-frozen lake, the sense of calm is sort of scary.

"Angela," I say. "We gotta go."

There's no one behind us and everyone in front of us has his or her backs turned. My feet are almost covered in icy water, and Angela still won't move.

If I don't do something, she'll stay in her seat and drown.

51

Six

I know I have to do something. Angela is frightened out of her mind. Ice-cold water swirls around my ankles. Around me, I sense the change from calm to near panic. Just a few seconds ago, everyone was sort of quiet, filing nicely toward the two open doors, one at the front, the other, over the wing, but the water is rising, already over my ankles, and I can hear the sounds of distress as people start to scramble for an open door. Suddenly, I remember some rotten poem one of my Lit teachers read to my class, something about "red in tooth and claw", and I get a fearful picture of what might happen if we don't get out of the plane in about a minute. If I don't get Angela moving soon, we're going to be fish food or clawed to death by people trying to get out.

I tug at Angela's arm, but she just won't move. It's almost like she's incapable of moving. I guess she's in shock. I've heard of shock before, but I never understood it. I always got the picture of somebody getting zapped by a lightning bolt or something. If she is in shock, I wonder why I'm not. Or maybe I am, and I just don't know it? The only thing I feel is a rising shiver in my chest, kind of the same feeling I got whenever I ran into a bear out in the bush when we lived up in Alaska. It's the sort of feeling you really don't want to get.

"We've got to go, Angie," I say. I stand up, but Angela still isn't moving. "Angie, get up. Come on. Let's go."

Angela isn't moving at all; the seats in front of me have emptied and nearly everyone has gone out the door. I can see the last few people disappearing out the hatch over the wing. I reach down and shake her on the shoulder.

"This isn't a joke. We're going to get trapped if we don't go NOW!"

I'm shouting, but the girl just clings to her knees harder than ever. The water has risen above my ankles. A picture of getting trapped in the back of the plane and sliding into the inky blackness makes me shudder. I take hold of Angela and give her a serious shake.

"Get up!" I shout. "We've got to go."

I'm feeling real desperation now because nothing I'm saying is moving her; she's petrified, and if we stay here any longer, we're in real danger of getting sucked down into deep water. I can't be worried about her thinking I'm feeling out her private parts any longer, so I just reach down to her waist and unbuckle her seatbelt. In one swift motion, I wrap my arm around her waist and pull with all my might. She isn't heavy, but the close quarters and the simple fact that she isn't using a single muscle to help me makes her seem like she weighs a ton. It doesn't help that I can't fully bend over to get hold of her because of the stupid brace, but I pull her limp body up against my chest, wrap my other arms around her waist, and begin dragging her toward the wing hatch.

The back half of the plane is almost filled with water. I catch a glimpse of a body floating in the water. I can't tell if it's Todd or the flight attendant, but a horrible image of fish nibbling at the flesh flashes through my mind.

I've always hated deep water. I have never been able to swim in lakes or out in the ocean. Just the thought of hanging like a floating spider over hundreds or thousands of feet of cold, black abyss where any kind of slimy creature sprouting a million teeth could be lurking down below, ready to snatch at my toes and drag me under, makes me shiver and cringe. I have no idea how deep this lake is, but based on how big it is, I'm betting it's more like Loch Ness than a bathtub.

I can't get the image of a huge, black creature lurking in the darkness out of my head. I pull at Angela's body with all my might because the water is up to my knees and she's dragging me back. Angela can't weigh more than a hundred and ten pounds, but her weight is enough to press the breast pad of the Boston brace into my chest, so I can hardly breathe. My fear of being sucked back toward the floating body gives me a boost of energy and before I know it, my arms have slipped up underneath Angela's armpits.

The thought that I'm accidently grabbing something I'm not supposed to grab gives me pause. I'm already scared but I'm even more afraid of Angela suddenly waking up from whatever shock she is in to find me fondling her chest. I stop, lean forward, sort of scoot my arms down toward her waist and start dragging her again.

The exit hatch is a little tougher to navigate with Angela leaning against my chest.

"Come on, Angie. Give me a little help here," I whisper in her ear. "We're almost out. You can do this..."

Angela begins to really sob, but I feel her finally take some of her weight onto her own feet. I let go of her waist and twist to see where I'm taking us.

The emergency ramp is inflated. It's a pretty big ramp and at least thirty people huddle against the edges as it floats on the water. The plane is now so low in the lake that the inflatable ramp seems to stick straight out like an obscene gesture. I can't see how the ramp is going to detach from the plane if it sinks all the way under.

Captain Sully's plane never completely sank. It sort of bobbled in the water, more than halfway under, but still sort of afloat, like a giant fishing bobber. Still, even if this plane only swamps instead of sinking, I'm not staying inside, not with floating dead bodies and the possibility of getting sucked back into the lake.

"Come on, Angie, let's get out of here." Angela continues to sob, but she's at least finally standing on her own feet. "We have to step out on the wing. It's okay. It's just a little under the water. We've already got our feet wet. Come on, you can do this."

I step out onto the wing, then put my left foot into the floating ramp, and immediately slip on the slick material. I grab the edge of the exit before I do the splits or fall. I carefully put my other foot into the raft and then slide down to my knees. It's safer than trying to stand. I reach back for Angela to help her get into the raft. She takes my hand without hesitation. She's not really looking at me, and I wonder if she even knows who I am. I try to help her get in gracefully, but everything is so slick and wet, she basically tumbles right over my shoulder. I grab hold of her by the waist again and more or less settle us both into the bottom of the raft on our knees. There's at least an inch of ice water in the bottom and I'm soaked up to my thighs. The water is truly glacial and even though I'm wearing a wool jacket and slacks and I've only been wet for a few minutes - I'm already shivering.

Looking up, I see Mr. Tan Jacket at the other end of the raft. He still holds the gun at the ready as he watches over us. The raft is about twenty feet long, but even at that distance, Mr. Tan Jacket is still a hovering raptor looking for any reason to claw at anyone he wants to hurt. He looks at Angela and me and then looks away as if he knows we're the last people out and he wouldn't have cared if we didn't make it out in the first place. We're obviously not that important. Glancing over at the other raft I see Mr. White Shirt and Soda Can Man in the front of that raft as well. They don't have any weapons to control the thirty or so people in front of them and I wonder if someone is going to try and drown those two. Looking back toward the shore, I see the sun setting and the light is nearly blinding me. Closer to me, I hear a voice.

"Here, let me help you."

It's the co-pilot. His uniform shirt is untucked on one side and his nose is bleeding heavily. He reaches out and takes my elbow.

"Sit over here – we need to try and keep the weight evenly distributed," he says.

The co-pilot guides me to the corner of the raft, the one closest to the plane, and then he directs Angela to sit right next to me. I'm a little surprised when she snuggles up under my arm. I'm not used to girls wanting to be anywhere near me, but I guess under the circumstances, she needs to be near someone, even if it is the lowest person on the social ladder. I'm not quite sure what to do so I just drape my arm sort of loosely over her shoulder. I get the mental picture of a guy on a movie date trying to slip his arm over his date by pretending to stretch.

Only Angela isn't my date, and this isn't a movie.

"Are you the last one out?" the co-pilot asks me. I don't answer. It's almost as if I can see his mouth moving, but I can't figure out what he's saying.

"Are you the last one out?" he asks again.

"I...I think...I don't know. Yeah..." I'm stammering, but it's not because of the cold. I just can't seem to get my thinking unfogged.

I wonder if this is what shock feels like. I wonder if there can be a sort of delayed reaction when it comes to shock. Sort of an after-shock. Aftershock? Makes me think of a cartoon character like Yosemite Sam or Bugs Bunny getting hit by a lightning bolt and then walking around getting buzzed every other step. For some reason, that makes me want to laugh, only somewhere deep down in my thinking, I know there's nothing funny about what's going on. I wonder if that's part of being in shock too. Random thoughts about cartoon characters jumping in and out of your head like popcorn going off in a microwave, blocking out the blood and guts in the real world around you. It's like everything is in slow motion, nothing makes real sense, and I can't quite figure out what's real and what's a dream. I see Misty crawling on her hands and knees toward me. That really doesn't make sense and I wonder why until she scoots next to Angela. What's even stranger, Misty takes my wrist and pushes my arm off Angela.

"Angie, Angie," Misty whispers. "Are you okay? It's over, you know. We're all okay."

That's right! Angela's her best friend. I'm not Angela's friend. But why would you take my arm off her as if I'm something disgusting? And how can she say we're all okay? Todd is definitely not okay. These thoughts sort of bring me back to reality.

"We are not okay," I say.

"I'm not talking to you," Misty hisses.

56

Misty flashes me a rather ugly look and I feel a hard sort of defensiveness ripple across my chest like a warm current. Whatever fogginess I've been breathing in, clears up in one glaring moment.

"I just got your friend out of a sinking airplane," I say flatly.

Misty doesn't answer. She just looks away. Before I can think of anything else to hiss back at her, the co-pilot speaks up.

"All right, listen everyone," he says loudly. "We have to detach the ramp from the fuselage." He says, "Please listen to me. The plane is sinking, and it could pull us down too. I'm going to detach the ramp, so try not to move too much."

The co-pilot turns back to the exit hatch. He reaches for a red handle at the bottom of the hatch. I can read the words "For Ditching Use Only" on the handle. The co-pilot pulls it, there's a sharp hiss, and I feel the ramp slide fully onto the surface of the water. The co-pilot pushes the ramp away from the fuselage of the plane and I see a rope still attached to the plane. It strings out from the ramp, but the pilot is fumbling over the edge of the ramp in the water. After a second, the rope disappears.

I finally look away from the sinking plane. The sun has finally dropped below the horizon. In the distance, I can see the shore of the lake. I take a quick look to the left. The lake is gigantic. It seems to be a long, thin lake about a mile wide, but who knows how long. It just seems to go on forever. The farther shore on the other side of the plane is a long way away. The shore across from us is much closer, maybe only a quarter mile away. The other raft is about twenty yards away and they have also detached from the plane. It looks like more people are in the other raft. A movement beyond it catches my eye and my heart takes a quick leap. There are two boats in the distance.

I'm not the only one to see the boats. Almost everyone begins whispering quietly at once. Mr. Tan Jacket turns his head and looks too.

"What's going on?" asks Angela. I'm surprised to hear her voice.

"I don't know," I say. "Looks like boats are coming."

"Someone's coming to help us," Misty says.

Angela pulls away from me. She crawls eagerly over to the other side of the raft to see better. Misty follows, and the co-pilot also turns to look at the approaching boats.

"They're not here to help us," the co-pilot says.

I look a little closer. There are two small boats with outboard engines racing up to us. In the lead boat, a dark-haired man with a long beard stands in the bow of the boat. He holds an AK-47. I know instantly what kind of rifle it is because of the curved magazine. I've seen them before in Africa, and I know the good guys don't usually carry those kinds of guns.

The co-pilot swears, and I really feel like using a much nastier word, but I keep quiet. Angela sinks down as low as she can get in the bottom of the raft. She draws her legs up to her chest and puts her head down. Misty crawls up next to her. I notice that neither of them is as close to me as Angela was when we first got out of the plane.

What is going on? I mean, I just saved Angela's life and now I'm back to being an overripe tuna sandwich! Why am I still the gross kid no one wants to be near? We are probably all going to get murdered and Misty is still more worried about me as a social disease than she is about radical terrorists. I'm not just a little bit mad, I'm furious. Why should I try to help anyone if all they're going to do is spit in my face after I drag them out of danger?

"This is all about you, you know," I whisper fiercely. Misty glares at me and clinches her teeth. "You're the Vice-President's daughter and we wouldn't be in this mess if it weren't for you."

"We wouldn't be in this mess if Todd had done his job," she hisses back. "Leave me alone."

"Todd?" I say, shaking my head. "What do you mean, do his job? He's dead. I mean, don't you care about that?"

I'm beginning to wonder why I had any sort of crush on this girl. Then again, she's probably just scared out of her mind and missing the point.

The boats pull up to join us. Each boat has two men, one manning the outboard motor, the other, at the front of the boat. I can see now that all the men are armed with A.K.'s. I see Mr. Tan Jacket stand up in the front of our raft. One of the boats bumps up to the edge of the raft and Mr. Tan Jacket slides across into the boat. He warmly embraces one of the men.

The second boat edges up to the other raft, the outboard motor slows to an idle, and I see Mr. White Shirt and Soda Can Man shuffle over to the edge of their raft. They climb into the second boat. Soda Can Man nearly falls into the lake, but a man on the boat grabs him and pulls him over. The bearded man says something to Soda Can Man who nods and leans over into the boat to get something. The second boat drifts slowly toward the plane, the outboard engine idling softly. The bearded man looks back at our raft as his boat drifts closer to the plane. For a moment, his eyes catch mine. There is a glint in his eye. I can tell this guy has stared death in the face so many times it has hardened him against it.

There is something in a person's eyes that always gives them away. Since my folks were missionaries, I've been around a lot of hard people in my life. I've sat in church next to murderers and drug addicts. Every time, it's something in the eyes that tells you instinctively that the person you're looking at has seen the darker side of life. You get so you can peg these kinds of people from just a glance, so I can tell that the bearded man has been in the company of the Devil - and they are on speaking terms.

Soda Can Man stands up in the boat holding a backpack. The bearded man nods his head, then looks back at Mr. Tan Jacket. Mr. Tan Jacket stands up.

"We will take your boats to the shore!" he shouts at both rafts. The word "boats" sounds more like *bowts*. "We will negotiate the release of our brothers in American prisons and you will go free. If you do not do what we tell you…you will die."

The bearded man says something to Soda Can Man. I see the man at the outboard motor directing the drift of the boat. They maneuver the boat until it bumps up against the sinking plane next to the wing exit that Angela and I had used. The plane is low in the water but tipped so the nose of the plane points up slightly as if it smells the sky and longs to get airborne again. Soda Can Man steps off the boat onto the wing. I can hear his feet sloshing in the ankle-deep water. He disappears into the open hatch carrying the backpack. A moment later he reappears without the backpack and jumps back into the boat.

The man at the outboard adds some power pulling the boat away from the plane. There is some discussion between the bearded man and Mr. Tan Jacket. Whatever language they are speaking is so rapid, I can't make out any distinct words. The language sounds a lot like both men are trying to hock up a wad of mucus in the back of their throats. That idea makes me grin. I think about the comedian who uses the puppet, "Ahmed the Dead Terrorist." The comedian asks him how to spell his name and he says, "A...H...Phlegm..." Another completely disconnected thought about ventriloquists and puppets when I need to be thinking about how to stay alive! More shock? I don't know.

I can see someone in the other boat tossing a towrope over to the other raft. A few seconds later, Mr. Tan Jacket tosses a rope into our raft. Someone at the front of our raft collects the rope and ties it to a small grommet on the leading edge of the raft. As soon as it's secure, Mr. Tan Jacket takes a seat. The driver at the outboard motor picks up the rpm and I feel our raft bog down into the water as the tow begins.

The shoreline is still a good quarter-mile away. The woods are thick to the water's edge, but there is a small clearing a bit north of our position. The shoreline is choked with driftwood that has been bleached white over time. It glows a little in the setting sun and I can see we are being towed to the shore by the clearing.

There is a sudden thunderclap behind me. A concussion wave nearly throws me forward, and several people scream. I look back at the plane and see a cloud of smoke rising from it. Soda Can Man obviously had a bomb in the backpack. The plane looks like it's been blown nearly in half, ending any chance it wouldn't sink to the bottom. In seconds, the nose of the plane tips nearly straight up, then sinks with a hiss of escaping air.

It makes sense. Mr. Tan Jacket and his crew know what they're doing. They flew the plane low enough to confuse radar, and I'm willing to bet they disabled the emergency transponder too. Now they've made sure the plane sinks to the bottom of a lake that's probably hundreds of feet deep. The terrorists are making sure there is no chance a search-and-rescue crew might estimate our position and spot the wreckage from the air or satellite. Isolated hundreds of miles from our coastal flight path and hidden in several million square miles of uninhabited forest, we may as well have been kidnapped and hidden on the moon. There is no way any of us are going to escape and walk to the nearest public telephone either.

Even if the terrorists are successful in their "negotiations," there's nothing stopping them from killing every single one of us. These are the kind of people that don't care about dying anyway. They could kill us all, leave the bodies under the trees, and it might be years before our bones are ever found.

But they aren't going to kill me that easily.

I figure we can't be anywhere near civilization, so escaping into the woods isn't going to lead to a rescue, but at least out in the sticks I'll live a little longer. Besides, I've spent a long time in some of the most remote places in the world. I've learned a lot about how to survive in wild places. In Alaska, I learned all about how to survive in these woods. As soon as I get the chance, I'm going to disappear into the dark. I'm willing to bet the terrorists know a lot more about how to survive in Somalia or Beirut or whatever rock they crawled out from under than they do about how to live out here. They probably don't know anything about how to track a quarry in the woods either. Besides that, I don't think they even know how many hostages they have yet. I haven't seen anyone doing a headcount, so if I slip away at the first chance, they probably won't even know I'm gone.

I look back at Angela and Misty. Angela is still hunched over, clutching her legs against her chest, sitting in three inches of ice water. Misty is huddled next to her, seated on the pillow-like edge of the raft - I guess so her sensitive little bottom isn't soaked in the lake water. She looks my direction and for a moment, I think she's looking at me, maybe trying to sort of say, "I'm sorry," so I nod my head. I'm

61

thinking maybe I ought to give her a little room to say stupid things when she's stressed out. I can afford to be forgiving, but I feel a sudden embarrassment when I realize she's looking past me at the sinking plane, as if I'm not even there!

I'm not feeling particularly attracted to Misty anymore, that's for sure. But I'm also feeling a mix of fear and frustration and just plain rage. I'm sick to death of guys like Stan, girls like Misty, and terrorists. They all think they can roll right over top of guys like me and I'm thinking, I got nothing to lose. If there's a way I can stab these sleazeballs in the eye, I'm going to do it. And the one thing I think I can do is take away the one thing they want most.

I mean, I'm not afraid of the woods or the dark or the cold, but I want to do something more than just creep away into the bush. I want to get even. I don't even know what I'm going to do when I do bail out either, but I wonder if I can drag Misty out of their hands. That would really spin them off. Of course, it's a million to one I can grab Misty and pull her away into the woods without drawing attention, but why not try? If you want to do a dance with the Devil, you gotta take the first step.

We're drawing close to the shore. The driftwood on the shore has been moved aside to some degree, and I can see this is where they must have launched after watching our landing in the lake. The other boat and raft are ahead of us. The lead boat drives right up to the shore, and Mr. White Shirt hops out onto the muddy edge of the lake. He turns to take hold of the towline while another terrorist gets out. Together, they begin to pull it onto the shore.

I suddenly see what I have to do. I got an idea. It's bat-brain-crazy too. Then again, what have I got to lose?

The sun has set so deeply into the edge of the horizon, I can't see it anymore. It's rapidly getting dark, the terrorists are busy trying to pull the first raft onto the shore, and our tow boat is still ten or twenty yards out, waiting its turn to land. If I'm going to do something to mess up the enemies' plan, this is the time. To my left, I see the piles of driftwood that are stacked much higher than where we are landing. I can see a half-dozen or more trees sticking out into the lake from the shore like natural piers too. I'm seated at the back of the raft, and everyone is looking at our tow boat as we drift slowly into shore. Slowly, I lean back into the edge of the raft. I look at the other raft. The terrorists on the shore are working together to pull it into the shore and no one is looking our way. I glance back at our towboat. None of the terrorists are looking at us from there either.

I lean over and hiss in Misty's ear, "Misty, you gotta listen to me."

"Leave me alone," she says loudly. My band director, Mr. Towns, looks over at us.

"You gotta listen to me," I say again. "This whole thing, you're the key. We gotta get away and fast."

"What are you talking about?"

"Look over to the left. You see that log? We gotta slip over the side in about five seconds, swim underwater, and get behind that log so they don't see us."

"What, are you crazy? I'm not going anywhere."

Mr. Towns leans back toward us and whispers fiercely, "Mr. Reynolds, shut your mouth and sit tight."

"This is all about her," I say. "Don't you see that? She's the daughter of the next Vice President. They want her. The rest of us are just...expendable. She's got to get into the woods and hide. This is our chance..."

"I said sit tight and shut your mouth, Mr. Reynolds. If you try anything stupid, we'll all get killed."

"We're all gonna get killed anyway," I snarl back at him.

Once again, that fierce sense of *I'm sick of being kicked around* comes roaring out of my mouth.

"They're gonna hack her head off with a knife on video for the whole world to see, and you're worried about me sitting still and being quiet? I'm not sitting anywhere." I look back at Misty. "This is all about you, Misty. They want to make hacking your head off the cover story on every newspaper in the world. They are going to chop you to pieces..."

"Shut up," she hisses at me. "Shut up. They're not going to..."

"You're the cargo they wanted," I snap back at her. "They said they wanted a cargo on our plane. Well, the plane is under three hundred feet of ice water by now, but they put you next to the emergency door to make sure they got you out alive. If you don't listen to me…"

"They're not going to do anything to me," she says. "They'll…they'll negotiate…"

"You really think that? Negotiate you for what? Money? They don't want money. They were just willing to crash the plane. They don't care about dying and they really don't care about killing."

Mr. Towns begins to crawl in my direction and I can tell from the look on his face that he's ready to physically try and take me down.

"Mr. Reynolds," he says through gritted teeth. "I said, sit down and shut up."

I ignore him and look back at Misty. There's no time to fuss around with Mr. Towns. He doesn't like me anyway. Actually, pretty much nobody likes me, so I really don't care what any of them think anymore.

"Misty, you've got to listen to me. I grew up in Alaska. I know how to survive out there. I'm going over the side before we get to the shore and I'm getting into those woods. If you don't come with me, they will use you like a bowling pin. Do you really want to have them cut your head off with a kitchen knife? These guys are ISIS terrorists."

"They won't do that," she says. "You don't know what they want."

"I know they've already killed four people and one of them was working for them. What does that tell you?"

Mr. Towns is close enough to reach me and I scramble up into a crouch, ready to push off over the side of the raft. Mr. Towns's face is contorted in rage. He's never liked me, and, in these circumstances, I can tell he wants to take out all his pent-up anger at students defying his authority over the years on me.

"I don't care what stupid things you think you learned in Boy Scouts," he snarls in my face. "This isn't Camping 101, you idiot. I'm not going to let you entice them into shooting all of us. Now, sit down."

Mr. Towns grabs my left wrist in a grip like a vice and tries to pull me back off the soft edge of the raft. I jerk my arm backwards. He holds on and tries to get hold of my other arm, but the bottom of the raft is just plastic on water, not a firm foundation, and he loses his grip. He falls face forward into the ankle high water at the bottom of the raft. In a second, he pulls himself nearly to his feet and tries to pull me down again. I hear a bunch of voices telling me to sit down, but I lean back toward the edge of the raft.

My movement pulls Mr. Towns forward again and his weight crashes into me. The edge of the raft plunges deeply under our weight and in the half second before I fall backwards into the water, I see that at least a half a dozen other people are going to go into the drink with us.

And the water is seriously ice cold. I instantly feel a sense of panic. The cold is so intense I feel every muscle in my body cramp up. It feels like thousands of needles are drilling into my skin. I have an instant, blistering headache and it's everything I can do not to thrash around in a panic. Mr. Towns' body pushes me down deeper, but he lets go of my arms. I push to the surface and take a harsh, ragged breath. I can hear shouts from the raft. Some people are leaning over trying to reach us in the water. I swing my head away from the raft and see Mr. Towns come up to the surface.

I gasp loudly, but instead of taking the hands from the raft that are trying to pull me up, I take a deep breath and plunge back under the water.

I swear it feels colder than the first moment I hit the water. It's everything I can do not to pop right back to the surface again to try and get away from the mind-numbing cold. But I stay under and swim as fast as I can toward a log that sticks out into the lake.

My eyes are open. I can see the log ahead of me and below I can make out the slope of the lake bottom dropping down into inky blackness. The lake must be really deep and again, I feel a sense of panic as my lungs scream for air. I have to make it to the log, slip under it, and not come up for air until I'm hidden on the other side.

If I can hold my breath just long enough.

Seven

I thought the log was only a few yards away, but it seems miles ahead of me. The back brace feels like a parachute in the water pulling me backwards as I struggle forward, and my greatcoat feels like it weighs a hundred pounds. The flimsy little lifejacket is suddenly very much a life jacket in my mind. I pull the silly inflating tab and I hear the faint hiss as it begins to fill with air just as my lungs are screaming at me to claw my way to the surface only it doesn't pop me right to the surface because of the greatcoat. Now I'm just sort of floating, but that's sort of a good thing - I can't risk coming up for air where anyone can see me. I can only hope the confusion of half a dozen people thrashing about in the water will mask my escape.

I have to get under the log. I'm not sure I can resist the urge to come up for air much longer. I shove my panic aside and pull harder at the water. The water is so cold and my muscles cramp, so it feels as if I'm pulling my way through a lake of caramel sauce. The log is closer. I nearly bump my head on it as I slide underneath.

My head breaks the surface and I exhale and inhale quickly. The sound of my breathing seems loud enough to scare away a grizzly. I'm positive the terrorists can hear me, so I nearly have a heart attack when Misty pops up from under the water right next to me – and she isn't making any attempt to be quiet.

"Oh my…oh snap…so cold", she sputters.

I can't believe she's here. I mean, I guess it makes sense that we all piled into the water, except I'm almost as shocked that she's following me as I am about how cold it is. And it's cold! I don't think I've ever felt anything so cold. It feels like heavy, wet hands are smothering me. The life jacket helps a little, but my legs cramp as I

67

cling to the log, my head feels like twenty ice cold marbles have been shoved up my nose and I'm spluttering trying to get a breath. I also can't believe Misty is floundering around next to me and she isn't wearing a life jacket.

We've got to get out of this ice water fast, so I slide my hands along the underside of the log, looking for any kind of branch or handhold to keep us from sinking.

"Misty...quit thrashing around," I hiss fiercely. "They'll...hear you. Take my hand."

Misty grabs my outstretched hand with both of hers. In her panic, she almost pulls herself over top of me toward the log. I slide back under the water underneath her, still clutching desperately for a handhold on the log.

My legs cramp so badly, I really can't tread water any longer. Just as I'm about to throw Misty off me, my hand finds the stub of a branch sticking out of the log. It's so slimy, it feels almost wetter than the water, if that's possible, but I grab hold of it as if it were the hand of an angel. I pull with all my might, manage to get my head above the water again and somehow, I don't let Misty slip away either. Now I know why I believe in miracles.

"Calm down," I hiss. "They'll hear us...just stay...c,c,c...calm. Might not even... know we're missing...yet."

Our heads are below the top of the log. I can't see the boats or the terrorists. I hear people shouting and the sound of splashing water. I feel a sort of craziness creep over me, something deeper than panic. I'm suddenly thinking they're nipping right at our heels. At any moment now, a terrorist is going to leap onto the log from off the beach and spray the water with automatic weapons fire. If we're not turned into Swiss cheese in the next few seconds, our arms and legs are bound to freeze up until we drop like lead weights and drown. Nothing about this situation is making me happy.

But nothing happens.

Misty is hyperventilating. Her teeth are chattering so hard, she can't talk. I can't believe she's even trying to get away after the way she looked at me on the raft. But she's here!

She lets go of my right arm and tries to reach the log. I can tell she wants to pull herself up on top, out of the water - but they'll see us if she does.

I begin to shiver violently. I have to get us to the shore and quickly, except we can't afford to make any noise either. I slide my other hand along the underside of the log and find another branch hanging down into the water.

"Misty...calm...calm down," I hiss in her ear. "I'm going to...pull us...toward shore. Quit thrashing...they'll hear."

"I gotta get out," she chatters. "Freezing...can't catch...my breath..."

"I know, I know. Just pull...pull yourself along...the log...Don't stick your head... above the log...they won't see us...We'll just pull in to the shore...Here...Hold onto my shoulders."

Misty obediently puts her arms around my neck and nearly pushes me under again, but I pull myself closer to the log, dragging her along with me. Working hand under hand, I pull us into a cluster of broken driftwood stacked on the shore. There is no beach, just a wall of twisted, bleached driftwood stacked at least ten feet above our heads. There is no way we can crawl out of the water without being seen. I'll have to slide us along the wall of driftwood and branches until we're far enough away to be out of sight.

This turns out to be a challenge. The driftwood is stacked in a heap and several large logs project out into the water, just like the first log we swam under. Reminds me of a pincushion sticking out into the lake water. To make our way across the face of the wall of driftwood, we have to push out into deeper water again to slip around the logs sticking out into the lake. The first log is sort of submerged maybe eight or ten inches below the surface, so it isn't too difficult to get past. We just sort of slide over it, but Misty's hyperventilating is so extreme I'm afraid she won't be able to hold her breath long enough to get past the next log because there's only one way to past it – by going under it!

I don't have time for explanations or warnings.

"Hold your...breath," I say.

I take hold of Misty's hands draped around my neck with my left hand and pull us both underwater - only to run face-first into a mat of tangled, slimy branches hanging underneath the log. Misty jerks backward and tries to thrash to the surface, almost unhinged with fear and cold. But we can't afford to make any noise or splashing in the water if we're really going to get away. Any sort of noise could bring the terrorists running our direction, so I yank her back down, pull her around in front of me and shove her around the tangle of branches and under the log by pushing her out a little way into deeper water. Once I'm sure she's clear, I swing under the log and pop up to the surface next to her. She's already clawing the surface of the water, trying to get to the shore. She's making way too much noise and I can't do a thing about it now. We're both past any ability to be calm.

Behind this log I see that we've reached the end of the driftwood pile. There is a small inlet here where the roots of living trees are exposed at the water's edge like giant black spider's webs. The inlet is far enough indented away from the driftwood that I can't see the place where the terrorists are unloading the passengers. I assume if I can't see them, they can't see us. Still, every movement Misty makes seems incredibly loud. My arms and legs feel wooden.

The roots of the trees on the shoreline look like a natural ladder, only as I get closer, my feet still don't touch the bottom. Looking down, I can't see the bottom of the lake in the gathering darkness.

Misty reaches the roots almost at the same time I do. I reach up and grab them, but I can't get any kind of foothold. The earth under the roots on the shoreline has been eroded away by years of wind and waves.

"This way," I sputter. "Come on."

I slide to my left and try again to get a foothold. This time, I manage to get my right foot twisted into some roots. My foot feels like a block of stone, slick and unsure. I don't know if my slimy foothold is enough to help me get out of the water. I heave with all my might, arms shaking in protest. The sound of water rushing off my body back into the lake seems deafening. My back brace is filled to the top with water. It gurgles and sucks me backwards as the water slithers out the bottom over my pants. My arms shake so hard I know I can't hold on for another second, but a sudden release of water from under the brace over my pants almost throws me forward.

I flop down like a beached fish, driving my face into the dirt. A blackberry vine snags my forehead. The little shiver of pain helps me overcome the mind-and-muscle numbing cold crushing me to the ground. The earth in my face is moist and black, filled with trillions of bits of decaying wood mixed with dark clay. It smells musky and strong, and the sensation of pain from the blackberry vine and the earthy smell keeps me just sane enough to remember that Misty is still slowly freezing to death behind me in the lake. I roll around to try and help her.

It's clear that Misty is totally exhausted. I grab hold of her arm with my right hand and pull with all my strength. Her muscles must be totally cramped because she's basically dead weight.

"Get your foot in the roots…gotta help me."

"I can't…can't breathe."

"Just get your foot in the roots…Come on…going to try and…pull you up but you gotta help me."

"Okay…Okay…"

I reach down with my other hand and pull. She gets about halfway out of the water and I reach around her waist and pull again. It takes twenty seconds of pulling and pushing before she collapses on the ground next to me.

I've never felt anything so numbing in all my life. I'm so cold it feels like the day Joey Sinclair in third grade punched me in the gut so hard my breath got sucked out of my lungs. It's the same crushing, burning sensation. I gasp and hack for a breath. Every muscle in my body shudders and quakes. I'm not sure if I can control anything.

Only I know I have to force myself to move or we will definitely die. If the cold doesn't kill us, the terrorists will.

Back in Alaska, I fell into the creeks around our trailer near Sunny Cove more than once. But I don't ever remember going totally under water, and we were always within easy walking distance of the trailer. Most of the time, I only got soaked up to the waist, enough to make me shriek like a little girl, but nothing so bad that I couldn't keep on fishing for a few hours. It was easy to get wet and keep fishing since I always knew a warm shower and an armchair by the fire was less than an hour away.

Misty and me, out here…we are fresh out of warm showers to look forward to now, that's for sure.

"We've got to…move," I chatter. I can hear my teeth making a drum cadence between every word. This is so insane. "Come, come…on," I say. "See us…if we…s,s,s…stay here."

I drag myself to my hands and knees and slog around the trunk of a tree. The weight of my wet clothes makes every movement feel like I'm trying to lift a twenty-pound weight. I don't get more than five feet before I collapse again. The effort I used to pull Misty out of the water has sapped my strength.

Misty crawls just past me and falls as well, just at the edge of a massive bramble of blackberry vines blocking the way into the forest beyond. The ground around us is littered with ferns, most of them taller than our bodies as we lay on the ground. The truth is, we're well hidden under the ferns, up against the blackberry vines. I'll bet if we don't move, they would almost have to step on us to find us.

"Stop…stop…moving…just…listen…for a minute."

Our combined breathing seems so loud. I feel my heart pounding in my throat. In the distance, I hear voices, only I don't hear any sound of someone crashing through the underbrush in our direction.

We might have gotten away without being noticed – for the moment. It's possible they may not figure out Misty is missing for at least a little while. I'm not sure how many people piled into the water after my little tussle with Mr. Towns - enough for us to slip away without being noticed right away. I can't imagine anyone who saw us fall into the water is going to say anything about where we swam off to either. I don't know, maybe Mr. Towns. He's a self-important turd, so I wouldn't put it past him. But I suppose even Mr. Towns wouldn't jump up and shout, "They went that-a-way."

72

I've got to get this shivering to stop. I pull my legs up as close to my chest as I can get. The brace digs into my thighs and I'm so cold I don't care. I figure the terrorists were all on the shore, pulling the rafts in. They weren't close enough to see who went into the water. Even if they figure out Misty is missing, will they figure out where we got out of the water? There's a huge pile of driftwood between the landing area and us; we're backed up against a wall of blackberry bushes and hidden under a mass of ferns. We can catch our breath...get the shivering to stop...in a minute...just a few minutes is all I need...

Jumping out of the raft and running off into the bush seemed like a pretty good idea at the time. Now - not so much. Reminds me of shouting at Soda Can Man, getting my face swatted off, and nearly getting Misty killed. Yeah...I'm just full of great ideas that crash and burn, or at least, crash and freeze.

What in the name of all that is holy am I doing out here? I haven't got a clue what to do next. The terrorists are Satan-level evil, but they're not morons. They'll figure out where we went. They wouldn't have planned this whole hijacking right down to the soda cans on the flight attendant's cart and then let us disappear into the bush. And the didn't drop us off in a lake five hundred yards from the nearest town either. It's not like we can just slip away and make a 9-1-1 call at the nearest gas station. We're up to our armpits in nothing but mosquitoes, trees and bears for hundreds of square miles in every direction - not to mention the fact we're likely to die from hypothermia before sunrise.

Great! Awesome new idea, Kyle! Congratulations! You just kidnapped the Governor's daughter, so you can curl up and freeze to death next to her.

Except for one thing. We're not under the muzzle of a gun anymore. That much we have going for us. They are not calling the shots anymore!

And I remember something else too. A story I read in homeschool, something written by Jack London about a guy in Alaska who can't get a fire started before he freezes to death. The whole idea of turning into a snowball and wishing I could start a fire brings it to mind. I read it during our first winter in Alaska. I had to write an essay about how the story symbolized man's arrogance in the face of nature or something along those lines. I just remember thinking the guy should have started the fire before he got too cold. But it wasn't just bad luck! He should have thought it through. He should have gotten warm long before he felt cold. And I'm feeling awfully cold, right now.

Too cold!

I'm too cold...We can't just sit here. We can't just take a few minutes to rest either. That's the trap. Like the guy in the story. If we sit still, we'll just fall asleep and turn into human popsicles during the night. We've got to stay awake, keep moving and get warmer.

Slowly, I lift my head and look deeper into the bush ahead of us. There's a sharp slope upwards. To our left the hillside gets seriously steeper. Directly ahead of us, the slope isn't as sharp. The underbrush in front of us is a tangled mat of blackberry bushes, broken alder saplings and devil's club bushes. The devil's club is a thick, light green vine covered with tiny thorns.

I don't have time to beat myself up for bad ideas. We've got to work our way through the wall of blackberry vines in front of us and it's going to tear us to shreds. But I know we can't get closer to the beach where the terrorists are, we can't move to the left because the slope becomes steadily steeper until it becomes a cliff dropping down into the lake and sitting still isn't an option. It's time for my next bad idea.

I snake my way forward past Misty's shivering body until I run into the tangle of blackberry vines blocking our way. The vines are as effective as barbed wire and just about as sharp. When I as a kid, we would often go fishing along the banks of creeks in the Alaskan bush. Most of the time, we simply trudged through the water, hopping from pool to pool, looking for the next big trout, but occasionally, we would run into a tangle of logs or a rapid, and we would have to hike out of the creek bed into the bush to get around the obstacle. Tangles of blackberry bushes and devil's club were common obstacles, like vast nests of green spiders crowded around the edges of water sources. In Alaska, I found the best way to get past it was to more or less swim through it by raising my foot as high as I could to trample the vines to the ground, sort of like using my legs like mechanical stompers. In this case, we can't afford to stand up, we can't push the vines down without making too much noise, and we can't use our feet at all because we're laying on our stomachs. We also can't just give up either, so threading through the blackberry vines into the bush beyond is our only option.

I find a broken branch on the ground. Carefully, I use it to push a blackberry vine a bit to my left. With my right hand, I carefully push another vine to the side, creating an opening just large enough to wiggle through. One of the advantages of being a cyborg is that the back brace is blackberry thorn-proof. After sliding past the first tangle of vines, I lean back, pushing the vines behind me backwards away from the opening I just scrambled through. I turn back to Misty.

"Okay, your turn. I'll hold this one back. You crawl in."

Misty drags her head up to look at me. Her chin shakes so hard I can see the flash of her teeth like a little strobe light in the twilight.

"Are you insane?" she whispers furiously. "There's gotta be...some way...around. That's like...barbed wire."

"I know," I say. "But they'll never look for us this way..."

"I'm not...crawling in there," she hisses furiously.

"So, what do you want to do? Go back?"

"Don't be stupid," she says. "I'm not going...I'm not giving up...it's easier...going this way."

"And that's...that's where they're going to look too," I chatter back. "They're not going to ...expect you to push through this. If you stay by the lake...gonna find you in an hour...that what you want?"

Misty looks back over her shoulder as if expecting the terrorists to pop up out of the lake like Navy Seals. She looks back at me, shakes her head, and then purses her lips. She is so exhausted and cold, she doesn't say a word; she just crawls forward. I push the first tangle of vines to the side to let her in and a few seconds later she is well into the bramble next to me. Once I let go of the vine behind her, we are effectively buried under a tangle of blackberry vines. It's not a perfect hiding spot, but if we stay still, we might just be overlooked. After a minute's rest I use the branch to create a new space and we press deeper into the bramble. The vines grate over Misty's woolen sweater, and I have to pull them out of her hair. One vine at a time, we push and wiggle and slide forward for about ten minutes until our breathing from the effort is ragged and harsh. We stop for a moment and listen, hearing nothing except the hiss of a light breeze in the trees above our head.

I'm out of breath and unfortunately the exertion hasn't warmed me up at all. They say that working out warms you up, and I say that's a lie made up to get people to buy gym memberships in the winter. My pants are sucked tightly to my skin like a slimy, ice-cold wetsuit. My shoes are filled with water and feel as heavy as lead weights. My hands are already bleeding from the blackberry thorns and I know we're in trouble. Darkness rapidly gathers under the ferns and brambles and even though I feel so cold I can barely move, it seems like it's already getting colder.

Blackberry bushes are more or less weeds in the Northwest. Even in Washington State, it's pretty much a nuisance, growing like green razor wire around every little run-off creek or pond. It's funny to watch tourists get so excited about ripe blackberries. I guess they must be expensive in the stores farther south because most of us locals don't particularly care about blackberries - except to cuss at the vines whenever they creep over into our yards. Tourists stop on the side of the road, tie up traffic, and nearly get themselves strangled to death, diving into a mat of vines after that one, juicy ripe one that's just out of reach. Most of the brambles are like a thick hedge; close enough to the water to make fishing for trout a real nightmare, and yet only about as wide as the width of the average driveway. So, it doesn't take us very long to thread our way through to the other side of this thicket. Twenty minutes after I pushed aside the first vine, we finally burst out of the other side of the bramble.

Misty's head hangs low and her hands are limp. I can hear her breathing shuttering in shivering fits. She doesn't seem able to say anything, as if the shivering is too severe to allow her mouth to form words. I suppose that's just as well - only you didn't hear it from me! She hasn't had a whole lot of good to say to me yet. I hear her whimper occasionally so it's clear she isn't going to be able to move much farther. I know a little about the cold and how quickly you can die from hypothermia, so I know I better do something quick or they'll find us all right – cold and dead.

"You know, in Alaska…my parents…Dad was a missionary pilot. We were stationed at a base in Taku Inlet…not far from Juneau, down in the south of Alaska…I learned a lot about how to survive out here…so…we gotta keep moving…Okay? So, we don't freeze…I'll try to do something to get us a bit warmer – but we gotta move, okay?"

Misty just looks at me. I can't tell in the twilight if she glaring or hopeful. It doesn't matter either way. We've got to get farther away from the lakeshore.

Taku Inlet was far from the tundra. I remember the little town we lived in because it was called "Sunny Cove", only I don't remember a whole lot of sunny days when we lived there. It was overcast and gloomy most of the year, so I suppose the name was wishful thinking. The bush around Sunny Cove isn't any different than the bush we're crawling through right now, so it's familiar to me, almost comfortable in a weird sort of way.

I learned a lot about survival when we lived there because I didn't have a whole lot of other things to do. My dad was almost always gone and after home school lessons with Mom, I was sent outside to find something to do. At first, I wasn't allowed to go far because there really were lions and tigers and bears in the woods. Okay, no tigers - but the phrase was something my dad used to say all the time. "Don't get too far away, son. There's lions and tigers and bears in these woods…Oh my!" I didn't figure out that sentence came from the movie *The Wizard of Oz* until nearly a year after the crash. Now it's like one of my favorite movies just because of that line.

Back then, I never saw a mountain lion, but I did run into bears on a regular basis. Most of the time, they were black bears - large enough to scare my pre-teen, little body into near hysterics, but not the deadly and dreaded Grizzly. Those monsters might kill you just for the fun of ripping something apart, and even the local native population avoids them. Right now, it's getting on toward winter, so I expect most bears are settling in to hibernate about this time. I'm more worried about terrorists than bears.

There was an old native guy from around Sunny Cove named George Black. George was really old. He was missing nearly all his front teeth, his face looked like a crinkled-up brown paper sack, and he smelled like a cross between tobacco and raspberry jam - and I loved him dearly. He nearly lived at the mission church. He was too old to fish on the commercial boats any longer and most of his family had disowned him long before he converted to Christianity and had gotten sober. He lived in a small trailer about a hundred yards from the church and pretty much every day that I wasn't flying with Dad, he would wander over to see what I was doing. I don't know what interested him so much about an eleven-year-old white kid, but he really took a shine to me. He taught me how to catch trout in the creek, how to skip rocks on the bay when the tide came in and how to survive in the woods.

George was always happy. He smiled a lot, which was funny, because he didn't have any front teeth. Nothing seemed to get him down either. Since he had lived in Taku Inlet all his life, he had a lot to teach about how to live in the bush. And his first lesson was that keeping warm and staying hydrated was more important than pretty much anything else.

My hands shake, and my fingers feel stiff. Misty seems lethargic, like she's going to shiver into a deep sleep any minute. I need to get us warmer and fast. There's only a few patches of snow on the ground here and there, but it will certainly drop below freezing before the sun rises in the morning. Of course, starting a fire is out of the question, even if that were easy. I can do it – George taught me half a dozen different ways to get a fire going without matches – but even if I could take the time to get one started, I'm far too close to the terrorists to risk it.

I can't see where the terrorists are pulling the passengers out of the rafts, so they probably can't see us either. I can hear the occasional muffled voice in the distance, nothing distinct, so I figure they probably can't really hear us either. I imagine if the noise from pushing through the blackberry vines hasn't drawn their attention yet, we might be in the clear, at least for a few minutes. It's time to make a better move. Now that we've gotten away from the lake and past the blackberry vines, it's time to make some real distance before it's lights out.

"Okay, Misty. We're going to stand up...get deeper into the bush before it gets too dark to see."

"I'm freezing. I can't...

"I know but if you...if you just start moving...get your blood moving...you know?"

It's not a very good lie, but I hope it's enough to get her on her feet. Like I said, gym memberships in winter! Still, she will probably feel better for a little because her heart rate is going to go up if I can get her moving. It won't stop her body temperature from dropping, or mine either, at least that's what George told me about the old wives' tale about keeping on the move when you're cold, but one way or another, we've got to make some tracks.

"Come on. Let's go..."

Carefully, I pull up to my knees and look back over my shoulder. I still can't see anyone, and I've already looked back at least twenty times. It's getting darker and I already can't see more than maybe fifty feet into the bush. In front of us, the slope is getting steep and we'll have to be careful not to fall backwards. That would be a pretty tidy little disaster, rolling down the hill, elbows over ankles. I peer into the gloom around the base of the trees and see nothing except ferns growing like mutant mohawks out of pillows of moss.

I stand to my feet and pull Misty to her feet. I look over my shoulder one last time and begin to walk. I try taking her hand, but she pulls away so violently, she almost falls over. She wraps her arms around her chest and almost sinks down into a crouch.

79

I'm suddenly not in a very nice mood. In fact, I'm pretty ticked off.

"Fine, you want to stay here?" I step over the last of the blackberry bushes onto a moss-covered log. "We made a big enough hole in those blackberry vines that an idiot could figure out we went that way. If they don't find it by flashlight, they will in the morning. We've got to move…"

"There's no place to go…"

"We can get deeper into the bush. They're going to be looking for you back there!"

"It isn't my fault…"

"I never said it was." I stop for moment and look back the way we came. "Once they figure out you're gone…going to start looking along the shore of the lake, okay? If we get away from the shore…find some place to hide…"

"What good is it going to do to hide? This isn't a game of hide and seek. They'll find us…"

"They'll find us for sure if we don't get moving in the next five seconds. I mean, what do you want to do? Stay here and…"

Both Misty and I duck down into a crouch suddenly at the sound of breaking branches in the distance. I swear under my breath again and grab hold of Misty's sweater at the shoulder. I start dragging her back up the slope behind us.

Now I can hear muffled shouting in the distance behind us. I pull Misty down into a crouch again.

"What are you doing?" she hisses angrily in my ear.

I shush her and turn to look back. I can clearly make out the beams of flashlights about a hundred yards behind us. They flicker and slice through the darkness like bolts of lightning. Another snap of breaking underbrush makes us both catch our breath.

"Wait a minute," I say quietly.

"We can't just sit…"

"Five seconds ago you didn't want to keep moving." She opens her mouth to toss something at me, but I shush her with a hand gesture again and then point.

"Look…see what I mean? They're looking along the shore."

I point back the way we came.

"This slope turns into a cliff right over there. They're not expecting you to go up there, so they're going to search along the edge of the water but…getting dark. They might think… must have…missed you in the dark….won't expect you to try and…climb up the slope in the dark and even if they do, if we get under a log or something…keep totally still, they'll probably walk right past us. It's our only chance."

Misty shakes so hard, I can hear her teeth chatter from three feet away. I'm not even sure if she can walk. She looks back at the lakeshore, turns to face me, and finally nods her head.

Without a word, we both get to our feet, and turn into the bush.

Eight

Misty stumbles after me. I turn and weave my way forward, step over a log, and then onto the forest floor. I pause to look back at her and wonder for a moment if she's really going to keep following me or not.

For whatever reason, whenever I'm around her, I feel embarrassed about who I am. It's as if I can feel her criticizing me without her having to say a word. I guess an attitude is like a force field, because I would almost swear on a stack of Bibles that her eyes are boring a hole into my shoulder blades with a very intense dislike. She's thinking about being soaking wet, freezing cold, and stuck out in the Canadian bush with the lowest life form in the jazz band. Crazy thing is, my social standing at St. Mark's, or lack thereof, is really the only thing she knows about me. Sometimes, it's really no fun being me.

When I first came to St. Mark's, I thought it wouldn't be that difficult to fit in. I mean seriously, I've figured out how to survive in totally different cultures, even when I didn't speak the language. You would think that coming back to America, speaking the same language, and eating the same foods, it should have been a piece of cake. It hasn't been! I found out in a big hurry that pretty much everybody in the country club crowd knows everybody else. It's a relatively small world. If they don't know you or your family or at least your trust fund manager, then you don't belong, and anyone who doesn't belong is pretty much social pond scum.

I hear muffled voices in the distance. The flashlights are getting closer. I can tell they are working their way along the edge of the lake, so we've got to get as deep into the bush as possible, get behind a log or a rock or something, and get down low. In the gathering

82

dark, if we stay very still, they just might miss us. That's the hope, anyway.

There are hundreds of fallen and broken logs and branches in our way. There are no paths or easy passages forward, and the ground is so thick with moss and decaying wood, it's like walking on a trampoline. I make almost no noise as I struggle forward, but I can hear Misty behind me. She's not making any effort to keep quiet, smacking tree branches out of her way and cursing under her breath. Fortunately, the terrorists aren't any quieter. This is a good thing because I swear, we sound like a herd of cattle tromping through the forest.

George always said I was like a walrus in the woods - loud, sloppy and obvious. Until this moment, I could never figure out why that was such a big deal. After all, in Alaska, we were trained to wander around shouting, "Hey bear" before we came around a corner, so we wouldn't surprise a bear. A surprised bear is a killer bear, so why George made fun of me for being so loud in the bush never quite registered in my city-kid brain. I remember asking him why he wished I could be so much quieter on the one hand and yet I was supposed to be loud enough not to surprise a bear on the other. That just didn't make sense. I mean, sure, if you want to be a hunter, you should probably learn how to really stalk around, but I have never had any interest in hunting. I don't like the taste of wild game; I've never killed anything other than fish and I don't want to either. All he would say was something like: *There's a time for everything.* I didn't get it then, but I think I get it now. If there was ever a time for being quiet in the bush, it's *now*.

George did try to teach me some stalking technique and I admit I'm trying to use it now. He said the way to be quiet is to sort of crouch, set your weight evenly, and step toe-to-heel instead of heel-to-toe. Stepping so deliberately from toe-to-heel allows you to feel if there's anything like a stick underneath your foot before you put weight on it. It also evens out your stride. It's slow going and I'm not really doing the toe, heel thing on every step. Still, I can hear every step Misty takes like a slap on the ear. Maybe it doesn't matter anyway. If Misty is going to walk like an elephant, no amount of soft stepping on my part is going to help. At least the terrorists are just as clumsy.

I press on for at least twenty minutes, glancing over my shoulder every so often to see if Misty is still behind me, hoping not to see a flashlight beam right on our tail. Straight above my head, the sky still holds on to the last purple glow of sunset. Here below the tree line, the shadows are closing in like a gliding black mist. Looking back again, I can't see any flashlight beams. We've obviously come a fair distance inland from the lake and they've continued following along the edge of the water. I can't hear their shouting anymore either. For a second, I think we might have gotten a real break. I take the first safe breath I've had since we first went into the water. When I exhale, I swear my breath feels as thick as a London fog, but I can't see it because it's too dark. We have got to find some place to hole up, and soon.

Eventually, they're going to come to the place where the slope becomes a cliff, and they're going to know they must have passed Misty in the dark. At that point, they'll double back and start looking deeper into the woods. I don't know what kind of tracking skills they have, but it won't be hard to figure out which way we went if they're paying any attention at all. There's only one way we could have gone! The slope on our left is steep and they'll know we didn't head back to the beach. They won't need any tracks to figure out we must have gone straight into the bush. Besides, even by flashlight, I'll bet it won't be hard to find the gaping hole we trampled though the blackberry vines. How long before they find that? A matter of minutes? Even if they don't find it right away, by morning, it will easy to see. How far can we get, groping around in the dark?

I fold my arms across my chest to try and conserve at least some body heat. After another fifteen minutes of shivering, I know it's a losing battle. My body heat is escaping faster than my uncle's money at Christmas. My teeth chatter in the breeze. I can see Misty's skin almost glowing in the twilight and it's so dark now I can't make out the details of her face. We have to try something, anything, to get a little warmer.

Suddenly, I nearly run face-first into a large pile of rocks. I step around the first big boulder and find a small space behind it next to the slope. Half a dozen broken limbs are piled up above the rocks, making a tiny hollow not much larger than an open broom closet. It's not going to work as a real shelter, but it will have to do for at least a few minutes. I stop and turn back to see if Misty has lost me in the dark.

"Careful," I hiss back in her general direction. "Get behind these rocks. We gotta stop here and try to get a little warmer."

To let Misty get into the space, I have to lay back on the slope. Misty curls up next to the rock pile, wrapping her arms around her body. I figure her own body heat will probably warm up the air in the hollow just a smidgen, enough to feel a little better for a few minutes anyway. I look back into the gloom, hoping not to see any flashlights or hear any voices. I can't hear anything except our own teeth chattering. The twilight has deepened to the point where I can't see more than six or eight inches in front of my face. It won't be long before it's truly pitch dark.

"Okay," I whisper. My teeth chatter so hard, I feel like I'm making a rap against a drumbeat. "Our clothes are soaking wet. We have to at least wring them out or we'll freeze."

"Wouldn't be…so cold if you…hadn't pushed me into a lake."

The last thing I want right now is get into a word fight. At least ten different feelings, none of them good, scurry across my mind like spiders running from raindrops.

"I didn't…I didn't push you!" I hiss furiously. "Maybe you'd be a lot warmer under the video lights…right before they cut your head off." I spit this out in one big gush and immediately wish I hadn't said it. I'm just so sick of her whining. When she doesn't answer, I regret it even more.

"I'm…look, I'm sorry…"

"Whatever," she says.

"I'm sorry...really...look, we gotta, you know, wring out our clothes...get some, like, insulation. I learned that...back in Alaska..." I feel really lame trying to explain to her what I think we need to do. I guess I'll just have to do it.

I take the limp lifejacket and my great coat off first. The lifejacket is just a useless piece of plastic so I kind of toss it aside. The greatcoat is more or less a rain-jacket, sort of thin with a plastic-like feel on the outside. Then my sweater. It's thin too. The truth is, neither the greatcoat nor the sweater is ever all that warm even when I'm not soaked to the skin. They are, essentially, decorative items for the uniform.

I wring out the greatcoat and the sweater and place them on the slope behind me. The sweater is wool, so it's supposed to be warm, even when it's wet. I wonder if that's why the uniform Nazis at St. Mark's made the fall uniform almost entirely of wool. Gotta keep the prep kids warm, even if they get soaked – wouldn't want a lawsuit because Little Miss Wonderful got wet.

Normally, I wear two shirts because of the back brace, and that is going to be an advantage tonight. I wear a white cotton tee shirt underneath the Boston brace to keep it from rubbing too many welts into my skin, only it doesn't always work all that well. Welts and bruises and skin rubbed raw are a simple fact of life in the brace. You get used to it.

Overtop of the brace, I wear the uniform long sleeve shirt. I'm already regretting having taken off the greatcoat and sweater because it's colder than a polar bear's tush, but I'm committed to wringing everything out, even if I have to get frostbite in the process. I've done it before too. I've fallen into enough creeks while out fishing with George to know that getting all the excess water out of your jeans is the fastest way to feeling warmer. Soaked jeans are like wearing a frozen suit of armor.

Misty isn't moving. She just sits and looks at me. I guess the idea of taking off any clothing in front of me isn't an option. Of course, it's 95% dark and I can only barely see her shape. I don't know what she's worried about – I wouldn't be able to enjoy the view even if she stripped down to her skin in the next ten seconds anyway.

"Squeeze out the water...then we have to try and get some insulation," I say almost breathlessly. The cold is so intense my tongue is having a hard time forming words. I figure if I keep talking, I won't lose my drive to get everything wrung out. "I knew this native guy...in Alaska...guy's name was George...he taught me what to do...if you fall into a creek or something...when you're out in the bush."

Misty doesn't answer. She just sits there so I'm guessing she's shivering to the point of falling apart. I can't see well enough to know, but my running narrative is having about as much effect as talking to a wall. She doesn't make any effort to take anything off and follow my lead, so I just decide to ignore her. I wring out the long sleeve shirt as tightly as possible. I can feel the goosebumps crawling up my bare arms like spreading lice. It isn't fun, but I know I have to get as much of the excess water out of my clothes as possible.

"You're crazy," she says.

"But I won't be as cold," I toss back.

I unbuckle my pants and start to peel my wet trousers down to my knees. Misty makes a noise and turns her back on me. I'm not trying to impress or anything; I just have to take my pants down to unbuckle the brace. I have to reach around behind my back blindly and pull the three Velcro straps that hold the Boston brace tight against my torso. I feel a sudden rush of adrenaline at how loud the Velcro sounds in the stillness. After loosening the three Velcro straps, I'm able to pull the brace apart, squeeze out of it, and set it on the ground. Misty's curiosity gets the better of her. With her back still turned to me, she glances over her shoulder at the brace.

"What happened?" she asks. "I mean, that you have to wear that thing."

"Born that way," I answer. I'm fumbling with my undershirt because my hands feel heavy and stiff from the cold. "My back is...kinda like a hunch back...I gotta wear that till I quit growing...so it won't get worse but...won't get much better either."

"Does it…does it hurt?"

I'm genuinely surprised at her question. We have not been on the friendliest of terms in the last few hours. I wonder how much of her question is curiosity and how much she really cares. I guess it doesn't matter.

"Yeah," I answer with a flat, matter-of-fact tone. "Hurts all the time."

"That sucks," she says.

"Yeah…is what it is."

Taking off the brace is always a strange sensation. No matter how much I exercise - and I exercise a ton - taking off the brace makes me feel suddenly weak. My body obviously depends on it to stand up straight instead of depending on my back and ab muscles, so my torso feels thin and frail every time I squeeze out of it. Whenever I take it off, I get a powerful temptation to slouch all the way over until I'm curled up like an armadillo.

The brace was obviously keeping me somewhat warmer too because the icy blast of the air against my wet under tee shirt nearly buckles my knees. I peel off my tee shirt and rub my skin roughly with the palms of my hands. It suddenly occurs to me how glad I am it's dark. Honestly, the idea of being half-naked with Misty has crossed my mind before only I wasn't standing with her in an icebox in my dream! Standing behind a pile of rocks in my underwear with my pants around my knees is really making me self-conscious. The sooner I can hide my whitey-tighties again, the better.

I wring out the tee shirt, lay out both shirts on a nearby fern, and tackle getting out of my pants. They are heavy with water and I have to sit on the slope to get my shoes off.

Each shoe is like a lead weight. I pour out the excess water, pull the tongue of the shoe up, and strip off my socks. I wring them out and place them next to my shirts. I start on my pants next. The first leg seems to be suctioned to my leg and it's everything I can do to get it off. The second leg is a bit easier because I can use the rest of the pants to get some leverage against the suction. Fortunately, the pants are woolen slacks, not jeans, so they don't weigh a ton or feel as slimy as jeans would feel. It only takes a minute to squeeze half a cup of water out of them, but that minute feels like an hour because the cold pecks into my flesh like a thousand rabid penguins.

"What are you…what are you doing now?" Misty is so cold she can hardly speak. "Now you…gotta put everything back on…just as cold…"

"Yeah but…George told me…said the key to getting warm is dead air…it's like insulation…I'm gonna fill up my pants and between these two shirts…ya' know, with some of these ferns and stuff."

Misty just snorts something derisive and keeps her back turned.

"No, seriously," I say in a hurry. "I remember George showing me this whole idea…we were out in the bush and he showed me a squirrel's nest in a tree. He said the squirrels used…every sort of dry tinder they could find to create a puffy, kind of a ball for a nest. He said the dead air between the twigs and leaves will warm up…sort of like making a fur coat. I'm not kidding; it's one of the first things he taught me. He made me practice making shelters and stuff. That's the key…lots of insulation."

It's an agony as I slip my pants back on. I decide not to put my back brace back on because it isn't going to help me stay warm, and I pretty much hate the wretched thing. If we don't make it out of here, I'll at least be without the brace. The pants are stiff and cold, but not as wet. I peel my wet socks back onto my feet and then stuff the bottom of the pant legs into the tops of my socks. Since the brace is off, my pants are two sizes too big for my waist and that's exactly what I need.

"I remember falling into the creek by our house," I say. "George made me wring everything out…then stuff my pants full of grass. He said it was like putting on a fur coat."

Reaching around, I find a fern and tear off some of the leaves. I stuff the material down into my pants, all the way down to my socks. I begin clawing for the driest moss and fern leaves my hands can find and continue stuffing my pants full. It only takes a few minutes to fill them all the way up to my belt with as much of the stuff as I can cram between my legs and my pants.

I stand up and zip my pants shut. Misty must have heard the zipper sound because she finally looks around in my direction. I'm bare from the waist up. I can hardly see her face in the dark so I don't expect she can appreciate my abs. The thought makes me chuckle a little.

"What?" she asks.

"Nothing," I say.

I pull on the wet tee shirt, tuck it in, and then pull my long sleeve shirt on and tuck it in as well. In the same fashion, I fill the space between the long sleeve shirt and my tee shirt with as much moss and fern leaves as I can. In a few minutes, I look like the Michelin man. Over top, I pull on the sweater, then the greatcoat and button it up as high as it will go. Within minutes, I do feel significantly warmer.

"See," I say. "It's scratchy but it's warmer."

"I don't know…I can't…"

"Listen, Misty. It's going to freeze tonight. Don't you get that? I lived in Alaska for almost three years. I've heard way too many stories about people getting lost in the bush and freezing to death. You're soaking wet."

It's finally dark, yet Misty is shivering so hard, I can see her shape quivering. I try another way…

"Listen, I can't see you in the dark, okay? Just take your clothes off and wring them out like I did. You've got a sweater on, right? I'll collect some ferns and stuff, you stuff it between your shirt and the sweater. It'll help. I promise. And then, you can put my greatcoat on over that. It'll help…really".

"I'm wearing a skirt."

"Yeah, but…you got, like…tights on…"

"Leggings, not tights," she says.

"Okay, but you can stuff them."

"They're skin-tight."

"Well, then, at least the top half of you will be warmer."

Misty says something under her breath. I'm not sure, but it sounded a whole lot like something rude and un-ladylike. The idea makes me smile.

"Listen," I say somewhat gently. "I'm not...you know...trying anything, I'm just trying to help. I can't see you in the dark anyway. It'll help...I swear..."

It's quiet for a few seconds. For whatever reason, I know it's time to just shut up and let her think it through.

"You gotta turn the other way," she says quietly.

"It's dark; don't worry."

"Just turn around."

"Okay, okay. I'm turning around."

It takes Misty a lot longer than I did to finish wringing out her clothes. I'm not exactly sure what she's doing behind me that takes so long, but I can't help wondering. What really makes me think I'm insane is that I can't help thinking about Misty getting nearly naked in the dark behind me. How in the world can I think about that at a time like this?

I get so frustrated with that kind of thinking - it just sort of jumps into my head at the worst times. It's stupid, ridiculous, even nuts. I swear, sometimes I feel like slapping myself in the face. We're nearly frozen to death, lost in the woods with terrorists trying to find us and kill us and I'm still imagining what Misty looks like in the buff.

That is so pathetic.

But the truth is I think about it all the time, no matter how hard I try not to think about it. Sometimes I think about it so much, I just want to scream. Or punch something. Of course, my mother taught me all the biology stuff since I was homeschooled most of my life, and I've heard the speech about how normal it is to think about sex and all that rot. But I know the rules! I know it's not right to lust all the time. Only, I really want to look, I mean, I really want to look.

And it's like a war in my soul.

I've been a Christian since I was seven and I really believe – and I just can't figure out how to be normal and not lust. Sometimes I think it's going to kill me. If God made girls so stinking beautiful, why am I not supposed to notice? I mean I know part of it is just being seventeen, but another part of it is trying to juggle my desire to drool every time I see a drop-dead beautiful girl with what I really believe. It feels impossible sometimes too because everybody at St. Mark's thinks sex is a giant game and the object is to score.

I don't have any friends at St. Mark's, not really, but I know enough of the other guys to know what they think. They think it's stupid to resist thinking about it. They pass porn around on their cell phones like parents give out candy on Halloween. I've seen some stuff that would probably get half of my gym class arrested. So I've wondered, many times, why I even try to be good.

Then again, if I'm honest, I do know why I try.

My dad made sure he introduced me to enough single mothers and people in Africa dying from the AIDS virus to make sure I knew why. My dad wasn't a big believer in just teaching me what the Bible says about right and wrong. He wanted me to see why some things are right and other things are wrong. He didn't protect me from seeing the darker places in the world. We left for the mission field when I was nine, so I found out what a prostitute was before I even knew what the word "sex" actually meant. Some of the missionaries we supported worked with human trafficking victims, and I saw some things that literally broke my heart.

So, the idea of getting some horrible disease or getting a girl pregnant scares the spit out of my mouth. I really want to wait until I'm married...but I also wish it was light enough for me to turn around and see Misty undressing too. I guess it's just something I've got to live with - one day at a time.

I shake off my thoughts about Misty's body and take a deep breath.

"Let's get up the hill a little farther."

Misty doesn't answer me right away. Suddenly, I realize her breathing has changed. I can't see her, but it sounds like she's trying to keep me from hearing that she's crying. I'm sort of stunned. I never really thought about what she must be feeling. I've thought about my own fear, my own cold, and my own ideas about what to do next. I never really put myself in her shoes. She's got to be on the edge of totally melting down. I reach out toward her and put my hand on her shoulder. She pulls away a little, but not completely.

"It's going to be okay," I say softly.

"They're going to kill us. They're going to find me. There's nothing I can do."

"We can get deeper into the bush..."

"It doesn't matter. They've got flashlights and guns...and we don't even know where we are."

"I don't see any flashlights right now. We've already gotten away..."

"But not for long. They're gonna to find us."

"They're not." I put a little bit of an edge in my voice. "They're not, okay? We just have to keep moving and they won't."

"Where are we going to go? We're lost, I'm freezing...they killed Todd. They poured acid on him."

"I know, I know. Misty, I know. But we can't just sit here and let them find us either. We have to keep going. We have to try."

"Even if they don't find us...what are we going to do? We're gonna die out here."

"No, no we're not. I've lived in these kinds of woods. I know what to do, just...just come with me. Okay? We won't go that far, okay? We'll just...we'll find a good spot to hide and then in the morning, we'll get so deep out here, they'll never find us."

Misty's sobs are real now. She doesn't try to hide it. I'm not sure what to do. I want to hug her, but I don't know if she'll let me. Instead, I just squeeze her shoulder a little.

"Let's just go up the hill a little. I know it's really dark but...hey...look at the sky."

I can't tell if Misty is looking up but I do. The stars are a riot of light. We must be a hundred or more miles from the nearest electric light bulb, so there's nothing to compete with their brilliance.

"See...it's not all dark. Come on."

Misty still shivers violently, but she slowly gets to her feet. Turning toward the slope of the hill, we begin to press forward

93

slowly. I can barely make out the ground in front of us. The slope of the hill is at least forty-five degrees. The trees are little better than darker shapes against a dark background, but we press forward, using our hands to guide us. Gradually, the darkness begins to brighten a tiny bit. The moon must be out behind the trees where we can't see it.

In a few minutes, I can feel myself warming up. The insulation isn't nearly as good as I would hope for, but at least I'm a little warmer. Ten minutes of scrambling forward passes us by, then another ten. In the gloom, I can see an uprooted, fallen tree. The roots stand nearly straight up like a wall.

"There," I whisper. "We can get under that tree, bury ourselves in some ferns, and get warm. Okay?"

Misty doesn't answer. I can see her outline, but I can't tell if she is even looking at me. When she speaks, her voice is so low I can barely make out the words.

"Okay," she says. "I'm so cold…"

"Yeah, me too. You get under here first and I'll try to cover you up."

I let Misty step past me. She huddles down under the trunk with her back against the roots. The slope of the hill is behind her and to her left, so I figure the roots will hide us from anyone looking up the hill from below in the morning. As soon as Misty is settled, I begin to feel around the ground for anything I can use to cover her up. There are plenty of ferns and dry moss, so I begin to tear out handfuls of everything I can reach. At first, I give her handfuls and she tries to cover herself. After a few minutes, I just sort of go about tossing whatever I'm finding on top of her. She doesn't resist or complain or make any noise at all. It takes me about fifteen minutes to really cover her up, or at least, I think I've covered her up.

"Are you covered?" I ask.

"Yes," she says quietly. "More or less."

"Okay…I'm going to crawl in there too. We can…you know…body heat. You know what I mean?"

She doesn't answer, so I take that as a good sign. I feel awkward trying to cuddle up with her under a log, but I know we need to keep each other warm. I don't put my arm over her or anything; I just sort of sit next to her back. I almost immediately feel her body heat. It's not exactly warm, but our teeth aren't chattering nearly as hard as they were when we wrung out our wet clothing either. After a few minutes, I put my arm around her.

"Don't," she says.

"Sorry…it's not like…it's just…we'll be warmer if we're…really close…or closer. You know what I mean?"

"Okay, just…you can just sit close. Right?"

"Yeah, yeah, that's good…" I pull my arm back and settle in behind her back. She doesn't pull away, so I expect my body heat is comforting. My back is bunched up against the tree roots and I'm not covered with much of anything.

It's going to be a long night…

Nine

I'm afraid to sleep. I've heard too many stories about what happens to you when you get too cold. First, your teeth chatter and you shiver as if nothing on earth could make you stop. Then, you do stop, and an overwhelming sense of fatigue pours over you like a warm, wet blanket. Your eyes get heavy, you fall asleep, and you never wake up. Hypothermia!

I'm not sure where the lines are crossed between hypothermia taking over my body and being just plain exhausted. I'm scared that we're not warm enough. I slip off my greatcoat and lay it on top of Misty. She doesn't move so I guess she's asleep. Over and over again, I reach around, tear out whatever moss or fern that feels dry, and pile more on top of Misty, or I try to pile it over myself. It's like trying to sleep under fifty individual washrags instead of one blanket. Every move I make dislodges something. One second the tip of my nose is so cold I swear it's forming into an icicle, so I try to bury my face under a fern, then my back feels like someone's pouring ice water between my shoulder blades. It's torture by temperature.

I'm still shivering from time to time, just not all the time. I don't know if that's a good sign or not. Misty seems to have fallen asleep although I can't tell for sure. I think I've done a pretty good job burying her. She's also shivering occasionally; I can tell because her breathing seems to shudder only it's not as bad as before. Gradually, I edge closer to her. I tell myself I'm getting closer because I want to keep her warm, except she feels so warm to me. I wonder who is warming up the other.

I doze off for maybe minutes at a time, only to snap awake again and again. I've never been good at staying awake even under the best of circumstances. A few times, I've tried to stay awake all night, but I was never successful. In Alaska, there was a small church at the mission headquarters and some of the pre-teens got together for an all-night New Year's Eve celebration one year. I couldn't stay awake past one in the morning, even with every episode of *Battle Star Galactica* running on video and an endless supply of pizza and soda. It's just not in me to stay awake, even for a good cause. I can't study past ten at night either.

My dad was like that too. He and Mom were polar opposites when it came to internal clocks. Dad was "lights out" at about nine every night but Mom was just getting started. She would often tease him about being a party pooper whenever he got up and headed for the bedroom at about the same time I was sent to bed. On the other hand, she was useless in the morning before about nine. My dad was up before any reasonable person, sometime around four, so Dad would often tease her just as much as she teased him. He called her "Mrs. Floppy Bear" in the mornings because she would curl up on a couch or a chair, dead to the world, while her coffee got cold on the table. Dad and I would both take turns lifting up one of her arms and dropping it to see how close she was to really being alive. She would groan and grumble and occasionally threaten us, all to no avail, because Mrs. Floppy Bear was our entertainment before dawn. We never got tired of poking her awake. I think she sort of liked it, too. In some weird way we all knew it was a game that said to Mom, "We think you're adorable." I don't know for sure, except she never got angry either.

My eyes droop heavily and in my mind, I see my mom curled up in a chair once again. I lift her arm, drop it, and then pull back slowly. It isn't my mother anymore. It's the flight attendant I saw Mr. Tan Jacket murder. I see her whole body flop off the chair and someone unseen drags her away. I turn away, disgusted and afraid, only to find myself treading in deep water. In the distance is a wave, so high, so dark, and so breathtaking, it looks like a mountain coming at me

97

as fast as a freight train. I dive only just in time, the crash of the wave above me is like a thunderclap and I claw my way to the surface. Gulping air, I see another wave bearing down on me, foaming and cruel, so I turn. And then I find myself suddenly on a surfboard, paddling furiously. The wave catches me, throws me bouncing and chattering down its hungry face. I turn the board; a furious spray shoots out from my turn. The green shoulder of the wave presses forward, now sparkling with yellow fire from a distant sun. I hurl myself up the face and now I'm flying, flapping my arms like seagull wings. Below me, the water disappears. I'm flying over a forest and there are wolves streaming like gray ghosts between the trunks of the trees. They snap at my heels, growling and frothing at the mouth. Their eyes are red and evil. I kick one away, but another takes its place, so I struggle to gain altitude. My arms feel so tired, so thick with cold and strain that I can't seem to rise. The wolves are near...nearer still...

I violently jerk back to consciousness. Misty's breathing is deep and slow and she's not shivering. I can feel her warmth on my chest. My back seems to be covered with ice. I try to fluff up the debris I stacked against us a little deeper for about the millionth time.

I hate dreams about deep water. Every time I dream that way, it's always waves crashing over me and I've barely got enough breath to get back to the surface before another tsunami comes my way. The weird thing is, I so often end up surfing the wave and yet I've never been surfing in my life. I've never even really seen surfing, except on television. For some reason, these dreams are always a mix of fear and exhilaration as if I could almost be having fun if I wasn't scared out of my mind. I have no idea what any of it means either.

I've gotten in the habit of thinking about my dreams when I wake up, hoping God will say something to me in a dream, like in the Bible. So far - nada...or if one of my dreams has been from God the message must have gotten mixed up on delivery, because all I've ever seen is either too bizarre to believe or so X-rated there's no way it could come from God.

98

My mother's favorite Bible story is about Joseph, who gets sold into slavery in Egypt. It was a dream that saved him. Actually, two dreams! The King's baker and his wine-taster get chucked into the same prison with Joe, they both have dreams, and Joe is able to figure out what the dreams mean because God gave him the interpretation. In the end, God tells Joseph what the king's dream meant and because of that, he was moved up to become the Prime Minister for the whole empire. From the prison to the palace in one clean sweep, just because of a dream. But my dreams have yet to mean anything other than the fact I had something too spicy for dinner.

A sharp crack wakes me up. I'm sore all over. I feel like one gigantic itch festival. My skin is on fire only it's not the kind of fire that keeps me warm. I itch everywhere, my back cramps from sleeping without the brace on, and I have to resist the urge to scratch myself bloody. What I do know for sure is that any sudden movements on my part could be deadly, so I listen intently. There is a breeze in the tops of the trees and Misty's breathing is still strong and steady, but nothing else. The sharp sound could have been a branch breaking in the wind or it could have been an enemy. Again, I calm myself and listen.

I hear nothing except the wind.

I realize I can see the ferns on the slope next to us. The long uncomfortable night must be nearly over. I must have slept a little because I remember the waves and the wolves in my dream. I push up a little until my head is clear of the debris I buried us under during the night and look around carefully. The creeping, cold gray of dawn slowly builds around us. I pause and listen again.

We have to get moving before the sun is fully up. The terrorists will figure out that no one could climb up the cliff face by the lake, so they will know we went straight into the bush. I don't think they know a whole lot about tracking or hunting, not that I know much better. Still, where we left the lake and scrambled through the blackberry bushes is going to be obvious in the morning light. It won't take them long to figure out which direction we went.

We need a plan, too. There's no way we can be anywhere near civilization. On the other hand, the terrorists had to set this thing up somewhere close, so they had to hike in or fly in somehow. There could be old mining or logging roads close by or some sort of track they hiked. If we could find it, maybe we can find a way out. Or did they fly in by floatplane? If they did, the plane might be hidden somewhere on the lake. Of course, that wouldn't do me much good because even if I could find it, they wouldn't just leave the keys in the ignition. Besides, even if I could trust my nineteen hours experience as pilot in command, stealing their plane wouldn't help the rest of the hostages anyway – if I didn't crash or get shot on takeoff.

Up to this moment, I've been running on adrenalin and instinct. I can't help feeling guilty somehow, like I got caught looking at naughty pictures on my cell phone and I'm going to the headmaster's office in a few minutes. Bailing out of the raft, making a run for it, it all seems wrong. Everyone else just sat there, doing what they were told. Me getting all crazy, jumping into a freezing lake, and somehow convincing Misty to follow me into a trackless, endless forest feels like I'm in real trouble. Mr. Towns was almost frothing at the mouth he was so mad at me. Did I get people hurt because I ran for it? Was I wrong?

I'm shaking now, not shivering. Shaking because I'm afraid, because I feel like I'm in trouble with everyone who is anyone in my life. What would my uncle think? He would have told me to sit tight, let the experts figure things out. And my dad? He was a Marine, but I'm not and running off could have put everyone at risk. Maybe they weren't going to kill her. Maybe they just want her for negotiation and now I'm putting her life, my life, maybe everybody on the plane in danger of getting killed because I wanted to play Marine and run off into the woods.

I can only imagine how Misty feels.

I didn't grow up in the governor's mansion and go to prep schools all my life. I wonder if the most difficult thing Misty has had to face was not being invited to a party. I'll bet her idea of camping is staying at a hotel out of town, too. I've nearly drowned her and if I'm

100

uncomfortable, covered in itch and dirt, she's probably feeling ten times worse. Or will be once she wakes up.

I shake my head and push all these thoughts into the background. I don't have time to second-guess myself right now. I don't have the luxury of worrying about what Mr. Towns or Stan or anyone might be thinking either. I can't help what is happening to the other passengers, and I'm not going to be responsible for whatever happens to them either. It's the terrorists who are responsible, not me. Feeling all sorry for myself and worrying about whether I should have turned left or right yesterday is stupid. If I've learned anything since the crash that killed my parents, it is that I can't fix yesterday. In fact, my dad once told me that everything I did five minutes in the past is as far away from me as King Tut. I can't fix the past...but I can do something about today.

"Misty," I whisper. I pull back from her a little bit. I don't expect she's going to want to cuddle.

Misty's eyes flutter. She wakes up suddenly and almost jumps away from me. There's enough light for me to make out her face. Her hair is frizzed out from being wet and uncombed, bits of dead fern cling to her sweater, and she looks confused as if she can't remember where she is and why she's huddled under a tree with me.

"What? What's going on?"

"Nothing, it's okay," I say quickly. Obviously, she's worried someone has found us. "I don't see or hear anything but...it's almost daybreak. We gotta get moving."

Misty brushes her hair back from her face and looks around. About a dozen different feelings seem to rush over her face, everything from fear to anger.

"What are we...what do we do?" Her voice cracks as if she is going to start crying again.

"Let's get to the top of this hill." I point over my left shoulder.

"What's up there?" she asks.

"I don't know but...we can't go back. They're going to search away from the lake and over that way." I point back down the slope and to the right. It's a flat grade stretching away into the shadows.

It's much easier going and I'm counting on the terrorists thinking we would run that way. "I don't think they'll think we went up this slope. It's really steep. They'll probably think we went the easy way."

Misty nods her head. It makes sense.

Carefully, I wiggle my way backwards out of the nest of debris I built up during the night and stand up. I stop again to listen and look around me. Dawn is just beginning, so I can still barely make out the trees. If the terrorists are searching for us, they will still need to use flashlights, at least for the next half an hour or so. I don't see or hear anything except the wind.

Misty scrambles out behind me. Standing up she nearly falls over because the slope is so steep. I reach out for her elbow to help her keep upright.

"Thanks," she says.

"I'm really...really sorry," I say. Misty just shrugs her shoulders and looks down at her feet.

"You didn't hijack the plane," she says softly.

"No, but...it was my idea to...take off, you know."

"I didn't have to follow either. Let's just...let's just go, okay?"

"Okay," I answer. "Here...put on the coat."

"That's yours," she says.

"I know, but..."

"But I'm a girl!"

"No...I mean, well...I've got a sweater and two shirts...I'm good. Really. Please?

I think she's not sure what to say so she finally just nods her head and puts on my greatcoat. It's too big for her, but that's a good thing because it almost comes to her ankles. I nod my head and since now *I'm* not sure what to say next, I just turn toward the slope. I'm a little hopeful now that Misty doesn't completely hate me. At least she doesn't blame me for having to spend the night curled up under a tree.

I look up at the slope and take a deep breath. It's so steep we're going to have to basically crawl to the top. I pick up my back brace and start picking my way forward.

"Why are you taking that thing?" Misty asks.

"If they find it, they'll know where we've been. But it might be useful, even though I hate it. It's got Velcro I can make into a fishing line, a piece of aluminum I could make into something. I don't know. Just feels right to keep it."

"How long have you had to wear it?"

"Since I was thirteen. I'm supposed to wear it until I'm eighteen."

"I thought you were eighteen."

"Not until January. Close enough, I guess."

The slope is hard going and within minutes, we're both breathing too hard to talk. At least twice, my feet slip out from underneath me, and I almost land face-first in the dirt before I catch myself with my hands. Every few feet, I turn to help Misty scramble up behind me. The sun is up and it's definitely above freezing. Before long, I'm feeling pretty warm. It's basically impossible to keep quiet because the slope is so steep. Neither of us can help snapping sticks and occasionally making a loud grunt.

An hour or so passes and we finally reach the top of the ridge. The last few feet are the steepest yet. I push the brace ahead of me and use the roots of a tree to pull myself the last few feet up to the top. I've been looking back on almost every other step and I haven't seen anything. I can't see the lake at all even though I know it's probably only a couple of hundred yards away, somewhere off to my left. Straight ahead of me over the top of the ridge, the slope begins to descend sharply. I can hear water flowing somewhere up ahead too. There must be a creek running downhill toward the lake in the ravine in front of us. I turn back to help Misty crawl up the last few feet.

"Almost there," I say.

As I take her hand, both of her feet slip, and she lets out a sharp cry. Fortunately, she's not that heavy and I don't lose my grip on her hand. Her shout was loud enough to echo, and I want to cringe. Misty frantically tries to get her feet under her, and I have to hold on with all my might to help her scramble to the top. Once she gets to the top, I stop to listen.

"Great," I mutter under my breath.

103

"What is it?"

"Listen…" I swear under my breath. In the distance, I can hear the muffled sound of voices. They must have heard Misty's little scream.

"I'm sorry," she pleads. "I didn't mean to…"

"Forget it. Let's go."

Together we plunge forward, but we don't get more than a half a dozen yards before we have to stop. The slope of the hill on this side of the ridge is basically a cliff. It's almost vertical and I hear another shout from the slope behind us.

"We're going to have to zigzag our way down…"

"That's crazy. It's straight down."

"Not really. Well…maybe, but…"

"Let's go this way…"

"We don't have any time…"

"I'm not going that way!"

I can tell Misty isn't interested in any argument. She turns and takes the lead, marching uphill along the top of the ridge, which is probably only about three feet wide. I just shake my head and turn to follow her. Almost immediately, Misty runs into a fallen tree that blocks her way forward. The crown of the tree hangs directly over the slope to our left and the roots stand straight up nearly ten feet on the edge of the slope leading back the way we came. The only way past is to creep around the roots, but that takes us back closer to the terrorists. I have no idea how close they are or if they will see us.

I curse again under my breath. There's nothing we can do except go around the roots or go back the way we came. I shoulder past her and start to make my way down and to the right to get around the roots. The slope is so steep, both of my feet fly out from under me and I land on the seat of my pants. I can feel the wet earth soak into my pants. I scramble to my hands and knees, still clutching the back brace in my right hand and start clawing my way down and sideways, trying desperately not to slide any farther than I have to get around the roots. Misty slips and slides behind me.

104

On the far side of the roots, I have to climb back up the slope at least twenty feet on my hands and knees. At the top, the ridge is undercut from erosion creating a vertical wall four or five feet high. I toss the back brace over the top, grab hold to a sapling on the top of the ridge with both hands and pull myself up. I turn and reach for Misty.

Behind us, I hear another shout. When I look back, every hair on my head pricks up. I can clearly see two men at the bottom of the ridge. I see them at the same time they see me. One of them raises a rifle and shouts.

I pull Misty to the top of the ridge with one mighty heave. Just as I turn to reach for the back brace, I hear a rifle shot. Three feet to the right of my head, a branch explodes and Misty screams.

Both of us fall to the ground. I crawl forward toward the farther drop-off on the other side of the ridge.

"Go, go, go..." I shout at Misty.

"I thought you said they wanted us alive."

"They want you alive...not me. Let's go."

The slope in front of us is nearly straight down. I look at the broken tree to my left and I know what we have to do.

"This way," I say.

I pull myself up on top of the fallen tree and begin to scoot backwards, holding on to the bark with my left hand. My right hand still holds the brace. Misty crawls up behind me and together we start sliding down the trunk.

The tree hangs nearly straight down the slope like a rope, three feet thick and covered with bark. Fortunately, most of the branches have been shorn off over the years, but it's slick and covered with moss. In seconds, my hands are black with decayed wood and the crotch of my pants is soaked. I can only imagine what Misty is experiencing, trying to scoot backwards down a moss-covered log in a skirt. Those leggings are only going to protect her so much.

Suddenly, my hands slip and I'm free-sliding down the trunk. I let go of the back brace and claw at the trunk. I feel my right index fingernail tear loose, and my face slams into the wood as I cling to the trunk like a cat on a rope. I can taste blood from a split lip.

I spit out a mouthful of rotten bark and look over my left shoulder. I can see the brace caught in a jumble of rocks below the end of the tree trunk, about twenty feet away. If I hadn't gotten a death grip on the tree, I would have slammed into the rocks and probably broken every bone in my body.

I look back up at Misty. She is ten feet above me clinging to the trunk of the tree. Her skin is so stained with black from the decaying bark of the tree trunk she looks like she's wearing fishnet stockings on her arms.

"Keep going," I croak. "Almost there."

I slide backwards a few more feet, wiggle over top of the remains of a limb, and finally reach the end of the trunk. There's a drop below me about six or eight feet and I know there's no way back the way I came. I push myself backwards until my feet dangle over the end of the log. I look over my shoulder again and slip farther back until most of my body hangs out into space and my arms and shoulders nearly scream at me from holding my weight. I look again over my shoulder and try to aim my feet at the least jagged rock I can see, but it's still at least five feet from my heels to the impact zone. My arms can't hold on any longer, so I just let go.

I hit the rock with a grunt and the angle is so steep, I tip over backwards and slam into an upright sapling. The impact drives the wind out of my lungs and I feel myself falling again. I grab the sapling and sink down slamming my right knee into a rock. The pain shoots through me like a bolt of lightning.

It takes me a full thirty seconds to pull myself upright. My knee throbs and cries but I don't think I broke anything. I feel weak all over. I look back up at Misty. She has reached the end of the log, clutching the trunk.

"You have to hang off the end and drop down," I say.

"I can't." Her voice shakes and I can see her lower lip trembling.

I pull myself forward and put my back against the sapling. I brace both of my feet as wide as I can.

"I'll catch you."

"I can't."

"Misty, you can't crawl back. This is the only way."

She doesn't answer. I can see her look back up the trunk. For a moment, I think she's too paralyzed to move. Suddenly, she simply lets go and slips over the back of the trunk.

I'm caught off-guard. Her body slams into my chest and I lurch back against the sapling. I fall to my right but somehow manage to keep my left arm wrapped around Misty's waist. My right leg hyper-extends into a rock again, and another flash of intense pain shoots up my leg. Misty's body slides down and wrenches my left arm. With a yelp, I let her go. She crumples into the rocks, reaching out with her hands to stop her fall.

I reach out and steady her with my right arm. Both of us heave air in and out of our lungs by the bucketful. I look back the way we came and realize it's a flat miracle neither one of us was killed.

I pull my right leg up and feel a nasty throb. Looking down, I can see blood staining my right pant leg.

"Are you okay?" I ask. My breathing is ragged and hoarse. "Can you get up?"

"My hand is cut but...I think I'm okay."

"Okay...we gotta keep going."

Misty doesn't bother to thank me for catching her and I don't say anything. I look down the slope toward the sound of running water. We'll have to zigzag our way down through the trees, but at least we will be hidden from anyone looking down from above. I look around and see the back brace. For nearly four years, I've dreamed about escaping the stupid thing and now I won't give it up. I pick it up and step down toward the trees. The first step sends a numbing shock into my knee. It feels like something is boiling under my kneecap, but I keep moving. After a few steps, the pain seems to simply sear like a steak sizzling on a grill instead of exploding with every step. It's an improvement.

Misty stumbles behind me. A couple of times, I step on a loose patch and nearly slide, catching myself on a branch. I can't help looking back. I can't see the top of the ridge through the trees. It won't take them as long to get to the top of the ridge as it took for us, because they won't be making any effort to be quiet. There's no way they're going to miss which way we went. We really tore up the tree trunk when we slid down, so we may as well have painted a big black arrow on the rocks. Still, I don't know if the terrorists will try to slide down the trunk or look for an easier route. Either way, we don't have a lot of time. It won't take them thirty minutes to get to the top, maybe ten to figure out which way we went, and we've already used up most of that time.

After about a half hour of zigzagging across the slope through the trees, I finally see the creek ahead of me.

"We're at the bottom," I say over my shoulder. "Almost there."

It's obvious the terrorists will kill me to get to Misty. They want her to negotiate for something – money or power or to get someone released from prison. The rest of us are expendable. Still, somehow, they have to be in communication with the outside world to get what they want. They may have thought of everything to keep from being found, but eventually, they are going to have to make some sort of exchange. That means the good guys are going to show up, so I just have to keep us alive for a little while longer.

We've reached the creek. If I weren't so tired, scared and cold, it would be truly beautiful. The water is noisy and fast, flowing smoothly over thousands of rounded stones. The grade is steep, so the water pours from one pool to another over mini-waterfalls, some nearly as high as I am tall. Broken logs point in from the forest on either side. On our right, I see a log wedged between two huge boulders. The end of it nearly reaches the other side of the creek. We might be able to get across without getting wet. I decide it's worth a try.

"Let's get across here," I say.

Misty doesn't answer. She's beginning to shiver again, and I can tell she's just blindly putting one foot in front of the other at this point.

The log turns out to be very old. It feels rotten when I step on it. I walk slowly to the end. There's a gap between the end of the log and the farther bank, not far, maybe three or four feet. I use the brace to help me take a swinging jump. Just as my left foot pushes off from the log, it collapses beneath my weight. Instead of clearing the water, my right foot lands in the stream. Fortunately, it isn't more than knee-deep. I nearly fall as my left foot swings forward, and I lose my grip on the back brace. It falls into the water, so I reach out with left hand to get my balance, reach back into the water with my right, and get hold of the brace before it's swept away.

I trudge out of the creek into the bush on the far side of the creek and turn back to see if I can help Misty. She hasn't even started across.

"Come on," I say.

Misty doesn't move. She just shakes her head. I can see tears welling up in her eyes.

"It's too steep on that side of the creek," I say. "We need to move upstream, away from the lake, so you have to come across."

Misty isn't moving. In fact, she's simply standing on the edge of the creek with her arms folded across her chest. Huge sobs flow over her.

I want to be mad at her. I want to scream at her to shake it off and get moving, but I can't. She's probably never experienced anything more traumatic than a broken fingernail and now she's witnessed people being murdered, she's overwhelmingly tired, and scratched up so badly she probably feels like she's been attacked by an electric sander.

I drop the back brace on the bank behind me and decide I've got to go and get her. Stepping into the water is like plunging my foot into a bucket of ice water. The current tugs at my pant leg and in an instant, I can't hardly feel my toes. The rocks are slick under my feet, but the water doesn't go much deeper than my thighs. It only takes me about three minutes to get back across the creek.

"Come on, Misty," I say softly. "I'll help you. We've got to get across and move-up stream. Come on."

I reach out to her with both hands. She starts to turn away, but I slip my right arm around her waist and simply scoop her into my arms. She doesn't resist. Instead, she wraps her arms around my neck and buries her head into my shoulder. At any other time, I would be thrilled. I'm holding the girl of my daydreams in my arms. I can smell her hair, and she smells something like the honeysuckle flowers that grow in my aunt's backyard garden in the summer. But I can't concentrate on that right now. I turn around and start carrying her across. The creek bed is a mass of slimy stones so every step I take is like trying to walk on bowling balls covered with snot. Misty may not weigh that much, but my arms are knotted up and screaming by the time we get to the other side. At least Misty seems to have taken control of her feelings.

"Thank you," she whispers.

"Don't mention it," I reply.

I set her down on the far bank and look behind me at the top of the ridge. Nothing yet!

There are some blackberry brambles creeping down to the edge of the water. Fortunately, they aren't too difficult to scramble past into the moss-covered fallen logs under the trees. I'm soaked again, up to my thighs anyway - but at least we're on the other side of the creek. Anyone looking for us will have to find a way down to the creek and then figure out which way we went. With luck, they will think we wouldn't cross. With even more luck, they will probably also have to split up, because they won't know if we went upstream or down.

We weave through the trees about fifty yards upstream until I find a large boulder crossed by a fallen tree. We slip under the tree and I look back. I can just make out the creek. Looking up, I can see across the creek to the cliff we nearly fell down. At the top of the ridge, I see a flash of color. Two of the terrorists are at the top of the ridge, looking down.

Ten

I'm pretty sure the terrorists can't see us. They are at least half a mile away at the top of the ridge, moving away from us. *Thank you, Lord*! I can barely make them out, but one of them is wearing a red jacket. I can see it flash through the forest green like a red strobe light as they move along the top of the ridge toward the lake. They must have looked over the cliff and figured we went back along the ridge.

That would probably make sense to them. The ridge is basically a cliff, and looking back at it, I can hardly believe we got down without breaking every bone in our bodies. I can't see the log we slid down, but even if the terrorists find it, I doubt they will follow, or maybe they won't realize we went that way even though the log is pretty messed up from our slide. They might not figure it out since I don't expect them to be expert trackers. After all, terrorists are basically elementary school bullies on steroids, not geniuses, and bullies are only cocky and confident when they're holding the guns. At least, that's what I want to think about them. Maybe faced with a slide down a rotten log hanging over a cliff face, they might wet their pants and look for an easier way down. That's what I hope for anyway. One thing I know for sure, at least Misty and I aren't cowards.

Maybe they'll miss the signs we slid down the log. The drop off from the end of the log we came down is at least eight feet and the forest is full of broken, torn up logs. Maybe they'll look at the cliff and figure we must have gone the easy way along the top of the ridge toward the lake.

Maybe…

Besides, it was a miracle I was able to jump off the end of that log without breaking a leg, and an even bigger miracle that Misty wasn't killed when she fell into my arms. The terrorists are going to have to search back along the ridge, probably all the way back to the lake until they can find a place where they can get down to the creek. Even if they find a way down, it could take them hours to get back to where we're standing, and they won't know which side of the creek we're on either. The northern side next to the ridge we just came down, is steep all the way into the creek. Searching the north side of the creek is going to be a bear. It's clogged with broken trees and blackberry vines that have spent the last century fighting their way over each other to get to the water's edge. The slope is steep too, so if they're going to cover that shore, they will have to slog knee-deep through icy pools of water.

The southern side we are on isn't nearly as steep and there's nothing to stop us from continuing our way south away from the creek and farther away from the terrorist's camp. But we could also go west, upstream, following the creek line. They won't know which way we went, so they will have to split up, not knowing if we kept going into the bush or pressed on upstream. With luck, I think we can put enough hours between us to finally get a break.

I turn back to look at Misty. She sits on a moss-covered log with her arms wrapped around her chest, shivering and miserable. There's a vacant look in her eyes as if she's awake on the outside, but mentally checked into a nightmare on the inside.

"It looks like they're searching back toward the lake," I say.

Misty looks like she's in shock. Her hair is frizzed and matted with bits of tree needles and dirt. She stares past my left shoulder, and I'm not certain if she can really hear me.

"Misty," I say as gently as possible. "Misty...are you okay?"

She just shrugs a little bit and continues to stare over my shoulder. I can see tears beginning to pool in her eyes and her lip quivers. I stumble closer to her and she almost jerks backwards.

"It's okay," I say gently. "I think they're going to take hours searching down toward the lake."

Misty nods her head and the tears begin to flow. She furiously wipes them away, trying to sweep away her feeling of helplessness. I kneel next to her and she suddenly looks intently into my face as her tears make muddy tracks across her cheeks.

"I'm not...I'm not giving up, you know," she says in a rush. There's desperation in her voice, as if she's trying to convince herself, and not me. "I'm not!"

"I believe you," I say quietly. "I do."

"I think you're right," she says. "They were going to kill me. They were going...going to put it all on video...and I had to run...I did." There's a grasping, troubled sound in her voice. It's sort of high pitched, like a shrill whistle.

"I know," I say.

"They'll keep coming...and I don't know what to do. Why do you...why do you think...what kind of a plan..."

"I don't have a plan," I say. "I'm just...sort of making it up as we go."

"That's not a plan...we need a plan."

"A plan for what? Right now, we just have to get as far away as we can get."

"Get away?...Yeah, you're right...that's a good plan."

"Right, it's a good plan."

"You think we can get away?" Misty nods her head over and over. "You think we can?"

"I do," I say confidently.

I feel something different suddenly. It's like I want to tell her without words that she can believe in me. I want her to...no! I need her to believe in me.

"They are not going to find us," I say.

I feel a warm stir in my chest. Looking into her intensely blue eyes and seeing her fear, I feel a surge of strength. I've only ever seen irritation in Misty's face whenever she looked at me before. Now I see something else, something like hope. She doesn't want to be weak and she's more afraid I'll see her desperation than anything else. But she needs me. She really needs my help, and I think she's terrified she won't be able to depend on me. Maybe she's afraid to ask. Or maybe what I see in her eyes is a plea that words can't really lay out. For a moment, she reminds me of a little child looking up at me for protection and something clicks down deep. Suddenly, I want to provide that protection as much as I want to breathe. At any cost!

"I think we should push on upstream, okay?" I reach out hesitantly...very slowly...and take her hand. She doesn't pull away. There's something different passing between us, something like a connection. She needs me, and I want to be needed – and knowing that is like getting juiced up on sugar! I'm starving, cold and miserably uncomfortable, but I'm finding a savage kind of energy I haven't felt before too.

"They won't know which way we went," I say. "They will have to move slowly looking for us, but we don't have to take our time. Let's just get as much distance between us and them as we can and then we'll hide."

I don't tell her that hiding isn't going to do us much good in the end. I don't tell her I expect they're going to keep coming after us no matter how long it takes because Misty is the prize. Right now, I believe we really can get away.

"That sounds good...okay," she says.

"Okay."

"We can get away. We really can. Right?"

"We can. I believe that," I say, nodding my head.

But when I look around, I swear the forest seems to press in on us like the invisible willpower of some green and brown sorcerer who resists us. Just reassuring each other doesn't change anything. Everything is really against us. This isn't a nice little fishing trip in the bush a half a mile from the base in Alaska. This is a real war and it's time to face it that way. It's like the Bible says: There's a time for everything under heaven, a time for peace and a time for war. And this is war!

My mind shifts back to fishing with George in Alaska. Our main strategy was to slog through the creek up to our thighs in glacier water, hopping from pool to pool, looking for the best places to drop our lines in for trout. Slogging through a stream is the fastest way to move upstream because the forest usually grows right to the water's edge and is filled with blackberry vines, devil's claw and bushes. It's quicker to just get wet and push on upstream, pool-to-pool. Whenever I went fishing with George, I just accepted the fact I was going to have tennis shoes sopping wet and filled with sand from the creek. It was a fact of fishing.

That's not going to work here. The cold is going to be just as deadly as the guys with the guns and besides that, walking in the stream would make us visible for half a mile both upstream and down. Better to trudge through the bush on the south side of the creek. We'll make better time that way, stay reasonably dry, and still be close enough to the creek to get a drink of water whenever we need. The water is probably pouring out of a glacier somewhere upstream and it's a thousand miles from pollution, so I don't think we have to worry about getting sick from drinking it.

"Come on," I say gently. "Did I ever tell you about when I lived in Alaska?"

Of course, that's a stupid question. I haven't really told Misty anything about my life. She and I have never had a conversation lasting longer than two sentences, most of which ended with her telling me to stick my head up my armpit or something similar. Not a classy way to put me off, but I got the message.

I figure that at least talking to her will help. She doesn't say anything, just stumbles along beside me, so I tell her about George and how he taught me how to survive in the bush. She doesn't respond, so I sort of string out the story for at least an hour. We don't really stop except to figure out how to get around the occasional stump or branch. After another couple of hours or so of stumbling through the bush, I'm beginning to feel a little dizzy. We haven't had anything to eat since the day before.

"What happened to your parents?" she asks unexpectedly. I'm a little caught off guard, so I glance over at her and don't answer right away.

115

I guess talking about something is one way to pass the time and get her mind off the shivers and the ten thousand spots on her skin that itch. Still, talking about the crash is not at the top of my favorite subject list. And it's not just because it still hurts so bad! I guess I just don't know whom to trust anymore.

Ever since I started school at St. Mark's, I've been the outsider. I don't fit in and I'm not exactly sure why. I mean I know I was homeschooled and I've heard every criticism about how all of us homeschoolers are wacked out social armadillos, but that hasn't been my experience. I've had to learn to socialize with different races, different cultures and different languages too. I expected the American high school scene to be a lot less complicated than figuring out how to speak French in Cameroon slang. I was wrong. In high school in the States, especially at an upper-class prep school, you're either "in" or you're "out" and no one is exactly sure what gets you "in". All I know for sure is that I'm not "in".

Going into St. Mark's, I sort of thought I would make the popular list, or at least, the "accepted" list. After all, I've spent half my life bouncing around the planet, living in some seriously remote places so you would think that was at least a little bit cool! I mean, how many seventeen-year-olds at St. Mark's have lived in New Guinea?

But it hasn't turned out that way. Everybody just sees me as the weird orphan kid.

"They um…died," I say sort of flatly. Of course, that's obvious. "I mean, in a plane crash…my dad was a missionary pilot, so we lived all over. I've lived in…Africa, Alaska…and for a few weeks, in New Guinea before the crash…They were flying in a small plane and…I don't know…maybe engine failure but…they crashed. It's been about a year and half now."

I've thought about the crash almost every day since it happened. I don't really know how to feel about it. That sounds sort of crazy, but it's true. One second, I'm feeling fine, the next I'm so depressed I can hardly see. Then I start crying sometimes out of nowhere and for no real reason, and I feel like an idiot. I guess it's okay to cry, except for

116

some reason, I don't want anyone to see. It's almost like I've got some kind of disease that everyone, including me, is afraid to talk about.

"That's horrible," Misty says.

I look over at her. She looks at me and nearly trips over a branch. In that moment, I can see she really does think it's horrible that my parents are dead.

"I'm really sorry," she says. "I heard you were, you know, an orphan but I didn't know...how. I just thought it was when you were a baby or something."

"Does it really make a difference?" I'm surprised to hear a little edge in my voice.

I haven't been too great at controlling how I feel for a while, especially when my parents are the subjects. The shrink my aunt sends me to see says I should expect to have flashes of emotion from time to time. I don't like thinking that he's right, so I try to pretend I've got everything under control. I don't like Dr. Shannon. He's creepy.

"No," she says hurriedly. "I just didn't know it was so close. You know, if you were a baby, you wouldn't remember so much."

"Yeah," I answer. "But I remember everything."

We struggle on for another fifteen minutes or so without saying anything. I feel angry and I'm not sure why. Misty didn't say anything mean. She just asked about the crash. Anybody would want to know. In fact, she's the first person at St. Mark's to even ask. I should feel great that someone even cares to know. But I don't. I've been dying to tell someone how I feel about everything and now that I get the chance I feel like crawling under a rock and screaming "leave me alone."

"I think about it a lot," I say suddenly. "I don't really have anybody to talk to about it, so I don't really know what to say. My aunt sends me to this psychiatrist, but I hate talking to him."

"I know what that's like," she says quietly. I look back at her again and she's staring down at her feet. I pull back a low-hanging branch and let her pass.

. "What do you mean?" I ask.

"I've been to a psychiatrist. He was sort of a jerk. I mean, all he did was scribble notes on a yellow pad and say 'tell me more about that'. I felt like I was giving a lecture."

"Yeah," I nod. "Yeah, that's what I'm saying."

"I'm really sorry about your parents," she says. I can tell she means it.

"Thanks," I mutter.

Dr. Shannon hasn't helped me much. I think my aunt and uncle are awesome for trying to help so I don't complain, but the good doctor is really a waste of my time. I expect he's a big waste of money too, although I don't have a clue what he charges to say, "tell me more about that".

I've prayed about the crash. I believe in just telling God everything, because I think He's tough enough to take anything I throw at Him – at least, that's what Mom and Dad taught me about praying. I've done that too – throw everything at God. About a week after the funeral, I went out into the woods behind my uncle's house and really let loose. I wasn't afraid to use the sorts of words that get you detention slips either.

That was the weirdest day of my life. I remember wandering out into the backyard of my uncle's house - he owns nearly five acres, so, even in Seattle, I was alone. There's this one big section of the yard that's sort of a leftover piece of forest and I remember looking up at the trees, my eyes so full of tears that the trees looked fuzzy and distorted. I remember that so clearly. And then I shouted, "Where are you God? Where? All my life they told me you were real. Now they're dead and I'm still here."

And nothing happened. I don't know what I was expecting, but no angels showed up. No lightning bolts or voices out of the sky either. I mean, I've read about Moses and him hearing the voice of God out of a burning bush and all that, and I've wondered: *why Mo and not me?* My mother read the Bible to me before I could read. In fact, I learned to read *from* the Bible. I've been in and out of that book all my life, but I've never had a vision or had a dream that I could say was from God.

118

So, I sort of stood there for a while, just listening. I could hear some ravens in the distance making their obnoxious croaking call. I could hear the breeze in the trees, nothing more.

After a while, I stumbled back to my uncle's house. My uncle and aunt and the girls were out doing some sort of errand, and I was there alone. I didn't think of my uncle's house as my home, not then, so I didn't know exactly what to do. It wasn't long after the funeral and I hadn't yet stepped foot into St. Mark's, so I didn't have a routine or even know where things were stored in the kitchen. I was still in someone else's house, so I sort of stumbled through the kitchen and thought vaguely about getting something to eat, only I didn't.

Then the doorbell rang.

It was so unexpected I literally jumped. I wasn't sure if I should answer it or not, but I figured it was probably some more church people dropping off food. They had been dropping off casseroles and homemade cherry pies with crisscrossed crust toppings ever since the funeral. As if my uncle and aunt needed any help. They were, after all, rich enough to buy a restaurant if they wanted. Anyway, I supposed it was the "church" thing to do to drop off pre-made dinners after a funeral. I guess "recovering" meant you were incapable of turning on a microwave oven or ordering takeout.

I remember not being in the best of moods when I finally flung the front door open. I snapped it open so fast the lady on the porch took a step back. I didn't recognize her since I had only been back in the country for a short while. She was something like thirty with short dark hair, dressed in a business suit, and I thought "sales pitch" at first.

"Hi", she said timidly. I didn't answer. I just stood there like an idiot. I was suddenly incredibly tired, and a mixture of overcoming sadness and anger threatened to explode out of my mouth like hot vomit, so I kept my lips tight shut. I didn't care that I was being rude. I just didn't care about anything.

"You must be Kyle?" she said. I just nodded.

"Well, I was just driving past. My name's Carla. I don't really know your family or anything. I mean, we're not like close friends or anything, but I see your uncle every week. At the office, you know?"

I finally managed to say something. "My uncle's not here right now…"

"Yeah, I was just driving past your house. I…um…I'm a paralegal in your uncle's firm. I heard about…everything…at the office."

"Yeah," I said. I didn't know what this lady was after, but I suddenly wanted to just slam the door in her face. I don't know what…but something stopped me.

"Anyway I…I don't want to sound weird or anything, but I was driving past the house…"

"You said that."

"Yeah and I was…well, I was praying. I do that a lot. I go to Calvary Community…well, that's not important. Anyway, I just felt like…God wanted me to stop and pray for you…if that's okay? I know it's hard to feel like God's close by when you've lost so much. But He's really here, you know!"

And I lost it. I mean, I totally melted down. There was simply no way this lady could have known that ten minutes before I had been shouting at God, wanting to know where He was.

And He was right there.

That's what He wanted me to know. He was really with me: Listening…hearing me. In that moment, I knew that God was real in a way I had never known before.

So, I didn't see any angels or anything, but I did meet a lady named Carla who just felt she needed to ring the doorbell at just the right moment. Yeah, I let Carla pray for me that day and I felt better. Praying was like pouring out everything inside and instead of feeling empty after I got it all out, I felt okay. I found out that just talking to God was a million times better than anything Dr. Shannon had to say.

This whole memory sweeps over me like a warm breeze. I can't ever think about Carla showing up on my doorstep without at least a little check in the back of my throat, like I want to tear up and swallow real hard. I think for a second about telling Misty the story and actually shake my head. That's not something I can tell anyone - not yet. That's just for me.

"What?" she asks.

"What do you mean?"

"You were shaking your head."

"Oh…I was just…thinking about the doctor my uncle sends me to see. He's just…I don't know, kinda creepy. Doesn't help, that's for sure."

"So why do you go?"

"Well…my aunt and uncle, they're really awesome. They really are, and I don't want…they're just worried about me, so if seeing the guy makes them happy, I'll go."

"That's cool," she says. "I quit going about a year ago."

"Why were you seeing a shrink?" I can't disguise my tone – I can't imagine why she would need to see a psychiatrist. I guess she senses that tone because she doesn't just spill her guts.

"Just some family stuff," she says quietly. "Are we going to keep walking forever? I'm really getting tired. Can we just stop for a while?"

"I don't know." I look back over my shoulder, almost like a reflex and of course, I don't see anyone. And why would I expect to see anyone? The terrorists were searching the other direction and even if they sent someone to search up the creek, they would have to creep along slowly to search for us, and we've been pushing through the forest for at least four hours or so. I can still hear the creek on my right and now, I'm worried we're getting too far away from it. I steer us back toward the sound of the water. There's a fallen log stretching at least a hundred feet in that direction, so I step onto it and start threading my way forward. Suddenly there's a blinding flash of light and a peel of thunder. It breaks out of somewhere over my head, and I nearly fall off the log. Misty lets out a yelp.

I hadn't noticed how dark it was getting since we've been focused on talking and walking for so long. Now that I'm paying attention,

I'm surprised how much the clouds overhead are sucking away the sunlight even though it can't be much past noon. I look back at Misty. She clutches her arms to her chest and I can tell she's freezing again even after hiking through the bush all morning. It if rains or snows, she's going to collapse. Okay...if it rains or snows, *I'm* going to collapse whether she does or not. It's time to find some place where we can hole up for a while.

We are both on autopilot. I'm guessing the terrorists have searched all the way back to the lake by now. I don't know if it's just the two that I saw or if others have joined the search. I think I counted seven from the plane and the boats, but there could have been more that I didn't see. How many would they need to watch the other passengers? How many did they send to look for us? Obviously, the two that I saw must have spotted us - the gunshot at my head sort of gives that away. But did they communicate with others who were searching too? I don't know if they have radios, but the shot must have alerted the others to all come running and help with the search. There's just no way to tell how many people are on our back trail. Maybe it's just the two of them coming after us.

"Wait here a second," I say to Misty. She is so exhausted she just slumps to the ground with her back to a broken stump. I walk over to the edge of the creek and peer around the trunk of a tree. I can see downstream at least half a mile.

Nothing.

I look up to check on the source of the thunder. The clouds are dark and hanging low. It looks like it's going to pour any second.

I want to keep going. I want to just push on until I simply drop, but I'm running out of steam. I'm getting dizzy from lack of sleep and food, and I can see that Misty is burned clear through. She is out of gas, and I can only hope the bad guys are not any better off. They were probably up half the night looking for us. I'm hoping they're exhausted and frustrated, not knowing which way we went.

Thunder rolls across the creek at me again. I pull back and walk over to Misty.

"Come on." I reach out my hand to help her up, but she shakes her head.

"I can't. I'm totally wiped out..."

"I know. I'm right there with you...I just looked back down the creek. I can see for probably half a mile and I don't see anyone. It's going to rain or snow or something soon and I think they're way behind us. So, we'll find a good place and I'll build a shelter. Okay? Maybe even get a fire going, but I need to find the right spot."

Misty closes her eyes and then nods her head.

"Okay," she says. I reach out with my hand and she takes it. And this time, she doesn't let go for a while.

Twenty minutes later the rain begins, only it isn't really rain. It's mixed with ice and a bone-cutting wind. It isn't a horrible storm, just cold and wet, but the clouds drain the rest of the sunlight into twilight. The only consolation is that our pursuers are going to be just as wet and cold. They will also have to move slowly in the gathering dark, trying not to miss us.

I'm thinking that pretty much any shelter will do when I see a huge boulder thirty yards in front of us. A large tree has fallen over it, creating a space between the stone and the log, sort of a natural lean-to. It's a perfect place to build a shelter.

"Look," I say. "Let's get under that tree."

Misty is so exhausted, she doesn't answer. Five minutes later, we're both under the log. It doesn't provide a lot of real shelter all by itself, so I start piling every broken limb I can find up against the boulder and on both sides of the log. It doesn't take long to build a reasonable lean-to. In twenty minutes, I've surrounded Misty, leaving a small opening under the bulge of the boulder that's just large enough for me to crawl through. Only I don't stop there. George's teaching about insulation applies to shelters too. His rule of thumb was to keep piling anything and everything onto your lean-to until you had a pile as deep as your arm, from fingertips to shoulder.

When I'm finished, the rain is really coming down. Fortunately, the trees are thick around the boulder and the shelter, which gives us the added benefit of a billion or so branches above our heads to block the rainfall. Even better - since I basically piled everything in an uneven way, the whole thing looks like just another pile of broken limbs. You couldn't tell it was a shelter unless you were right on top of it.

Satisfied, I crawl inside.

"Feel a little better?" I ask. Misty scoots back and leans against the rock.

"Pretty cool," she says. "It's really a lot warmer in here already."

"It's your body heat," I say.

"Yeah...body heat," she says. "I'm just a walking hot water bottle...just what I always wanted." She grins a little, and I'm impressed. She's at least trying to lighten up.

"Something like that," I say. "It's a small space and your heat sort of bounces off the rock and it warms up the air."

"So...I guess you'll have to sit pretty close...if it's all about body heat," she says. She's giving me a funny look and I'm suddenly aware of how small the space is.

"Well...it should keep the rain out anyway," I say. A drop of water splashes onto my forehead.

"Spoke too soon," she says. She smiles for the first time since we fell into the lake. And then she moves closer to me. For a moment, I feel like I can hardly breathe. Her eyes are so blue and she's looking right at me – as if I'm really here, instead of the person she always looks past. I swear there's some sort of electric current radiating out of her, like I'm sitting next to a live coil. It's hard to breathe again.

"I'm sorry," she says quietly.

"Really?...I mean...why? I mean..."

"I haven't been very nice to you. And I'm sorry."

I'm not sure what to say, so I just sort of shrug. For some crazy reason I feel shaky and rigid all at the same time. I'm almost afraid to move. I keep looking away from her face, but every time I look back, she's still looking at me as if she never looked away.

"Can I...sit closer?" she asks.

"Oh...yeah...okay."

She scoots right up next to me and then quickly leans her head over, right onto my shoulder. I'm so stunned I don't know what to do. It's like seeing a baby deer wander into your backyard and you're afraid to move or even breathe too loudly for fear you might scare it away.

I'm not thinking exactly either. It's more like falling into a rhythm that just feels natural. I slip my arm around her shoulder and simply hold her. She snuggles even closer, her warmth spreading across my chest and I'm afraid I might quit breathing and die. I've dreamed about holding this girl, written in my diary about it, and here I am. It wasn't exactly what I imagined, covered in dirt and far from comfortable. But despite the cold, the constant itch of a thousand cuts and scrapes, and a gnawing reminder that I haven't eaten since yesterday...for the first time in a very, very long time – I feel...good.

Eleven

We sit quietly for about an hour, listening to the rain assaulting our shelter. I feel something warmer than Misty's body heat in my chest. I want to protect her. No...it's stronger than that...I need to protect her. Looking down at her, feeling her forehead resting just below my collarbone, and the scent of her hair, stirs up something almost primitive in my heart. Her breathing is calm and deep and I think she might be almost asleep. I want to go on holding her.

"Hey," I say gently.

"Hmm," she answers. She doesn't seem to want to pull away from me, so I don't move my arm even though I'm getting a real cramp in my shoulder.

"I think maybe we can risk a fire. Maybe just for a little bit, until it gets dark. They might see it after it gets dark."

"Are you sure?" she asks. "How are you gonna do that?"

"It's getting pretty nasty out there. I don't think they're moving too much. The weather is going to slow them down and it's going to be dark in a few hours."

"We don't have any matches or anything."

"It's worth a try."

"You gonna rub some sticks together or something?"

"No. Nothing like that. I don't think that works."

"Something else you learned in Alaska?"

"Yeah. "

I sit up, pull my arm away from her shoulder reluctantly, and start untying my shoe.

"You can start a fire with your shoe?" she asks.

She flashes a funny little smile at me and I realize she's being playful and again, I'm impressed. I mean I've had a crush on Misty

126

since I first saw her, but she was always at a distance in the country club crowd. I sort of expected her to be...I don't know...soft. Her reaction after falling into the lake and how she was talking last night kind of clinched my thinking about her too. I haven't been expecting her to put a brave face on things, not out here in the wild. I haven't been exactly thinking, "spoiled little rich kid," not exactly, but I've been thinking something along those lines.

Now that I think about it, that's not very fair to her. After all, she's kept moving for nearly 24 hours despite being half frozen and lost. She complained a lot last night, but that could have just been the shock and the cold. Maybe she's a little tougher than I thought. I look back at her and smile.

"Nah...but George taught me how to make a fire drill."

"What's that?"

"Well, it'll be easier if I show you. I gotta say...it's kind of hard to do. Actually...I've only done it right once. Every other time, George had to finish it off for me. He was really cool...George was. Pretty much every week he would hang out at the base...that's the trailer where we lived...we called it the base..."

"Why'd you call it that?"

"That was where we had the radio. It's where we lived. Dad was flying from a floatplane and we had all the radios and stuff in the trailer. I was...homeschooled."

"Really?...That's kind of cool. I've been to Day School my whole life. I totally wish I could have stayed home."

"It was boring, actually. I mean, my mom was great and everything, but you can get everything done in, like, three hours every day so I was way ahead by the time...y'know...when the crash..."

I shrug my shoulders. Misty pulls her legs up toward her chest and wraps her arms around her knees and I finish taking my shoelace out of the loops. The quiet is sort of tense.

"Well, anyway..."

I sit back holding the shoelace and look up at the log above our heads. "This is a cedar tree. You can tell because of the bark. It's kind

127

of stringy. George always said it was the best fire starter…you want to help?"

"Sure," she says. She smiles a little again. "What can I do?"

"Try and tear off some of the bark. Just get a couple of handfuls of the driest stuff you can reach. Then you sort of rub it between your fingers and strip it down until it's like thin little threads."

"Okay."

"We'll make a little pillow out of it. That's the tender."

Misty sits up on her knees and reaches overhead toward the trunk of the tree. As she reaches up, I have to look away. I don't mean to notice, but Misty has a gorgeous chest and I feel really embarrassed that all I want to do is stare. I can't for the life of me figure out why that would catch my attention right now. There's a whole ten-page essay worth of reasons that I shouldn't even notice that sort of thing in this situation, but whatever animal lives behind my eyes doesn't make any sense.

I look past her to the boulder behind her left arm. There is a dry place under the curve of the boulder where I can see some dead branches. The boulder has protected them from rain and they look as dry as a bone. I crawl around Misty and pull out four or five sticks. Each of them is about a quarter of an inch in diameter, perfect kindling.

Misty has pulled out several handfuls of bark. I'm relieved that she isn't stretching up toward the log anymore. I shake my head like a puppy trying to shake off water and sit back next to her. I begin to fish around in the mat of sticks and bracken that makes up the walls of our lean-to. I'm looking for a green branch about two feet long.

"Okay, just…um…start shredding that. Get it as fluffy as you can in a sort of ball. That's the fire starter. See…what I'm going to do is make some really hot…um…like ashes and then we put them into the cedar pillow and blow. It should catch fire. That's how it works."

"Where do you get the ashes?"

"That's what the shoe lace is for. I'm going to make a little bow, like a bow and arrow." I've found a perfect branch. It has a few leaves still attached so I tear them off. It only takes me a few seconds

128

to tie the shoelace between the ends of the branch, making a tiny bow.

"Then I take this really dry piece here, snap it off so it's about eight inches or so. Like this. This is the spindle. It's gotta be really dry so this is perfect. Now...I need another dry piece, something sort of flat for a base. Like a baseboard."

I search around again under the boulder and I can't find a flat piece of wood. There's a larger piece, except it's round and about two feet long.

"This will have to do. I need to find a rock or something."

"Here," she says. "I just moved it because it was under...I mean, it was poking me."

"Cool, that's perfect." The rock is oddly shaped, sort of like an avocado, but it has a reasonably pointed end. I start hacking on the two-foot piece until I've made an indentation about the same size as the end of the spindle. I have to check the fit a few times, but in five minutes, I think I've got it perfect.

"Okay, almost ready. You almost done with the fire starter?"

"I don't know. What do you think?" She shows me a handful of cedar bark about four inches across. The strands of bark are still way too thick.

"Hmm...could you shred it a little more? The smaller and softer it is, the better. It needs to look like a ball of hair."

Misty goes back to shredding the bark. I turn around and start leveling out a place near the entrance to the lean-to for the fire. I've made enough fires with George to know you need plenty of ventilation. I also know that using a bow and spindle takes a ton of work, so I want everything ready to make the fire so we don't sweat it out, manage to get some hot ash and then find out we don't have any firewood for the actual fire. That would be a dip-wad thing to do, so I start snapping the dry sticks I found under the boulder and stack them up like a little teepee. By the time I've got a decent teepee, Misty has shredded her two handfuls of cedar bark.

"That's perfect," I say. "Now for the hard part."

I've used the bow and drill at least half a dozen times, but like I said, I only ever got it right once. Every other time, George had to finish the job. This time I've got to get it right without anyone's help.

Bow and drill fire starters are easy enough to understand, but difficult to get right. The first thing I do is tear off some big, flat, green leaves from one of the branches making up our lean-to wall. I put the leaves next to the dry log I'm going to use as a base. These will hopefully catch the ash I'm going to make with the spindle. I take off my outer shirt too because I'm going to need it to hold the top of the spindle.

"The trick is to keep steady pressure on the spindle. You loop the bow string around the spindle like this and put the end of the spindle into the dent you made on the base board."

Misty leans in a little to see what I'm doing. She still holds the fire starter. In the confined space, I can feel her breath on my neck. It's warm, so why do I get goosebumps?

"So, you've got to keep pressure on the spindle and you can't just hold it. Best I can do is wrap my shirt around my hand and sort of press down on the top, like this. So now, you just saw the bow back and forth until you get some hot ash."

My first attempt to spin the spindle just spins it out of the loop. My second effort isn't any better and inside of ten minutes I'm feeling frustrated enough to want to put my fist through a wall. Every few minutes, I lift the spindle to see if I've built up any hot dust, but I don't see anything. I finally get the hang of sawing on the bow without popping the spindle out of the loop. I really pull at the thing for at least ten minutes until Misty suddenly yelps.

"Oh, look…smoke."

"Awesome," I answer. I quickly roll the base log over, shake a tiny bit of hot dust onto one of the green leaves I had set aside, and lift up the leaf carefully.

"Here," I say. "Let me have the fire starter."

Misty hands the shredded bark to me and I tip the hot dust into the middle of it. I start blowing, slow and steady into the pillow of bark. At first, nothing happens. I'm irritated, but I keep blowing.

After about the sixth lungful of air, I see a tiny tendril of white smoke.

"Oh my gosh," Misty says. "This is really going to work!" She's genuinely excited and I smile.

I keep blowing on the pillow and the smoke gets thicker. I have to turn my head away to get a breath without taking in a lung-full of smoke. I blow a little harder. With an audible "pop," a single tiny flame bursts out of the middle of the bark.

"Aha..."

"Awesome! This is so cool."

"Yeah. Check it out."

I carefully put the pillow with its tiny flame into the middle of the teepee of dry kindling that I had set up. Very carefully, I add some twigs and blow a little more. In a few minutes, we have a real fire going and I'm so stupid excited, I'm dizzy. There's something so real about getting the fire going.

It's such a simple thing – it's just a fire, yet, it feels like a life preserver or like we lit up a huge neon street sign that says, "we're going to make it." Even when I was a kid, the campfires we would light out in front of the Alaska base always mesmerized me. I could see the darkness and the forest just outside the circle of the fire's light and I thought about how the fire kept everything scary and dangerous far away. I got visions of ancient natives or cavemen huddled around the flames, just inches from a thousand creatures that wanted to eat them, and I would get a shiver. For so many thousands of years, the only thing that kept us from being eaten or frozen was a tiny little flame. And here, now, we've got one and it isn't just a thought about Indians and cave men. It's real; we're here and the dark and the cold and the creatures can now be driven back - just because we lit a fire. It feels pretty cool!

Misty scoots closer to the flames and we each take turns warming our hands. It's such an amazing thing! You don't think about how incredible a flame is when you're riding in your uncle's BMW with the heater blasting away the Seattle chill. Out here, this tiny little flame is already warming up the space and it feels a lot like heaven. I can feel the warmth reflecting off the boulder and I'm already so much warmer. I feel a distinct sense of relaxation, even comfort.

I have to keep feeding the little fire because the wood we have to burn is so small. I don't think we can keep the fire going for more than an hour or so unless I try to burn the big piece I used as a baseboard. I don't want to do that if I can help it because the fire might get too big. We're taking a risk as it is.

"Thank you," Misty says quietly. I turn to look at her. She is staring into the flames, not looking at me. I look back at the fire myself and sort of shrug.

"We can't let it burn for long, you know," I say. "But we can warm up some rocks and bury them and that'll stay warm for hours."

"No, I mean...thank you for everything. I'm really sorry too." She turns to look at me. I'm almost afraid to look at her so I keep staring into the flames.

"I'm sorry I've been mean to you." She already said that once today, so I wonder if she thinks I don't believe her or something. I don't know what to say to reassure her either.

I've spent the last year-and-a-half feeling like the ultimate outsider, so I guess I just don't know how to be accepted. That is so weird. I suppose I've daydreamed about Misty finally taking notice of me, but now that I'm on the good side of the fence, I don't feel very good about it. I mean, I wanted so bad for her to like me, but just talking about the crash and George and thinking about where I've been and what I've seen, I just can't see how Misty could ever understand what I feel so I just sort of shrug my shoulders.

"Yeah," I say, almost under my breath.

Suddenly, I don't just want someone to invite me into the "cool" crowd. I can accept that she really does feel bad about stomping on me, but how can she possibly understand what it's like to lose both of your parents? I've lost everything – my home, my parents. I'm an alien in her world. I can wear the uniform and play in the stupid band, but I'll never be like Misty and she'll never know where I've been. Knowing that makes me sort of angry.

"It's okay," I shrug again. I really don't want to talk about anything anymore. I just want to get warm and not think.

"No, it's not," she says. Her voice is steady, but I can hear something almost fierce in her tone. "I know what you're feeling…"

That doesn't sound quite right and out of nowhere, about a thousand different ugly feelings come swelling up in my throat like someone reached out and choked me. I was just getting comfortable, just beginning to think everything was cool and she says she thinks she gets it? How many dead parents do you have, girl? If it wasn't for the fact that my mom drilled it into my head not to pop my feelings out of my mouth - because shooting back at stupid people makes you just as stupid…man, I would be shooting right about now.

"What…what do you mean?"

"Well…I had a problem once and it was kind of the same thing…in seventh grade. There was this girl, Kelly Thompson; she was wicked."

"I'm sorry…that's like…I don't know…" Sometimes people can be clueless. Her dad is about to become the Vice President. Mine's dead!

I admit I'm feeling irritated and I should probably keep my mouth shut. She has a look on her face like I just slapped her but telling me about some kid in seventh grade who picked on her and hurt her feelings is about ten million miles away from what it feels like to find out that both your mom and your dad were killed on the same day.

"I know what you're thinking," she says in a rush. "But really, I mean…It's the whole story, only I've never really told anyone." She crosses her legs Indian style and seems to come to a decision. "Kelly was really mean, she stole my friends, told everybody I was making out with Dean Alveada and I wasn't, but no one would believe me. She made fun of everything I did."

She's throwing her words out in a gush, like she has to keep going before she gets scared and stops. For whatever reason, this is a big deal to her and she's rushing so she can't change her mind. I

133

don't know what to say. I just turn and look back at the flames. She's quiet for a second, takes a breath and tries again...

"I'm not really good at talking about it...I just..."

Part of me wants to be nice, but the other part of me is currently being strangled by fifty different feelings I didn't even know I had.

"I don't see...how you can say you know what it's like," I say.

"That's not the whole thing." Her voice trembles a little and I turn to look at her again. I can't figure out why someone making fun of her in seventh grade can be such a big deal or why she wants to compare it to my feelings about being an orphan.

"My sister," she says. "My older sister, Mary. She was really protective and...she tried to get this girl to leave me alone, you know? But Kelly just wouldn't back off. And then she started posting all kinds of stuff on the Internet about me and Mary. It just got so bad..."

"Yeah...well, that's no fun." I try to keep any hint of sarcasm out of my voice. I'm really trying to just be nice and listen. I've never really experienced being bullied in school because I was hardly ever in school until just a year-and-half ago. The only bully I ran into was my dad when I didn't get my assignments done. That's not the same animal.

Misty isn't looking my way. She stares into the fire and I can see tears forming in her eyes. I wonder why someone lying about you on the Internet can be so traumatic. Maybe it's a girl thing. I know girls can say some nasty things about each other. They are masters at using words like weapons. I decide to try and soften my tone.

"Sounds like...you were really hurt by all that."

Misty still doesn't look at me. Suddenly, a huge tear falls down her right cheek. She doesn't wipe it away. She just keeps staring into the fire. When she speaks, it's in a whisper.

"I've not really talked about it to anyone...except Dr. Morris."

"The shrink?"

"Yeah...didn't help much. See...Kelly just...pushed it. Spread all kinds of rumors and even...published some pictures. I guess she had a camera in the bathroom."

134

Wow. I've heard of vindictive teenagers but taking nudie shots in the bathroom and posting them on the Internet is pretty much an all-time low.

"This Kelly girl sent out nude pictures of you?"

"No...not me. My sister. And then...they were printing them and everything. Mary was fifteen, so it was child porn. The police got into it. It was...beyond horrible and then..."

Despite feeling like her story had exactly nothing to do with how I felt about losing my parents, I want to find out what happened. I'm starting to feel a little bit like a moth staring at a flame.

"And then what?"

Misty sort of shrugs one shoulder and shakes her head a little. She finally wipes the track of her tear off her cheek.

"I found her. That was...the hardest thing, I think."

"What do you mean, 'you found her'?" I ask.

"Mary stayed home from school. She said she was sick and I think my parents knew she just needed a break, you know? But when I came home...she drank a whole glass full of...pool acid...and she was dead."

I am literally stunned. I can feel my mouth drop open. I've heard some horror stories before, but *pool acid*? Oh Lord almighty! The thought is so shocking, I feel like I've been slapped in the face. And I know what it feels like to get slapped!

Misty turns to look me full in the face and I can tell she wants me to understand in a way that Dr. Morris with his worthless diploma on the wall never could understand.

"It's my fault..." she says, and there's a plea in her tone.

I can't imagine what it must have been like for Misty to find her sister dead from drinking a glass full of pool acid. I can't help but get a horrific picture in my mind. Did the acid eat a hole in her body? Even as I picture that thought, I'm horrified I would even picture it at all. No wonder she was seeing a shrink. At least for me, the crash happened a hundred miles away. I was doing homeschool work, busily finishing off a book report on *Huckleberry Finn* when I got the news. I didn't have to watch the plane slam into the side of the mountain. I never saw the fireball. I didn't have to identify their charred remains.

But Misty *found* her sister. And then to think her sister had only gotten involved to try and get the bully to back off Misty's back...no wonder she thought it was her fault.

"I am so sorry," I say. "I'm sorry I didn't think you could understand. I just thought it was a story about someone picking on you."

"I haven't talked to anyone about it before. I wasn't sure how to start." Misty shakes her head. She closes her eyes firmly for a second, then looks at me again. There's a powerful energy of hope in her eyes mixed with fear, and now I know why.

"I'm really sorry. I didn't know. I mean...I was thinking something totally different. You never told Angela? She's like, your best friend."

Misty shifts her weight, pulls her legs up, and rests her chin on her knees like she's taking a rest after running up a hill. I guess getting that story off her chest was a whole lot like running a marathon. Pool acid! I just can't get the whole image out of my mind.

Misty sighs deeply as she looks into the fire. I can't figure out what to say, but I notice the flames are getting low, so I put a few more pieces of wood on the lowering flames. The fire cracks and spits a little.

"Angie's awesome," Misty says. "But she..." Misty looks over at me and gives a little shrug.

"She wouldn't get it," I say knowingly.

I nod my head and again, something passes between us, something like a chill or a tiny buzz. I know! I know what she's feeling in a way a hundred other people can never know. I know the sinking feeling of dread, like the bottom of your gut has fallen away, and everything that matters has drained out of you.

"But I get it," I say softly.

"Yeah...I think you do," she says.

I know I need to do something. I can feel it. She looks at me and I know what's going through her mind just as clearly as if she were

136

telling me, word for word. She's afraid she's said too much. She's afraid she trusted me too quickly. And she desperately wants to know that I'm going to tell her she's okay with me. She needs to feel safe.

"I won't tell anyone," I say.

"Thanks."

"I know why you don't want to talk it."

"I can't forget it. I think about it…"

"All the time," I finish.

"Yeah…every day," Misty whispers. "I don't know why exactly, but I kind of don't want Angie or anyone to know."

I nod my head because I know what that feels like from the inside out. Normal people just won't understand. It's not normal to have your parents, or your sister, torn away. It leaves a hole in your soul, an emptiness that lingers…like a scar that you can't see.

I feel something like a rush in my chest and all I want to do is take Misty into my arms and just hold her. I'm so drawn toward her that I lean forward…and then I hesitate. I'm afraid my breathing is too loud, and everything seems to slow down. I can't take my eyes off her face and the odd thing is, she doesn't turn away. Something is happening, something deeper that I can't explain. I lean farther forward, resting my weight on my right hand, and she doesn't pull back.

And then, I kiss her.

Twelve

I've never kissed anyone before. I've dreamed about it and wished for it since I was, like, twelve, and first realized that girls were simply the most beautiful creatures on earth. And it's better than any daydream. Her lips are soft and moist. My eyes are shut, and I can smell her fragrance like the rosemary bushes that smell so strongly after it rains. She opens her mouth a little to pull me in closer. I shut my eyes and an electric current quivers through every square inch of my body. I'm not sure what to do with my hands. Okay, I know what I *want* to do with my hands, but even though I'm kissing her, I don't feel like I have a right to put my hands everywhere I want to put my hands.

There's something about pressing my lips against hers, something sort of magical. It's another kind of connection I wasn't expecting…but my right wrist is beginning to hurt from leaning on it and the pain is beginning to distract me from the kiss. I just don't want to back away.

My mom and dad kissed in front of me all the time when I was a kid. My dad would be in the kitchen and suddenly cry out, "What's that, Kyle?" As soon as I looked away, he would swoop my mother into an embrace and "slap a lip lock on her," as he used to say. I would always fall for it and my mother would always make up an obviously fake effort to get away from him. When they finally came up for air, he would grin at me and say something like, "Just showing you a good example of how a man loves his woman, son" and my mother would punch him in the shoulder. He would overreact to her punch and say something like, "Love hurts" or, "Oh no, husband abuse!" I always loved how playful they were – like little kids in the

138

kitchen playing house and I thought how much I wanted that in my life.

Thinking about my parents and the pain in my wrist finally forces me to pull away. She smiles a little, as if we were just caught making out by her best friend. I'm not sure what to say, so I sit back a little farther and start fishing around for a stick to put in the fire. I really want another kiss.

"Misty," I say, feeling a little shy. "I've never...well, I've never kissed anyone before so..."

"Never," she says playfully. I feel a little embarrassed. I'm seventeen and I've never kissed a girl before. That's particularly frustrating because from what I hear around school, most of my male classmates must have started making out when they were in fifth grade or something. Based on the stories I've heard in the locker room, it's a miracle most of them have not fathered thirty-six kids by now too! I'm betting their stories are about as real as space aliens secretly running the White House, but I still don't have a whole lot to brag about – that's for sure.

I shrug my shoulders and continue to poke our little fire with a stick. "Well...yeah. I just, I don't know..."

"What do you think," she interrupts. I look up at her and I swear I could keep my eyes on her face for a hundred years. Her small smile is enough to cause my toes to curl up too.

"Wow," is all that I can get out of my mouth. I feel my lip trembling. Misty just smiles and slides a little closer. She leans forward and suddenly, forcefully; I'm kissing her again. This time, I lean forward and put my hand around the small of her back. I feel her put her hand on my neck. I reach out with my other hand and caress her beautiful black hair. Even with bits and pieces of bark and twigs, I swear, her hair is as soft as velvet.

We don't break away for at least five minutes and even then, I don't want it to stop. I pull away again and smile. This time, I keep caressing her hair and looking into her eyes. She doesn't seem to want me to stop either. In the firelight, with the rain drumming softly in the leaves above our heads, I think I'm in the middle of the most beautiful moment I've ever felt.

I don't know how long we just sit and stare at each other, but a popping sound from the fire reminds me that it's nearly dark. I feel awkward because I don't know what to do next. I mean every movie I've seen - after the kissing part – everybody ends up naked! And it's not like I don't know how everything works. That is one key advantage to having been homeschooled. I got more of the birds and the bees than most pre-med majors. My parents had the philosophy that taking the mystery out of sex would help prevent me from getting into it before I got married. In one way - that sort of made sense. After all, it's the forbidden fruit that looks the tastiest. Still, there may not be any mystery for me in terms of biology, but the feelings are so intense, my hands shake.

The problem is, I swear, I'm always thinking about sex and that just drives me crazy. Being here, alone with her, a thousand miles from anyone who would know what we're doing, makes it a thousand times worse too. So, I'm thinking about it – a lot.

Even though I grew up on the mission field, I've thought about sex pretty much every waking moment of my life since I was thirteen. When kids at school hear my story about being a missionary kid, they usually think I'm totally clueless or something. But my parents were not what most people would think of as "prudes". They were really open about everything and not just in homeschool biology class. I mean my dad was so blunt it made me red in the face. He used to say that a woman's body had a more powerful effect on a man than heroin, which is why a normal guy is going to get his switch flipped on by a woman until he's 104 – then he'll just die! "Death," he said, "is the only cure for the woman virus. Get used to it, pal."

I once told him all about how much I was thinking about sex and how it was making me feel guilty and irritated and stupid all at once. He told me that being a Christian doesn't mean you don't think about sex – it's just HOW you think about it that matters. One of my dad's favorite sayings was, "It's not the package that's the problem, it's the

140

delivery!" He used that phrase to explain almost everything. So, it's not sex that's the problem, it's crossing the lust line that's the issue. God Himself is pro-sex. And He'd better be - He invented it! There was a reason Adam and Eve were naked.

So, Dad and Mom drilled it into my head that sex is for a man and his wife only. He used to say, "Keep Mr. Happy in your pants until you say, 'I do.' That's the deal. That's what's right and a real Marine does what's right – not what he feels like doing in a hot moment." Dad was cool like that. He knew it was on my mind, but he didn't make me feel like I was a leper because I thought about it thirty times a day.

"I don't know about you, but I'm really hungry," I say. Misty smiles big and I feel my face flush.

"Me too," says Misty. "But I don't see a whole lot of options."

"Maybe there is," I say. "I got an idea...here...help me with this..."

I turn around and get my back brace. On the back of it are three long strips of nylon Velcro straps. "If we can, sort of, peel these apart," I say, "we can make some fishing line. I mean, it won't be perfect, but it might work."

"You really think we can catch some fish?"

"It's worth a try. That creek out there...it's perfect. I must have caught a hundred cutthroat trout in creeks just like it in Alaska. And this one's a hundred miles from the nearest fisherman. It's probably loaded with fish."

"I've never been fishing before," she says. "But I love fish. Especially Salmon."

"It's funny," I say as I put the brace in between us with the straps facing up. "I love fishing, but I don't really like eating fish."

"I love fish. Why don't you?"

"It's not steak."

This makes Misty really giggle. I grin and pull one of the nylon straps up to get a good look at it.

"No, seriously. It just doesn't have any...substance, you know?"

"That's why it's so good. It's light and it doesn't make you feel bloated."

"Always gives me heartburn."

As we work on tearing off the Velcro straps and peel them into long threads, I tell her a little more about George and what I learned in Alaska. The more I talk about it, the more I miss it. Of all the places my parents flew me off to over the years - Alaska was my favorite place. I've never seen anything like it. Washington State is a close second, but I think maybe Alaska is where I'm going to end up. It's where my heart is, that's for sure.

I've been fishing in other parts of the world, so I know there is nothing like Alaska when it comes to fishing. I figure Washington State and maybe British Columbia are probably just as good, at least I hope so. In so many other places, you sit for hours on the edge of a lake, hoping for a bite while you either bake in the sun or freeze. So, slogging through a creek in Alaska, pool to pool, is like heaven in comparison - cold and beautiful and pretty much a fish in every pool. It is something else.

"I went fishing in Alaska like three or four times a week year-round. What you do is drop the line right into the waterfall or just where the water is coming into a pool, right where the bubbles are still heavy. The fish are waiting for stuff to wash downstream so as soon as they see it, they hit it. When I was a kid, I didn't even have a fishing pole. George would just give me about six or eight feet of line; he would tie it to the end of a branch and that was all it took."

"I've never been fishing before," Misty says.

"Never? Really?"

"Yeah, I mean…my dad's a lawyer or he was anyway. So, he was always somewhere else, you know? And, after my sister…we just didn't do things like camping and stuff. Actually…I've never been camping either."

"So, what do you think about camping now?"

"Better than last night, but I think I like camping out at the Hilton better."

"I know what you mean."

142

It doesn't take very long to make a thread about eight feet long. The Velcro straps are made of tough nylon threads and it's really strong, so I'm not worried about a fish breaking the line. Still, it's bright white in color, so it will really be a stroke of luck to catch anything. I just hope that by dropping the line right into the rapids it will be just tricky enough to fool a trout.

"What about a hook?" Misty asks.

"Yeah, well...we'll have to make one. Um...do you have, like, a bobby pin or something?"

"A bobby pin? I haven't seen one of those since I was eight years old."

I feel a little stupid. What do I know about girl stuff?

I toss things around in my brain for a second, looking for an idea. The pull-tab on my zipper is too small. I've read about old Indian ideas like making hooks out of shells or sharpened sticks. I'm thinking along these lines when a crazy idea pops into my head. Suddenly, I'm thinking my teenage obsession with all things sexual may have a silver lining after all.

"Okay...um...well..." I look down at the fire and I can feel my face flush. I'm not really sure how to say what I need to say.

"Well, what?"

"Can I...I mean...do you have a..." I look up suddenly and just blurt out what I'm thinking. "Do you have an underwire in your...bra?"

Now it's Misty's turn to blush. She is so obviously shocked that she sits back a little. She blinks a few times and I'm afraid that my question has really crossed some sort of invisible line. It's one thing to make-out in a lean-to in the rain, it's another thing to start talking about taking off your bra. She obviously thinks it over and decides my motives are above the line because she finally nods her head.

"I do," she says and then just sort of stares at me. I'm not quite sure what to say.

"Um...well...If I can get the wire I can, like, bend it into a hook." I can't help but grin. "I'll just...look away...while, you know..."

143

I do some sort of unconscious sign language thing with my hands, rolling my fingers over each other and Misty suddenly bursts out laughing. I'm so relieved that I laugh too.

"Okay," she says. "You can turn around now."

She uses the same sign language roll of her fingers and I blush again. I turn around and try to occupy my eyes with the lean-to wall and it doesn't help because I can hear everything. I swear that's almost worse than if I was just looking. I can't help but picture everything with every rustle of fabric and every breath I hear. It's pretty much everything I can do to keep my mind on something else...*oh look! It's a branch...and look! It's another branch...*

"Got it," she says. I turn around. She holds out her bra towards me and I hesitate to take it. I've seen bras before, only I've never touched one. My parents were open about sex and stuff like that, but I was never allowed to fold my mother's underwear. My dad said it was disrespectful. So, I've seen one...never touched one!

I reach out and take the bra. It's black and has lace on the sides and I'm a little surprised to feel a serious adrenaline rush spin through me when I touch it. That's so weird because it's just a piece of cloth, only I know what it was just touching and it's still warm to the touch. And I can't help but let my eyes fall to her chest, wondering if I can see anything now that her bra is gone. I'm a little disappointed to see nothing at all since her St. Mark's shirt is very effective.

I feel really guilty too!

How am I supposed to keep from having sex when all I ever do is think about sex? I mean, I really believe what I believe, but just touching her bra is making me short of breath, among other things. My dad told me that he stayed pure until he married Mom and I want to do the same thing, but this is driving me bat-spin crazy.

One thing that really stands out in my memory is how my mom thought my dad was the greatest man in the universe. She was forever talking about how awesome he was, about how, "when God invented men, he wanted them all to be just like your dad" and stuff like that. I never saw them fight either. I'm sure they did because I do

144

remember some tense times. They just made sure never to fight in front of me.

My mom had it hard growing up too. Not as bad as my dad's life, but her dad cheated on her mother and then left with the other woman. The whole idea of sex outside of marriage was a real trigger for her. She said any guy who couldn't control himself before he got married couldn't be trusted to control himself after the wedding either! "But your dad would never do that," she said. "You want to know why I know that? Because he waited for me, so I know he can control himself. That's why I trust him, Kyle. Trust is what real love is based on, son. Don't ever forget that..."

So...I've got my issues, my thought problems, and I know I'm not the sharpest tool in the shed, but I know I want what my parents had. I want to be like my dad and the more I miss him, the more I want to be like him. Maybe he wasn't as perfect as I remember. Maybe I'm making him out to be something like Superman, but I don't care – he was my hero. He was able to keep himself out of bed with anyone until he married mom and if he could do it - I can do it.

"Thanks. I'll give it back...in a second. I don't want to really tear it up or anything."

I put the bra on my left knee and find a sharp stick to cut open a small hole in the fabric at the bottom of the cup. When I've done that, I pry out the wire. It's not too hard to do, except I feel bad about tearing up her underwear. The wire is sturdy, and I have to use a rock to bend it into a suitable hook. The wire is far too long for a hook, so I crimp it about half way through its length and then bend it over and over again until it snaps off. I use the rock again to bend the top end of my hook until it folds over into a small loop. It's far from perfect, but I can tie it to the line, and it's sharp enough and big enough to catch a fish.

"Kyle?" Misty says. I look up from my project and I know I'm still seriously blushing. "Can I have that back now?"

I laugh again because I don't know what else to do. I hand her the bra and then turn around. Despite my arguments with myself, I can't help glancing over at her.

In the firelight, I see her back toward me. She has her shirt pulled up halfway. Now, I've seen more skin than this on a summer Saturday at the pool, but for some reason, this is different. She stops suddenly and looks back over her shoulder, and I glance away as fast as I can. I don't know if she saw me looking and I'm scared to look again.

"Kyle," she says quietly. I don't turn around. I'm caught for sure! If there was a gopher hole close by, I would drag myself in and pull it shut behind me.

"Yeah," I say.

"You can turn around now."

I turn slowly, and she has her shirt firmly in place. I nearly sigh with relief and since she doesn't say anything, I guess she didn't catch me peeking. She smiles at me and the look in her eye tells me: *I'm busted!* Still, she doesn't say anything. I'm not sure if that means anything or not.

"Well…it's getting dark soon," I say quietly. "I guess it's now or never."

"How are you going to catch anything without bait?" she asks.

"You'd be surprised what I've caught trout with. I once went fishing with a piece of masking tape and I caught one."

"So, what are you going do?" she asks. I shrug my shoulders.

"Look for something. I'll tell you what. Let's go worm hunting."

"Euh" she says. "I don't do worms." She wrinkles up her nose in disgust and I have to laugh again. She's never been camping, never been fishing, and we're stuck under a log, in the rain, a thousand miles from the nearest Hilton. This is going to be fun.

We definitely need to go worm hunting first. Fortunately, the shelter is just a big pile of branches and ferns that I piled up against a log that was fallen over a boulder. Where the log touches the ground, I can see a fair pile of wood rot. It's probably the best place to find worms, so I dig in with both hands. It only takes ten minutes of grubbing in the dark, rich-smelling wood rot to find four huge earthworms.

"You ready to fish?" I say.

"Never been," she says. It's sort of nice to see a little joy in her face for once. Neither of us was expecting anything fun on this little adventure.

"Well, we better go," I say. "It's getting dark pretty fast."

"What about the fire?" Misty asks. I hadn't thought about it until now.

"It's pretty low. I don't think it's going to catch the lean-to on fire. I mean, everything's soaking wet on the outside."

"No, not that," she says. "It's almost burned out."

"Oh, well, that's no big deal. So long as there's some hot coals, we can get it going again. Those coals will last for hours, believe me."

"Okay." She grins and sort of smiles at the same time, like a kid asking Santa for something she knows she's never going to get in a million years. "Let's go."

As we crawl out of the shelter, I'm immediately assaulted by how cold it is. I didn't realize how our little fire in a confined space had warmed us up. Misty immediately wraps her arms around her chest and I can see her breath. The rain is now little more than a cold mist that clings to our foreheads. It may not be raining or snowing, but we will likely be soaked to the bone in twenty minutes.

"Whoa," she says. "It's really cold out here."

"Yeah. Proves how good our little shelter is, huh?"

"That's for sure."

"Let's try this and get back inside as quick as we can." I find a small alder sapling that's about four feet long and maybe an inch in diameter. It only takes me a second to snap it off at the base, strip off its leaves, and make a perfect little fishing pole – nice and springy. I tie the line to the end of the pole, take one of the worms, and impale it on the hook. I sort of bunch the whole worm onto the hook by stabbing it, looping it back and stabbing it again. I want the whole worm to cover the hook, so only a small length of worm is hanging freely. It's not a perfect set-up, but trout are not the Einsteins of the fish world. I gather up the length of the line in one hand and start marching toward the creek.

147

"Let me take a look first," I say, holding up my hand signaling her to stop.

We can't be too careful. It's drawing down toward evening. We may only have less than hour to see if we can't get anything to eat. I peer around a tree and look downstream. I can see for nearly a mile before the creek curves to my right. There is no one in sight. Looking behind me, I'm happy to see that I can't make out our shelter or see even a flicker of the fire. Still, I decide to move upstream a few hundred feet to a huge boulder that's nearly the size of a small car. Behind it I see a beautiful pool about ten feet by maybe twenty. The creek falls into it perfectly, making a gorgeous cauldron of frothy water. I figure I can drop the worm right into the falls and let it flow naturally with the current.

"That's perfect," I say, pointing at the little rapid coming into the pool. Misty just nods her head.

After carefully stepping over a few boulders at the water's edge, I balance myself as best I can, and toss the baited hook into the stream. Nothing! Again and again, I drop the worm into the icy water. Just as I'm about to give up hope, I feel a wicked pull on the line.

"Yah!" I exclaim. I'm so surprised, I yank the line back too hard. I literally fling a fair-sized trout onto the rocks next to the creek, almost at Misty's feet. She squeals as much in delight as surprise.

The fish immediately begins to flip back toward the water.

"Grab it," I hiss. I'm still trying to keep my voice down. "Grab it with both hands."

Misty does the strangest little tap dance as the fish flops ever closer to the water, almost like she's trying to block the fish without touching it with her hands. I want to laugh, but I'm scrambling over the boulders to get to the fish before it gets back into the water.

Misty finally crouches down and grabs the fish with both hands. It flips out of her hands twice before she finally just pins it down under her hands. She looks up at me in triumph and I nod my head approvingly.

"My first fish," she says.

"Nice," I say. I guess the issue of who actually caught the fish *isn't* an issue.

There is something so awesome about a freshly caught cutthroat trout – especially when you haven't eaten in two days, people are trying to kill you, and there's a drop-dead beautiful girl holding it with both hands. I can't help really laughing.

We keep fishing for another thirty minutes or so. There's no talking. The stream is loud, so we would have to nearly yell to be heard. Without saying anything, both of us know making a lot of noise is a bad plan. There's no way to really know if we're safe or not.

I have to move to three other pools before I manage to catch another fish. It's now really getting dark. I help Misty string the fish onto a stick through the gills to carry them and roll my fishing line up to the pole. We wash our hands in the icy water and carefully make our way back to camp. I'm careful to keep looking downstream.

It was fun to watch Misty dance around the fish, but I'm not forgetting why we're stuck out here. I wonder where Mr. Tan Jacket is tonight. I wonder if they've hurt any of the other passengers. Without Misty, did some other passenger get beheaded on video? I keep glancing downstream, wondering where the two terrorists are that I saw this morning. I hope they're freezing.

Misty and I scoot back into the shelter. The fire has burned down to a patch of shimmering coals and it's really warm inside. I am so grateful to get out of the cold. I didn't realize I was shivering. Misty curls up with her back to the boulder, arms wrapped around her knees.

I hold up the fish in triumph. "Dinner is served."

"Sounds good," she says. She's obviously tired and she's doesn't look at me or the fish.

It only takes me a few minutes to convince the fire to flame up again. The coals are still wicked hot. The real challenge is cooking two trout over an open fire without a knife to gut them first! I finally resort to simply tearing them apart with a combination of a sharp stick and my teeth. It's gross but I figure if people can eat sushi I can

149

at least get the guts out of a trout. I toss the guts into the fire, impale the fish on a stick and start roasting. In less than an hour, we are both reasonably full. Only Misty hasn't said a word and she hasn't really looked at me much either. I'm getting the sense that something is wrong. On the other hand, maybe picking tiny trout bones out of a half-charred fish doesn't lend itself to conversation. Maybe there's nothing to worry about. I figure I need to say something.

"It's going to get really cold tonight," I say. Misty doesn't answer, but her eyes suddenly begin to well up with tears. I don't know what I said.

"What's wrong?" I say.

"Nothing," she answers. There is a definite change in her voice. I'm not sure what to do because it doesn't look like there's nothing wrong to me.

"Are you okay?" Misty flashes me a look that is radically different then how she's been looking at me over the last few hours.

"No...of course not...this is...insane. Don't you get that?"

"What?" I'm a little perplexed. "The fish was pretty good, wasn't it?"

"And they're still coming after us too."

"Oh...yeah...maybe they are..."

"Maybe? This is crazy. What are we supposed to do? Just catching a couple of fish doesn't solve anything..."

I feel real anger flood into my face. "Well we're not dead yet."

"How far do you think we can go? This isn't a fishing trip with George." There are real tears falling onto her cheeks now.

I'm not sure how to answer. I just built a shelter, found a way to get something to eat, we're reasonably warm, and she's freaking out. Less than hour ago, she was telling me all about her deepest secret and kissing me - and now she's like a porcupine. And all I said was, "It's going to get really cold tonight." I can't figure out what to say.

She turns her face away from me, brushes away the tears from her face, and I'm not sure what to do. I sit back and toss a few more sticks on our little fire.

150

I don't want to keep the fire going at night. When we were coming back from our little fishing trip, I couldn't see the fire shining out of the lean-to, but it wasn't fully dark yet and the fire had burned down low at that point. If we keep the fire going full flame after dark, it's going to be like putting a target on our foreheads because I know how dark it gets when you're a hundred miles from the nearest electric light bulb.

Misty sighs heavily and shakes her head. I don't know what to say so I figure I'll talk about what we need to do next. "I'm going to warm up some rocks," I say. "They'll hold the heat for a long time, you know."

"Whatever."

Obviously, that wasn't the right thing to say either. I feel another stab of anger. I mean I'm doing the best I can here. If it wasn't for me, the terrorists would have her already. And how many of the other idiots at St. Marks would have been able to build a fire with a fire drill? I'd like to see Stan try. I've seen the way Misty and every other girl looks at him too. Bet he couldn't figure out how to make a fishhook from a bra.

I've already set aside a half a dozen small round stones about the size of potatoes, so I push them into the middle of the fire with a stick. They will be nearly red hot in less than an hour and I'm reasonably confident I can just let the fire burn down to the coals. There should be enough coals in the morning to relight the fire after sunrise.

I've got to do or say something. I know I can't just make it all go away by saying just the right thing. She's just scared and cold and uncomfortable. I only know that because I'm feeling that way myself, only I'm not mad at Misty because I'm cold. I'm mad at Misty because she's mad at me all of a sudden and I didn't do anything.

When I was growing up, my parents had a rule called the "speaker-listener" rule. I don't know where they picked it up, probably in some relationship book Mom was always reading, but they made it a house rule. The idea is that most people who are mad really just want to be heard out. So, whenever one of us was feeling

151

angry, everyone else was supposed to carefully repeat back whatever complaint the mad person was spewing until the mad person felt they had been heard. Funny thing was, it usually worked.

"Okay," I say carefully. "You're really worried about them finding us and...just catching a couple of fish doesn't really help all that much." Misty looks away from the fire at me, a funny look flashes across her face.

"I'm not saying the fish were bad or anything...they helped," she stutters. I've practiced this sort of thing with my mom a thousand times growing up, so I know you don't just repeat things back word for word. You have to sort of make sure the other person knows you're listening.

"They helped - sure," I agree.

"Yeah, I mean...we got something to eat."

"You're right...better than being hungry," I say.

"But they're still coming. Where are we supposed to go? Even if they don't find us...we're stuck out here. It's freezing out there...this is so insane!" She shakes her head harshly as if she's trying to wake up. And I get it now. For whatever reason, I just get caught up in whatever I'm doing in the moment. Building a lean-to, making a fire, catching a fish – whatever. It's, sort of, one step at time in my mind, but she's thinking about twelve other things at the same time. Mom told me girls were like that – and she was a girl, so she would know. She said she was always thinking about feelings and what's going to happen if this or that and it's all jumbled up and confusing in her head sometimes. Well...it *was* in her head...before the crash.

"I'm sorry," I say. "I'm sorry about the crash and...being out here. I'm sorry about your sister too...and I don't know what to do either. I'm just trying... you know?"

"I know, I know," she says. "I'm just...this is just so crazy." Her voice has softened a little.

"Yeah, it's crazy," I say gently. "It really is...but we're sort of okay right now, right?"

Misty seems to think about that for a minute. She finally nods her head and takes a big, deep breath.

"I'm sorry," she says. "I'm just…really tired. You know?" I suspect she's really scared too only she doesn't want to go that far. Maybe there's nothing more to say. I scoot over closer to Misty and carefully put my arm around her shoulder. Maybe just being near her will help.

And I suppose it does, or at least, it seems to help a little bit. She doesn't pull away from me. Instead, she settles herself as best she can with her back against the boulder, and she doesn't push my arm away. We sit like this for a while, staring into the dying fire.

When the fire burns down to coals, I notice that my arm is falling asleep. I suddenly think about how scared she must be.

"It's going to be okay," I say quietly.

This is a lame thing to say and I don't know why I let those words escape over my lips.

"I hope so," she says softly.

Okay…maybe that wasn't the worst thing to say.

"I got an idea about how to keep pretty warm tonight," I say.

Misty just shrugs one shoulder, but then she leans her head over on my shoulder. That one little move fills me with hope.

"If we bury some hot rocks from the fire under where we lay down…it should keep us pretty warm."

"Okay," she says. "Whatever you think."

The rain has stopped outside and it's not quite dark yet. I slowly pull my arm off her shoulder.

"I'll be right back," I say.

I slip out of the shelter and begin rooting around under some fallen logs nearby. It doesn't take long to find a couple of armfuls of reasonably dry debris – dead ferns, tree needles and bits and pieces of dry bark. I load this into the shelter in armfuls until I'm able to cover the floor behind the fire with a layer about three inches deep that we can use like bedding. I dig three holes through the bedding down into the soil about three inches deep. I then fish out the hot rocks from the coals with two sticks, bury the rocks in the holes, and then push the bedding back in place.

"Kyle," she says. I move over and sit next to her again. "I'm sorry I got mad. It was just…everything, you know?"

"It's okay," I say. "Let's just try to get some sleep."

"I'm glad it's so warm in here," she says. "When we were out fishing, I was, like, this is really cold out here."

"Well, these rocks should stay warm for a long time."

"Thanks," she says.

She looks at me and gives me a little half smile. I reach over and put my arm around her again. She leans over and puts her head on my chest. I lean back until I'm fully lying on the brush and she slides back with me until we're laying side-by-side in the gathering dark. I begin to caress her hair. I feel the warmth of the rocks beneath us, bleeding up into my back like an electric blanket. I'm amazed how warm it is, how close she is, and I'm still wondering about it when I fall asleep.

Thirteen

It's a long night. A full day of running on an empty stomach and then a cold rain has seriously depleted my energy. This is why people get a cold after getting wet and lost in the woods. Sometime during the night, I give up any pretense and snuggle up behind Misty as close as I can get. She doesn't move, so I guess it's all good. I can't tell if she's asleep and I'm not really sure if she's still irritated with me. Actually, I'm not sure if she's mad at me at all or just freaking out because of "everything" or just sort of nuts. I like girls, I really do – but they don't make *any* sense.

I try to force every ounce of warmth to flow out of me and into her. Fortunately, the rocks I buried beneath us keep the ground reasonably warm. I feel so much warmer curled up behind her that I'm worried I'm taking up her body heat instead of giving her mine. I'm still worrying about it when I finally drift off to sleep.

I don't know how long I'm out, but when I wake up, my back is freezing. Misty is probably warm enough because I'm curled up at her back and the boulder in front of her is likely still reflecting some heat from the fire. Our little campfire has burned down to a tiny circle of coals that shimmer with a sort of alien-like glow. Outside the shelter, I hear the low moan of a swift breeze in the treetops. I'm shivering again, but I had purposely covered the floor of the shelter with at least a foot of dried ferns and leaves because I knew that during the night, we were going to need to cover up. Misty shifts a little in her sleep as I carefully push myself into a seated position. She faces the boulder and she doesn't seem to be shivering although her hands are tucked tightly under her chin. I suppose the boulder has held at least a little of the heat from the fire and with me curled up behind her, she's reasonably warm.

Still, I carefully begin to cover her with some handfuls of dried fern. She moves a little but doesn't wake up. After covering most of her lower body, I push and pull the bedding until I've made a little mound like a ridge to go behind my back. It won't be much of a cover, but it's better than nothing. I scoot back behind Misty and then half-roll backward, so I can pull the brush behind my back up as close to me as possible. It's not as cold as before, so I carefully put my arm around Misty's shoulder and lie still.

In the quiet, watching Misty's steady breathing in the eerie red glow from the coals, my mind is thrown back to the problem we're going to face again in the morning. The enemy is still out there, lurking in the shadows like demons in the night and I don't even know how many of them are after us. I only saw two yesterday, but for all I know, they've sent reinforcements. Mr. Tan Jacket doesn't strike me as the kind of man who gives up easily. I think Soda Can Man was more of a follower, but Mr. Tan Jacket is the most wicked one of them all. His eyes reminded me of the black, dead eyes of a Great White shark, merciless and cold. Great Whites are just killing machines and Mr. Tan Jacket is no different. He will stop at nothing to get Misty back.

I imagine that back home, everyone is freaking out. When was the last time a Vice-Presidential candidate's daughter was aboard a highjacked airliner a month before the general election? The media must be going insane, interviewing everyone from the latest expert in terrorism to the former gardener at Governor Woods' house who probably doesn't know anything except that he had once seen Misty playing in the pool or something. The news people will be hovering around the Woods house like a pack of rabid dogs and I'll just bet the other political party will have something to say about the election. *Governor Woods, how can you go on with the election if your daughter was kidnapped or maybe killed? What kind of a person are you, Governor Woods – you should resign immediately as the running mate.*

I don't really know much about the election, nor do I care. I'm not old enough to vote anyway. I haven't followed it much since I've been a little busy with my parents' death and trying to fit into a

156

completely different world at St. Mark's too. It's not been on my mind all that much. Everybody at St. Mark's knows who Misty is because her dad is the Governor and the Vice-Presidential candidate, and it's gotten around the school what a hardhead Governor Woods can be. Based on his reputation, I'm willing to bet the Governor isn't going to resign. He will hole up at the Governor's mansion in Olympia and wait out the storm.

I've never met the Governor or even seen him, except on television. I think I saw Misty's mother pick her up once from St. Mark's. I can't be sure about that because most of the kids at St. Mark's either get picked up by the help or, if they're old enough, have their own new BMW or whatever to drive. Misty's old enough to drive, only I've never seen her in the driver's seat. I don't drive yet even though I'll be eighteen soon. Never got around to it where I've been living. I know more about flying a plane than driving a car.

Most of the kids at St. Mark's have drivers pick them up in Lincoln Town cars and big, black SUVs. I think I'm the only student in the school who takes the bus. Not a school bus – they don't have that sort of thing at St. Mark's. No – I walk to a city bus stop and commute with the regular folks. My uncle doesn't have time to pick me up and neither does my aunt. They don't really have time to teach me to drive either and even if they did, I don't know how I would feel about them buying me a car. There is some life insurance money I'm supposed to get when I turn eighteen. I don't know how much it is, and I try not to think about it. I don't like the idea of thinking of my parents in terms of how much money I'm going to make off their death.

My arm is going a little numb, so I readjust my weight and continue to watch Misty breathe. The more I think about it, the more alien she seems to me. Not just because she's a girl either. It's the whole upper-class thing that's getting to me. I've figured out how to use the half-a-dozen forks you find on the dinner table and I've figured out how to dress when I go with my uncle and aunt to the country club, so I don't stick out like a sausage at a synagogue anymore. But until tonight, Misty wasn't in my circle of friends and now that she is at least sort of my friend – I'm guessing here, but I think the kissing thing gives it away - I'm not sure how to deal with it because I still feel like such an outsider. I wonder if she's mad enough at me to regret the making out part.

The truth is, I don't have a circle of friends. That's really the truth too! I mean, I've heard people say, "I don't have any friends", but what they really mean is, "someone hurt my feelings and I want everyone to feel sorry for me." In my case, I really don't have any friends. There are a few guys who nod their head at me when I come into the band room and one or two others might even say "hi," but I don't hang out with anyone at all – unless you count my cousins, but they're just little girls. The truth is, I know I can't blame anyone for me being a loner except me.

It's not like I don't want any friends. I'm just not the kind of person that makes friends easily. I've spent half of my life moving from one incredibly remote place to another. When you're homeschooled, and the nearest social group is a church filled with native folks who don't speak more than twelve words of English, you don't find a lot of opportunities to make any deep friendships. George was more like a weird old uncle than a friend, and my soccer mates in Cameroon were more like co-workers than friends. It was more or less me and my parents...until the crash.

I'm not really getting back to sleep. My brain is spun up on memories and thoughts about my lack of a social life and I can't get past the fact that my skin is one gigantic itching pad. No matter how I move my hip or position my shoulders, something is digging into me and I don't want to flop around. By some impossible miracle, Misty is asleep even though we're trying to sleep on a bed of nails. Even though three quarters of my body is warm enough with the pile behind my back and Misty's warm body in front of me, the tip of my nose and ears are still being stabbed with icicles. I try cupping my hand over my mouth to blow some warm air on my nose and it doesn't help much. Besides, my breath smells like the inside of my left shoe and I'd rather have icicle nose than breathe in that stink. I think whatever sleep I had before the glacier formed on my nose is all

I'm going to get. Still, I don't move as much as possible. At least, one of us may feel a little bit better in the morning.

Suddenly, I think about my uncle and my aunt. I haven't thought about how they must be feeling. I can't believe I didn't think about it until now. I've been so focused on running it never occurred to me they are probably pretty upset. Part of me wants to believe no one really cares about me and I'm all alone. But I know better. My uncle and my aunt and my little cousins took me in without a single complaint when my parents died. They've been a real blessing to me.

Uncle Jack and Aunt Helen were devastated when my parents died. Aunt Helen was like my mother's sister even though they were not biologically related. In fact, Uncle Jack met Aunt Helen at my parents' wedding. Mom and Aunt Helen were best friends from Jr. High through college. She was Mom's Maid of Honor and Uncle Jack was my dad's Best Man. It's a cute story about how they met, got married four years later, and I ended up the ring bearer at their wedding. I wasn't much more than four years old then and I have exactly one little memory of it – something about trying to hold the pillow carefully. I guess you don't remember much when you're four.

Aunt Helen was there for my mom, sort of like Uncle Jack was there for my dad. Mom and Aunt Helen met in Jr. High. Mom told me that Jr. High was like sinking into a black hole for her. Her father had cheated on her mother and then ran off with the other woman. Her mother, my grandma, was barely able to keep a waitress job and my mother's whole world was on fire back then. She never saw her father again after he left. I have no idea whatever happened to him and her mother died of cancer before I was born. With that kind of life, she really clung to her best friend.

Mom wasn't popular in school. She was really skinny, and she didn't fill out until she started high school. The other girls were mean, but Aunt Helen was different. I think Mom and Aunt Helen talked to each other pretty much every day of their lives until Mom married Dad. When my parents and I went off to the mission field, I think it was just as hard on Helen as it was on Mom.

159

At the funeral, Aunt Helen was crying so hard I thought she was going to suffocate, so there was really no question about where I was going to live. She saw me as an extension of her best friend and she has been nothing but wonderful to me since I came to live with her family. She worries about me all the time, talks to me nearly every day, and Uncle Jack is just as cool.

I didn't think about how they must be feeling right now. Another airplane crash? Another Reynolds killed or missing because of an airplane? They must be in shock. And since Misty was on the plane, I'm willing to bet some reporter found the story about my parents and connected the ironic little dots. Are they fending off some guy with a microphone and a camera trying to make a sad story even sadder, so the reporter's station gets the better ratings on a story that every media outlet on the planet is reporting? Aunt Helen doesn't hide her emotions very well, so I hope my uncle is threatening everybody with a nasty lawsuit if they even step on his front lawn.

My uncle is a former Marine Sergeant, so he won't be weepy or anything like that! At the funeral, he never shed a tear. Instead, he took control of himself to honor my parents. He put on the stone face of a Marine drill instructor, fierce and proud, a look that threatened death to anyone who might doubt his loyalty and love for my dad and mom. It was a look of sadness and power that I'll never forget.

My dad and Uncle Jack were both Marines, but they were opposites in terms of personality. Uncle Jack is steady and controlled, very thoughtful, and a little withdrawn. It makes sense that he became a lawyer. He's the guy with a very sensible, evenly controlled life – not much different than being in the Corps. I'll bet he plans how much toilet paper he's going to use on his daily visit to the porcelain throne. My dad, on the other hand, was a risk taker, a man of action who itched under routine. He was almost a little wild.

I suppose that makes sense when you think about my dad's background. He grew up in foster homes since he was born. Uncle Jack was the big brother, the steady voice in his world where harmony didn't exist. Dad didn't have any family except for Uncle Jack and he isn't even a blood relative. Since neither of them were

160

adopted out, they stayed together from one foster home to another until Uncle Jack joined the Marines. It was an uncertain way to grow up.

One foster family my dad was probably closest to lived near a small, rural airport. There was a man there, Randy Harris, who owned an aerial advertising service. He flew a small aerobatic bi-plane and flew advertising banners over local football stadiums during games. He was a retired Navy pilot and he owned the advertising business to make just enough money to keep his bi-plane in the sky. When my dad was fifteen, Randy hired him to help get the banners in the air.

I never met Randy, or the foster family dad was living with back then. The way my dad describes it, a lot of foster families are like cheap motels – all the essentials, nothing too memorable. I don't even remember the foster family's name. I wonder if Dad even told me their name when he told me the story.

Whatever!

What's important is that Randy had more impact on Dad's life than anyone else when he was growing up...except for Uncle Jack...and my Mom...and I guess me too.

From what I heard, Randy was a rough-talking, grouchy former sailor who swore like a logger, but never missed church on Sunday morning. He was also incredibly devoted to someone he cared about, and it just so happened my dad grabbed Randy's attention. Randy really took him under his wing. He taught my dad how to drive his truck ten months before his sixteenth birthday, so he could drive around the airport to help launch the banners even though he couldn't get a license to drive off the airport property. That would have been cool. I've been seventeen forever and I'm no closer to getting my license than I am to getting to the moon.

The way my dad described it, flying the banners was some kind of nuts. They started by setting up two fifteen-foot wooden poles that had a "Y" on the tops. They set them about thirty feet apart in a weed-infested patch of dirt that ran next to the runway. My dad would lay out the banner on the ground, take the loop end of the rope tether from the banner, and string it through the "Y" on the top of the two poles - sort of like making a clothes line fifteen feet off the ground. Then Randy would take off on the runway. Dad said there was a grappling hook attached to the tail of the bi-plane with a long rope. The bi-plane had an open cockpit, so Randy would wrap up the trailing rope with the grappling hook and hold it with his hand during takeoff. Once he was in the air, he would drop the hook so that it trailed out behind the plane. Randy would circle around the airport and drop in low over the side of the runway. My dad's job was to sit in the truck on the other side of the runway and spot for Randy as he made his pickup run. When the bi-plane was just shy of the poles, my dad would signal, Randy would pull nearly straight up, and if everything went right, the hook would catch the line between the poles. It sometimes took two or three runs until the banner caught. My dad said he never tired of the thrill of seeing that bi-plane shoot nearly straight up at a hundred and twenty knots.

I think there's no way I'm getting back to sleep. My thoughts drift all over the place. I'm so uncomfortable I can't lie still, and my arm is going numb hanging over Misty's shoulder. I sit up and scoot over to the remains of the fire. There is still some warmth in the ashes, so I decide to relight the fire. It's still dark outside, I'm getting cold, and I'm willing to risk it. I can't imagine the terrorists are stumbling along the edge of the creek, working through the barbed wire tangles of blackberry bushes and dodging boulders and fallen trees in the dark. Even with flashlights, that would be a chore. Of course, they might have night vision goggles for all I know. I never thought of that and the idea does make me pause for a second. But what are the odds they would have night vision goggles? I'm a little more worried about hypothermia or, at least, getting a nasty flu or cold. We've been cold and wet for quite a while, so I think keeping warm until the sun comes up is more important than worrying about night vision goggles. They will likely be on our trail as soon as the sun is up so keeping a fire past dawn is out of the question. I'll just keep the fire small.

I carefully scrape off the top layer of ash with a stick. In a few seconds, I find several coals that are still hot. I don't see any obvious signs of actual fire, but the heat is still significant. I reach up to the cedar log overhead and pull off some strands of dry bark. It only takes a handful of bark and some determined blowing to get a small flame going.

It's still pitch-dark outside. I have no idea what time it is or how long I have to wait until dawn. I haven't got a clue what to do next. I don't know where we're running to in the first place. I just know we're running away from people who are trying to kill us. Or at least, trying to kill me. If they catch up to us, they'll kill me on the spot because I'm not the prize. They'll just toss Misty over their shoulder like a sack of rice and carry her away, leaving my body to rot under a log somewhere. They don't need me.

Since they're combing the bush looking for us, it makes sense to think Misty is who they are after. I believe that. But if Misty is their prize, what will they do with the rest of the passengers? And if they don't care about anyone but Misty, what will they do when they get her? On the other hand, there's something odd about their Misty fixation. If all they wanted was to kidnap her, why go through all the trouble to land an airliner in a lake and then take the rest of the passengers away in boats? They could have just taken her and let the rest of us drown.

It seems like they want something more than just Misty. Or, at least, there's something more about her than I can see. Whatever it is, terrorists hold hostages for demands, so they must have some way to communicate with the outside world to make their demands known. I don't know what kind of terrorists we're dealing with either. I've seen enough news reports to know these guys are insane enough to just blow themselves up. It's just as likely that even if they get whatever it is they want, in the end, they'll just kill us all and kill themselves in the process. A lot of Muslim terrorists are willing to do that sort of thing.

My mom and dad were willing to die for what they believed in. The difference is they were killed in a plane crash because of

163

mechanical failure or weather, not because they flew into a building on a suicide mission. In New Guinea and West Africa, we ran into Muslims all the time and they always seemed like decent people to me. Well, except in New Guinea and I think that's because we were not far from Indonesia, which is the largest Muslim country in the world. There were stories pouring out of the Indonesian islands about mobs burning down churches and beheading pastors all the time. It was scary because it wasn't that far away.

I asked my dad about it. Why were so many of the Muslims we knew reasonably quiet people who just went about their business every day, but some Muslims were blowing themselves up? He didn't answer me right away. In fact, he was sort of grim when I asked him. He said he needed to think about it before he answered and then, I didn't hear anything from him for nearly a month.

But then one day, Dad came back from a flight with a passenger and he called me over to meet the man.

"This is Abdul," my dad said. "And that's not his real name either...He's on his way to Jakarta, so he's going to be staying at the base tonight. Do you remember asking me about Muslims? Well, Abdul will tell you all about it."

Abdul was a former Muslim, about fifty years old. He had a long, white beard and his English wasn't the best. Abdul wasn't very tall, and he probably didn't weigh a whole lot more than I did, but there was something powerful about him. There was an atmosphere or invisible kind of energy around him that made me want to just be quiet and listen. You could just tell he had suffered a lot and seen a lot. Over the years, I've met a few guys like Abdul, people who knew God in some powerful way, like the old prophets in the Bible. It was like the Spirit of God hovered around him, intimidating and certain like the warmth from the sun.

He told me how he had grown up in Pakistan, a Muslim from birth, raised to become a soldier in the Taliban. He was wounded and captured by Americans during the Afghan war. The funny thing is that before the Taliban, he had gone to university in Pakistan, so he had advanced training in engineering and science. He told me he

164

thought he was smart enough to debate one of his prison guards who happened to be a Christian.

"Happy mistake," he said. "No matter I say, he know to say back...many facts. I see Jesus is true God, not Allah."

Abdul renounced the Muslim faith, became a Christian, and that decision cost him everything – his family, his health, even his name. He explained to me that Muslims fear going to hell more than anything else.

"We know, even little ones know, we must do Allah's commands. If we do not, hell when we die. But everyone know, they broken many commands. Everyone know. Qur'an say...Allah hate sinners."

But there was one way anyone could know for sure they wouldn't go to hell. If someone dies fighting for the cause of Allah, he will go straight to paradise. It was the only guarantee in the Qur'an. Even worse, everyone was taught it was a holy duty to Allah to fight for his cause anyway. In fact, in the Taliban, Abdul said, men didn't hope to survive and go home; they hoped to die and go to paradise.

"So, many blow up on themselves," he said. "Maybe worse. But is not right. God will forgive because Jesus die on the cross. Bible say, John 3:16; For God so loved the world He gave His only Son, that whoever believes in Him will not perish but have everlasting life."

So, Abdul dedicated his life to tell other Muslims they didn't need to fear hell any longer. Jesus is the answer. He planted secret house churches all over the Muslim world, traveling under false names, risking his life every day. Yet he wasn't a fearful person. He smiled so often when he talked to me that day I wondered if he had some sort of medical problem. I was amazed at his strength.

I don't know what brand of Muslim these guys happen to be, and I don't care. What I do know is they are totally ruthless. I saw them kill people without a second thought. They are not interested in surviving and going home. They are interested in getting whatever they want and then killing everyone they can kill – even if they have to blow themselves up to do it. The landing in the lake proves it. It was absolutely insane, maybe one chance in fifty we would survive.

No one who really wants to get out of an operation alive would have taken that kind of risk.

Even though they obviously want to capture Misty, once they get whatever it is they want, they'll probably kill her. In the end, whatever their plan, they are not going to negotiate. So, there's only one thing we can do – keep running. I don't know how long they will be willing to keep on after us but giving up is not the better deal. I'm sorry about what is probably going to happen to the rest of the passengers but giving up isn't going to save us - or them. Our best bet, our only bet, is to keep moving.

I look into the little flames and wonder how far we can get. We're headed due west, so maybe we can get to the ocean. Maybe we can make a fire on the shore, make a lot of smoke like an SOS, and flag down a fishing boat or something. I glance over at Misty. She sleeps deeply, and I wonder how she can be comfortable at all. She must be awesomely tired to sleep so hard. It's strangely comforting to just watch her sleep. Thoughts about terrorists and cold and fears about what we're going to do next seem to drift away as I watch her slow, steady breathing...slow...steady...

I wake up with a jump. I don't know how long I've been asleep. My fire has burned down to a bed of smoldering coals again. Misty has shifted a little in her sleep. I sit up slowly and look out through the opening in our shelter. It looks a little less dark than it did whenever it was I fell asleep. I crawl over to the entrance and take a longer look outside. I can see the trunks of the trees now, so dawn must be creeping over the edge of the world.

I scoot back into the shelter. We're going to have to get moving soon. I took a big risk building the shelter, making the fire and fishing for dinner. I think it was worth the risk because we've at least gotten something to eat. Most importantly, we've really warmed up. It's all good, but there's no way to tell how long we're going to be safe here. For all I know, the terrorists really do have night vision goggles and have been trailing us all night. They could be right outside, and we wouldn't know it. It's time to get a move-on. If we can put some more real distance between the lake and ourselves, then I can build another fire.

"Misty," I call softly. "Misty. We better get going." I gently shake her left leg. She wakes up suddenly, scattering the ferns I covered her with the night before. The look in her eyes is a mixture of confusion and fatigue.

"It's okay," I say. "It's okay. It's just morning." Misty shakes her head a little to get the cobwebs out. She wraps her arms around her chest. From the look on her face, I'll bet she's thinking about hundred thousand or so aches and pains she's feeling. Sleeping on the hard ground in the cold is never fun.

"It's getting cold," she says.

"I know, but it's colder outside; trust me. I relit the fire last night, so I don't think we have to worry about hypothermia or anything like that."

"Can you light it again? I'm freezing," she says. I'm tempted to just do whatever she wants, and I admit I'm a little afraid of what she may do if I say "no."

"Well, I'll tell you what," I say. "Let's get moving for a couple of hours and I'll find some place where we can light another fire."

"I'd rather get warmed up," she says. "Let's just get the fire going again. It'll only take a minute or two."

"That's not it," I say. "They're probably going to be looking for us now that it's daylight."

"You didn't have a problem with the fire yesterday," she says and there's definitely a note of irritation in her tone. "What's the big deal? You said it yourself. They weren't looking for us in the dark. They're probably a long way away."

"I don't know, maybe...or maybe they had night vision goggles."

"So why did you relight the fire last night?"

"Well..." I'm sort of at a loss. "It was cold and..."

"And I'm cold right now," she says. "So, it's okay when you're cold, but not when I'm cold?" There is a definite edge in her voice now.

167

"It's not that...I know but...I think we've stayed in one place too long. I don't think they have the night vision stuff, it was just something I thought of...but they're going to be looking during the day. I just think we need to get some more distance between us and the lake."

"What difference is that going to make? If they're going to find us, they're going to find us. I'd rather be warm."

"And I would rather be alive!" I sort of spit this out at her. "Look, I'm sorry. I really am..."

"Whatever," she says.

"I'm sorry, okay? Here...look." I reach over to the boulder. There are dozens of clumps of gray, green moss growing on the surface. I peel off a few handfuls.

"If we put a bunch of this inside my back brace we can make a sort of cocoon. And then...if we put some of the hot coals inside it, it'll smolder for hours. Then, when we find another place to stop, I can just use the coals to get another fire going. I just think we need to keep moving."

I begin to stuff as many handfuls of moss into the cavity of the back brace as I can find. I'm sort of using the activity to keep from arguing. And from even looking her in the eye! I don't know why she can't understand that keeping on the move is way more important than starting another fire. I get that it's cold, we're uncomfortable, and the idea of a nice big campfire to stare into while we're warming up is really appealing. But I'm not convinced we're anywhere near safe and she just doesn't seem to care. I'm really second-guessing kissing her now.

Misty sits still with her arms crossed over her chest while I basically stuff my brace full of chunks of moss. It's uncomfortable knowing she's glaring at me, so I just concentrate on peeling moss. After a minute or two, I shuffle over to our dead fire and begin digging around in the ashes with a stick until I find eight or ten hot coals. Some of them have bright spots that wink out as soon as I push them out of the ash and the others are completely black. All of them are still too hot for me to pick up with my bare hands, so I know they'll last for quite a while smoldering in the moss. I dig out a little hollow in the pile of moss I've made inside my back brace and then use two sticks to put the coals into the hollow in one big heap. I then cover up the heap with moss and push some more in until it's tightly stuffed.

"That should smolder in there for hours," I say. "It should still be hot, and we can just blow on it to get it hot enough to make a flame."

"I gotta go," Misty says.

For a moment, I'm confused.

"Go? Go where?"

"No, I mean I've gotta go."

"Oh," I say. "Well...um..."

"And I can go by myself. I don't need help," she says sharply.

"Yeah. No...okay."

I'm a little embarrassed. I can't help picturing the process in my mind because there isn't a toilet around the corner. I'm not sure if I should recommend something for toilet paper or warn her against using skunk cabbage leaves for toilet paper, which is a bad idea. I made that mistake...once. Skunk cabbage has big, flat leaves that look so inviting as a form of toilet paper. George didn't warn me and when I had to go number two in the bush, I tried it. What I didn't know is that skunk cabbage has tiny little thorns that are so small, they look like fine, white hairs. They even feel soft on your fingertips but believe me, on the more sensitive side of your anatomy - they are anything but soft. I remember letting out a howl that would have scared a grizzly. I couldn't sit right for days.

Based on Misty's facial expression, I decide that warning her about skunk cabbage leaves is a bad idea.

"Okay," I say. "I'll just...I'll go down to the creek and get a drink. Meet you there...in a minute."

My face feels flushed. I'm not embarrassed that she needs a toilet. I'm just sensitive because she's so irritable. I mean I understand all the stress about being lost and everything, but like three times in less than twenty-four hours, she's either flared up or melted down. She just doesn't seem to get the fact that being comfortable is not an option when people are trying to kill you.

I pick up the back brace and crawl out of the opening to our shelter. It's still very early in the morning and I can't see much more than a few feet in any direction. It's colder outside the shelter. Stepping out makes me realize how warm we were all night. I can see my breath, so I know if we hadn't had the shelter and the fire, we would probably have frozen to death last night.

Misty crawls out behind me. I turn to look at her, but her arms are still crossed and she's not looking at me. With her breath floating like a cloud around her chin, she looks like she's wearing a cloudy harvest wreath on her head.

"I'll see you down at the creek," I say, and I move away as quickly as I can before she can answer. As soon as I've passed a tree and I'm out of sight, I slow down.

I don't know what to do with Misty. Before the crash, I used to daydream about being with her, and now that I've been close enough to taste her tongue I'm not so sure I want to be so near her anymore. She's being a raging pain. And I'm just doing the best that I can. I mean, what does she want me to do? It's not like I can just snap my fingers and make it all go away. She just doesn't seem to get it. We can't waste daylight sitting around a campfire just because it feels nice.

The bush around me is still waking up from the night. The trees are so thick, the weak dawn light can't quite break through to the ground making everything seem sort of unreal. The shadows are still harsh and black. I stumble on a branch and nearly drop the brace, so I stop for a moment and shake my head.

Who am I kidding? I have no idea what to do except to keep running. I don't even know where we're running to in the first place. I managed to catch a couple of trout yesterday, but if they figure out we're following the creek, we'll have to give up on it and run into the bush. Will I be able to find another stream, so we can catch more fish? How far can we go without enough to eat? How long before we simply freeze to death because every day is one day closer to winter?

There are already patches of snow on the ground and yesterday's half-frozen rainstorm is only the beginning of misery when it comes to winter on the Canadian Coast. Living in Alaska taught me that much.

I decide that Misty's idea about "needing to go" applies to me too. Fortunately, I don't need toilet paper. I set the brace down and reach for my zipper. Out of habit, I snap my head from side to side a few times just to make sure no one is watching. I've always been the guy with bathroom stage fright. Every other guy can slide up to the urinal and get down to business, but if there is the slightest possibility someone might see me – I'll clam up and I can't force a tinkle to save my life. It's even worse whenever I've needed to go out in the open air. I don't know why I'm so worried. Habit, I suppose.

After getting the job done I briefly wonder about hand sanitizer and the thought makes me chuckle. I pick up the brace and start walking toward the sound of the creek.

Yesterday afternoon, I found a place where I could get down to the edge of the creek without having to wade through a tangle of blackberry vines. I retrace my route from the day before and in a few minutes, I can see the short drop-off from the forest floor to the creekbed. As I get closer, I see the light of daybreak increasing. I set the brace down on the edge of the drop off and carefully step down onto the bare, wet stones at the bank of the creek bed. I'm just about to kneel to take a drink when I hear something to my right. I turn to look and feel a spine-numbing cold run down my back that has nothing to do with temperature. Standing in front of me, ankle deep in the creek is the terrorist in the red jacket.

And he raises his rifle to take aim at me.

Fourteen

Red Jacket isn't more than ten feet from me, ankle deep in the creek. He holds his rifle one-handed, aimed somewhat unsteadily in my direction. In his other hand, he holds a radio. I feel a rush of fear and sickness crash over me as he whips the radio up to his mouth and shouts something into it using whatever language he's speaking. I snap my head to my right, hoping against all hope that Misty is nowhere to be seen, and I almost cry with relief when I don't see her.

"Where is she?" he shouts. He clips the radio to his pant pocket with one swift motion and then takes the rifle with both hands. He angrily jabs the gun my direction.

"Where is the girl?" he screams. His eyes are wild. He stumbles forward on the rocks, splashing madly in the water.

"I don't know," I shout back. He's almost on top of me and there's absolutely nothing I can do. I'm going to die in the next few seconds and I know it.

The terrorist is just a few feet in front of me. He launches the butt of the rifle into my stomach and I crumble to my knees in the icy water, grabbing my stomach and smashing my left knee painfully on a rock. The breath is knocked out of me and my lungs clamp down like two sheets of fire in my chest. The pain of the blow makes my eyes water and I can hardly see. I feel the man grab a handful of my hair. He jerks my head backward and sticks the barrel of the rifle into the soft space under my jaw.

I'm going to die, I think.

The terrorist is so close; I can see drops of water glistening in his beard. I hope Misty heard the shouts and took off running. If I have two seconds left to live, my last prayer is that she will get away.

"Where is she?" he yells again.

Maybe I can convince him to search in the wrong direction. If it's the best I can do to try and save her, I better make it good.

"We got separated yesterday," I spit back at him. My voice sounds shrill in my ears. "I fell asleep under a log. I haven't seen her since yesterday. We were on the other side of the river. She's probably over there somewhere." I wave my hand wildly, pointing behind him at the other side of the creek.

The terrorist lets go of my hair, so he can take the rifle with both hands. He shoves the barrel up against my forehead. I bounce back from the force of getting poked on the skull by a piece of steel and for a second, I see a scattering of stars in my eyes.

"You're lying," he screams. "I don't need you to find her."

He puts the rifle up to his shoulder in firing position and I see his trigger finger move into position. I shout something, some sort of savage snarl of defiance and fear because I'm not going to die without a fight. I dive headlong into the pool at my left just as he fires. The sound of the shot is so close and so loud, my ears instantly ring nearly dead and numb from the concussion. The pool I land in isn't more than knee-deep. The terrorist turns to take another shot at me and there is nowhere to go.

Suddenly, some massive force from behind the terrorist flings him forward. He drops the rifle into the water and I'm so shocked, I hesitate for just a second. Then I look behind my enemy.

Misty stands on the bank of the creek, holding a broken branch that she has just used to softball the terrorist in the back of the head.

I choke out a shout but before I can think, the terrorist is standing up in the knee-deep water. He spins around to see who hit him from behind. Misty pulls back for a second swing, but she's too far away. Her swing goes wide, and the terrorist just laughs. He takes two lunging steps toward her and then punches her full in the face. She crumples to the bank. Without a thought to stop me, I simply launch myself at the terrorist's back. I don't know what I'm doing or what I hope to achieve. I'm just lashing out with all my might.

I wrap my arm around his neck and pull with all my might. He's surprisingly strong. For one wild second, I'm surprised by the strong smell of garlic that I take in being so close to his head and beard. He thrashes wildly and then elbows me hard in the gut. I've already been socked in the stomach with the butt of the rifle, so the second blow is agonizing. I can't help but loosen my grip on the man's neck only I don't completely let go. I'm dead if I do!

I literally hold on for dear life! The terrorist twists to try and get a hold of me, but I don't let go. He catches his foot on something under the water and both of us fall backward into the shallow pool.

The water is liquid ice. Combined with getting punched in the gut and nearly shot in the head, the shock of the water takes what little breath I have away in an instant.

I gasp wildly for air. The terrorist shoves himself up out of the water. He flails his arms like a breaching octopus and I can't hold on to him. I lose my grip on his neck and fall backward into the pool. It's only a few feet deep, but the current is so strong, I'm nearly upended.

The terrorist twists around to face me. He grabs me by my shoulders and forces my head under the water. The water is so cold, my lungs immediately scream for air even though I've only been under for a few seconds. The terrorist leans his full weight onto my chest. I close my eyes tight shut. I see bright sparks. The current drags my feet upwards and I begin to slide under him, but he doesn't let go. He's determined to keep me under until I drown, and he outweighs me by at least forty pounds.

I feel a stone under my right hand. With one last desperate plea to get back to the surface I grab the stone and swing my arm with all the strength I have left. I feel the rock hit the man in the ribs. For one brief second, his grip on me loosens. The current slips me right underneath him and I come up to the surface just as my lungs feel like they're going to explode.

The instant I break the surface, choking for air through a haze of ice water and fear, the terrorist turns to grab me again. I still hold the rock, so I swing it again. I feel it crunch into the side of his head. My arms cramp from the freezing-cold water, so I know I didn't hit him with enough force to really hurt him. But it's enough to stun him for a moment. If I don't stop him, he's going to kill me.

174

I drop the rock and fling my whole body at him. I wrap my right arm around his neck and wrench him to the side. We fall into the pool and now, I have the terrorist's head underneath the water. I lean into his left shoulder and hold him under the water with all my might. The water pushes hard against my back, so I dig my heels into the rocks and push back against the current. The terrorist twists and turns, trying to get out of my stranglehold on his neck, but I just squeeze harder. He grabs at my right leg with his arms, but I've got him at such an angle that he can't get his feet set to get any leverage on me.

I'm vaguely aware of the sound of the stream pouring over the rocks behind me. I can't take my eyes off the blurry view of the man's head in the water under my arm. He twists again, a little weaker, and then suddenly he shudders violently, almost like a bolt of electricity has hit him. Then...he stops shuddering as suddenly as he started.

Now there's nothing, no movement. His arms no longer grip my leg. His body feels heavy in the water...and I know he's dead. I hear a voice on my right near the bank of the creek, but I also hear a strange sound coming from my own throat. I can't let go of him and I can't quit thinking of that horrible shudder. The voice at the bank is louder, more insistent. Misty's voice!

"Kyle," she shouts. "Kyle."

I turn to look at her. She stands ankle-deep on the edge of the bank. The left side of her face is bruised, her left eye puffy and nearly swollen shut. I remember the terrorist hitting her so hard that she dropped like a sack of potatoes. Thinking of him hitting her, I feel a stab of fear. Where is he?

But I'm still holding his head under the water. I look down and then yank my hand away as if I had suddenly realized I was holding a snake. His body drifts away from me. It catches on the shallow rocks at the edge of the pool and he doesn't get up. He doesn't jump out of the water and attack me. He doesn't do anything - because he's dead.

And I killed him.

175

"Kyle," Misty shouts. "Kyle, we gotta go. We gotta go right now."

I turn slowly to look at her again. My hands shake, but it's not from the cold water. I keep feeling the death shudder over and over like a horrible twitch, a living thing that's attached itself to my hands. Only it's not a living thing. There's a dead man in my skin, like a leech that's ready to bite down and cause that death rattle to snake its way up my arm...again and again. I'm hyperventilating and a strange noise that sounds like a repetitive moan comes out of my mouth. It's almost like I'm watching myself from a distance and I don't know what to do with my hands. I somehow want to throw them away.

"Kyle, please," Misty pleads. She no longer shouts. I can see tears in her eyes. We have to get away from here. We have to get away from...from him. I can't make myself look back, but it doesn't matter. I can see his body in my mind, caught on the rocks like a dead fish, bloated and rotting in the water. The thought makes me shiver again.

I force myself to move my legs. I shake so hard, I'm afraid I'm going to collapse so I keep my eyes on Misty and take a step...then another. She's only ten yards away, but every step feels like it takes ten minutes. She reaches out to take my hand and I don't reach back. I can't touch her with my hands...my hands...and the shudder.

It's not like the movies. You watch the good guy kill the bad guy and you pump your mental fist because the dirtbag got what he deserved. But you're just watching a fraud, an actor who will get out of the water after they shoot the scene. It's not like that. Not for real. You don't feel the death twitch in a movie. You don't feel like every muscle in your body suddenly refuses to work after you stuff a man's head under the water so hard and so long that you squeeze the life out of him. When you see it onscreen, you don't feel like throwing up. On a screen, it's just an action sequence, one actor pretending to kill another actor and no matter how much gore they show you in a movie – it's no big deal. But killing a man with your bare hands feels so awful, I think I've forgotten how to breathe.

I stand in front of her for a moment, but I don't really see her. She takes my hand and I sort of jump, like I've touched a bare electric wire for just a second.

"I'm sorry," she says. "I'm so sorry. You were right. We should have just taken off as soon as we got up. I'm so sorry." She squeezes my hand and I suddenly realize that she's seriously crying.

"We've...we've got to go," I say slowly.

"That's right. We gotta go," she says. I nod my head only I can't seem to connect what I'm saying with what I need to do next. I shiver again, and I realize I'm soaked and freezing. I'm having a hard time catching my breath. I don't know if that's from the cold or because I can't get the picture of the dead man floating in the creek behind me out of my vision.

Misty squeezes my hand again. Behind her, I see the white color of my back brace sitting where I left it at the top of the bank on the edge of the forest. I let go of her hand and walk toward the brace, away from the creek, away from him. The brace gives me a goal and it isn't until I'm standing right over it that I finally turn and look back. The body must have washed downstream over the edge of the pool where we fought because I can't see him. Misty kneels, takes hold of my hand again, and then reaches for the brace. I know the brace is important and that thought gives me a new energy. It's important because we have to live. I want to live.

Misty stands up holding the brace and together, without a word, we just turn and crash headlong into the bush.

I don't know where we're going, so we simply run. I don't let go of Misty's hand and we plunge deep into the forest...away from the creek...away from him.

The terrorist screamed something into his radio, so I have to believe that his buddies won't be far behind. The thought of more terrorists causes another adrenalin rush in my chest. I banish any thought of slowing down. We run as fast as we can, twisting around rocks, now running along the length of a fallen log. We leave the sound of the creek far behind. I expect they'll keep working their way up the creek looking for us, so I head south, away from the creek, away from wherever they were taking the rest of the passengers and parallel to the lake. I can only hope they're not much for tracking because the way we're flying through the brush, a blind monkey could follow our trail.

A nasty stitch in my side finally slows me down. We both heave in huge, cold breaths. I look back the way we came, and I don't see anything except shadows and trees. I can't hear the creek either. I have no idea how far we've come. I'm still really cold even though the running has gotten my heart pumping. My clothes are sopping wet.

I let go of Misty's hand and look around. I look up at the cloud-filtered sunlight streaming through the trees and I think: *being alive is so weird!* I mean, what does it mean to be alive anyway? I take in a million little sensations from my skin and eyes and ears every second of every day and filter them through my brain. Only a tiny fraction of those impulses will make it to my conscious thought. I don't know how or why my brain does that. I can't even figure out who the "I" is that somehow can think about my own thinking. So why am I alive...and he isn't? Is it just chemistry? Being alive must be more than lungs full of air. It was so quick – maybe three minutes and everything about that person is gone. I know he was a terrorist trying to kill me – a bad guy...but a person...alive...and I took that life...I took it...I killed him...

I'm not sure what to do, so I sort of mechanically take off both of my shirts to wring them out. My skin instantly bursts into a million goose bumps and I'm almost glad. The sensation is so real, so...alive. And I need to feel alive right now. My hands are so stiff I can't really get a good grip on the shirt to wring it out, so Misty takes both shirts out of my hands and starts squeezing them. Somehow, she knows I'm in a sort of dream. Was this what it was like to find her sister?

"You look really cold," Misty says. She finishes wringing out my shirt, hands them back to me and then strips off her sweater. She takes it and starts rubbing me down with it. It's not much, but it does help a little.

"Thanks," I say through chattering teeth. I start pulling the wet shirts back on, but I'm so cold, my hands feel like wooden sticks. It's difficult to get the shirt over my head, so Misty helps me. It's so crazy...I'm almost winded getting my tee shirt on.

"You better wear the coat for a while," Misty says.

"No...for you..." I'm so cold now my mouth feels heavy. I'm not sure how much farther I can go without getting warm.

"Don't be silly," she says. "I'm not soaking wet. Just put it on...there."

I admit it feels so much warmer than I thought it would feel. My whole body wants to snuggle into it, so I wrap my arms around my chest.

"We better get going," I say. Misty shakes her head and sets the back brace down.

"Your pants too. We gotta squeeze out as much of water as we can, or you'll freeze...a friend of mine told me that," she says with a little smile.

It's a sweet thing to say and I want to smile back. I just can't smile. Instead, I feel like I'm going to cry. I've never felt so guilty, so sick to my stomach about something I've done. I've felt guilty before when I got caught lying to my parents or when I got caught with a porn magazine once...nothing like this. I know I had no choice. I know he was trying to kill me, but just knowing all of that is true doesn't take away the feeling.

I pry off my shoe with the toe of my other foot, then peel off the other shoe so I can strip off my pants. It's funny...I'm not thinking about the fact I'm standing in my underwear in front of the girl I've been daydreaming about for a year. Instead, I'm thinking about how she's trying to take care of me. And that matters...a lot.

"I'll wring these out," she says.

Everything seems so harsh and bright, like how stupid it is to wring out the pants, only to put them back on when they're still clammy and cold. Misty hands my pants back to me, I pull them on and I swear I can feel every square inch of the fabric grate over my skin. I lean over to put my shoes back on and think how weird it feels

179

to nearly suffocate from leaning over to tie them. Thinking about suffocation isn't any fun, so I concentrate on the fact I'm at least a little bit warmer. I know being warmer won't last too long if we don't get moving. We have to put as much distance as possible between the creek and us.

I take one last look back. The sun has fully risen and there are clouds overhead, so I can't see very far. But that also means they can't see us very well either. Both Misty and I are basically dressed in dark blue, a color that blends easily into the shadows among the trees.

We turn and start jogging farther away from the creek and the terrorists. Again, without saying anything aloud, we just sort of know our best bet is making distance, so we settle into a quiet walk-jog rhythm for at least two hours.

We haven't had more than a toasted trout for nearly two days. Despite the survival shows on television, I know a lost person in the woods isn't really in danger of starving for weeks. George told me that. He pointed out that people in the Bible would fast for forty days and live to tell the tale. So, fasting may not kill you right away, but that doesn't mean you won't feel hungry enough to think about eating mud. It's a lack of water that can kill you. We've had creek water all day yesterday, so I'm not worried about dehydration. It's a lack of food combined with fear and hours of hard-going over uneven ground that's going to wear us out - if the cold doesn't get to us first. After a while, I begin to think we're going to have to stop soon or we're going to collapse so I keep my eye out for another place to make a shelter and get a fire going. I don't know if my nest of hot coals is still cooking in the belly of my back brace or if I'll have to take an hour to make another fire drill. Better hope not!

I wonder if the other terrorists have found Mr. Red Jacket floating face down in the creek. Did they find him, or did he get caught up against a rock like a piece of driftwood? How many terrorists came running when he called out on his radio that he had found us? They're going to be enraged when they find him dead. If they find him! He could be lodged under a rock, caught in the current until he turns rotten and pasty white. The thought of his eyes, all milk paste and wide, staring blankly up from the water makes me shudder. I feel my stomach threatening to come up my throat even though I don't have enough material in my stomach to barf even if I shoved three fingers down my windpipe. Fortunately, I keep it down.

The ground steadily rises under our feet. The light coming down through the tree canopy is still muted from an overcast sky, but it's noticeably brighter. I shiver constantly as we thread our way past a seemingly endless minefield of broken branches, rotten stumps and boulders. We're going to have to stop soon because just keeping on the move isn't really making me warmer. My clothes are damp, which might be worse than if they were sopping wet. I don't know for sure. I'm betting the damp clothes are refrigerating my body temperature down to danger levels. I've given up holding Misty's hand to clutch my arms across my chest.

Another half an hour crawls by and I'm beginning to stumble. Ahead of us, the trees are noticeably thinner. After a few minutes, it becomes clear that some sort of clearing is ahead.

The terrorists on our trail are not going to give up. Mr. Red Jacket must have stumbled up the stream all night looking for us. We can't hope they'll just be content to torture the other passengers and leave us to wander in the woods. Misty is too important to them and now, I've taken out one of their men. The terrorists were the wolves, we were the sheep, and now they know we can bite. They will be enraged for sure.

"Wait a second," I say to Misty.

"What? What's the matter?"

"There's a clearing up ahead." I point forward.

"Okay. So..."

"So, we'll be exposed, you know," I say. "I mean, let's just be careful."

"Oh...Okay."

I really slow down the last few feet and sort of creep up to the edge of the tree line behind a stump. To our right, I can see that the rise in the ground we've been climbing all day is the bottom slope of a pretty big mountain peak. I couldn't see it before because the forest was so thick. I can see it now because we're not really facing a clearing. It's a jumbled mess of snow, rocks and broken trees from a small avalanche in front of us. The debris field is at least a mile-long scar from the peak at our right down to where we stand and then past us to our left by about another quarter mile. It's like a silent, white and black river, probably twenty yards across - a real mess.

"Looks like this didn't happen very long ago," I say.

"It smells like mud," Misty says. "Kind of stinks."

The avalanche churned up a bunch of trees, making a bank of dirt and upended tree roots. It reminds me of the logging roads I saw back in Alaska. When the bulldozers first punch a road through the bush, they just plow up everything into huge piles of roots and mud, like big retaining walls between the rest of the forest and the road. I've seen these piles get twenty feet high, well over top of the cab of a bulldozer. Over time, if the new road doesn't get covered with a thick bed of gravel, this berm erodes because of the rain and snow until the roadbed becomes a great big river of mud. Pretty much the only thing that moves on a fresh logging road without a gravel base is a bulldozer. When George and I went fishing, we sometimes followed these new logging roads back into the bush looking for a creek to fish. We had to crawl along the piles of mud and tree roots on the edge because the roadbed itself was usually three feet deep in wet, black muck. But I also remember that so many of those piles of broken trees, roots and dirt made a lot of little caves. Could be a good place to hole up for a while.

Misty steps forward and I pull her back.

"Wait a second," I say.

"What? What is it," Misty sounds a little surprised and tired. I know the feeling.

"If we just walk across, we're going to leave a bunch of footprints in the snow. They'll know exactly where we went."

"Oh yeah. You're right," she says.

"Let's go that way," I say, pointing to our left. "It looks like the end of the snow right over there. I'll bet if we get over to the other side, we can figure out a place to make another shelter and then, you know, we can see them coming…because…"

"Because they'll cross over the snow in the open," she says with a smile.

"Yeah," I smile for the first time since yesterday.

We turn and make the ten-minute walk to the bottom of the avalanche field. The snow and mud sloshed up into a thick bulge at the end of the slide. Huge boulders and logs are bunched up in a wide pile like a border of jagged cobblestones, so we can pick our way across to the other side of the field without stepping in the snow. In ten more minutes, we are ready to jump off the last boulder at the edge of the bulge into the forest on the far side of the field when I see something odd in the snow.

"Whoa, check it out," I say, pointing at a patch of snow at the edge of the debris field.

Mangled in the snow is a small deer. Obviously, the avalanche caught the poor thing in its plunge. It's been rolled through rocks and snow for who knows how long, so its legs are twisted in a half a dozen unnatural ways. It has burst open, stringing its innards out on the snow like a bloody pile of worms. Misty makes a retching sound, but I'm not thinking about a gut pile. I'm thinking about venison steaks.

"Here," I say. "Help me get it out of the snow."

"That's so gross," she says.

"Yeah, but it's fresh. I don't see any maggots and it's been in the snow. It's like finding it in a freezer."

It doesn't take me long to pull the body out of the snow. I don't actually need Misty's help. Since the deer has been basically crushed, I can pull out the guts with my hands. It's squishy, smelly work, but I'm not planning on eating the intestines.

"I can't believe you're touching that," Misty says.

I just grin and finish cleaning out the gut cavity as best I can. There is some leftover gunk, but without a knife, it's the best I can do. My hands are covered in blood and dirt, so I use handfuls of snow to clean them off. In a few minutes, my hands are nearly as red from the cold as they were from the blood. I'm thinking about our next fire now. I'm not fool enough to build one out in the open, so we need to get back into the trees and find a good place to make another shelter.

"It looks like snow's coming," I say.

Misty looks up. The weather looms overhead like a crouching ghost, threatening to smother us with fog filled hands that are heavy with snow.

"I think we'd better stop and make a fire sooner rather than later," I say.

"You think we're safe enough?"

"Yeah...if we get on the other side of this debris field, we can see someone coming a long way out. Let's go..."

The deer isn't heavy, maybe thirty pounds, but I can't very well drag it through the bush for hours. Besides, building a fire during the day makes more sense anyway. At night, having a fire is like building a strobe light beacon for anyone to find us. At least during the day, we can cook some meat, warm up some stones, and make ourselves as comfortable as possible for a long, cold night. I figure we've walked at least three hours away from the creek and with the snowfield at our backs, we can probably see them coming. It's time to build another fire.

I grab the deer by what's left of its back legs and move into the bush on the other side of the debris field. We hike up the slope next to the edge of the debris field and it doesn't take long to find a suitable place to settle down for a while. It's a group of three trees growing close together. Next to the trees, the avalanche has tossed up a rootball, a few boulders, and some snow, making a cozy little space where the debris looks fairly dry under the lowest branches. Kneeling by the trees, we will be completely out of sight. I can even see out from between the trees across the snowfield if I stand up and I'll still be well-concealed. I'm not planning on building a shelter for the night just yet. I just want to get out of the wind, out of the cold, get warmed up, and polish off some roast venison before it gets dark.

I let go of the deer, wiggle my way under the branches, and stand up to get a look at the snowfield. As I suspected, I'm completely concealed. I can see across the snow and debris field clearly for at least a hundred yards. I can see to my left and right twice that distance, so it's unlikely that anyone is going to come our direction without me seeing them coming a long way off.

"Okay," I say. "Let see about getting something to eat."

"Like what?" She seems honestly revolted. "You don't think I'm going to eat that thing, do you?"

I shrug my shoulders. "More for me then," I say with a smile.

I get on my knees. I pile up as much dead leaves and bracken as I can until I make a reasonably comfortable place for both of us to sit. All and all, under the trees, backed up against a wall of mud and snow and seated on a cushion of dry, dead plants, we're pretty snug. I stand up and look across the snowfield. There's no one in sight.

"Kyle," Misty says. She speaks so quietly, I have to turn around and kneel back down to hear her. "Thanks for taking care of me."

Taking care of her? She's the one that's been taking care of me since the creek. I've been so cold, so hungry, so scratched up, scared, and nearly sick with guilt that I've forgotten how pretty her eyes are.

"Well...I sort of like you," I say. "A lot..." She smiles and looks away from me.

"I'm so sorry...about yesterday and...sort of arguing and...I just..."

"It's okay," I say. I reach out to touch her hair gently. "It's okay."

"You were right. We should have taken off right away...I'm so sorry...about what happened."

Suddenly, I feel physically weak as if every muscle in my body just gave up and quit. I must have been running on adrenaline and an animal-like terror, and now that I can let my guard down for a minute, it all comes flooding back to me. Mr. Red Jacket, the death-shudder under my hands in the water...leaving his body in the current...running. I feel so tired. My head feels like a block of iron wobbling on a stick.

"Are you okay," Misty asks. I don't look at her. She bends her head lower to try and catch my eye. "I know what it's like, " she says.

185

"When I found my sister, I remember what it felt like." I look up and I believe her.

"Does it get any better," I plead. She nods her head.

"I've learned to live with it," she says. "I have bad dreams sometimes, but I don't think about it all the time anymore." She absently picks up a small twig and begins to snap it into tiny pieces. My eyes are drawn to her fingers snapping the twig. "I just kind of stay really busy. I'm in the band and student council and I practice all the time."

"And that helps," I say.

"So far," she answers. She drops the twig and leans forward toward me. "That… and having people who understand."

"I think I do," I say.

"I know you do," she says. She leans forward and presses her lips into mine with a sudden, almost fierce energy.

Fifteen

My first task is to get a fire going. This doesn't turn out to be easy. After twenty minutes of sifting through the black moss stuffed into the cavity of my back brace, I am finally able to break one of the coals down until I find a hot spot. It takes another half an hour of blowing and trying to get some tiny needles to ignite before I finally get a flame going. Still, it's better than rigging up a fire drill again.

Cutting anything reasonable to cook off of the deer's body turns out to be a difficult chore without a proper knife. I smash a number of rocks against one another to try and get a sharp chip. Unfortunately, pretty much everything turns out to be as dull as a teaspoon. I finally bend the aluminum shaft off the front of my back brace. Once I snap it off I have a bit of a sharp edge. It isn't much, but I'm able to hack off some of the flesh from the rump of the deer. I impale a few pieces on a green stick and start roasting. The smell is nearly intoxicating.

Honestly, I don't like venison. I don't like any sort of wild meat. I'm a fan of dead cow and anything more exotic than chicken or beef makes me queasy. I've tried venison before, but the gamey, wild taste is just gross. In Alaska, we had deer and even bear occasionally. I swear the bear tasted more like seafood than anything else. My dad said that was because most black bears spent their time on the beach rooting under the rocks for crabs all day. The deer we had was so wild-tasting I just couldn't get more than a few mouthfuls down before I thought about barfing. But right now, I'm so hungry, I'm thinking about venison sushi.

"You know," Misty says. "That smells really good."

"So, you're not too grossed out to give it a try?"

187

"Not anymore. I've always liked venison. We had it at Thanksgiving every year because my grandpa loved to hunt."

"At Thanksgiving? My dad always called Thanksgiving 'dead turkey day.'"

Misty laughs. It's nice to hear her laugh.

"I can't stand venison," I say. "...but I'm hungry enough to eat the stomach out of a dead rhino so..." Misty laughs again.

"That is not a picture I want to have in my mind right now."

"Sorry."

"Why don't you like venison?" she asks.

"I don't know. Just tastes weird, you know, a wild kind of taste. My dad called it 'gamey.'"

"That's why it's good," Misty says. "More for me."

"I thought you said you weren't eating because it was so gross."

"That was before I smelled it cooking."

I may not like the wild taste of venison, but I've never felt this hungry and tired either. I'm a little worried about spoiled meat, so I really cook it until it's more like deer-jerky. The first bite tastes a lot like heaven and I have to resist the urge to eat too fast. Misty's revulsion at the thought of eating a mangled deer has fully disappeared. She eats the charred piece I hand to her in four quick bites. I cut up some more meat, roast it over the fire and hand her some more. It's slow going, hacking off one small piece of meat at a time, roasting and eating it. That may be in our favor. I imagine our stomachs have shrunk to the size of prunes, so we're better off eating slowly anyway. We have to eat slowly because of the wait time on the cooking.

I've never really gone hungry before. The longest stretch I've ever gone without a decent meal has been an extra-long flight with my dad and even then, we had crackers or beef jerky to keep us going. I don't think I've ever missed more than one meal in my life. In the last two days, we've missed all except one meal and that was only one small trout each. I didn't realize how hungry I was until I started cooking. The smell of venison feast is so awesome.

In West Africa, we once stayed at a mission station in Cameroon for a few months. It was a remote base about an hour by air from anywhere. The area was desolate and most of the people we saw were very poor. I don't remember ever seeing an overweight person. Everyone was thin. There was a small medical clinic at the compound next to the airstrip. It was a simple, white stucco building with three rooms, a concrete floor, and what seemed like the only working toilet in the country. I distinctly remember the toilet because only the mission staff could use it. The locals were used to relieving themselves in whatever bush was nearby and I wonder if they even knew how to use a toilet anyway. But I'm not thinking about the toilet right now.

"When I was ten, I lived for a while in Cameroon, West Africa," I say.

"Wow, really," Misty says. "What was that like?"

"I was just thinking about it because we're eating this. I was just thinking that I've never missed more than one meal in a day before, not until now. I've never been this hungry. I'm even willing to eat venison."

"I don't think I've ever missed a meal at all," she says. "Why were you thinking about Cameroon?"

"I was only ten," I say, shrugging my shoulders. "Most of the people we saw didn't eat more than once a day, if they were lucky. Everybody was really thin."

"Really?"

"Yeah. I remember once I was in the clinic, kind of in the back room, and I was eating a sandwich my mom made me for lunch. And there was this kid watching me. I mean I didn't see him at first because he was outside. I was by the back door and he was kind of spying on me because the door was open a little. I didn't see him right away, but when I looked at him, it was like...I don't know...I felt sort of sick. He was really thin. His arms and legs were all skin-tight and you could see the bones. Pretty much everybody looked like that over there, but this kid was different. He was...looking at

189

me sort of like he had never seen that much food before or something. I couldn't even eat."

"What did you do?"

"I offered him the sandwich, but he wouldn't take it."

"Why not?"

"I don't know. He just looked at me for a second and then walked away. I guess he was just sort of amazed that I had so much to eat in the first place. But he wouldn't take my sandwich."

"I wonder what he was thinking?" she says. "Maybe he didn't take it because he didn't want to feel, you know, like a beggar or something."

"Maybe," I say. "But I just remember feeling like…like I was so spoiled, and I didn't even know it."

"I've never even been out of the country before," Misty says. "I've only been to Anchorage and that's still America. We've never even gone to Canada and that's like, three hours from Seattle. I don't even know what I would do in some place like Africa."

"I've been all over," I say. "West Africa, Alaska, New Guinea. And when we traveled, we stopped in all sorts of places. I've been to Holland and France and Australia."

"Where did you like living the best?" she asks.

I have to give that some thought. When I was in the middle of it, I didn't want to be anywhere but back home. My dad used to tell me, "Don't forget this son. You'll never get to see anything like this someday." But when I was kicking up dust playing soccer with an underinflated ball next to a mud hut in Africa, I was too busy complaining to think – "Hey, I'm in Africa, man."

"I don't know," I say. "Probably Alaska. We lived there the longest, like almost three years."

"That's not much different than Seattle," Misty says.

"Not where we lived," I say. "We lived up there for almost three years at two different mission stations. The first wasn't far from Anchorage, but the second was called Sunny Cove. That's where I met George and it was a long ways from electricity."

"You didn't even have electricity?" she asks.

190

"Well, sort of. I mean, not like hooked up to electric lines and stuff. We had a gas-powered electric generator and batteries and stuff like that, so we had lights, but not all the time. They had a couple of trailers, kind of like mobile homes, but we didn't live in them. That was where we kept the radio phone and weather computers and things like that."

"Where did you live?"

"We had a couple of log cabins. They were really cool. It smelled like cedar all the time."

"I love that smell," Misty says. "I have a cedar hope chest in my room. It's really old and every time you open it, you get this sweet smell."

"Yeah, I love cedar. It's probably my favorite wood."

"Our barn is made of some kind of wood. I don't know if it's cedar, but I love the smell there too."

"Barn?" I say. Misty's dad is the governor of Washington State. I'm not picturing a barn at her house.

"Yeah, well, not at the Governor's residence. It's at our real house. That's where we have a barn. It's one of my favorite places. Me and my sister played there, like, all the time. We have chickens and ducks and after...you know...after she died, my dad... got me two sheep."

"Sheep," I say surprised. "No way, really?"

"Yeah, they were so little when we first got them. I went to the barn every day. When we first got them, I had to feed them with a bottle."

"That's cool," I say. Misty's voice has softened almost to a whisper. Obviously, the sheep mean a lot to her.

"I named them Mary and Sunshine," she says. I can tell she's a little shy telling me about her sheep. "It's kind of...It's not very high school to have a sheep named Sunshine, you know. I mean, if I had a dog, nobody would think it was weird."

"No, but who cares?" I say. "I think it's nice." No one knows better than I do how cold and mean people can be on the social set at St. Mark's. I figure it's pretty much the same at every high school in

191

America. Sometimes, I feel like the weakest animal in the barn. Everybody pounces on the weakest animal in the barn, so I don't blame Misty for keeping her sheep a secret. At St. Mark's, you have to present the image of Ivy League maturity or you'll get crushed. Once again, I'm touched that Misty feels like she can tell me something like this.

"I don't tell people about them," she says. "I told Angie. She was cool about it, but sometimes, I feel like having them is like keeping my old Barbies. We don't get to go there as much anymore because Dad became Governor and we moved into the residence. But whenever we do go, they always run to me when I come home. They...follow me around when I take them out into the yard. It's not like having a dog or a cat. They're different and I don't even know why."

I look at her with a new tenderness. I feel like I understand something about her that no one else can understand. The image of Mr. Red Jacket floating away from me in the water flashes across my mind and I shudder again. I imagine what it was like for Misty to find her sister and I know what it was like...you feel like you can't breathe. You feel like your legs won't work, like you can't tear your eyes away even though the sight is so horrible you want to slam your eyelids shut and never see anything again. But when you shut your eyes, you still see it, like it's tattooed in ugly, bright colors on the insides of your eyelids. It makes perfect sense to me why Sunshine and Mary are so important to her. And so secret! That's something just for her. Two warm little creatures that needed her almost as much as she needed them.

We've been through so much in the last twenty-four hours. We went from making out to fighting in less than an hour, but I think it's just the stress, not something wrong with Misty. I don't really know anything about her. What I know now makes me realize she is so much deeper than I thought.

"I never had any pets," I say. "We never really stayed any place long enough and...so many places, you don't see any pets. Maybe up in Alaska someone might have a dog or something, but in Africa and New Guinea…animals were for food."

"I used to eat lamb chops all the time," Misty says. "I can't anymore."

"That makes sense," I say. "When we were in…"

Crack.

The sudden echoing sound causes us both to snap our heads back to the debris field. How long have we just been sitting here eating toasted Bambi while the terrorists have been closing in on us? I picked this little mini-camp because the debris from the avalanche had piled up around our trees, making a tumbled over, muddy, snowy wall. I carefully straighten up until my eyes are barely able to see over the edge of the wall. On the far side of the snowfield, I see movement.

I swear quietly under my breath. There are two men moving out of the bush. One of them is clearly Mr. Tan Jacket and both hold rifles. Mr. Tan Jacket squats down looking at the ground. He gestures to his left, my right, and I realize what he's doing. He's following our tracks. He knows we walked to the bottom end of the avalanche zone.

Something cold and wet touches my cheek. It's snow! And it's not because a little fell off the tree above me. It's starting to snow.

I swear again.

I duck down and scramble on all fours back to the fire. It may be a small fire and I can only hope the tree limbs above our heads have broken up the smoke, but they might see the smoke at any second. Or smell it.

"We gotta get outta here, right now," I say.

There is no disguising the panic in my voice. I can't believe I was so stupid to stop and build a fire in the first place. The man I killed got off a message on his radio before I took him down, so they must have found him. They must have been following our trail for hours.

"What are we gonna do?" she says. "Where are they?"

"Other side of the snow field," I say.

I take the metal piece of my back brace that I was using for a butcher knife and break up the fire. I want to get the burning pieces scattered so putting them out won't make too much smoke. There is a small patch of snow on the edge of our little campsite. I drop the metal piece and use both hands to scoop up a handful of snow.

"Help me with this," I say. I toss the snow onto the smoldering remains of our fire. There is a sharp hiss and some white smoke, but that's better than a black smoke plume.

"We've gotta run. Right now," Misty says. She scrambles to her feet, but I grab her skirt.

"I know," I say as calmly as I can. I want to just run like a scared rabbit too. I'm pretty sure they're going to find the campsite no matter what we do. "Let's not make it easy for them. It'll only take a second."

Misty hesitates. I wonder if she's scared enough to just abandon me and run crazy into the woods. I share the feeling, but she kneels back down. Together, we scoop and dump snow until our hands are red from the cold and we don't hear any more sizzle. It only takes a minute, but I swear it feels like a half an hour.

I toss the back brace under a bush, grab the aluminum shaft and get up. Without a word, I take Misty's hand and pull her after me. I'm not worried about leaving a trail. I just want to get as far away from the campsite as we can, as quickly as we can. The snow falls quietly around us, thicker every minute. There's no way to avoid making tracks in the fresh powder. The snow is falling fast, so we can hope it will be fast enough to fill in the tracks we're making. Otherwise, we may as well be lighting a neon sign with an arrow pointing our direction. Our only hope is to gain distance.

It will probably take them fifteen minutes or so to follow our trail to the bottom of the debris field. They won't miss the gut pile I made from the deer. Since I dragged the stupid thing most of the way to our campsite, they shouldn't have any trouble finding their way to our last stop either. That should take another fifteen minutes or so. Half an hour – that's all the time we have to make ourselves scarce. I'm really cursing myself for dragging the deer. But, on the other hand, our bellies are full, we've really warmed up and the deer feast has given us both some much-needed energy.

We fly along at a frantic pace until we're both sucking in wind like a vacuum. We stop for a second, then, without a word we set out again, quick this time, but not running all out. They're going to know exactly where we are going. We can't go to the right because that would take us into a snow-covered mountain. We can't go to the left because we will eventually come out at the lake. From what I remember, the lake was miles long. Our only real option is to go straight ahead, and the terrorists will know it. They don't even really have to track us. Simple logic will tell them which way we're headed, and I wonder if we shouldn't do something unexpected when I hear a shout from behind us. I look behind. Obviously, they are not trying to sneak up on us.

I still hold Misty's hand. The look in her eye is unthinking panic. Her hand shakes. There's nothing we can do except run.

The forest around us is rapidly turning white. I look up and see the clouds flowing down like a gigantic wave of white and gray trying to drown us in its foam. There's no way we can hide our trail, so we simply run. The air grows colder but seems all the worse because I'm running, trying to heave in a breath past my fear and fatigue. My lungs burn from the cold. I feel mucus running freely out of my nose because of the cold, but I don't try to wipe it away since one hand is holding Misty's and the other is frantically trying to push branches and fern leaves out of my way as we run. We're nothing more than terrified prey and the wolves are closing in.

I jump onto a log. It makes a long, thin trail in the general direction we're running and running on top of a log beats tripping over broken stumps and stones any day. I let go of Misty's hand and race along its length. At the end, I look around for her. She balances her way along the length of the log behind me, looking down at her feet. She looks up in my direction for a second, loses her footing, and falls with a surprised yelp.

Her voice echoes through the trees like a bullhorn. I wince, and I'm worried as much about the sound as about her falling. I run back along the length of the log. Misty is pulling herself up to a seated position on the ground next to it.

"Are you okay," I ask.

"I think so, yeah," she answers. She brushes the snow from her hands and tries to get up. "Ughhh...oh, man that hurts," she says.

"What? What's wrong," I say.

"It's my ankle. I think I twisted it."

"Here, let me help you," I say. I offer my hand. She takes it and I pull her to her feet. She balances on her left foot and tries to take a step with her right. The look on her face tells me all I need to know.

"I really twisted it," she says.

I'm cursing myself for running along the length of the log, but there's nothing I can do about it now. I look over my shoulder behind us. I don't see anything except snow falling in the woods. The snow shower makes the trees look dark and creepy, like black things with claws lurking in a hazy film of white. Even worse, the snow shower seems to be slowing. That means our tracks won't be filling up. We've got to keep going.

"Can you walk on it?" I ask.

"I'll try," she says.

There's no way she's going to get back up on the log, so I hop down, put her arm over my shoulder, and hobble forward. Misty tries to put weight on her foot, but it's a losing battle. In three steps, even the slightest weight on her ankle equals an uncontrollable cry of pain. I'm afraid it's worse than a sprain. Her slight cries of pain become real tears. Every effort she makes to get past the discomfort and try to walk is real agony. I manage to hold her upright, but there's no way to keep from leaving an obvious trail in the freshly fallen snow.

I know they're right behind us. I know we can't outrun them and I know we can't disguise our trail. Misty is putting almost her entire weight on me and the ground is uneven and slippery. I don't have any kind of a plan or hope to escape. I'm down to instinct, like a wounded, dying animal. My breath is ragged. Every breath I pull in is like icy shards cutting streaks into my throat. Misty's breathing is

196

uneven and fast. She twists around on nearly every other step, trying to look back over her shoulder.

I have to stop, just for a minute. Misty balances on her left foot and I look behind. The snow has nearly stopped falling and visibility is still clouded by a white mist. I don't see any movement, but I can see our trail like a dark scar on a white sheet pointing back into the woods.

My breathing evens out a little and I know it's time to keep moving. I have no idea what to do other than to keep stumbling forward. The ground slopes away to our left and there are more large boulders in this area than I've seen so far. Some of them are as big as a house and I'm looking to our right, just beginning to think we might have to just find a place to hide when Misty suddenly gives a sharp little cry and pulls back on my arm.

Directly in front of us, the ground gives way and disappears. A few more steps and I can see why. A harsh, deep ravine cuts through the forest right in front of us, curving away to our left toward the lake and blocking our way as effectively as if we were facing a razor wire fence. There is no slope down to the bottom. It's just a cliff at least fifty feet deep. A stream of foamy white-water splashes loudly at the bottom. The ravine is a ragged gash in the side of the mountain. It slices into the slope for at least a quarter of a mile up the slope before it blends into a waterfall that shimmers across a sheer wall of rock on the mountainside. If we stumble along the top of the ravine and then try navigating across the boulders at the base of the waterfall it will take an hour of hard going against the slope, fully exposed to anyone following our trail because of the break in the trees at the edge of the ravine. And if we go that way, I'll have to nearly drag Misty along with me, making us even slower.

Looking the other way, the ravine only seems to cut deeper into the ground and it curves away from our view. I can only hope it slopes out at some point beyond where I can see. There's no telling how close they are behind us. I can imagine our trail is so easy to follow, they've been running to catch up with us. They know we don't have any weapons, so we're easy prey. There's no way I can

197

fight them off. Killing Mr. Red Jacket was nothing more than survival instinct. Trying to make a stand against two armed men who are better fed and better rested with nothing more than my bare hands is just suicide.

I swear rather loudly. I look back to my right, then left again. I've just decided our best bet is to travel downhill when I see a thin, fallen tree crossing over the ravine about a hundred yards up the slope from where we stand. At any other time, the idea of trying to cross a fifty-foot ravine on a log barely four inches in diameter wouldn't even cross my mind. I'm just about to give up on the idea when I hear a shout from behind us.

"They've found us," Misty shouts.

I look back over my shoulder. The snow has stopped falling and the misty white haze in the air has nearly vanished. I can clearly see two dark figures running through the woods in our direction.

There's no time to hesitate. I pull Misty's arm harder into my shoulder, put all my strength into lifting her, and run toward the log. I can almost feel them behind us, like dogs nipping at our heels. I don't think they're going to shoot at us because it's obvious I'm supporting Misty. Any shot at me and they risk killing her...and she's the prize.

We're at the log. It is a tree that fell across the ravine from our side so we have to step around the exposed root ball to walk across. One look at the trek across the ravine and Misty pulls back.

"I can't, I can't," she cries.

"We don't have a choice," I shout in her ear.

I don't have time to be gentle. We either get across the log or they will catch us. And I don't mean to be harsh - but they won't kill her, they *will* kill me - on the spot. There's no time to hesitate! The log is so thin on the other side; if we can get across the ravine, I might be able to dislodge it. That might slow them up.

"You can't be serious!" She is fully yelling at me now. She tries to pull her arm off my shoulder, but I won't let go of her wrist. "Let me go," she says.

"What are you talking about," I say.

Now I'm angry. Misty finally pulls her arm off my shoulder. I turn and stare at her.

"You are what they're after. Don't you get that? They don't want me. If they catch up, they'll kill me on the spot."

"I do get that," she shouts back. "You go. They won't come after you."

"I'm not going anywhere," I say.

"They'll take me hostage. They'll make some kind of deal."

"You don't know that!" I'm nearly screaming at her now. "We've already seen what they're willing to do. What if they just want to torture you on video and rub it in your father's face? What if once they get what they want, they just blow your head off?"

Misty's face is ashen and shocked. She grits her teeth and shakes her head almost violently left and right.

"I can't...I'm afraid of heights and my ankle...I can't..."

I look past her shoulder. The terrorists are close enough I can almost make out the details on their faces. We don't have any time. I take Misty by the shoulders and look her right in the face.

"I'll be right with you," I say. "All the way. I'm going to hold on to your waist and help you keep your balance. But we gotta go. Now."

I turn Misty around, get right behind her and wrap my arms around her waist. I don't have the luxury of thinking about how intimate this position is because I have to admit I'm scared nearly to death. Heights don't bother me – it's the sudden stop at the end of a fall that bothers me. And looking down, I can see a mouthful of jagged rocks seething in a froth of white-water foam. One false step and we're both dead.

"One step at a time," I say. "You can do this."

Misty's breathing is rapid and shallow. She hobbles out to the edge of the log and then looks back over her shoulder. I follow her look. The terrorists are no more than a hundred yards away. Both run against the uneven slope. We only have a few minutes to get across. If we can, we might be able to duck behind the trees on the other side. There's nothing stopping them from crossing the log, but I figure a few well-aimed rocks should discourage them, at least for a little while.

Misty puts her weight carefully on her right foot. She puts her right arm on mine, leans into me, and takes a step onto her left foot. She moans and grips my arm like her hand is a vice. I step in behind her. Every nerve in my body is on high alert. My hands shake and it's everything I can do to resist the urge to look behind me or push Misty to go faster. She takes another hobbling step, then another. Behind me, I can hear the terrorists shout in their own language. I look back for a second. They're right on top of us - maybe sixty yards away and moving fast.

"We gotta go faster," I shout.

"I'm trying not to fall," Misty shouts back.

She takes another step. The whole tree shudders under our feet. Misty screams and I don't blame her. We're more than halfway across but the log is getting so thin, every step is causing it to bounce.

"Almost there!" I yell.

"Stop there!" someone shouts.

I turn my head. Mr. Tan Jacket has taken aim with his rifle.

"Stop there!" he yells again.

"Keep moving!" I shout at Misty.

She leans harder against my right arm, takes another hopping step. The whole log bounces and we're nearly thrown up like bouncing on a trampoline. I swear loudly. Misty screams again, lets go of my arm, and flails wildly with both arms, trying to keep her balance. I bend my knees and steady Misty at her hips the best I can. In another three steps, we will make it across.

I cringe even lower when the first rifle shot booms in my left ear. I hear the whine of the bullet over my head for a split second before the slug slams into a tree on the edge of the ravine. I grab Misty's waist with both hands, push her with all my might, and literally launch her toward the far side of the ravine. She shrieks and crashes into the muddy side of the ravine on her stomach. I lose sight of her because my movement causes the log to bounce even harder and I'm slightly airborne for a moment.

Sixteen

I literally scream like a four-year-old girl as my feet bounce off the surface of the log. I fall so fast I don't have time to think. My arms slam against the wood, but I swing away underneath it and almost into the void. I lash out with both arms, slide across the rough surface of the log, and I almost lose my grip. Somehow, I grab hold and pull into the log with all my strength, slamming my face into the wood. There's a sharp pain in my nose, I taste blood, and I think at least one of my fingernails has ripped away. Misty screams in the background and every muscle in my body explodes with tension as I cling to the side of the log.

Somehow, I've swung almost completely under the log, but my arms hug the tree to hold me up. My heart beats so hard I swear anyone within twenty feet must be able to hear it like some booming timpani.

"Kyle, Kyle!" Misty shouts.

I can't turn my head to see her. Real terror grips my chest, I shiver all over, and my arms suddenly feel too weak to hold me. My legs flail out into nothing except empty air and I dangle out into space like a spider on a thread. Thank goodness I've been such a workout fiend because of the back brace or I wouldn't be able to hold myself.

My face is flush up against the wood. I manage to turn my head. Misty has scrambled away from the edge of the bank. She is on her knees facing me.

"Keep going," I croak. "Get behind the trees."

"Kyle!" she yells, reaching out to me.

On the far side of the ravine, I hear another rifle shot. Misty shrieks, jumping backwards as the bullet rips a hole in the log about

201

six inches from my left hand. They're not shooting at her - they're trying to kill me! I start scooting myself, arm over arm, toward Misty. The bark of the log digs into my forearms painfully. Another shot whizzes by my left ear and smashes into the bank behind me, inches from the back of my head.

I'm at the end of the log. The bank is so steep the dirt on the edge is mashed up against the back of my head and my legs still hang into nothing but air. I'll have to turn around somehow if I'm going to get any kind of footing on the ravine wall. I'm just turning around when I see Mr. Tan Jacket's associate run to the other end of the log on the edge of the ravine. It's the guy with the long black beard I saw at the boats.

Blackbeard shouts something and points his finger at me. He has a clear shot. He raises his rifle, takes aim, and I know he can't miss!

Instantly, I swing around to face the ravine wall in total panic. Above me, the log rests on the muddy top of the ravine. There are some exposed roots hanging out of the mud just below where the log sits. I fling my right arm forward, catch one of the roots, and scramble upward, hand over hand. I still can't get any footing on the ravine wall so it's all arm strength. I dig my knees into the mud, slam my face into the earth, and even try to use my chin for traction. For five seconds, I flail my arms and knees and tense every muscle in my body to get up the embankment because any second now I'm going to feel a bullet tear the heart right out of my chest.

But the shot doesn't come. I suddenly feel both of Misty's hands grabbing my shoulders.

They can't risk a shot at me if Misty is so close! She can't lift my weight, but her strength helps stabilize me. I dig my knees into the mud on the top of the ravine and scramble the last few feet over the top on my belly. Misty falls backward trying to pull me up.

"Run!" I shout at her. "Go, now. Get to the trees."

Misty frantically gets to her feet! She instantly screams trying to put weight on her foot. I know a sprain can be painful, but with this much terror and adrenaline I would think she could deal with it! Her ankle must be actually broken.

"Go!" I shout again.

Misty hobbles forward, falls, and simply starts crawling on her hands and knees. I look behind me. Blackbeard is already halfway across the log. He is close enough; I can see the satanic glint in his eyes. His teeth flash white, framed by his coal-black beard, like a phosphorous gash in an oil slick. He moves to raise his rifle into firing position and the movement makes him sway on the trembling log. His smile vanishes, but he quickly regains his balance.

Behind Blackbeard, Mr. Tan Jacket has taken a few steps onto the log. He doesn't seem to like the idea of heights and even from thirty feet away I can see his face turn pale. He glances at me, but he is seriously concerned about the drop beneath his feet. That's when I get an idea.

I flip over onto my back, dig my elbows into the dirt, and use both legs to push the end of the log bridge. There's still at least ten feet of the tree resting on my side of the ravine. It's thin and springy like a frozen length of bungee cord, so I'm not sure if I can push it completely off the edge. Maybe a little push is all I need. I strain and shove with all my might and it hardly moves.

Blackbeard sees what I'm doing. I'm fully exposed, so he raises his rifle slowly, trying to get into firing position while still holding his balance. Mr. Tan Jacket shouts and tries to turn back. The movement causes him to flail wildly and he loses his grip on his rifle. It pitches away into the ravine and he shouts his head off in terror. I realize I can't push the tree over the edge, but I figure I can make the trampoline idea work for me. I quit pushing and start kicking the log with both feet.

Blackbeard tries to crouch down and sit on the bouncing log, but it's too late. With a horrible cry, he spins off into the ravine. Mr. Tan Jacket dives back toward the opposite side of the ravine. He manages to catch a root from the root ball of the tree bridge, but his whole body swings off the side of the log. He slams back into the log, impaling his ribs on a sharp stick that protrudes from the side. I see the bright crimson of serious bleeding. Somehow, Mr. Tan Jacket holds on and he doesn't tumble into the ravine after Blackbeard.

I'm not going to hang around to find out how badly Mr. Tan Jacket has been hurt. He dropped his rifle, but that doesn't mean he doesn't have a backup, and it doesn't mean he hasn't got a dozen friends already coming through the woods to help him either. It does mean we can keep running.

I roll over and get to my feet in one swift motion. Misty isn't that far ahead of me. She stops and looks back at me. I pound my feet into the forest floor and run from the edge of the ravine. I stop for a split second to loop Misty's arm over my shoulder and look back. Mr. Tan Jacket has somehow pulled himself back onto the far side of the ravine. He clutches his left side, trying to stop the bleeding. I can see blood staining his shirt and pant leg even from here. In a few seconds, he's going to realize how seriously he's been hurt. I lunge forward, nearly lifting Misty off the ground. We stumble wildly through the bush oblivious to branches swatting us in the face, just running scared.

Twenty minutes of crazy-running later and I stop to catch my breath.

"I don't think he's right behind us," I say between gasps of air. Misty leans over, clutching a stitch in her side.

"Why not?" she asks. "They're not giving up trying to find us."

"Trying to find you," I say. I immediately regret it.

"I didn't ask for any of this," she snaps. "It's not my fault."

"I know, I'm sorry," I plead. "I just...he's probably not right behind us because he was bleeding pretty bad."

"I could see that."

Misty pulls her arm off my shoulder and tries to take a step on her bad ankle. She yelps in pain and sits down heavily on a log. She shakes her head in a wasted attempt to keep from crying. The tension and fear are obviously tearing her apart.

"I'm sorry," I say. "He didn't look like he was in any shape to keep after us."

"How is that supposed to make me feel better?" she yells. "We've been running for two days. What are we supposed to do now?"

Her voice has gone from a yell to a shriek. I glance nervously behind us, more out of habit than anything else. I really don't think Mr. Tan Jacket is snapping at our heels. He was bleeding badly.

"We keep going," I say.

"Going where?" she yells. "We don't even know where we are. I wouldn't be here if you hadn't dragged me into a lake."

I'm feeling frustrated with her. Getting all freaked out isn't helping anything. So, I decide to yell back.

"Well what do you want to do? Give up?"

"I don't know," she screams. "You brought us out here."

"This is not my fault."

Part of me wants to just back off and let her pout. Another part of me is just plain mad. I'm tired of being the bad guy every time her feelings get twisted up in a knot.

"I didn't drag you into the lake. You jumped because you knew I was right."

Misty doesn't answer. She wipes her face with her hand, smearing dirt across her cheek, and looks away from me. I'm not about to be ignored. I step around to get into her line of sight and bend down so I'm nearly in her face.

"I just killed a man to try and protect you!" I yell. "I had to drown another guy, but you didn't think it was time to get moving then either, did you?"

Misty doesn't answer. She doesn't look defiant and angry anymore. Her tears seem different suddenly. I've seen this change before because she's probably sorry, but I'm not in the mood to care.

"We're not making the same mistake twice," I say harshly. "We need to keep moving and you can either sit here and feel sorry for yourself, or you can come with me."

Misty looks up at me and she's switched back to being angry.

"You wouldn't just leave me," she snarls.

"That's not what I meant."

"That's what you said. You said I can either sit here or come with you."

"I meant..."

I lean back, stand up straight, and turn around. I can't seem to get my thinking straight. I didn't mean I was going to leave her. I just meant…

"I just meant…we can't just sit here. We've got to keep going."

"You said you were going to leave," she says flatly. "If that's what you want to do, then leave."

Her last words are really loud.

"I did not. This is a pile of…this is stupid."

I stomp away from her a few paces and shake my head. I look back and Misty isn't looking my way. She crosses her arms, sets her chin defiantly, and the look on her face is a mixture of fear and anger and pain.

I remember more than a few times when my mom had that same look. Crazy thing was - my parents never fought in front of me, but I always knew when they were in battle. The look on my mother's face was a dead giveaway. She could never hide it from me.

What's really weird is they always told me about their fights after the fact. It was bizarre. They had a rule – *don't fight in front of Kyle!* And then they had another rule – *always tell Kyle all about it, give him a blow-by-blow description so he can feel embarrassed and freaked out!*

I guess it was their way of teaching me how to be real and get through fights. Now that I'm in the middle of it with Misty, I'm starting to see why they did that.

A lot of parents hide what's happening in their marriage. Maybe they're scared of what might happen if their kids find out they're not always in control. Maybe they're just embarrassed. My dad used to say too many parents want to be their kid's friend instead of a parent. My folks would rather I knew all about the fights they got into. Dad used to say, "You're never going to learn how to fight unless you learn how to do it right."

Weird people – boy do I miss them!

Looking at Misty with her closed-off, defiant body language, I'm forced to admit – it's back to the whole speaker-listener thing…again. Whenever I got crossways with my parents, they would make me use it with them because it was based on the Bible verse James 1:19. In fact, my mother made me memorize James 1:19 and my dad made me recite it to him over and over again whenever there was a disagreement around the house. Honestly, I used to hate it. Whenever voices got raised or I felt like storming off to my room, my mom or dad would make me quote that scripture. There were not a few times where I quoted it through clinched teeth. It says, "Everyone must be quick to hear, slow to speak and slow to anger, because the anger of man does not bring about the righteous life that God desires."

It got under my skin and I admit I got busted a bunch of times for abandoning "the rules" and just mouthing off when I was mad. My dad called the rules, "the shut your mouth and open your ears" rules. I didn't like being made to use the speaker- listener thingy, but I watched my parents avoid screaming matches many times. I've seen plenty of other families where screaming fits were about as normal as using the bathroom once a day. So…if it works, don't fix it…

I turn around and walk back to where Misty sits. She won't turn her face to me.

"Okay," I say carefully. "So…you think I was threatening to take off."

"That's what you said," she growls. "If after everything you want to take off, then just go. Just go."

"I didn't say…okay, so you think…if I want to go I should just go."

"Well, that's what you want. You don't really care if they find me. You're just trying to get away yourself."

That really stings. I kept her from freezing, I found food for us twice. I built a shelter, built a fire, not to mention fighting for my life twice. How can she say I don't care? I can feel my face flush. But my dad's voice keeps ringing in my head, "Control your tongue, Marine."

"So…" I say very carefully.

I really work to keep the tone of my voice as neutral as possible. I've done this before with my mom and even the slightest hint of sarcasm got me into huge trouble – not to mention I've actually made

207

my mother cry because I was too harsh. That's something you don't forget – especially when your mother is now dead.

"You think I don't care if they find you and...all I care about is taking care of myself."

"That's what it feels like," she snarls. "I'm just...I don't know what to do. I don't know...where are we running and my ankle is killing me...how are we supposed to get...out of this...and..."

She trails off into some more tears. I decide to press the listener thing...

"You feel really...you don't know what we should do."

"Yes," she says firmly. "Yeah...I mean, we can't just keep running. Where are we running to? Oh great..."

Misty looks up because snow starts falling again. "This is just great. It's snowing again. I'm freezing. This is insane!" she screams the last word at me as if she can launch every ounce of her frustration at me with a single word.

"You don't know where we're going and...it's really cold."

"What are you doing?" she yells again. "You sound like an idiot."

I really have to bite my tongue. This isn't working the way it did with my mom.

"I'm just trying to listen. Just trying to understand you, okay?"

"What do you want to understand?" she asks. "How can you not get it?"

"I get it, okay? You're cold, you're scared, you're hungry. I get it."

"You don't get it," she says coldly. "You just think we can run away and everything's going to be just fine. You can make a fire with a shoelace – so what? That's not going to get me out of this mess."

"Get you out of this mess?"

I'm starting to feel like I did when I stormed off to my room and slammed my door. This "repeat back until you understand" stuff is starting to make me gag.

"This isn't all about you, you know? They don't want me alive. Did you ever stop to think about that? There's a reason I had to kill two people today! Did you hear me? I killed two people to try and get you out of this mess."

"I didn't ask you to kill anybody," she says.

"I didn't have a choice," I turn around and stomp forward, shaking my head. Big, puffy flakes of snow fly off my hair like a dog shaking off soapsuds.

"Fine," she says. "Just leave. That's what you want to do anyway."

I stop, close my eyes, and try desperately to get control of my rage. I remember...his face under the water, blurry and white. I remember his death shudder in my hands and suddenly...my anger just snaps like the crack of a whip...snaps into revulsion.

She'll never know what that shudder felt like. Suddenly, I hope she never does know what it feels like. She's just scared. She's lost, people are trying to kill her and with a messed-up ankle, she's in pain.

I turn back to face her. The snow is really starting to fall. I look past her, and I don't see any terrorists running with guns through the trees.

"I'm not going anywhere," I say softly. "I don't want to leave you, Misty. I'm not trying to make you mad either. I'm just...I'm just as scared as you are."

Misty isn't ready to look at me yet. I walk back to her and sit next to her on the log. She still won't look up at me. I remember my mom telling me that sometimes she just needed to vent and sometimes how she let things go came out all twisted. My dad used to say, "Girls think with their feeling."

"I'm not going anywhere," I say again. "I'm not trying to make things worse, okay?"

Misty doesn't answer. She brushes snow off the surface of the log and begins to pick at the bark.

"I'm sorry I yelled at you," I say. "You're afraid we can't just run. I get that. We have to do better than that."

Misty nods her head. She continues to pick at the bark. The snow is falling so fast, it's beginning to pile up around her fingers no matter how often she tries to brush it aside. I'm starting to feel colder.

"Misty," I say. "I'm sorry I yelled at you and I'm sorry I...I'm sorry if what I said... sounded like I was going to just take off or something."

"That's what you said," she says, looking up at me.

I know that's not what I said but arguing about it isn't going to make her feel any better. She's just afraid and I don't want to be mad at her for being scared.

"If I did...then I wasn't thinking, or I was just blowing up or something. I'm sorry."

Misty looks back at her bark picking, then looks back at me.

"I've never been stuck out in the woods before," she says quietly. "I've never even been camping before."

"Yeah," I say. "You said that."

I look up at the falling snow. If everything weren't so crazy, it would be beautiful. The falling snow seems to muffle everything and the quiet is almost something you can touch, like putting a fuzzy blanket over your head.

"Well, we can't be that far from the ocean," I say.

"What do you mean?"

"Well, the flight path from Anchorage to Seattle is right over the west coast of British Columbia. When they took over the plane, they turned us inland for like, about 45 minutes before we landed in the lake."

"I wasn't really paying attention," she says.

"Yeah, well, there was a lot to think about," I say. "But I think, you know, if we turn west, we can make it to the ocean."

"What's that mean?" she asks.

"Like you said," I say, "I can make a fire with a shoelace. If we can get there, we can make a big fire, make a lot of smoke, and some plane or boat will see it. Or we can just keep moving down the coast. There's bound to be a fishing cabin or something like that."

"Yeah," she says hopefully. "Maybe...do you really think so?"

"I don't know how far it is," I answer. "But we can find another creek, get some fish."

"You really think so?" she asks. "Do you really think we can make it?"

"Yes," I say confidently. "Odds are Mr. Tan Jacket has either had to call in reinforcements or he turned back. Either way, we're probably in the clear – at least for a little while. The snow should cover over our trail too."

"Mr. Tan Jacket?"

"That's the name I thought of."

Misty stops picking at the bark on the tree. She shakes her head, scattering the snow off her hair. She wipes her face with both hands and then looks steadily at me.

"About...what happened this morning," she says. "I'm...I'm really sorry." The anger, fear and frustration have left her voice. "I'm sorry about...what you had to do."

I shrug my shoulders and look away. I don't know what to say or how to feel. I've spent most of my life wishing I could be a U.S. Marine, but Marines are trained to kill people in battle. Until today, I never thought about what it would feel like when you actually did it.

"I didn't mean to make you feel like it's all about me," I say.

"It's okay," she says. "I don't really think...I mean...I just felt, sort of, hopeless...you know? Everything is so..."

"Crazy?"

"Yeah."

I look back at her. Her face is smeared with dirt. Snow sticks to her eyelashes and her teeth chatter a little. That chatter makes me think about how cold I am too. We've been sitting still way too long.

"Let's just get out of here, okay?"

"Okay," she says. "Do you really think they've given up?"

"No," I say quickly, shaking my head. "They're not giving up. But I figure Mr. Tan Jacket is seriously hurt. Even if he could get hold of someone on his radio, it's going to take them a while to get to him if he lives. Then, they've got to find us and with this snowfall, I think our trail is going to get covered, at least up to this point."

211

"So, what do we do?" she asks.

"Well, I think we should quit running in a straight line for one thing. There's a mountain to the west so I figure we can head east for a little while, find a place to set up a shelter again, and get a fire going. It's a start."

"Okay."

"You're ready?" I ask.

"Yeah."

Misty hobbles to her feet, puts her arm around my neck, and we start walking - this time to the east. It feels downhill, so the going is a little easier, but the snow is beginning to fall heavily.

After an hour of staggering through the snow shower, the temperature has fallen so far that every step is an agony. We are chilled to the core. We have no choice. We have got to find some place to get out of the cold. If we don't get a fire going soon, we are both going to start hallucinating and eventually freeze to death. Misty hasn't said more than a few words since we started walking again. Her body shivers beside me. We're in real trouble.

I find a boulder about the size of a Volkswagen with a few trees growing next to it. There is a very small area at the base of the boulder that is still almost free of snow because of the trees. It's not an ideal location, not as perfect a set-up as the log by the creek last night, but it will have to do.

I brush as much of the snow away as I can and set Misty down with her back against the boulder. She isn't as protected as I would like, but I'm hopeful I can make something of a shelter. The forest is littered with fallen trees. Some of them are so big it would take a bulldozer to move them. Others are no more than saplings. I drag half a dozen of these smaller logs over to Misty, lift one end, and prop them against the top of the boulder. It's not much, but in a half an hour, I have at least created a space large enough for the two of us. The logs don't totally keep out the snow, so I start piling smaller branches on top. In another half an hour, I have something reasonable, but the temperature has dropped even further since I started working. I've sacrificed making a fire to build a shelter and I wonder if that was a big mistake. The snow continues to fall rapidly.

My hands feel like wooden clubs. I can't seem to get my fingers to grip anything tightly. Misty is so cold, she sits against the boulder with her legs drawn up to her chest. She has buried her face into her knees and I can hear an occasional whimper. If I don't get a fire started within a few minutes, it might be too late. My mind seems to have slowed to a crawl and I suddenly can't remember what step in making a fire I should be doing next. My temptation to crawl under the shelter of the logs and curl up against Misty is so strong I almost start crawling in. What stops me is a memory.

My dad wasn't a Navy Seal - he was a Marine. He used to joke and say that the Seals were almost as tough as the Marines; of course, I could tell he had no end of respect for them. He told me all about Seal training, about how the men would stay in the ocean for nearly a week until they were so cold, they began to hallucinate. That sort of torture in their training was intentional. They had to get to a place where every single action, even something as simple as taking a step, was completely deliberate, a conscious choice. Normally, we walk and move unconsciously, but when you get to a point of serious cold, you have to be so deliberate that you're literally telling yourself to put one foot in front of the other. That's where I'm at now.

My dad said he did Marine survival training up in the high Sierras in California and his instructor was a Seal. It wasn't as intense as Seal training, just seriously cold. His instructor made plenty of fun of the Marines for not being tough enough to get through it. He also taught them how to make it. He told them that when they got to a place where they had to tell themselves to take the next breath, "You're actually only at 40% of what you can really do. It's the 40% rule. When you get there, you still have 60% of your strength left, even though you feel like you can't take another step. It's then, only then, that your real strength comes out. You have to mentally, deliberately force yourself to the finish line."

I used to listen to my dad's stories with absolute fascination. Navy Seals. Marines. Tougher than the rest! The best of the best! I wanted to be in that group, but my back brace made that dream impossible.

Until today.

I shake my head. One step at a time, I will force myself to build a fire. I clear a space at the edge of the shelter next to the boulder out of the wind....one brush with a stick...then the next brush...and the next. One movement at a time...one decision at a time.

Misty is literally moaning behind me. We don't have much time. I have already set aside the driest wood I could find when I was dragging logs over for our shelter. I tear at the bark and rub it between the palms of my hands because my fingers won't work fine enough to break down the bark into a fine bundle of tender.

One movement at time. I talk to myself: "Set the bundle under the shelter to keep it out of the snow...make the spindle...untie your shoe...one loop at a time...pull the lace out of the loops in your shoe...reach for the base."

It's an agony. Somehow, I manage to get everything set up. I lean over the spindle. I pull the bow back and forth. I'm so cold that the rotation of the spindle almost mesmerizes me. I tell myself over and over, "40%, Marine! You're only at 40%."

I've always loved campfires. The smoke makes such beautiful shapes that weave and dance in the light. I love watching it curl and break into pieces and then form again.

Smoke!

The spindle has made just enough hot dust to make a tiny stream of smoke. The sight and smell bring me back. I clumsily pour the powder into the bundle and then blow. The bundle smokes, catches flame and five minutes later, we have a fire.

Seventeen

Misty is groggy and almost asleep by the time I get the fire going. I have a hard time getting her fully awake and I realize how close to freezing we must have been. From what I've heard, hypothermia is a deceptive way to die because it isn't scary. Your shivers sort of disappear and you just feel like going to sleep. "But if you do," George told me, "You'll wake up in heaven."

The snow still falls steadily, and the temperature is dropping nearly as fast, so I can't worry right now about anyone finding us. If we don't get warm, it won't matter if they find us because all they will find will be meat popsicles. If Mr. Tan Jacket called in reinforcements, it's going to take them some time to get to his location. Once they do, they'll have to try and track us, but I'm hoping the snowfall has covered over our trail decently. Besides, we're not running in a straight line away from them anymore. I've turned us to the east, back toward the lake. Add it all up and I think we might have at least a few hours before we have to keep our heads down again. In the meantime, I stoke up the fire. The hiss of melting snow makes me think about frying bacon and the thought doesn't comfort me.

"Misty, you need to wake up," I say.

She hasn't moved since I started propping up the logs for the lean-to. Her arms are still wrapped around her knees, her face buried in her arms with a mess of raven black hair scattered everywhere. I brush back her hair and gently shake her.

"Misty, come on," I say. "I've got a fire going."

She sighs quietly, raises her head, and half-opens her eyes.

"I'm really tired," she says.

Her words seem slow, as if every syllable is being made around a mouthful of marbles. "I don't feel very cold, you know."

That's a really bad sign. She doesn't make any move to brush the hair out of her eyes either or any effort to get closer to the fire. She's on autopilot. I touch her cheek and it's ice-cold.

"Come on, " I say, scooting close beside her. "Let's get a little closer to the fire."

I half push, half lift her a few feet toward the flames. Her arms sort of drop to the ground. It's almost as if she isn't thinking about them at all.

"I'm fine," she says slowly. "Really. I'm just tired. The fire's out there. I just want to stay here."

"I know," I say calmly. "But you'll feel better this way. Come on."

I push her again. She isn't resisting me, but she isn't helping either. I guess since I've been moving around dragging logs and sawing on a fire drill, I'm in a little better shape. Still, I'm shivering so hard, I'm afraid I'm going to break a tooth, but I don't feel any shivering in Misty at all. George told me the first sign of freezing to death is when you stop shivering and you stop thinking it's cold.

The fire isn't very large and the hiss of falling snow makes me worry it'll go out. I'll have to keep it stoked up higher than I want. Still, I would rather build a big fire with the risk rather than freeze to death.

I scoot Misty far enough out of the lean-to for her to feel the warmth of the fire. It doesn't take long for her to perk up. She starts warming her hands against the flames, but I notice that she isn't making any effort to brush the falling snow out of her hair. I force myself to get up, step away from our little fire, and stomp around looking for more wood, and it doesn't take long for me to start shivering so hard, I feel like I'm going to shake into little pieces. I keep pulling and dragging branches back to our boulder. I stack another set of long, slender branches from the top of the lean-to over to the top of the boulder, making a kind of secondary roof to block as much of the snowfall from over the fire as I can. I also stack even more branches onto the lean-to, remembering George's instructions to put an arm's-length amount on top of a lean-to to create some real insulation.

In an hour, I'm covered in a thin layer of ice crystals. My hands ache and look red. Within twenty yards or so of the lean-to I've found about as many loose branches and ferns for insulation as I can find, and I've rooted around under enough logs to build a reasonably dry stack of wood for the fire. It should last us through the night, so I guess there's not much more I can do.

Misty looks up at me and smiles when I finally kneel down and crawl into the entrance of the lean-to.

"I'm really sorry about what happened today," she says.

"Let's just get warm," I say. I don't want to talk about it, so I change the subject. I slide next to her behind her right shoulder and look into the fire. "Are you feeling better?"

"Yes," she says. "I was so tired for a while. Just tired of everything, you know?"

"I know what you mean," I say.

"You know, when you were trying to get the fire going, I was sort of, I don't know, zoned out. I was so cold, I felt like I couldn't move. I'm sorry I wasn't helping."

"That's okay. There wasn't anything you could have done really."

"What did you mean when you kept saying, 'One more step, Marine'."

I'm really surprised.

"I didn't know I was saying anything," I say.

And I didn't know she had been paying attention either.

"Yeah, you kept saying, 'One more step, Marine' and sometimes you would say, 'Keep moving, recruit'. What was that all about?"

I lean back a little from Misty's shoulder and rest my back against the boulder. We are far enough under the shelter of the lean-to to keep the snow off our heads. The reflection of the heat of the fire fills the tiny space in the lean-to and I'm reasonably comfortable for being half-starved and after having been nearly murdered twice in one day. I suppose I can talk about something other than our next move.

217

"My dad was a Marine," I say. Misty shifts her body and leans back against the boulder next to me. "That's all I ever wanted to be when I was a kid." She looks at me with interest, so I tell the story.

My dad joined the U.S. Marine Corps with written permission from his foster home guardians at the age of 17. Since he was an orphan without any family to support him going to college, he joined the Corps so he could get the G.I. Bill. He was surprised, he told me, when he totally fell in love with the Corps. The sense of honor and belonging was something he had never known before since he had been shuffled from one foster home to the next all his life.

He served four years as an air traffic controller and gained the rank of Corporal. Instead of re-enlisting, he decided to step out, go to college, get a degree, then go back to the Marines as an officer.

"Only it didn't work out that way," I say. "My dad started teaching private pilots how to fly Cessnas and he met my mother. He said he couldn't live without her, so he decided to become a commercial pilot instead of going back to the Marines."

"That's romantic," Misty says.

"That's what my mom used to say. Anyway, then I was born."

"So, he talked about the Marines?" Misty asked.

"Oh, yeah," I say. "All the time. We had to have a Marine sticker on every car. He even had one on his plane when we were ten thousand miles away from anyone who would even care."

"So that's why you want to be a Marine?"

"Wanted to be," I say. I pick up another branch and shove it into the fire with a little more force than is absolutely necessary. Some sparks pop out of the flames.

"You don't want to be anymore?" Misty asks.

"I can't," I say. "That's why I wear a back brace. Or I did until I tore it to pieces today."

I shift a little, so I can unbend one leg. Sitting crisscross always makes my legs go numb.

"I have this disease. It's called Scheuermann's Kyphosis. It's a genetic thing where the bones in your back are shaped like wedges instead of squares. That's why I have the hunchback I was telling you

218

about. You know, when I first got it, they said it wouldn't keep me out of the Corps because it's not like I have a weak back or anything; I just needed the bones to grow right."

"Well, if it's not a problem, why can't you be a Marine?"

"Because somebody lied," I answer a little harshly. I've given this whole thing a lot of thought. "The doctor that put me in the stupid thing was an orthopedic surgeon and he retired as a doctor from the Navy. I totally believed him. That's why I worked out all the time so that when I got rid of the brace, I wouldn't be all weak and stuff. I wanted to toss the brace away one day and join the Marines the next. Only it didn't work out that way."

"What happened?"

"A couple of months ago, I went in to see the recruiter. I'm a senior. I'm supposed to get out of the brace in a few months, so I figured I would get the ball rolling, you know? So, I went to MEPS, that's the Military Entrance Processing Station, did the whole physical and then...they failed me."

I put another branch on the fire. The snowfall has slowed to just a few flakes every few minutes. I shift my position again, pull my knees up, and lock my arms around my shins. I stare into the flames, lost a little in the weaving light, lost in the past.

"I guess it's worse than the doctor said it was or something. I mean I worked out for years, so I didn't look...weak or anything, but my right shoulder is obviously lower than my left. They spotted it, took a bunch of x-rays and said – 'Go home, kid.'"

"I'm sorry," Misty says. She puts her hand on my shoulder. I just keep looking into the fire.

"That's all I ever wanted to be," I say. "We went to the mission field when I was nine and I've lived all over the world. But I listened to my dad and I daydreamed about being a Marine. I worked out. I started taking college courses online when I was fifteen. Heck, by the time I graduate from St. Mark's I'll already have an Associate's Degree."

"No way, really?" says Misty.

219

"Yeah. After the crash...I sort of stayed in my room all the time. Taking online classes was kind of...I don't know...took my mind off everything. I thought once I joined, an Associate's Degree would bump me up to, like, Lance Corporal right out of basic. I was so pumped...until August and the whole MEPS thing."

Misty stretches out a little, and then leans onto one arm so her bent legs are laid out lengthwise to the fire. The snow has basically stopped falling, a few flakes drift around like albino fireflies drifting in the breeze. The reflection of the heat of the fire fills our little shelter. We're both finally warm and reasonably comfortable...just not at the Hilton.

"I never thought about joining the Army or anything like that," Misty says. "It just sounds too, like, physical, you know?"

"I guess," I say.

I don't want to say something stupid like, 'That's because you're a girl' because I've known plenty of women who are tough enough to be Marines. It's just that Misty is definitely not one of those kinds of girls.

"It's not that bad."

"As far as you know," she says. "I've seen a few Youtubes about it. It looks brutal."

"No, just really intense. I got to try it out, so I know."

"What do you mean, 'try it out?'" she asks.

"I got to go to this Marine prep school kind of thing called Devil Pups for ten days. We got yelled at by the D.I.'s just like the regular recruits. It was pretty cool."

"Really?" she says with a little smile. "Is that why you're so intense?"

"I'm not intense," I say. "I'm just...determined."

Misty laughs. It's so nice to hear something lighthearted. I smile in return.

"Well...Devil Pups was kind of intense," I say.

"What was it like?"

"Ah well...it was really a lot of fun..."

I unwrap my arms from around my shins, stretch my legs out next to Misty's and look at her. Her face has lost the panic that clouded her eyes just a few hours ago, but I can tell she's still on the edge. We're not going anywhere until probably sometime tomorrow, it's not dark yet, and there's nothing else to do so I tell her all about Devil Pups.

It was in the summer right before my fourteenth birthday and just a few weeks before I was diagnosed for the back brace. We had just come back from the mission field for a summer furlough. Since my parents were missionaries, we got to stay in this nice Christian conference center in the San Jacinto Mountains just outside of Los Angeles called "Peaceful Pines". We stayed in a huge, two-story cabin with our own kitchen, every board game known to mankind, and no television. Needless to say, as an almost-fourteen-year-old who had just flown in from Alaska, I was ready for a little more than board games and no TV. I roamed the woods around the camp and begged my parents to take me into the nearby town of Idyllwild pretty much every day.

I was bored and starting to become a raging teenage pain in the neck - simple as that! My parents needed a solution before it came to serious confrontation, so my dad thought of the Devil Pup program. He knew all about it from his days in the Marines. Basically, Devil Pups takes teenagers to Marine Corps Base, Camp Pendleton and teaches them a little something about how to be respectful instead of a raging teenage pain in the neck. It's what my dad knew I needed. The Devil Pups website says the program is all about building self-confidence and character, but the real deal was a little more intense.

Dad didn't tell me exactly what I was getting into either. He said it was nothing more than a ten-day opportunity to tour Camp Pendleton. What he didn't tell me is that I was going to pretty much do everything the Marine recruits did, except carry a weapon. And when I say everything, I mean everything. Five mile runs, fighter town, crawling up mountains with a pack so heavy you could fall backwards and literally not be able to get up…yeah…everything.

My dad signed me up and a week later, I was on a bus heading for Oceanside, California. I remember realizing I was in for something a little different than a nice tour of Camp Pendleton when we pulled into a parking lot off of John Basilone Road and I saw a line of Marines standing in rigid 'parade rest' position waiting for us. When the bus stopped, the ugliest, meanest gunnery sergeant I've ever even heard of climbed onto our bus and started screaming at the top of his lungs that we had better get off of "his" bus before he ripped our heads off and urinated on our brains.

I have never seen forty teenagers get off of a bus so fast. But it wasn't fast enough. Gunnery Sergeant Raymond and half a dozen other Marines were everywhere, bellowing two inches from our ears so loudly and so fast, we couldn't make out a word they were saying. All I knew is that I was in trouble.

The next few days were a blur. I did so many pushups and leg lifts that my arms and stomach felt like they were transformed into rubber. One of the things I remember most vividly was going to the bathroom or "the head" as the Marines call it. Gunny Raymond marched us into the head where I saw a line of ten toilets and no dividers. He placed ten of us up in front of a toilet, made us stand at attention, and said, "Sit, poop and get out. You have five minutes."

I remember thinking, "That ain't happening."

Having to do my business sitting half-naked next to nine other teenage guys was nerve wracking. In fact, I was so constipated by day three I was ready to give way into my trousers. That was also the day I figured out what they were trying to teach us. If you want to survive, you have to learn to get past what makes you feel uncomfortable - and that's just a choice of the will.

"So, by the fourth day, we were getting it done and having full-on conversations at the same time."

"That is so gross," Misty says.

"Maybe," I say. "But that was the only five minutes where we didn't have a D.I. hollering in our face about something."

"That does not sound like a lot of fun to me," she says.

"Getting used to sitting on a toilet was easy compared to the gas chamber."

"The gas chamber," she says incredulously.

"Yeah, they gave us gas masks, showed us how to make sure they were tight on our face and how to clear them if the gas got in."

"They really made you go into a gas chamber?" she asks. "That's crazy."

"It was better than that. Once we got inside, someone had popped off a smoke bomb so there was smoke everywhere and you couldn't hardly see. Then, the DI tells us to take the mask off, say your name and where you were from, then put it back on and clear it like they showed us. So, I do. I get it all cleared, I'm breathing fine and then...well...I was the first guy into the room which means I was going to be the last guy to get out of the room. They started us out and some Marine starts pulling our gas masks off."

"No way," Misty says.

"I'm telling you, I felt like four billion bees slid down my throat and started stinging my lungs at the same time."

"That's horrible."

"I totally panicked and opened my eyes, so I got this blast of tear gas. My eyes lit on fire. I felt like a gallon of snot poured out of my nose."

"Oh, that's so gross," she says, laughing.

"I'm like, crawling over the guy in front of me. It was everyone for himself, but I couldn't find the door. It was like a slipperyslide. Everyone was covered in sneeze juice and I'm like, bouncing off of walls with snot pouring down my chin."

I mimic my movements that day with my hands. Misty is in full belly laugh.

"So, I feel these arms grab hold of me and throw me out the door. I'm still swinging my arms and hacking up a lung. It was awesome."

"That's horrible. How can you still want to do that?"

I guess that's a good question. At the time, all I wanted to do was go home. Now, all I do is wish I could go to MCRD and do the real thing.

"I don't know...there was something about it," I say. "When I got off the bus, I thought I was in for it, but by the time we graduated ten days later, I had something else. I felt like I belonged. I felt...special. I wasn't a real Marine but...still, it felt like I was a part of it. A part of the Corps."

And I did. I know now that I can never be a real Marine. But I had ten days - ten special days. They ran us into the ground, screamed everything known to man in our ears, made us crawl through the mud and jump off a forty-foot tower into a swimming pool. They called us maggots and scum-beasts and they said the highest compliment they would ever give would be to say, 'You would make a good Marine'."

And that's what Gunny Raymond whispered in my ear on graduation day. When I tell Misty, she nods her head.

"That's cool," she says. "Really." Misty pulls her legs back into a criss-cross. She picks up a twig and starts tearing it apart. "And I don't care what the recruiter said," she says. "You're a Marine to me."

Once again, just when I thought I had her all figured out, Misty takes me by surprise. I'm not sure how to take it. Part of me wants to throw out my chest and say "ooo rah", and another part of me wants to cry. The wrong half wins and I feel my eyes start to well up. I try to cover it by turning to grab another handful of branches for the fire.

"What are you going to do now?" she asks. "There's no way to get past the back brace?"

"No," I say. "I've already tried. I got my doctor to write a letter and I got a response the day before we left on this trip. It's no-go. They're just...it's not going to happen."

"So, what are you going to do?" I shrug my shoulders. I have certainly given this a lot of thought, but that doesn't mean I really have it figured out.

"I don't know," I say quietly. "I thought about...being a missionary. I've been on the mission field since I was nine. It's not a mystery to me."

"Where would you go?"

"France," I say without hesitation. "I've only been there twice, but there was something about it. And I love the language."

"Do you speak French?" she asks.

"Non, pas de tout…" I answer. "That means, 'No, not at all'."

"But you can say: 'not at all.'"

"Well, that's about all."

Misty laughs and leans back against the boulder. She stretches, arches her back, and pulls her arms high above her head showing me every inch of her figure. I nearly choke. I've seen beautiful before, but I swear, when God invented beautiful, He must have been thinking about Misty. I clear my throat and tear my eyes away just as she finishes her stretch and looks back at me.

"So," she says, "You would go to France and be a missionary? I believe in God, you know?"

"So do I," I say.

"Do you want to be a missionary because…you know, your parents and the crash and everything?"

"I guess. Well, a lot of the missionary kids I knew didn't stay on the field. As soon as they were old enough, they went back. I know one girl we met in Africa…as soon as she was eighteen, she took the first flight back to Atlanta. I heard from someone that she's a college student now and doing all sorts of stupid stuff."

Actually, I heard it was worse than stupid stuff. A friend of my mother's said she had had an abortion and then tried to commit suicide. I don't think talking about suicide with Misty is a good idea, so I don't say anything.

"So, why don't you want to come back?"

It's the question I've been asking myself since the crash. When I was out there living in a log cabin in Alaska or a half-built mud hut in Africa, all I wanted to do was go home and join the Marine Corps. But after the crash and moving in with my uncle's family, I found myself daydreaming over and over again about all the places I'd been. Now that the Marines have decided I'm not good enough for them, my daydreaming about the mission field has become an all-day

225

habit. But there's more to it than just memories of jungles and Alaskan forests.

"Because I really believe," I say quietly.

I stare into the fire and realize I wasn't answering Misty's question. I was answering my own question.

"I believe in God," Misty says again. "We don't go to church a lot anymore, but when me and my sister went to church, we just...loved the Sunday School. It was like our favorite thing. And when my sister died, my mom was really mad at God. But I wasn't. I remember thinking, 'God didn't do this. Mary did.' I don't know why, but it seemed like I believed more after she died than I did before."

"Yeah," I say softly.

I'm listening to her voice, but in my mind, I'm back in New Guinea on the day they told me my parents were dead. It was like a hole the size of the Grand Canyon opened inside my chest. But it never crossed my mind to think that God wasn't real. I couldn't figure out why God would let something like this happen, but I never doubted that He was real.

"I know what you mean," I say. "I didn't like Sunday School. I was so sick of the same stories and the same songs and it was like every church on the planet had the same photocopied worksheets about how Zachius was a wee little man and a wee little man was he..."

I look up and Misty smiles at me. "I remember that song," she says.

"Well, I didn't start believing because of Sunday School. Or even because of my parents. I remember when I was twelve or thirteen, I don't remember exactly, but we were at some kind of conference in California. Maybe it was the same time I went to Devil Pups, I don't remember, but we went to this little Christian and Missionary Alliance church one night and there was this guy talking about evolution and the Bible. He was a doctor, not a pastor, and I don't think I really understood what he was saying. He talked about all kinds of evidence and fossils and how there wasn't anything in science that went against the Bible. But what got to me was when he said, 'The Big Bang Theory says that absolutely everything came from absolutely nothing for absolutely no reason at all. So, you either believe everything came from nothing or you believe everything came from God. And everybody knows that nothing can't do anything.' That was, like, really wild to me."

Misty doesn't say anything, but she glances up when a snowflake touches her forehead. I follow her eyes. Another snow shower is beginning.

"You should get in behind me," I say to Misty. I scoot to my right to give her room to crawl back into the lean-to.

"Thanks."

Misty pulls her right leg out of her criss-cross and I see her wince. She leans forward and massages her calf.

"That's really hurt, isn't it?" I say.

"Yeah, but I don't think it's broken," she says.

"Why not?"

"Because I broke my other ankle when I was twelve and it was way more painful than this. It's probably seriously sprained. It's really swollen."

I lean forward to look. I can't help but notice the rest of her leg too. Misty must have noticed.

"It's only the ankle that's hurt," she says.

I pull my eyes away and look down at the fire again. I don't know what to say, but Misty just laughs.

"I guess. Maybe," I say.

I try to look back at her without sliding my eyes along the entire length of her outstretched leg. When I glance at her face, I see a look of shock and terror.

I whip my head around.

Mr. Tan Jacket stands just outside of the circle of our firelight, clutching his right side with his arm. There's dried blood on his pants and in his other hand he holds a gun, aimed right at my face.

I just recognize the look of fury and hate in his eyes when he pulls the trigger.

Eighteen

The bullet tears a nasty furrow into my left shoulder as it singes past me and lodges in the lean-to pole right behind my left ear. Hot blood boils out of the wound and spills down my arm. Misty screams and I fall backwards, clutching my wounded shoulder. Pain stings through my arm from shoulder to wrist in a split second and I can't help crying out. Misty leaps forward to try and cover me with her own body. Mr. Tan Jacket stomps forward like a soldier on parade until he is right on top of me, his gun pointed in my face.

"I missed on purpose," he snarls through grit teeth. "Just so you can bleed."

He pushes the weapon closer. At this distance, he can't miss even if he tried.

I'm really going to die this time. I wonder for a split second if the pain of dying holds on or if you just sort of float away. Mr. Tan Jacket purses his lips as if reminded of something unpleasant. He snarls with a vocal explosion of frustration and rage like a rabid dog, but he doesn't fire yet; Misty is not in the path of his shot, so keeping her from getting killed can't be the reason he hesitates.

"I should kill you now," he says.

His black eyes bore into mine. There is nothing except emptiness and hate in Mr. Tan Jacket's face. I begin to tremble. My arms feel weak, as if they are made of frozen gelatin and will crumble at any moment. I've daydreamed enough about being a Marine, being a hero in battle. But facing a man holding a gun in my face, a man I've already seen heartlessly kill people, I feel more along the lines of crying like a six-year-old kid who is afraid of the dark than anything else. Misty holds onto the crook of my right arm since I'm clutching my shoulder with my hand. She has her hand over her mouth, eyes as wide and round as a DVD disk, shaking with wracking sobs. Knowing she is there, knowing she is watching, makes me determined to make a stand. I grit my teeth and narrow my eyes until I'm almost daring him with my look to pull the trigger. I don't know what to say or do. I only know if I've only got three seconds left on this earth, I'm going to make it count.

"Semper Fi," I say quietly.

Mr. Tan Jacket brings the barrel of the gun to within four or five inches of my forehead. The cold drops of the falling snow touch my upturned face, melting on contact. For one split second, everything seems deathly still.

"I have killed many of your Marines," he says. "In Iraq." But he doesn't fire. Slowly, he backs away. "But you are just a boy. I heard you talking."

Mr. Tan Jacket glances over at the fire. He circles around the fire to the mouth of our little lean-to, never letting his aim stray from my face. He leans back against the boulder and involuntarily winces in pain. Obviously, the wound in his side is serious. I hope he's bleeding to death! Not a very Christian thought – but right now, I don't care…

"Her ankle is hurt," he says. "So, you will live long enough to carry her. But if you try anything, I will kill you."

A confusing wave of hope and fear slides over me like a quivering, cold electric current. Somehow, I've been given another chance to keep breathing. I look over at my shoulder. It's not really a bad cut at all, more like a scrape. I've been hurt worse falling off a skateboard. It's just that this scrape came from a bullet – and that makes it scary. I better push my advantage with Mr. Tan Jacket or it won't last long.

"If you kill me…you won't be able to carry her," I say. "You don't look so good."

"I won't care then," he says. "You carry her, you live. You try to run again, we all die."

I believe him! I believed from the start that Misty was the prize; now I'm certain of it. His obsession with finding her, even with a nasty gash in his side and after losing a lot of blood, doesn't make sense unless Misty is the whole reason for the hijacking in the first place. He has at least fifty or sixty other hostages, some of them from the wealthiest families in the Pacific Northwest, but he's out here – looking for her while shivering from the cold and risking death by infection. Misty is more than an obsession – she's the reason for the whole operation. I just don't know why.

The snowfall is now a snow shower. Thick, white blotches of snow fall so thick and fast, I can barely see Mr. Tan Jacket on the other side of the fire. The hiss and crack from the fire is so rapid, I'm genuinely afraid the fire is going to be drowned out. My recent effort to put some sticks between the boulder and the lean-to to act like a mini-roof over the fire is practically useless.

Misty sits up next to me, staring at Mr. Tan Jacket with a look of loathing and contempt. She brushes the snow out of her hair. Within seconds, she's covered up again.

"I don't think we're going anywhere in this," I say. "We'll freeze to death if we don't keep the fire going."

"You think I don't know?" Mr. Tan Jacket asks. "I come from the mountains in Afghanistan. I know the cold."

Mr. Tan Jacket slowly slides forward, closer to the fire. Shockingly, he puts the gun into his coat pocket. I'm too stunned to think of what to do before he suddenly lashes out with his gun hand, now that it's empty. He grabs Misty by the hair, jerking her back toward him. She shrieks as her right arm plunges into the fire. I jump to my feet. Misty scrambles out of the fire on all fours, but Mr. Tan Jacket doesn't let go of her hair.

"Let go, let go, I'm burning!" Misty yells.

"Let her go!" I yell.

I crouch down ready to literally dive right over the campfire at him. Since he's put the gun away, I figure I'll take him down.

Mr. Tan Jacket, using his free hand, pulls out a huge pocketknife. He flips it open with his thumb, yanks Misty's head back with a vicious jerk, and slides the blade of the knife up to her throat. She screams again and collapses back into Mr. Tan Jacket's chest.

"You will keep the fire going," he says. "If you don't…or you try to run…I won't kill her. I will just carve off pieces of her filthy face."

"If you hurt her…"

"I will, and you can do nothing," he spits back at me. "I don't care to die, but you care if she lives. We want her at the camp…negotiation, you see."

I still crouch across the fire, tensed and ready. Mr. Tan Jacket's eyes blaze like burning black coals and I know he will cut her to ribbons if I don't do what he wants.

"Get the wood," he says. "You better try to keep the fire covered. You wouldn't want the snow to put it out…bad things will happen if you do."

I slowly straighten up. "I keep the fire, you leave her alone?"

"Depends on the fire, doesn't it?" he asks.

Misty moves slightly. Mr. Tan Jacket nicks her chin with the tip of the knife and Misty groans. Her hair is such a wild mess I can't even see her eyes, but I can see the bright streak of blood dripping down her neck.

"Okay, okay," I say, throwing my hands out, palms forward. "Alright. I'll get wood, keep the fire up. Just leave her alone."

"We shall see," he says. He doesn't move, but he doesn't hurt her anymore either.

I move slowly, afraid to spook him into really hurting her. I know he wants her to survive. I'm just not completely convinced he won't cut her face into hamburger just because he hates me. I pull out what little dry wood I have already put near the lean-to and stoke up the fire. There's no sense keeping it small any longer. He wants a fire – fine! I'll give him a Fourth of July bonfire!

The snow falls heavily and since I don't have any gloves, my hands are red and painful from the cold. I step away from the fire and begin thrashing around in the nearby underbrush looking for wood. I have to find branches buried under other branches or fallen trees for any hope of finding something dry. Within a few minutes, I

231

begin to shiver violently. I shove one hand into my pocket while working with the other. In a few seconds, my fingers are so cold I can barely stand it. Frostbite is a very real possibility, but I have to keep working. After about half an hour, I have a pretty good armful of reasonably dry wood.

Back at the camp, I see that Mr. Tan Jacket has retreated into the lean-to. Misty sits directly in front of him in the entrance. Neither of them speaks. I can still see the knife in Mr. Tan Jacket's hand. He doesn't have it touching her skin, but in one swift motion, he could stab her if he wants.

I drop the load of wood next to the fire and head back into the woods. I set up a system, alternately warming my hands under my armpits, kicking logs over with my feet, using my left hand first, then my right to pull out anything promising. In an hour, I have piled enough dry wood next to the boulder to probably last most of the night. The boulder only affords so much protection for the wood and the fire from the snow, but it's not a complete failure. The fire still burns strong although there is a muddy trail drifting away from the lean-to into the forest floor. There is already a snowdrift at least waist-high piling up at the back of the lean-to.

This isn't a bad thing. George told me that natives learned long ago how snow is a great insulator. That's an irony, considering that snow is fluffy ice. But there is a reason that igloos worked as shelters. Once the snow gets to a certain thickness, warm air will get trapped in pockets. A good snow cave won't be toasty, just warm enough to keep you from freezing to death. I expect the lean-to is going to be almost completely covered in a couple of hours. I also expect Mr. Tan Jacket isn't going to invite me inside either. Not that I really want to be anywhere near him. Still, I've got to figure out some way to keep myself from freezing to death or getting frostbite. Just sitting in front of the fire with my back to the boulder isn't going to be enough.

Misty appears to be lying down now, but the terrorist is as vigilant as ever. I see his eyes glint out of the dark like smoldering coals, never wavering as he watches me work.

The snow isn't letting up and it's getting dark fast. I wander out into the snow again and gather some longer branches to make another small lean-to, just large enough to slide into by myself. It takes a lot longer than I want. After an hour or so of shivering and piling branches up against the boulder, I'm fairly satisfied with my creation. Every few minutes, I glance over at the other lean-to and every time, I see Mr. Tan Jacket glowering at me from the shadows. Not once do I look over that I don't see him staring at me. He doesn't say a word and Misty still lays in a fetal position deeper in the lean-to, not far from the killer's feet. There's no chance to talk to her and I've got nothing to do except try and get out of the cold myself and wait for morning.

I stoke up the fire and slide into my mini-shelter. It doesn't feel much better than being in the open wind and the ground is like ice. Still, it's better than just sitting in front of the fire. There's nothing to eat and nothing to do except wait. I wrap my arms around my chest and stare at the flames. My shoulder stings from the bullet cut and I'm exhausted. It suddenly occurs to me I haven't heated up any rocks to bury underneath me like I did the first night. I curse at myself and pull back out of the little shelter.

I fish around at the edge of the boulder where there isn't any snow for some rocks. I find half a dozen, place them carefully in the fire, and add some more wood. The sun has set, the twilight fades, and the lonely dark of night sinks down on us like a cold, wet blanket. I glance again at the lean-to. In the flickering light of the fire, I see that Mr. Tan Jacket hasn't moved. He still stares at me and for a second, I wonder if he's asleep with his eyes open, but he finally blinks. He doesn't take his eyes off me.

"What are you doing?" he asks.

I jump because I'm not expecting his voice. I'm not in the mood for conversation, but I suppose I better answer.

"Warming up rocks," I say. "Bury them just below the surface and you can feel the warmth all night."

"Very clever," he says. "You think you're smart?"

I don't answer...because I want to tell him that if stupid had a face, it would be his. Instead, I use a stick to roll my rocks around in the flames. I wonder if I can throw one hard enough and accurate enough to plug him right between the eyes. Unfortunately, I was never any good at baseball and if I miss, he won't kill Misty or me – he will just carve her up like a turkey and make me watch.

"If you do what I tell you," he says, "I will let you live."

"Why would you?" I turn to face him since I've really got nothing to lose. "Why should I believe you?"

"It is good for negotiation, yes?" he says. "The Vice-President's daughter and her boyfriend. Good headline, don't you think?"

Except I'm not her boyfriend. Until forty-eight hours ago, I was more or less an annoying piece of gum on the bottom of her shoe. I'm not going to tell him that and I don't hear Misty saying anything to correct him on the boyfriend issue either. I can't tell if she's asleep or just scared to death.

Here's what I know for sure. Mr. Tan Jacket is a cold-blooded killer and he isn't afraid to die for his cause. It was absolutely insane to land a passenger jet in a lake and not expect to cartwheel into fifty thousand pieces of aluminum and body parts. I think he was as surprised as anyone else that we survived. He's just a suicide bomber with a short-circuit in his trigger switch. I think he only wants to negotiate to get someone like the Vice-President close enough, so he can hit the real trigger. He might keep me alive, so I can half-carry Misty back to wherever he has the rest of the passengers holed up, but in the end, he'll kill us all.

I turn my face back to the fire. Mr. Tan Jacket doesn't seem to want to talk anymore, so I ignore him. I turn my back on him and scratch out a shallow trench in the ground of my little shelter. I turn back to the fire, fish out the rocks with two sticks, and bury them in the trench. I slide into the shelter, roll onto my side, and curl into a little ball. I'm under no illusion I'm going to sleep, but I can at least try to stay warm.

It's colder than last night. It's not just the snow that's making it cold. An icy yet gentle breeze begins to pick up, like a thick layer of

234

cold air trying to sneak in under the falling snow. A tiny trickle of warmth comes from the rocks I buried beneath me and the top of my head is warm because of the fire, but I'm back to the dripping, icicle nose again. My nose isn't going to feel dry for a second…all night long. It's so insane to be lying ten feet away from a murdering psycho.

Despite everything, I'm a little dozy and while I try not to think about it, I can't help seeing Mr. Red Jacket's face in the water again. My hands begin to tremble, and I relive the shudder of his last gasp at life once again. I wonder if that memory will ever fade or if every time I try to sleep, it will come back to me, like my own personal demon, lurking in the dark, waiting to pounce on me every night. I wonder what the difference is between Mr. Tan Jacket and me.

After all, we're both killers.

I killed a man…no…two men. I'm only seventeen and I killed two people with my bare hands. I drowned a man. His struggle in my arms was a desperate grasp at life, a final begging with the last of his strength for just one more lungful of air…and I just held him down. I didn't give him a chance. There was no do-over, no chance to say, "I'm sorry – just let us go and I'll let you go." And then, I pushed at the end of a log until a man fell shrieking to his death onto razor-sharp rocks. I saw the terror in his eyes when he fell into the ravine and I didn't stop pushing at the log. I didn't give him a chance either. I just killed him.

I know they had guns and they were trying to kill me and kill Misty too. I know I had a right to stop them from killing me. I know there's pretty much no chance they wouldn't have killed me if I hadn't stopped them. It just doesn't help to know all that. I feel so sick, like there's an eerie, dark emptiness inside my chest, a vacuum that's sucking away my ability to keep from trembling.

So, I can't help the tears. I don't want to cry, and I really don't want the scumbag sitting in the dark behind me to know I'm crying. But I can't help it. It's not going to get better. I can't just go home. I don't have a home to go to anyway. My parents are dead. I don't really have any friends. I hate the stupid school I'm forced to go to. I

235

hate having a twisted up back that hurts me every single day. I hate that I'll never be a Marine, that Mr. Tan Jacket is going to frog march me somewhere, only to smash my skull into bloody puzzle pieces with a bullet in the end. And I can't get that feeling of the death shudder out of my fingertips. It's like having touched something so foul the very thought of it brings back the smell, and no matter how many times you wash your hands, you can't seem to get the stink to go away. It's because the smell isn't on your hands – it's in the heart. The smell of death is in my heart.

I close my eyes and think about my dad. Thinking about him calms me and my tears finally stop. What scares me now is how I'm having a hard time seeing Dad's face in my mind. In fact, I don't see his face anymore in my memory. It's more like an impression or a sense of him that comes to me as I think of him. If I had to tell a sketch artist what he looked like, I would probably fail. I only know now what he felt like in my heart – powerful, dependable, always confident and ready. I always felt uncertain about my own decision-making powers because Dad always seemed to know what to do. I never had to decide anything really - Dad decided.

A few minutes pass, or maybe it's an hour or more – I can't really tell. I open my eyes and peer through the web of sticks and branches I piled up to build my mini lean-to at the light from the fire. I watch it slowly gnaw away at its fuel. Clouds of steam and smoke billow upward, drawing my drowsy vision into thoughts of foamy waves crashing against a distant shore.

After what feels like half the night, the fire burns lower. I have to keep it going or there will be a penalty I don't want to pay. I wiggle halfway out of the lean-to and add some branches to the flames. Just this much exposure shows me how dreadfully cold it really is tonight. I can see my breath in clouds almost as thick as the smoke from the fire. I'm nearly driven back into my tiny shelter from the pressing cold. It's still cold inside, but now I know it's not as cold as being out in the open air. That's at least one thing I can be thankful for…I guess.

Thankful. What a rotten word. When you're curled up in a ball under a pile of branches that only barely keeps a deadly cold from consuming your flesh in frostbite, it's a little hard to be thankful. But, the thought of being thankful for at least a little warmth gets me to thinking about Dad and Mom again. And that's a good thing.

My parents were like the Thanksgiving police. They were always happy, even though they gave up very lucrative careers in the airline industry to fly little puddle jumpers into some of the most remote places on earth. That's why I was trained to say "thank you" for just about everything because we were not in the missionary pilot business as a family for any wonderful salary or benefits. Every little good thing that might come our way, no matter how insignificant, was considered a gigantic blessing. There wasn't a whole lot of salary and benefits in living for months out of suitcases and taking "bucket baths."

Yeah…I had to learn to be thankful for bucket baths. That's what my mom called it. She would boil some water on whatever excuse for a stove we had and use the boiling water to half fill a ten-gallon plastic bucket that was once filled with laundry detergent. Then, she filled up the rest of the bucket with cold water to create a warm mix. She would hand me a plastic cup we had carried all the way from a McDonald's we once visited in Atlanta and she would tell me to "thank God for bucket baths."

A bucket bath begins by standing stark-naked with one foot in the bucket. You scoop up some water with the cup, pour it all over, soap down, and then get another scoop of water to rinse off. It was always my goal to get this procedure over with as soon as humanly possible, so I could get a towel wrapped around my nether regions as quickly as I could. I became an expert at the two-minute bucket bath because this exercise can be a seriously chilly experience. There was also the fear that whatever sheet we had hung over the bucket bath arena might just blow away when I was in mid-soap. Bucket baths were an exercise in extremes too. One second, I was groaning with pleasure at the warm water sliding gloriously over my skin. The next,

I was gritting my teeth against the blast of cold air that sent sheets of goose bumps over every square inch of my body.

And it was also an exercise in faith! Since many of the places we lived in had outhouses instead of actual bathrooms, our bucket bathroom might be a corner behind the house or trailer hidden by an old sheet mom would hang up on a tree limb, so the chances of embarrassing exposure to local eyes was high. We even did bucket baths under the wing of the airplane on occasion.

I first had to take bucket baths in West Africa. It was an incredibly dusty, windy place. It seemed like after every bucket bath in Cameroon, I ended up dirtier than when I started. The dust would blow up on my wet skin and coat me in a fine, flour-like powder that tasted like cow manure. The dust looked a lot like the foundation make-up my mom used too. My dad and mom insisted that I not only take a bucket bath…everyday…in every kind of weather…but they made me list out ten reasons to be thankful every day. Like I say – Thanksgiving police. I never put the bucket bath on my thanksgiving list.

Until I saw Jean-Paul!

I was maybe ten or so, maybe eleven…don't remember…when I saw Jean-Paul. We had been in Cameroon for about eight months when a local woman brought him into the mission station. The Cameroon mission station had a two-room medical clinic, a church building, a small tin airplane hangar next to a dusty strip of dirt we called a runway, and two mud huts where we parked our sleeping cots.

The medical clinic was like a hotel in Paris as far as the locals were concerned. Short-term mission workers had built it. The short-term guys were mostly middle-class people from the States who come out for a few weeks every year to do work projects for missionaries. In this case, they had carted in enough western construction materials to build a clinic that had an actual concrete floor and…glory of glories…real toilet paper and a working, flushing toilet. Like I said – hotel in Paris!

So, people came from miles around to admire the concrete floor and the flushing toilet. Actually, they came because our two Canadian nurses were the only medically trained people in the whole district. This is why Jean-Paul ended up there.

Jean-Paul was a premature baby boy who weighed no more than three pounds. My mom tried to shield me from the sight of him, but I was a ten-year-old boy with nothing to do but homeschool. I couldn't help sneaking into the clinic through the back door to see what all the fuss was about. The nurses were frantic trying to keep Jean-Paul alive.

He had been born to a poor famer's wife about eight days before he came to the clinic. The mother died because of the hard birth. The father thought the baby was cursed because the mother died, so he literally threw the baby out into the village trash heap. I found out later this wasn't an uncommon experience.

A local girl felt sorry for Jean-Paul. She fished him out of the trash heap, but there was really nothing she could do for him. That part of Cameroon was very rural, very dry during that season of the year, and it wasn't like she could just pop on down to the local grocery store and buy some formula to feed him. She did the best she could and tried to feed him cold tea by squeezing drops into his mouth from a dirty cloth. Since Jean-Paul had been left in the trash heap for about twelve hours, he was covered in bug bites, dirt and manure and that caused a horrible skin infection.

That really got my attention at the time because his skin was covered in pus-filled bumps. The girl who rescued him had no way to clean him off since water was at a premium. That's when it hit me. I had grown so used to nice showers and bathtubs and plenty of hot water in the United States. I took clean water and showers for granted, so I was grumpy about having to take bucket baths. Watching Jean-Paul slowly die from a skin infection because he had never had a bath changed my attitude in a hurry.

They put him in a little burial shroud after he died during his second night in the clinic. I remember the very next bucket bath I took too, right under the pilot's side wing of the airplane. I remember saying, "Thanks for the hot water, Mom."

"You're welcome, sweetheart," she said. "Where did you get your smile today?" I sort of shrugged my shoulders.

"I don't know," I said evasively. "I guess it's just a good thing that I get to clean my skin."

"Oh," she said knowingly. "You're right, baby-face. That's why we need to be thankful, even for the little things."

Suddenly, a harsh, croaking voice shakes me awake. I must have fallen into some sort of sleep thinking about Mom and Jean-Paul.

"Get up!" Mr. Tan Jacket shouts.

This is not in Cameroon! I'm curled up in a ball under a pile of sticks in the snow.

And Mr. Tan Jacket wants to kill me.

Nineteen

I roll over and look through a crack in the branches of my lean-to. Mr. Tan Jacket stands outside the other shelter, still clutching his side, and I can see the dark stain of dried blood on his shirt. Even from a distance, he looks pale and sick, like a Halloween mannequin made up to look like a murder victim. I can only hope he dies for real. Misty sits at the edge of what's left of the fire, warming her hands over the coals. The fire has burned down considerably, but there are still red-hot coals shimmering in the early morning light.

I scramble out of my shelter and Misty looks up at me, smiling a little. I'm not sure what to do or what to say. It's not like I can suggest we all have breakfast and talk over our agenda for the day. *Oh look – isn't it a lovely day, camping in the woods*! I mean, what do you say to the terrorist hovering like a bird of prey over his prime hostage? I don't suppose saying "good morning" is the right thing to say - so I say nothing at all.

The snow must have stopped falling in the night. Above me, the clouds are thick and low, gray and heavy, and a white blanket cloaks the rocks and bushes all around us. The trees are so heavy with snow it's difficult to make out the shape of branches and twigs. It looks like a billion lumps of cotton stacked up to look like trees. Strangely, it doesn't feel as cold as it did the night before. It's almost as if the wind has been squashed into the snow under the heavy hand of the clouds. It's still cold, but I don't feel an icy blast.

I step over to the fire, uncertain what to do. I'm afraid to say anything to Misty and I'm equally afraid to even look at Mr. Tan Jacket. I spread my hands out toward the coals and look at Misty. She has extended her leg toward the fire and her ankle is seriously

241

swollen. If it's not broken, it's one wicked sprain. I can't imagine she is going to be able to walk two feet on it.

"How's your ankle," I ask quietly.

"It's throbbing," she answers. "I'm really sorry."

"There's nothing to be sorry about," I say. "You took a bad step. It's not your fault."

"But I slowed us down," she says in almost a whisper. "How's your shoulder?"

I kneel beside her. I know Mr. Tan Jacket is listening intensely, so I lower my voice into a harsh whisper. "It's okay," I say. "It's really just a scratch. It's no big deal...but your ankle looks pretty bad...don't worry, I'll carry you if I have to..."

"You just might," croaks Mr. Tan Jacket.

I look up at him. He leans against the boulder next to the lean-to, still clutching his wounded side and there are beads of sweat on his forehead. He must have a blazing fever to be sweating in this cold. I don't know how seriously his side was punctured, but obviously, some sort of infection has set in. I wonder if I can stall him or move slowly enough so he just drops dead before we get anywhere near any of his buddies.

Looking at him, I can't be sure I'll get that lucky. Some men are so filled with meanness and evil, they won't die like normal men. It's almost as if their inner darkness is a sort of energy source, like feeding on the black blood of demons. It's like he's not human at all.

"I'll bet you're hungry," he says, looking at me. "That's too bad."

Mr. Tan Jacket pulls something out of his jacket pocket, slowly, as if he wants me to watch like it's a magic show. It's a handful of nutrition bars...or maybe they're candy bars. He opens one and makes a big show of taking a bite. This guy really hates me. What kind of terrorist tortures people by making them watch him eat? You would think he could do better!

I shake my head and look away. I'm not going to let him watch me drool like a puppy hoping for table scraps. I'm hungry all right...but I'm not going to give him the satisfaction of knowing what

242

my belly feels. I don't like nutrition bars anyway! They taste like cat poop covered in peanut butter.

I look back just in time to see him accidently drop two of the bars in the snow at his feet. He looks down quickly and then back at me as if I'm an animal that might suddenly scamper under his feet to try and get a mouthful.

As if!

He stoops to pick up the two bars, but his face blanches from what I can only guess is serious pain or nausea and he nearly falls over. He gives up reaching for the bars and leans back, panting slightly.

"You hope I'll just die," he says knowingly. He narrows his eyes as he stares at me. "I won't give you the satisfaction, inshallah."

He kicks the two bars toward Misty, and I flinch so hard, I nearly fall backwards because I'm not expecting it. He laughs but stops almost immediately with a harsh grimace of pain.

"Open them," he says to Misty. "Not him! You eat them...and take your time."

Misty hesitates. She glances back and forth between Mr. Tan Jacket and me. There's a tension so thick and real between us, it's like watching a tennis match. Beads of sweat stand out on Mr. Tan Jacket's forehead; his eyes narrow and I know he's thinking it over. How can he get Misty back to his base without my help? If he just kills me, the odds are he will die in a day anyway or at least get so sick he won't be moving anywhere. He needs me...and man, he doesn't like it.

There is open warfare going on between my gaze and his, like tiny, invisible swords flickering back and forth. His face is telling me all I need to know...if he was up to it, he would peel my skin off with a rusty spoon, one square inch at a time.

For a second, I feel like a kid in trouble, shaking and afraid and completely helpless because he must go to the Headmaster's office. I've got to face the facts. We're caught and I'm not my dad and I can't do anything! I'm nothing really. Nothing special. If I'm honest, it doesn't take any special kind of brains to pile up a bunch of sticks and call it a shelter! I'm just a kid running sacred through the bush without any clue what to do or where to go. So, I got nothing…nothing except an ugly, harsh feeling of defiance rising in my chest, a feeling so strong and warm, I can almost taste it on my tongue.

Yeah…the truth is, I'm so hungry I would probably try to chew the tail off a living mountain lion if I had the chance. But there is this thing in me that doesn't want Mr. Tan Jacket to have any satisfaction, any thought he can get to me in any way, shape or form. So, I'm going to defy him, fight him any way I can, as long as I can.

"Misty," I say, but my eyes don't leave Mr. Tan Jacket's face. "You should eat those…"

"What about you…"

"He doesn't get any," Mr. Tan Jacket croaks.

"That's cool," I say. "Not hungry anyway."

"You're lying," he says.

We both know it's true, only I'm not going to back down. I very deliberately take my eyes off his face and look at Misty.

"Don't worry about me," I say to her. "I'm good."

I look back at Mr. Tan Jacket, my face hard. I didn't twitch when he was eating and I'm not going to show even the least little bit of interest in Misty eating right in front of me. For whatever reason, I know it's important he doesn't see me flinch.

Misty hesitates. She looks at me and I know she's balancing how hungry she is with how mean it is to eat in front of me. Hunger wins out. She tears off the package and basically wolfs down the first protein bar. She tears open the second one and nearly inhales it.

"I'm sorry," she says. "I'm just so hungry."

"No worries," I say. "That's okay.

My little boxing match with Mr. Tan Jacket is over and I'm not sure who won. I didn't whine or beg, and I wonder if that's what he was hoping. Would I turn into a snot-nosed little boy, whimpering about being hungry while the girl got the food? If that was his plan, it has backfired on him big time! I don't think I barely blinked the whole time Misty was eating.

"It is time to go," says Mr. Tan Jacket.

"Where do we go?" He seems amused by my question. "How are we supposed to get over that gorge? You remember that?" I'm feeling reckless again.

He nods his head to the east, down the slope from where we're standing. "That way. To the lakeshore. Let's go."

I help Misty get to her feet. She tries to take a step on her bad foot, but it's no use. She lets out a hard grunt and shakes her head.

"It's no good," she says. "I'm sorry."

"It's okay," I say. "Put your arm around my shoulder. We can do this."

We stumble three-legged away from the dwindling fire. The snow is about four inches deep, not enough to really bog us down, just enough to cover the tops of my shoes. In five minutes, I can feel the ice water soaking into my socks. If I survive this, I wonder how much frostbite I'm going to have. Part of me wants to take this journey painfully slow in the hope Mr. Tan Jacket will die or at least pass out from whatever infection is currently chewing on his intestines. Another part of me wants to move just fast enough that he won't notice how far we've drifted ahead of him until we can make a break for it. I twist a little to see how far behind he might be tailing. I'm disappointed to see he is keeping up, less than twenty feet behind us.

Misty's breathing is labored. I wonder if she's coming down with a cold or something worse, like pneumonia. We've been soaking wet, alternately hot and freezing, and half-starved for nearly three days. It's a wonder we both aren't in a coma.

"Are you okay?" I ask in a hoarse whisper. I don't know if we're allowed to talk.

"No," she says. "I feel like I have a fever. I'm aching all over."

"I'm sorry," I say. "I really am."

"What are we going to do?"

"Keep walking," I say with a grunt.

Misty looks up at me and I see her expression out of the corner of my eye. It's something like...I don't know...almost admiration. I'm not really expecting that. Noticing it triggers something in my chest, something warm and strange. Strange...but familiar too. I grew up feeding on a belief in honor, courage and commitment. It was engrained in me, like the fibers that make up my bones. Seeing her look, knowing she depends on me – it makes me want to crawl over broken glass on my hands and knees for her.

"You're not alone," I whisper in her ear. "I'm right here. I'm going to stay with you."

"Thank you," she says quietly.

I don't answer because I don't need to. Her respect has somehow added an energy into my step. I feel like I could carry her around the world. But I've got to be careful too...No matter how much I want to just soak in the emotion I'm getting out of Misty, I've got my eye trained on the terrain right in front of me, so I don't trip over something. I won't be helping much if we both end up rolling elbows over ankles down a hill!

"He's seriously wounded, you know?" I say. "He might not make it much longer."

"I heard him moaning last night," she says. "And there's a weird smell around him."

"Really?" I ask. "Did you notice how he's sweating? He's probably got a nasty infection."

"He never takes his hand off his side. It's like he's trying to hold everything in place or something."

"Maybe he is. Maybe he'll drop dead, save us the trouble."

"Maybe," she says. "He seems really sick."

"We'll have to stay sharp. If we get a chance...if we get far enough ahead or he nods off or something..."

"I'll be ready," she says. She looks up at me again. "I'll be ready because...because you're here..."

Wow. Now I wish we hadn't had a fight yesterday. I don't know how she could have got it in her head that I would really leave her out here. In my mind, it was never an option to do anything except take care of her - no matter what. I hope she knows that now. I think she does.

246

I wonder why I'm so crazy about taking care of her. I want to think it's because of how I feel about her, but I wasn't feeling so hot about her yesterday. In fact, I was so fizzed I really wondered why I had convinced her to run off in the first place. I guess it's back to that sense of duty and honor my dad drilled into me again.

Honor! Courage! Commitment. The Marine Corps central values, pounded into the heart of every recruit. Of course, not everyone who makes it through boot camp really lives up to those values. There are bad Marines...and there are guys like me who believe in those values even if we will never get an Eagle, Globe and Anchor pin.

I believe in those values and not just because I wanted to be a Marine. Dad used to tell me, "A Marine is as a Marine does, son. It's all about the heart." I think those same values are in every page in my bible too. The whole Christian story is about God making the ultimate sacrifice for the human race. There can be no greater example of honor, courage and commitment than Jesus Himself. So...I can't be a Marine...doesn't mean I can't be a spiritual Marine. And right now, Misty needs my help.

Of course, she had the guts to jump out of the raft and she kept going even when we just about fell off a cliff. And she didn't go crazy after I killed a guy right in front of her. So she doesn't need help because she's weak. She needs my help because she needs it...and I want to protect her. The more she hangs on my shoulder and says stuff like, "I'll be ready because of you," the more I feel like doing anything for her.

"Misty," I say slowly. "I know this is...stupid...but..." I stop before I can say what I'm thinking. I feel like an idiot.

"But what?" she asks. I want to say, *nothing - it was nothing*, but I don't.

"Well...I want to know if...if you'll go to the Christmas formal...with me."

Misty laughs quietly. It wasn't hoping for that reaction. Obviously, she's thinking about how weird I am. We're slogging through the snow, a terrorist has a gun pointed at our backs, and I'm asking her to go to the Christmas formal. I can suddenly see why everyone thinks I'm a dweeb. I remember how I made a fool out of myself on the plane and I suddenly wish I had kept my mouth shut.

"I'm…yes," she says. "Yes, I would love to go to the formal with you." Again, that's not the reaction I was expecting. She smiles at me and I can tell she's really touched. I guess talking about the Christmas formal is enough to get her mind off the cold and the fear, at least for a moment.

"Really, that's…that's awesome."

"I just hope we can go."

"We will," I say confidently.

I pick up my pace a little with a new confidence. I don't know where we're going exactly and I'm not in any hurry to get there, but I feel a new sense of purpose. It's not about going to a formal. It's about knowing that by asking her, I somehow finally managed to get past being the kid everyone thinks is a total putz. At St. Mark's, Misty is at the top of the social pile. There isn't a guy on campus who wouldn't die to go out with her. I mean it was insane enough to try and just talk to her on the plane. Everyone knows I'm about as popular as a dog turd so, for me, her saying she'll go out with me is about as monumental as a modern eruption of Mount Rainier (which would be monumental since it's a volcano hanging over the Seattle skyline like a potential category five lava hurricane).

I wonder if maybe I can slip around a log or a boulder and ditch Mr. Tan Jacket. After all, he's in no shape to run. Misty's on one leg, but I bet we could get away from him. I carried Misty across the creek the other day. She's not that heavy. Maybe I can just scoop her up and run. I'll bet I can get far enough before my arms quit. I twist my head to look back but I'm disappointed to see that Mr. Tan Jacket still slogs along behind us. He's even made up a little of the distance. He's too close for us to make a run for it. I wonder if he can hear us whispering. As if to answer my question, he grins at me.

"You're not thinking about…how do you say…making a break, are you?" he asks. He smiles at me, but his smile stops at his eyes. His stare is filled with a maniac-like glint, anything but amused.

"It's 'making a break for it,'" I say.

"Ah, yes," he says. "But do not try. It will not be good if you do."

I trudge forward silently for about ten minutes. I hear falling water before I see the drop-off to the ravine. I'm not sure what he expects us to do next; my feet feel like two blocks of ice and I'm getting a cramp in my side.

"We need to stop," I say over my shoulder. "I need a rest. Besides, how are we supposed to get across this?"

Mr. Tan Jacket doesn't answer right away. I take another six or eight steps before I can't really go any farther without falling over the edge. We are obviously farther east than where we were yesterday when we crossed over the ravine. The walls of the ravine are not as steep here and the drop is nowhere near as deep. We could probably crawl down and step across the creek if we really had to.

I stop at the edge and let Misty slip her arm off my shoulder, so she can sit on a log. She brushes the snow off the top and looks back at Mr. Tan Jacket. I turn around and shrug.

"We need to take a break," I say.

Mr. Tan Jacket just nods his head. He gestures with the gun for me to sit next to Misty. As I sit next to her, I put my arm around her shoulder and simply stare back at him, willing him to just die. He looks even sicker than he did when we first got up this morning. Even from twenty feet away, I can hear his ragged breathing. Drops of sweat bead on his forehead and the gun in his hand seems to be slightly shaking as if he's finding it almost too heavy to keep steady. He leans against a tree rather than sitting down and I wonder if he's worried that if he does sit down, he won't be able to get back up again. He isn't clutching his wounded side any longer either. Is it because it's infected and the pain of touching it is overwhelming? He obviously notices what I'm looking at.

"You are not worried about me, are you?" he asks mockingly. He carefully lowers his weapon and slips it into his jacket pocket. I wonder if the weight of the gun, his fever, and whatever infection he's fighting off are getting too much for him. "I don't think you have anything to worry about," he continues. "I will get you both to my brothers, inshallah."

249

"Inshallah," I repeat.

"It means…"

"I know what it means," I interrupt with a little edge in my voice. Misty instinctively puts her hand out on my knee, like a warning.

"You do?" he asks. "And why is that?"

"I've heard it many times before," I say. "In Africa. And in New Guinea."

"I'm impressed," he says. "So, what does it mean?" He shifts his weight and I see him wince in pain.

"It means, 'if Allah wills it'," I answer.

"If God wills it," he says, correcting me. Again, I feel that nasty, rebellious irritation rise inside my chest. Everything seems to focus between us, like an invisible current of electricity streaming between my eyes and his.

"Not my God," I say quietly. Misty takes in a sharp breath. I feel her hand tighten on my knee and I know she just wants me to shut up. "I don't have to kill anyone to prove I'm good enough for heaven." I'm treading on very thin ice and Mr. Tan Jacket has the gun. But the flash of emotion I see on Mr. Tan Jacket's face isn't anger – it's amusement.

"You are weak," he says. "Your god is weak. The filth of America will be burned, and you will all submit to Allah…Inshallah."

It's everything I can do to restrain myself, but it isn't Misty digging her fingernails into my knee that's keeps me from saying anything. It's something my dad taught me a long time ago. Something I haven't thought about until just now.

There are two scriptures in the book of Proverbs that Mom and Dad made me memorize when I was fourteen – Proverbs 26: 4 and 5. In our homeschool at the time, we were studying apologetics and he said these two scriptures were the key. Apologetics comes from a Greek word, which means, "to answer" and it is all about knowing the reasons why we believe what we believe. I had to study evolution and the basic beliefs of every major religion in the world. And then I had to show why what we Christians believed made more sense. Since I had to write a paper and do a presentation on the subject, I not only memorized the scriptures, I memorized the basics of apologetics too.

My dad told me the real key to apologetics was Proverbs 26: 4 – 5. It says, "Do not answer a fool according to his folly, or you will be like him yourself…Answer a fool according to his folly, or he will be wise in his own eyes." It means that if you answer an idiot using the same tone of voice and the same kind of argument he is using, then you're just being an idiot too. But if you answer, "according to his folly", that means, if you sort of hold up a mirror and show the fool why what he is saying doesn't make sense…well, then, the fool can't be "wise in his own eyes."

My parents were missionaries so my homeschool program was loaded with this sort of stuff. When we went to New Guinea, I did a whole section on Islam because that is the dominant religion in Indonesia, which is right there in the neighborhood. But getting into an argument with a terrorist holding a gun who has already proven he will kill someone without a second thought is really answering the fool according to his folly. I figure I've said enough already, but I can't help dropping one last little grenade.

"My God died for me," I say carefully. "…and He promised me heaven if I trusted Him."

"You're a fool," he spits back at me. "Jesus did not die for you. Allah made it seem so, but he didn't die, and he was not God. He was a prophet."

"That's not what He said," I answer quickly. Misty shifts in her seat, almost begging me with her body language to be quiet. "Jesus said He was the way, the truth and the life."

"Shut up!" he yells. He is obviously no longer amused. He pushes away from the tree he was leaning on and the movement nearly causes him to collapse. His face visibly pales. "Get up!" he yells again. "Get moving."

Misty stands, but I'm slower to get to my feet. I keep my eyes locked on his face and I feel a hot, ugly defiance rising in my throat like steam under pressure. Mr. Tan Jacket isn't holding the gun – it's in his pocket. He's obviously feverish and weak, ready to collapse at any second. If I rush him right now, if I just tackle him - I'm willing to bet he'll fall like a stone. I tense my body and get slowly to my feet.

I must be broadcasting my thoughts. Mr. Tan Jacket's face changes ever so slightly, he begins to reach for the gun in his pocket and Misty snaps her face my direction. I hesitate for just a split second and then leap forward.

But Misty screams and grabs hold of my arm.

"No! You're gonna get me killed!"

And I can't believe she grabbed me!

I spin nearly completely around and almost drop to my knees. She must realize what she's done because she lets go of my arm, but I've lost the element of surprise. I fling myself forward, floundering over my bent knees and six inches of snow.

Since Misty grabbed my arm, I'm not stable enough to hit him with a full-body tackle. I stumble to my left and try to pull him down with my outstretched arm. He turns just enough to keep me from getting a full hold on his waist, but the movement is enough to topple him back into the tree he had originally been leaning on. I hear him gasp in pain. Being thrown into a log when you've got an infected laceration in your gut must be incredibly painful, but it isn't enough to take him down. I skid onto my knee, spin around, and swing my fist in a wild roundhouse that catches nothing but air.

I'm on both knees now, staring up at him. I struggle to get to my feet when the first shot explodes the air in front of my face. The sound is so loud and so close to my ear, I instantly feel deafened. A harsh ringing stabs into my ear and I cower back. Mr. Tan Jacket roars and steps forward, the gun leveled at my forehead. He swings it at me like a club and the barrel catches me in the temple. It cracks so hard I see a thousand sparkles in my eyes. The blow rips open a gash in the side of my head. I feel the hot cascade of a lot of blood pouring out over my cheek. I fall sideways into the snow, throwing my arms out instinctively to catch myself. I see the brilliant red of my own blood outlined on the snow. I turn back to face him.

Again, I know I'm going to die and everything seems to be crawling along in slow motion. I can see Misty screaming behind Mr.

Tan Jacket, but I can't hear anything except the ringing in my ears. I guess the shock has dulled my thinking too because I don't really feel afraid. I'm almost curious about how Mr. Tan Jacket is going to kill me. But he doesn't shoot right away. He is absolutely livid, that's for sure. He grits his teeth and the look of hate in his eyes is almost like a flame. He points the gun right at my forehead and shouts something I can't make out over the horrible buzz in my ears.

Twenty

Mr. Tan Jacket shouts at me again. This time, I hear something that sounds like a kid in a swimming pool trying to shout underwater. I still can't make it out clearly but there is something. Maybe I'm not permanently deaf after all. He steps closer, jabbing the gun at me and gnashing his teeth as if he's arguing with himself about whether to kill me. The ringing in my ears lessens just a bit and I can finally make out what he's saying. It's like swimming in a pool full of syrup.

"Get up!" he roars. "Get on your feet."

I'm still stunned from being pistol-whipped. I shake my head very slowly, start to get up, and I glance back at Misty. She has her hand over her mouth as it she's trying to either not throw up or not scream. It's flooding back to me now.

She tried to stop me! She grabbed my arm!

Grabbing me wasn't a reaction, it was stupid! She didn't want me to get *her* killed? She just nearly got *me* killed. What was she thinking?

I stagger to my feet. Mr. Tan Jacket, still holding the gun, holds my eyes for a split second and then he slashes at me with the knife he has in his other hand. It slashes downward on my left hand. The blade lays out an inch-long gash just below my thumb. For a second, I'm fascinated by the sight of the cut. The skin is textured and sort of milky white, like cooked pasta, and it hangs loosely over my exposed flesh. It's like my body hasn't figured out I'm cut yet, and the blood hasn't filled up the gouge. I slide down to one knee, barely able to keep from falling over and the pain hits me like a freight train. I instinctively grab my wounded hand with my good one and slide forward until my chest rests on my knee. Blood pours out from beneath my palm and I can't be sure he hasn't cut a major vein.

"Make the wrong move and I cut off your ear next," he snarls. "Get her! Get moving."

I stagger to my feet, still stunned by the searing pain in my left hand and the ringing in my ears. But Mr. Tan Jacket isn't done yet. He wants to make it clear that he's in charge. He swings the butt of his gun at my head like a club and I'm too dizzy to flinch. The blow hits me full force, right behind my right ear, opening a half-inch gash in my scalp. Another river of blood flows over my ear and down my neck and I fall face-first into the snow, too stunned by the blow to even try and stop my fall. I hit the snow face-first, so hard my breath is knocked out of me. My lungs clamp down, my chest burns like liquid fire in my chest, and I can't get a breath. I gulp harshly, trying to re-inflate my lungs. Mr. Tan Jacket continues to scream his head off at me.

"Get up...Get up!" he screams. "The jinn will pour boiling water down your throat for all eternity. Get up. Get up before I send you there right now."

"Don't kill him!" Misty screams. "Please. Don't!"

"Shut up," Mr. Tan Jacket screams at her. He points the gun back at Misty. "I can kill you now."

"Please," she wails. "Don't kill him. Just don't kill him. I'll do whatever you want."

"I'm up," I shout. I stagger quickly to my feet, gasping for air. Too quickly! I stagger to my left and nearly run into a tree. I clutch my left hand to my stomach and throw out my right hand in a gesture of pleading.

"You still need her," I croak. My lungs still cramp, waiting to fully inflate. I gulp as much air as I can. "You still...need me to help...her walk...I'm up...I'm up."

Mr. Tan Jacket swings his head back my direction, his teeth grit. He still points the gun at Misty. He hesitates, thinking it over for one long, slow moment. He grunts something I don't think even he understands and then slowly lowers the weapon. I can tell he's still too sick to really hold it steady for long. My chance to catch him is past. After being pistol whipped, stabbed and clubbed in the head, I'm not in any shape to challenge him again. He spits angrily.

"Get moving," he growls. "Follow the edge…to the lake. Get moving."

I focus my vision on Misty and stumble forward. Blood has dried or frozen to my cheek. I can feel the slick on my chin like I spilled gravy over my face and let it dry in a cold wind. I don't know how much my scalp is bleeding and my left hand throbs. I press it deeper into my stomach. I hope the direct pressure will stop the bleeding.

"I'm so sorry," Misty whispers. "I'm sorry…I didn't mean to hold your arm…I'm sorry."

I don't say anything. I'm so dizzy and hurt I can barely register what she's saying. I somehow manage to stay on my feet. I stand next to her, but I don't reach over and put my arm around her shoulder. My lungs still protest being mistreated, the gash in my head stings like acid burning my skin, and I'm having a hard time thinking clearly. Misty cries softly next to my left ear and I think I should say something, only I don't say anything to comfort her.

She grabbed my arm!

She tried to stop me, so she wouldn't get herself hurt. She tripped me up and nearly got me killed. What in the name of all that is holy was she thinking? Even if it was some sort of reflex, where did it come from? Why would she try to stop me at all? What's with, "You've going to get me killed"? What about getting *me* killed?

A flurry of conflicting emotions rain into my mind like hail hitting a tin roof. I feel alternately amazed and royally ticked off. I can't seem to get hold of which feeling is the right one, so I just stand there, waiting. Misty looks hopefully at me, but I just glare. Her face drops.

"Move!" shouts Mr. Tan Jacket. "No stopping. Let's go."

"I'm sorry," she says again.

I'm still trying to figure out what to think and how to feel about it. I just turn to the side – more of an obedient shuffle really – and she slips her arm over my shoulder almost reluctantly. I don't put my arm around her waist or take hold of her arm on my shoulder. I just take a step forward. She hops forward awkwardly trying to hold herself up with her one arm around my shoulder and I make no attempt to really help.

I just can't believe it. I can't believe she grabbed my arm. I just can't figure out what to do or say or think. I thought she was just scared and spouting off, but what if I'm just making excuses for her? Am I just another secret service agent to her – someone who better do the job right and if I don't and I get my head blown off she might be seriously put out? Is that what she thinks? Didn't making out with her mean anything? Or was I just some kind of distraction? She didn't just try to stop me – she shouted that I was going to get *her* killed. What's going on in her head?

"You're really tall," she whispers. "I can't really hold on very well."

"Well," I say savagely, "I wouldn't want you to be put out."

I can see her out of my peripheral vision. She snaps an ugly look my direction.

"I didn't ask to be here," she says. "I'm sorry. I'm sorry he went all crazy on you, but you didn't have to…dive after him." I just shake my head.

"I heard what you said," I say in a fierce whisper. *"You're gonna get me killed!* That's what you said and then you grabbed me. He nearly killed me, not you."

"I didn't ask you to charge him," she says. "What kind of crazy are you, anyway?"

"He's sick. He's weak. He can barely hold that gun up. If I had hit him by surprise, he wouldn't be standing and you and me…we'd be outta here again. On our own."

"I didn't know what you were going to do," she hisses. "How was I supposed to know? I'm just trying to…I just want to go home."

"Yeah. I know. I've been trying to keep you alive for three days."

I lower my voice, almost as if I know I shouldn't say what I'm thinking out loud, so I need to keep it so soft she might not hear. But

257

I say what I think anyway. "I've got a life too...Is everything about you?" I say.

I know I've crossed the line, but I just don't care. I've faced certain death a half a dozen times in the last three days and somehow, I'm still breathing, but everything comes down to Misty. I still can't figure out what she's thinking.

Misty tries to slip her arm off my shoulder. I stop and reach over to get hold of her hand.

"I don't need your help," she says loudly.

"What is the problem?" says Mr. Tan Jacket. He walks a full twenty feet behind us – just far enough behind us that I can't surprise him, but close enough for him to shoot me.

Misty yanks her arm off my shoulder. She tries to take a step on her ankle and nearly shrieks in pain. Her ankle is almost certainly broken, not just sprained. I stand back and let her try to take another step. Her face nearly turns the color of the snow. There's simply no way she's going to put any weight on her foot.

I can't help being mad at her. On the other hand, I don't want her to die either. I shake my head and step in to take hold of her again. She tries to back away, but without one working foot and standing in six inches of snow, she falls on her rear end with a surprised grunt.

"Pick her up," snarls Mr. Tan Jacket. "No more talking. Just move."

I glare at him, then turn to look at her. She's angry. I'm frustrated she hasn't taken one second to think about how I feel. Maybe she's selfish...maybe not...I don't know. Still, she was always the one they wanted and both of us know it. So, we're right back to the beginning, just like the day of the crash. We're wet and cold, Misty is scared and angry, and terrorists herd us with guns like a flock of sheep going to the slaughterhouse. Somehow, some way – I've got to do something.

Without a word, I reach out my hand. There's nothing to say now even if I had the courage to defy Mr. Tan Jacket's order not to talk anymore. She looks at my hand and I look at it too – a compromise, a hope, maybe just a way to get away from the cold water I'm betting is working its way into the seat of her pants. Whatever else my offered hand represents, it's a way out. I just want this whole nightmare to be over. We need it to be over and fighting between ourselves isn't helping.

Misty hesitates. She reaches up, takes my hand and I pull her upright. I sling my arm around her waist and we balance for a moment.

"Sorry," I whisper right in her ear. "I didn't mean..."

"I said, shut up!" snarls Mr. Tan Jacket.

I turn my head to look at him. He has the gun in his hand, but it's not aimed at us. It hangs limp against his right thigh as if it's a pendulum weight that's lost all its swing. He clutches his stomach with his left hand. His eyes are unnaturally wide and his lip trembles. He's in a bad shape; maybe not bad enough to drop him on the spot, just bad enough to keep him in the game and on the edge. He's far enough back that if I tried to rush him again, he would have time to get the gun into position and kill me. There's nothing to do except put one foot in front of the other and see what happens next.

I lean a little to pick up some of Misty's weight. We step forward and march down-hill toward the lake.

There's less snow as we shuffle along. An hour passes, maybe it's two. It's all a sort of dream now, like my mind is only registering every other minute. It's hard to keep track when everything is just more of the same rough ground littered with broken trees and rocks covered with snow – at least there's less snow. The patches of wet ground between sheets of snow are getting larger. The sky overhead is steel gray and there is a hint in the air as if another snowfall sits expectantly on the edge of falling.

I don't look back and I don't have to either. Mr. Tan Jacket's breathing is so harsh I can hear him gasping for air, even above the sound of the creek. He's like the horror film version of *The Little Engine That Could*. Puff, puff...toot, toot...only it's a hacking wheeze.

We only stop for a minute when I get the first view of the lake. Mr. Tan Jacket herds us forward with a simple grunt and I'm so tired, I just fall in like a sheep in front of the sheep dog. I'm not sure what we're supposed to do when we get to the lake. I'm guessing he wants us to follow the shore and I'm not about to tell him why that's a bad idea. The shore of the lake is covered with piles of driftwood and tangles of blackberry bushes. If he wants us to cover a lot of ground quickly, following the lakeshore isn't the way to get it done. Or maybe he's lost, and the lake is the only landmark he knows to find his way back.

We reach the lake about midday. It's hard to tell the time, because the light is so dim from the heavy clouds. I stop about twenty yards from the shore, right at the feet of the tangle of berry bushes I suspected would be there.

"Turn here," says Mr. Tan Jacket. I look back. He gestures toward the creek. "Go across there. Then keep going."

My arm is killing me from holding Misty's weight. My feet are freezing from shuffling through snow, so I'm not looking forward to getting my feet even wetter. Fortunately, or maybe not - the creek isn't deep and there are plenty of stones to step on. We cross over in just a few minutes and stop on the far side. I look back at our enemy.

"We need a break," I say. "Just a drink or something."

"Fine," he points at the creek. "Get a drink. Lap it up like a dog. That is what you are. A dog."

I know he thinks that's insulting, and I guess in the Middle East it would be, but I couldn't care less if he thinks I'm a dog. I've met a lot of cool dogs. There are bomb dogs in the Marines who have rank. I think Mr. Tan Jacket's a life form lower than pond scum – he doesn't even get to dog level in my view. Still, I figure it's in my best interest to keep that thought to myself.

I unhook my arm from Misty's waist and help her kneel on the edge of the stream. She balances on her knees in the small river stones at the edge of the creek, leans out, and puts her hands on a large stone. She puts her weight on one hand, gathers up her hair with her other hand, and leans down to get a drink. I kneel beside her and do the same thing. The water is so cold it's hard to feel like I've had enough to drink. One sip seems to close my throat. I have to concentrate and make myself really get a stomach-full. I don't know when I'll get a chance to quench my thirst in the near future.

I lean back and sit on the bank. Misty finishes her drink and sits next to me, leaning on one hand. We look back across the creek at Mr. Tan Jacket. He has slumped down against a tree, still clutching his side. He must have put the gun in his pocket again. For the moment, he doesn't demand that we get up and keep moving, so I guess he needs a break too. I notice he's not getting a drink of water and I wonder if it's because he's afraid he'll pass out if he leans over or if he's so sick, he doesn't feel thirsty. Either way is fine with me.

"I didn't mean it," Misty says quietly. She looks down and begins to absently pick at the pebbles on the creek shore. She tosses one into the water. "I didn't mean… don't get me killed…I was only…it just came out weird. I just didn't expect you to go all crazy, you know?"

I'm not sure what to say. Everything's been such a blur. Right now, all I can think about is that my left hand and my head are throbbing and ice-cold water is seeping into the seat of my pants. I hate that feeling. I also don't want to rush back into marching to my execution. I look over at Mr. Tan Jacket again. He stares back across the creek at me, no less aware than he was five minutes ago. My hope that he'll just keel over isn't happening. I look away, hoping he will give us some more time to rest.

"Everybody says stuff when they're freaked out," I say. "Everything's crazy right now. Just…forget it."

"I'm sorry about your hand," she says. "Does it hurt real bad?"

I pull my hand away from my stomach. It's not bleeding anymore. Somehow, I lucked out. Mr. Tan Jacket's slash skinned my wrist rather than cutting deeply. A half-inch peel of skin bubbles away from the cut, exposing the white and pink flesh. I'm tempted to tear off the flap, but on second thought, I think I'll just leave it alone.

"Ohhh, that looks nasty," Misty says. "I'm really sorry." She reaches for me slowly as if she's afraid I might smack her or something. Instead, I don't move at all. She lightly touches my wrist just below the cut. "I'm so sorry," she says softly.

I look at her closely. She's really worn out. Dark circles have formed under her eyes. Her hair is frizzed out, like a spray of muddy water springing out of her scalp. But her gaze is hopeful as she reaches for me.

"It's okay," I say. "I didn't mean to say you were, like, selfish or something. I don't know, you just yelled something. It's no big deal. It's okay…really."

Misty nods and pulls her hand back. I look away and close my eyes. I listen to the sound of the creek splashing in front of me and I wish I could just sit here and listen forever. I've always loved the sound of falling water. When I was a kid, I would sometimes just sit at the edge of the creek near our house and watch the water for hours. The sound and the endless, changing swirls of color in the water was mesmerizing and calming. But now I hear another splash that isn't natural.

I look up. Mr. Tan Jacket has moved into the shallows on the other side of the creek. "Get up," he croaks. "There is not much time."

He's right – there's not much time. I think this is it. I think I'm going to be Misty's crutch for another couple of hours and then I'll "outlive my usefulness" as my dad used to say. It's funny, but I'm not afraid. I'm almost looking forward to it. I guess you can be so tired, so cold and so uncomfortable, you don't really care about dying.

I get to my feet, help Misty up, and we start trudging through the bush once again. This close to the lake, the layer of snow on the ground is patchy. There are plenty of places with no snow at all and despite the fact I'm not in any hurry, we seem to make pretty good time. In a less than two hours, we come to the first creek Misty and I crossed after we first escaped.

I look up the creek back toward our little slippy-slide adventure over the cliff. I can see the cliff, not the log, and looking the other way there is a tangle of blackberry bushes at the edge of the lake, frosted with snow like a green and white mist on the horizon, and the lake is steel grey under threatening clouds. Not far from here, I somehow managed to pull Misty out of the freezing lake into another nest of blackberry bushes and it seems like it all happened years ago.

There's something quiet and still about everything around me that has nothing to do with the weather or the snow. We're nearly at the end now and I can't pretend it's going to end well, at least not for me. If I run now, he'll just shoot me in the back. And how can I run if there's even a small chance I can do something for Misty? She's the one they want. I'm the raging pain in their neck that took her away in the first place. They've already killed guys for a whole lot less.

I look back at the creek in front of us. The water foams and snarls around the rocks in endlessly changing swirls, black and cold, like the fingers of the angel of death. I want to enjoy the sight, only I can't help seeing the terrorist under my hands in the water. The shudder...his body floating away. I need to think about something else.

"We're almost there," I whisper in Misty's ear. I turn my head to look into her eyes. "Thank you." I say quietly.

"Thank you?" she asks. "I didn't do anything..."

"You made me feel...like I was...someone," I say.

"What do you mean?"

"I'm the guy, you know...everybody thinks I'm so...odd," I say. "You're the girl that everybody wishes they could take out. But I guess...not much of a first date."

"Maybe it was the best date I've ever been on," she says. "Do you want to know a secret?"

"Sure."

"I've never kissed anybody before," she says.

"No way," I say surprised. I just naturally figured with her popularity, she would have had plenty of make out sessions in her experience.

"It's true," she says. She looks away from me, out at the creek. "And I'm glad it was with you."

Behind me, I hear Mr. Tan Jacket. "Cross over," he says. "There is not much time."

No, not much time left. Everything seems so clear and real. I've been next to Misty for miles and suddenly I feel her warmth next to mine as if I hadn't really noticed it before. I smell her scent and I'm keenly aware of how soft the curve of her hip rubs against my side. I put my arm around her waist again and this time, I feel something like electricity flow through my fingertips. Even the air I'm pulling into my lungs seems especially sweet. I can smell the wetness of the snow. Not much time left…

I'm shaking as I step onto the first stone in the creek bed. It seems like that horrible dream you have when the monster is snapping at your heels and every step you take seems like you're pulling your feet through a thick paste. But this time, there really is a monster at my heels and every step I take is one step closer to a bullet in the back of my head. The hair on the back of my scalp stands up.

Some kind of feeling, something harsh and swift swoops up in my chest. I've faced death half a dozen times in the last few days and I've fought against it but now, I feel like giving in. I don't like facing it head-on. I'm so tired; if I'm honest with myself, I'm scared too. Not terrified, like a guy facing a werewolf. Not horrified, like I felt when the terrorist was dragging the flight attendant's body away. No…more like unsure. See…I believe in heaven. I believe Mom and Dad are there, waiting for me. I believe so much I'm not afraid to die…I just don't know how to die. I don't know if it really hurts. I don't know what happens…after…so I'm scared…of the process. I don't know the steps from taking your last breath to getting…*there*.

Suddenly, I just give up trying to get across the creek on dry feet. What's the point? When you're dead, you don't know you're feet are wet and freezing. I twist quickly to my left and scoop Misty up into arms. She makes a surprised noise and quickly throws her arms around my neck. I step into the water and it's brutally cold. In three seconds, I can't feel my toes. I just slog forward, not caring about the cold or the wet. The water reaches above my knees. I feel a rock roll under my foot and I lurch to my right, but I don't drop her.

"I'm glad it was you," she whispers.

She puts her head on my shoulder, I plow through the surging water into the shallows on the far side of the creek, and step onto the far bank, dripping and yet almost unaware of being wet.

264

"Me too," I say. I've run the race from feeling like I'm in love with her to so mad I could spit a nail at her. I don't want to say anything stupid, not if I'm going to be dead in an hour. "I'm glad it was you too."

I set Misty back onto her good foot. I put my arm around her waist again and we start hobbling into the bush on the bank, both bending a little to get past some low hanging branches. It's steep on this side of the creek and I have to pause a half a dozen times to catch my breath. Every time I look back, Mr. Tan Jacket is right behind us – just far enough away to keep me from having any thoughts of jumping him and just close enough to blow my head off if I try to run. At least he's far enough away where I can risk talking. Of course, he's gonna shoot me anyway – so why should I care if I break his no talking command?

"I believe in heaven," I say.

"Me too," she says. "I never stopped believing – even after my sister died. My parents quit going to church though..."

"I asked Jesus into my heart when I was nine, so I know I'm going there. That's what we were doing all over the world. Telling people that believing in Jesus was the way to get to heaven."

"I know," she says. "I went to this thing called Vacation Bible School once."

"Really?" I'm surprised.

Vacation Bible School is sort of like a summer day camp a lot of churches do, but I wasn't expecting someone from Misty's side of the world to ever go to one. Most of the Vacation Bible School programs I knew about were held at little neighborhood churches, a long way from high church and country clubs.

"Yeah, it was really neat," she says. "I was, I think, like six or something. It was fun, it was all about faraway places and we sang songs from Hawaii and stuff."

"Yeah, that was the *Surf's Up* one. I remember that one."

"You do?"

"Yeah. There's all kinds of themes. Churches do different ones every summer. But I remember that one."

265

"It was...well, I remember that we all prayed, and they asked us if we wanted to ask Jesus into our hearts. I remember..." She pauses. The ground is uneven in front of us and I wonder if she's just concentrating on where to hop next.

"You remember what?"

"It's kind of...well, I think...yeah...you...you would understand. I just felt like I really...like God was really real that day. Do you know what I mean? Literally there! I knew I needed to ask Him into my heart. Ever since...I mean, we don't go to church and we never talk about it. Especially after Mary died. But I've always believed God was with me. You know?"

"I do know," I say. "I know exactly what you mean."

Ahead of us, the trees thin. It hasn't taken very long to get from the creek to the place where the rafts first came to the shore of the lake. I guess when we first escaped, we really ran deep into the woods, away from the lake and the mouth of the creek. We hobble out of the trees and I recognize the muddy embankment where the rafts came ashore. There's no sign of the rafts or anyone else. They must have marched the hostages back into the trees to keep them out of sight.

"Turn here," croaks Mr. Tan Jacket. "Follow the path there."

Misty looks at me. I can see it in her face. She knows I've probably only got a few minutes to live. She pulls back from me slightly. We stand there with our arms wrapped around each other's waists for a moment. And then she leans up and buries her lips into mine...deeply...desperately.

266

Twenty-One

This kiss is no experiment. Through the press of her lips to mine, Misty is speaking to me, telling me secret things. My fear, my fatigue, my loss of hope all seems to evaporate like melting snow from her warmth as she holds me tightly. I want it to go on and on. I want to sweep her away from this ugly place, but a harsh voice tears us apart.

"Enough," Mr. Tan Jacket snarls from behind us. Still, I hesitate to pull away from her.

"I said, enough."

Slowly, I pull my face away from hers. She looks into my eyes as I pull back; her expression is hopeful and sad and longing all at once. Tears well up in the corners of her eyes. She gently touches my face with her fingers and I sense so many words, so many things she wants to tell me. I know now about her sister and the lambs and her feeling so alone after Mary died – her secrets. And she knows, at least a little, about the crash, about my loss. We've shared so much more than a shelter in the woods or a fire in the snow. There's something different between us, something that gets us past the misunderstandings, the hurt feelings and arguments we also shared in the last few days…something deeper than disagreement. I can see it all in her look. I can feel it - forgiveness and hope and desire, all in the touch of her fingers on my cheek.

"Start walking! Now!" shouts Mr. Tan Jacket.

I turn to look at him and that hot streak of defiance burns warm in my chest once again like a living creature that wants to escape with a roar. Mr. Tan Jacket holds the gun loosely at his side, but he's still just far enough away to keep me from rushing him. Besides, we've got to be close to wherever his team is camped. Even if I could get the drop on him, I don't think it would do me much good. It's just the end of the line for me now. No more lakes to jump in. No more shelters to build.

And now there's an echo in my mind, like a faraway voice, a voice of panic and protest that threatens to overwhelm me. Only I won't give into it like some little kid sliding into a temper tantrum – I'm not going to blubber and beg. I'm not going to listen to that temptation because there's a louder voice ringing in my heart. Actually, it's not really a voice. It's more like an extra sense – what my mom would call a sixth sense and my dad would say is the voice of God. I think it is God, speaking to me, calming me. He doesn't say if I'm going to live or not. I just know it's okay either way.

So, I look back at Misty. A lone tear slides down her cheek. I brush it away with my hand and smile softly. "We're almost there," I say. "It won't be much longer."

"Almost there," she whispers.

Her lips purse as she really tries to hold back the tears. Both of us know - it really won't be much longer. Whatever they plan for her, whatever is going to happen to me – it's a hundred yards away. I slip my arm around her waist, lean to my right to take up her weight, and we hobble forward for the last time.

The track the terrorists stomped into the brush from the lake to the trees is clear to see like an animal trail trampled into the mud. The ground swells up like a rising wave for about a hundred yards and the track slices across it like an oil slick. At the top, nestled back under the trees, there's a huge green tent, and a second tent, significantly smaller than the other. The rafts that brought us from the plane to the shore are stacked next to the larger of the two tents. There are even four, plastic, portable toilets a few feet from the larger tent, set on the ground like green tombstones tipped this way and that on the uneven dirt. The moment I take all of this in, there's a shout from the front of the larger tent. One of the terrorists I don't recognize has seen us. He leaps to his feet and shouts a second time.

268

From behind me, Mr. Tan Jacket answers in whatever pagan gibberish they're speaking.

"Stop," he says to us.

I stop slowly, as if in a dream. I don't let go of Misty. Instead, I crane my neck around to see what Mr. Tan Jacket is doing. I half expect him to shoot me right away. Instead, he gestures with his gun toward the smaller tent.

"Take her to that tent," he says. "Go in. Go now."

I look back at the tent and Mr. Tan Jacket says something that sounds urgent to the guard at the larger tent. The guard replies, nods his head, and whips out his radio. He jabbers something into the receiver and quickly turns to run somewhere out of my view. Whatever Mr. Tan Jacket wants, it's urgent.

It only takes a minute to get to the second tent. It's at least a third smaller than the big tent and tall, more like a pavilion than a tent. There's a small gas-powered generator behind it too. Obviously, something that needs power is going on inside. I've seen a lot of gas-powered generators living in the outlands. My dad used to make me shut them off at night and that's no easy task when you're afraid either lions in Africa or bears in Alaska are going to eat you the second the sound of the generator shuts off. I remember when the generator was running, there was at least some comfort that lions and tigers and bears would be scared off by the noise. But once I shut it down, the buzz and rumble of the engine was nearly instantly swallowed up by the colossal silence you only hear in the most remote places of the world. I don't know why the memory of running back to the comfort of the trailer after shutting off the generator is suddenly so clear in my mind. I guess when you're really scared your mind tries to distract itself.

The tent opening is a six-foot long zipper, currently unzipped. I take a deep breath, push back the flap of the tent with my hand, and help Misty hobble inside. There's a cot taking up the edge of the tent to our left. On our right is a flimsy card table holding up a bulky white box. There are two plastic folding chairs behind the table and a stack of large black plastic crates. The table doesn't seem strong enough to hold up the box, but before I can figure out what it is, Mr. Tan Jacket comes in behind us.

"Put her there," says Mr. Tan Jacket. He gestures at the cot.

A half a dozen ideas flash through my mind in a split second. He's only three feet from me. Can I drop Misty and tackle him quick enough or will he pull the trigger the instant he sees me flinch? Should I sit with her? Should I set her down and then dive at him? Maybe I can set her down and then dive for the door? But what are they going to do to her? I can't just run, and I can't just stand here.

Slowly, I twist around and help Misty sit on the edge of the cot.

"No," she pleads. "Don't hurt him. Please. Don't do anything to him. I'll do anything you want. Just leave him."

"Shut up!" Mr. Tan Jacket spits back at her.

I just stand up straight. I may not be a real Marine, but I'm a Marine in my heart – just like my dad. And there is no way I'm going to cower.

"Get on your knees," he says.

But I don't. I won't!

I just stand still - at attention. My dad used to tell me stories about great Marines like John Basilone and Chesty Puller. Basilone was awarded the Medal of Honor and the Navy Cross. And Puller! He was awarded the Navy Cross five times and is the most decorated Marine in history. Chesty didn't even understand what the word "quit" meant in the English language. Before I found out that my back was going to keep me out of the Corps, I used to daydream about being as tough as Puller or Basilone. Today is the day I'm that tough. I will not move. I set my face with the nastiest expression of disgust and defiance I can make. I stare into Mr. Tan Jacket's black eyes and I don't move a muscle.

Mr. Tan Jacket narrows his eyes. Slowly, he raises the gun and points it directly at my forehead. The mouth of the barrel seems like the pit of a deep well and it's only a few inches from my forehead.

"No, please don't," pleads Misty.

I hear Mr. Tan Jacket's harsh breathing and my heartbeat pounding in my ears. I grip my fingers around my thumbs to keep

270

from shaking. My knees feel weak and I can hardly take a breath. But I will not move, and I won't make a sound.

It seems like we just stand here for hours, but it's only a few seconds. Mr. Tan Jacket's hand shakes slightly from the weight of the gun. He doesn't fire, and I don't flinch.

"*Those who deny Allah, for them will be cut out a garment of fire: over their heads will be poured out boiling water…*" he whispers slowly. "That is Surah 22:19 from the holy Qur'an."

Suddenly, Mr. Tan Jacket lowers the gun. I let out a breath in a whoosh, but I still stand at attention. I didn't realize I'd been holding my breath.

Mr. Tan Jacket steps back toward the tent entrance and reaches behind himself with his other hand to pull back the flap. He leans his head a little to throw his voice out of the tent, then shouts something in his language. He never takes his eyes off of me. He drops the tent flap and turns his head back to face me.

"Your fate in hell is worse than any torture," he says.

Behind him, two men enter the tent. One is obviously one of the other terrorists. He's dark-haired and carries an AK-47. His eyes are really close together and he's all muscle – reminds me of the big, silent muscle men in gangster movies. The other guy is much older, a balding white man, probably pushing sixty. The white guy's face is ashen, like the drug addicts I saw crouched in the alleyways in the Philippines when we stopped there once. The ones we saw, they had been doping for a long time; their skin was all pasty white like the underside of a wet toad - sort of shiny and slick. This guy looks that way. What hair he has on his head is gray and thin too. He's not carrying a weapon and his eyes seem to flit back and forth as if he's constantly looking for an escape route.

Both men stop cold as soon as they enter the tent - something unspoken and powerful runs between Mr. Tan Jacket and me.

"Is that the girl?" asks Paste Face. "It is too late. We should have had her two days ago. We don't have enough time."

"It will be enough," says Mr. Tan Jacket.

271

"I'm not so sure," Paste Face says. "I don't think this is going to work...I'll...I'll...have to look at the charts." He shuffles behind Mr. Tan Jacket and goes to the card table. "...and I'll need power."

"What for?" asks Mr. Tan Jacket. "Doctor, you have done this thirty times."

So, Paste Face is a doctor! He looks like he's been doctoring himself with some sort of drug for a long time.

"I need to recalculate," Doctor Paste Face answers. "This was supposed to happen no later than yesterday."

"What difference does it make?"

"It makes all the difference. We've already injected the others...you want this to peak at exactly the right time, don't you? I need to know what she weighs, and I need to check the charts and my laptop is dead. I have to plug it into something other than a tree! And she hasn't eaten in a few days, it could mean..." Mr. Tan Jacket throws up one hand to stop the doctor from talking.

"That's fine," he says. "Just do it." Mr. Tan Jacket has yet to take his eyes off me. He now turns to the other terrorist – Mr. Muscles. "Start the generator."

Muscles leaves and a few seconds later, I hear the generator buzz to life. The doctor takes a laptop out of a crate and sets it up on the table.

"You look terrible," says Doctor Paste Face. "What happened?"

Mr. Tan Jacket pulls his left hand away from his side and slowly lifts the bottom of his jacket away from his torso. Doctor Paste Face takes in a sharp breath. Even I wince, and I've been hoping Mr. Tan Jacket would drop dead. The wound is obviously infected. No wonder his face is pale. It's a miracle the man is on his feet at all.

"I'll need to treat that right away," says the doctor.

"Her first," he says.

"Yes, of course..."

Dr. Paste Face turns to one of the stacked crates on the ground behind him. He pulls out a bathroom scale and sets it on the ground in front of the table. Behind Mr. Tan Jacket, Muscles comes back into the tent. Mr. Tan Jacket says something to him. He nods and hands Mr. Tan Jacket his rifle.

Before I know what's happening, Mr. Tan Jacket takes two steps my direction and unexpectedly smashes the butt of the rifle into my gut.

I crumple to my knees instantly. Pain, like a hot liquid, floods from my belly into my groin. I retch some sort of acid-like bile into my throat. I grit my teeth to the point of grinding them into pieces. I'm just beginning to raise my head to get a breath of air when Dr. Paste Face and Muscles grab Misty from behind. A shriek of surprise flies out of her mouth. She struggles helplessly against them and I can't react; I can't do anything – I am hurting so bad. The doctor holds some sort of white cloth firmly over her mouth. Her arms fail in panic until her eyes slowly dull out, she drifts into unconsciousness, and her arms go limp.

Before I can fully register what is happening, Mr. Tan Jacket swings at me again with the butt of the rifle, catching me in the cheek. A lightning bolt sears through my temple so sharp and so sudden, I'm knocked completely onto my side. I don't even have enough instinct left to try and stop my fall; I just hit the dirt full-force. I don't even know why I'm still conscious, but I can dully see the dirt in front of my nose. My right arm flops away from me as if it's trying to escape the pain in my body. My hand claws at the ground, like a spasm. I can feel the grit in my palm and I swear I must be missing a book-sized chunk of my skull. If Mr. Tan Jacket had been in full health, his swing to my head would have killed me for sure. I'm hurting so bad; I wish he had killed me.

My vision seems to go in and out of focus and fuzzy glittering stars swell up in my vision. My head throbs at a higher and higher pitch. I'm sure my skull is going to explode into a fireball of blood and brains any second. I wish it would explode and end this agony. If I could breathe, I would scream. Mr. Tan Jacket stands triumphantly in front of me. He hands the rifle back to Mr. Muscles, kneels, grabs a handful of my hair and pulls. My head hurts so badly, I can't tell if he's pulling a handful of my hair out by the roots or not. His pull on

273

my hair is like yanking on the bit in a horse's mouth. I've got no choice. I'm forced to my hands and knees, neck bent back, blearily looking into Mr. Tan Jacket's shark-like eyes.

I'm swimming against the blackness that wants to swallow up my mind. Unconsciousness is a few seconds away. He pulls my head backward as if he's testing how far he can pull before my neck snaps in two. Weakly, as if pushing my hands through liquid glue, I raise one hand and limply grab hold of his wrist. He leans forward, his gnashing teeth just inches from my face.

"You will drown in your own blood," he snarls at me. "When I cut your head off, the whole world will see."

My mouth hangs limp. The pain in my head is so agonizing, I can't think clearly. I'm not even able to be afraid. If cutting my throat stops the pain in my skull, then it's worth it. *Get on with it, dude!* I just want the pounding to stop! Suddenly, he lets go of my hair and I fall back to the ground, gasping against the bone-splitting pain pressing so hard behind my forehead. I'm certain my eyes are going to pop any second from the pounding.

"Do what you have to do, doctor," Mr. Tan Jacket says. "I'll take this one's head as soon as you're done."

"I can't guarantee…"

"There was never any guarantee," interrupts Mr. Tan Jacket. "Make your calculation and get it done."

"We should have evacuated twelve hours ago. Even if I can get the dosage right, they're right on top of us."

"Then you better hurry."

The doctor hesitates, shaking his head, but the look on Mr. Tan Jacket's face is far from patient. Finally, the doctor just shrugs his shoulders.

In a fog, I see Muscles lift Misty's unconscious body and cradle her in his arms. Muscles steps onto the bathroom scale and the doctor crouches a little to look at the result.

"Okay," he says. "I got it."

Muscles puts Misty back on the cot and then steps onto the scale.

"All right, I got it."

"How long?" asks Mr. Tan Jacket.

"Just a few minutes," the doctor answers. He goes over to the laptop and punches a few keys, looks at the screen, then reaches into a crate. He carefully removes a syringe and a vial. "The vaccine is a little trickier to calculate – especially in terms of timing."

"Not the vaccine, use the virus." The doctor stops prepping the syringe and looks up.

"What are you talking about?" he says. "We give her the vaccine. You mean him?" he says, pointing at me.

"No," says Mr. Tan Jacket. "I mean her. She gets the virus."

"That wasn't the plan. This is…ah…not what…"

"Do it now," Mr. Tan Jacket says firmly. He glances quickly at Mr. Muscles, just a flick of his eyes and the doctor doesn't miss it.

"Plans change doctor," Mr. Tan Jacket says coldly. "We've already paid half your fee, but I make the plans."

Mr. Muscles shifts the AK-47 ever so slightly. His gaze seems to bore into the doctor.

"Of course, of course," says the doctor. He licks his bottom lip nervously; his eyes shift quickly around the tent from me to Misty to Mr. Tan Jacket. "Plans change. That's fine. There's not a problem, right?" He holds up the syringe and the vial as if showing them he's being honest. He sets both on the table and then reaches back into the crate. For a moment, he fumbles inside, seems to change his mind, and then carefully shows Mr. Tan Jacket a second vial and syringe.

"Here we go," he says. "You want the same timing?"

"Obviously," says Mr. Tan Jacket. The doctor nods, preps the syringe and shuffles over to the cot.

I'm afraid to move, but I twist my head a little to see what the doctor is doing. The pain in my head has settled down into the worst migraine headache I've ever felt – it's like a baby porcupine crawled up my nose and started rolling around inside my nasal cavity. It's gut-sickening agony. To try and see better I move my head again and despite my best efforts, a full groan escapes my lips. I'm really hurting. The cold ground almost feels good on my screaming skull, so I sort of roll my temple back and forth trying to suck up some of the coolness.

The doctor pulls down the corner of Misty's skirt, swipes the top of her cheek with an alcohol wipe, and gives her the shot in one swift, practiced motion. He steps away and walks back to the table. Mr. Tan Jacket mumbles something to Mr. Muscles.

"That should do the trick," Doctor Paste Face says. He puts the vial and syringe down on the table. "Now, we should take a look at that wound…"

Suddenly, Muscles swings the A.K. into firing position. The doctor must have been anticipating something, because he leaps to one side just as Muscles fires. I'm surprised the old bat is so agile. I guess when you're dodging bullets your youth comes back to you. The doctor rolls over and comes up with a gun of his own that he must have had hidden in his waistband. He fires three times. Mr. Tan Jacket yells and falls backward out of the tent. I'm yelling something too, lashing my hands and knees against the dirt, trying to crawl out of the way. Muscles doesn't notice me since he's falling forward, dead as a stone. I can't tell if Mr. Tan Jacket was hit or not before he flew out of the tent.

"Plans change," yells the doctor. He fires three more shots at the tent flap and someone outside the tent shrieks. I can only hope it's a terrorist getting his scalp rearranged by a bullet.

Still sick and dizzy, I roll to my knees. My hands shake. I look at Misty on the cot. She's so completely unconscious, she hasn't moved. I can see her chest rising and falling with her breathing, so I know she wasn't hit. I look at the terrorist and think for one brief second about going for his rifle when I hear the doctor right behind me.

"I knew it," he wheezes. "I knew…stab me in the back…too good to be true…always is for me."

I look at him, hunched on the ground behind the card table with his back against the crates. It's obvious he's in trouble. A huge bloodstain spreads slowly across his chest. His shirt is already soaked in red. His face was already deadly pale and now it's turning a sick shade of blue. He holds the gun, aimed squarely at my head.

"They'll be coming...for you," he says. "Cut your head off...mercy to kill you now." He seems to consider that idea for a moment. He curses and then coughs harshly. Blood splatters from his mouth onto his chin. He wipes the blood away, looks at his hand, and then shrugs.

"Not much time," he says.

"Let us go," I whisper. "I can carry her..."

"She's dead already," he says.

A cold nausea sweeps over me. All I've been doing for days is trying to keep us alive. I crawl over to the cot completely ignoring the fact the doctor aims a gun at me. She isn't dead! She continues to breath. I whip my head around to face the doctor.

"What did you do to her!" I yell. "What do you mean, 'she's dead already?'"

"They think so," he says. "Supposed...to give her the virus...about three days...starts and then contagious...for about ten days...half the others have it...already."

"What was it you said?" I yell. "About a vaccine. You can give her..."

"Already did," he sputters. I can hear blood gurgling in his throat. "They...double crossed...me, didn't give her...but they think..."

Outside, I hear shouts. Someone is coming. The doctor almost lazily aims the gun past me at the tent flap and fires three more rounds. I crouch away from the sound. The doctor simply sets the gun down on his knee. He fumbles to pull out a second clip from his pocket. He pops the used clip out of the gun and snaps the new one in to replace it. I scramble on my hands and knees to the card table. My headache still pounds so harshly, I'm afraid to get to my feet.

"Please," I plead. "She's gonna be okay, right?"

"They'll...be here..." His eyelids start to drop. Real terror drops onto me. I scramble forward and take a hold of his shirt.

"No!" I yell in his face. "No. Stay with me."

He doesn't answer. I'm not sure if he's gone or not, but I can't wait either. I jump to my feet. The motion sends a wave of dizziness

277

over me, so I fight for a moment to stay on my feet. Suddenly, I feel a sharp twinge in the back of my calf.

Behind me, the doctor chuckles softly. I look down and realize he's stabbed me with a syringe. His eyes are open again and he has the gun raised, aimed at me. I step backward a few paces.

"What the…"

"You…really want…help her?"

"Yes," I say desperately. "What do I do?"

Outside the tent, I hear shouts. I look that way and then back at the doctor. There's no time. I've got to grab Misty and run.

"You'll live now," he says, dropping the syringe. "Leave her…run."

"I can't…"

"You can't carry…she's dead weight," he says. "They want…her found alive…anyway. Rescue should be…almost here."

"What do you mean…?"

"Shut up!" he says savagely. "I've got…a minute…you…listen." He aims the gun at the tent entrance. "Changed the plan on me…" he laughs lightly. "Should have known…I was dead weight…but I'll…last laugh."

He gestures at me with his free hand to come near. I'm still half-whacked from getting my brain beat in by the butt of a rifle, so I sort of hobble halfway back to him, all shaky and sick like a guy having a seizure.

"A-1 Storage," says Doctor Paste Face. "Bellingham…number three…1776…you got that?"

"What?" I splutter helplessly. "How does that help…"

"Repeat it," the old man hacks loudly. "Repeat it back."

"I don't…"

"A-1".

"Storage…uh…Bellingham…"

"Number three…"

"Is that a unit?"

"1776".

"1776…what is that?"

The doctor gestures at me to come closer. I kneel in front of him, almost hypnotized by the nearly-black blood dribbling down his chin.

"Don't trust Woods..."

The doctor's voice is literally gurgling. Blood bubbles out of his mouth with each word and his eyes seem to fade as I watch.

"Go," he croaks. "...before change...my mind."

He gestures with his head at the back of the tent. I scoot back and nearly fall over my own knees. I stumble to my feet and I don't care what he says – I'm going to pick her up and run. I don't care how far I get either – I can't just leave her.

"Leave her," the doctor croaks. I step toward Misty and the doctor shoots. The bullet buzzes so close to my side, it feels like an invisible electric eel sliding past my waist. I crouch down reflexively.

"I can't just leave her!" I scream back at him. "You're going to die anyway. Let us go."

"Stupid kid," he says. "Want her alive...rescue team...find her alive...the whole...point...run..."

He fires at me again. The bullet shreds a quarter-inch hole in the tent canvas behind me.

I look desperately at Misty, then back at the doctor. Outside, I hear shouts and men running. Suddenly, a hail of bullets tears through the top of the tent canvas. I fall flat on my belly, but they're shooting high. They're afraid to hit Misty...the doctor must be right!

But I can't just leave her.

The doctor fires again, the bullet searing the air close to me. He's driving me toward the back of the tent – away from Misty. I glance back at her, then back at him. He's going to die any second and by the look in his eye, I know he's going to shoot me if I don't bail out. I hesitate for one more second, then furiously elbow-crawl like a man on fire toward the back of the tent. I lift the bottom of the canvas. Overhead, another volley of bullets slams into the top of the tent. I look back at the doctor. He takes aim at the front of the tent and squeezes off a round. He looks at me.

"Don't trust Woods...Go!"

279

He squeezes off another round and I'm under the tent. The ground outside is slushy. Heat from the generator has melted enough snow to make a slip-and-slide of black mud and ice. I'm terrified and sick with guilt from leaving Misty behind. I pull myself hand-over-hand, through the mud until I'm right behind the generator. I roll to my hands and knees. A few feet away is a log. Behind me, I hear the doctor fire again, but then he curses. He must be out of ammunition.

There's nothing more I can do. I can't go back for her. If he's right, the terrorists will simply leave Misty unconscious on the cot. If he's right, then not far away, I should find a rescue team.

If he's right...

Twenty-Two

I crouch behind the log like a wounded, hunted animal – afraid to move, more afraid to stay still. My head pounds and the fuzzy glitter of stars in my eyes glow so brightly I'm having a hard time seeing. Behind me, I hear shouts. The generator still hums and puffs an acrid white-blue smoke. I can see the puff from the exhaust rising above the log. Any moment now, they'll realize the doctor is dead and I'm missing. Any second now, and they'll figure out I slipped under the back canvas of the tent. I glance down at my shirt. It's covered in sticky, cold mud, like having a frosting of half-frozen dog turds lathered onto my chest. I must have left a swipe of mud three feet wide pointing directly at the log. Any idiot can see exactly which way I went. But still, I don't move.

I can't believe I'm alive. And I can't believe I left her. I've spent three days trying to keep Misty alive and now I'm running into the bush again – but without her. It's like being at the funeral again. I'm stuck, paralyzed, because I don't know which way to go, what to do, how to feel!

Behind me, at the tent, a shriek of rage and desperation cascades into the trees and the sound jerks me back to my senses. I recognize Mr. Tan Jacket's voice. He shouts and spits something in his native language and it's enough to get me moving. I fly to my feet. My toes bore into the dirt as I scramble, head and shoulders bent nearly double, away from the tent. I run crouched over, slapping wet branches away from my face for at least a hundred yards before I look back.

The top of the smaller tent has been shredded by gunfire. Mr. Tan Jacket and two other men stand in front of it and he shouts and gestures with his hands like a man completely out of his mind with rage. Mr. Tan Jacket looks my way and in one fatal second, we lock eyes. Just as he takes a step in my direction, I tear my gaze away from his, fling myself into the woods and run.

I swear he's snapping at my heels like a rabid wolf. I flail forward and then leap off a broken log into a small depression that runs like a valley between two mounds of earth. I don't think - I just run. Fear, like a drug, shoots through my arms and legs and I swear I've never run so fast in my life. I'm the wounded animal again…they're the wolves…and they're coming…

I keep running for at least twenty minutes, glancing back over my shoulder over and over again until I'm winded and faintly sick to my stomach. I stop for a second and look back again.

Nothing. Nothing but trees.

Why aren't they right behind me?

Something clicks in my mind: *why bother with me?* Misty is the prize; I've known that all along – so I'm not important. Mr. Tan Jacket may want to torture me because I speared his perfect little plan, but he's got the girl now.

So, they won't be after me. I'm dead weight, unimportant, a nuisance, and Mr. Tan Jacket has better things to do now.

I thought they wanted Misty to hold her as a hostage or kill her live on the internet - only it isn't about leverage or a viral video; I know that now after what I overheard, after what the doctor did. They wanted to intentionally infect her with something.

But why? If they wanted to kill her, wouldn't it make a bigger splash to parade her in front of a video camera and then hack off her head? And why were they arguing about how the doctor had already "done it" thirty times? Done what? Infected thirty people…but why? I mean, even if the whole hijacking was about infecting everybody with some sort of biological weapon, why spend so much time and effort to track down Misty? They could have put a virus in our in-flight snack or put it in the ventilation system – unless it's something

282

that can't be made airborne. I guess that's possible, but why not infect Misty at a restaurant or when she was asleep in the hotel in Anchorage? Why argue about the vaccine and infect some people and not others?

I look back again and still, there's no one following me. I don't hear anyone, I don't see anyone, but they couldn't have been a hundred yards away when Mr. Tan Jacket saw me. They *should* be right on my heels.

Just thinking about that makes, the hairs on the back of my neck stand up. I may not see them, but I feel them, like they've all got invisibility shields on and they're right behind me. I almost bounce away, like a scared jackrabbit and I don't quit making my legs hammer up and down until I suddenly burst out of the trees into a sizeable clearing. The absence of trees and brush makes me feel disoriented – so I stop. I feel exposed, like standing on the edge of a cliff with the weight of a vast and empty space only a step away.

I'm seized with cramps in my stomach, so I lean over, resting my elbows on my knees as I gasp for air, light-headed and shaky. I don't know how far I've run from the camp, but I'm basically out of energy. My legs feel like I'm walking on stilts made from dry spaghetti noodles. I swear my legs are going to snap any second just from holding up my weight. I haven't had anything to eat since yesterday and nothing to drink since earlier this morning when we stopped at the last creek. I look behind me again.

Still – nothing but trees.

For some reason, even though I saw the look on Mr. Tan Jacket's face, even though I'm pretty sure from his point of view nothing short of skinning me alive, slowly, is going to soothe his rage – they're not coming after me! I've been running like a frightened antelope in a stampede for thirty or forty minutes, making no effort to be quiet or cover my tracks, just blind panic, yet I haven't seen any sign on my back trail that they're following me. I haven't heard anything either. They're just not coming after me. I'm home free.

So why don't I feel any better?

There was nothing I could have done! I couldn't have carried her. What was I supposed to do? The doctor gave me one choice; Doctor Paste Face was going to shoot me himself unless I ran! Whatever he wanted to do with Misty was already done. I did the best I could. I couldn't have done anything else. I had no choice.

So, why am I disgusted with myself? Why do I feel so sick inside? I'm having a vision of myself standing like a shield over Misty as the terrorists rush in – but it doesn't end well. All I can see is a stupid kid getting blown in half. Just standing there wouldn't have done anything to help her. I didn't have a weapon. Even if I could have thrown her over my shoulder and run – how far could I have gotten, stumbling under her hundred and fifteen pounds of dead weight before they gunned us both down? And if I had tried to carry her, how could I have gotten her out of the tent when there was only one entrance guarded by guys with guns - not to mention the dying doctor who was already shooting at me on the inside? I was able to slip under the back canvas of the tent – what was I supposed to do with Misty? Drag her limp body under the canvas by one arm like a dead fish?

But I can't convince myself. Horrible, gut-wrenching guilt pours over me. I feel the sting of tears in my eyes. I want so badly to go back, to find her, to do something, anything, to make this horrible feeling go away. Some Marine I turned out to be! Marines don't leave someone behind!

I turn around as if I'm going to go back, but I know that's stupid. They'll kill me the second they get sight of me. I turn around the other way, as if I'm going to go forward, but I don't know where to go. I don't know what to do. Frustration, like a head of steam in a boiling teapot, shoots out of my mouth in a roar. I shout something in an unknown language, something savage and desperate, until my throat feels raw. The echo swirls away until it's swallowed up in the stillness. I turn around again, daring myself to just grab a stick and charge the terrorist camp like a medieval knight on a one-way mission. Instead, my foot catches a root and I fall to my knees.

I'm a little stunned by the fall, so I just stay still for a while, on my knees. My heart thumps heavily in my ears, my breathing comes quick and shallow. I look up at the tree line, my vision blurred by tears and I think, *I've been here before*. I remember crying out that day at the funeral, looking at the trees through the blur of tears in my eyes, calling out to the God I believed in but couldn't see or hear or touch. And He answered me. Not that second and not with angels of fire or lightning from heaven. Still - when a total stranger knocked on my door, I know it was His answer.

So, I know what I have to do - I have to believe!

I haven't done a whole lot of praying in the last few days. You would think with everything I've been through, I wouldn't have neglected to talk to God. But I've hardly said a word to Him. I don't know why. It's like I've been on autopilot - just one foot in front of the other, don't think too much, don't feel too much…and don't pray. I mean, I don't know what to expect if I pray anyway. Prayer isn't like magic or the absolute guarantee everything is going to turn out smelling like jasmine on a summer day just because you talk to God. My dad warned me a thousand times about that sort of thinking. He once told me to remember that every person Jesus healed back in His day, 2,000 years ago, is currently dead! That picture really stuck with me. I had never thought of those miracles that way before – but it's true. They all died of old age or something, even though the finger of God Himself had touched them. So, just getting a miracle in the moment doesn't mean the natural course of life won't take over. And Dad reminded me, over and over again, how many great prophets and preachers prayed their little hearts out and didn't get what they wanted.

Prayer, he told me, isn't about getting what you want; it's about getting what God wants. Suddenly, not praying seems like the dumb thing to do.

"So, what do you want, God?" I ask aloud. "What do you want me to do?"

I look down at the mud and snow at my knees, shake my head, and look back at the trees. The air is so cold, it feels like acid in my

285

lungs and I hate what I'm *not* doing, because I *need* to be doing something - running or fighting or dying, not just kneeling with my knees in the mud wondering…and waiting. I mean, I believe, I really do, but for so long and in so many ways, God seems so indifferent to me. It's like, I know He's real, but all my babbling prayers in the dark feel like just so many words hitting the ceiling. I've prayed so many times, asked for so many things, and the world carries on without taking any notice of me. It's as if God continues to touch and move things behind the scenes like an unseen chess master, but my little part of the whole thing is too small to matter.

No…I don't believe that, I don't want to believe that – it just feels that way whether I believe it or not. And sometimes, feelings are too real to explain away.

"What am I supposed to do now?" I ask aloud. "I know you don't…you know…throw a voice out of the sky anymore but…I need something. If you just want me to quit, if you just want me to die…this whole thing - is this just how I'm supposed to die? I mean, God, that just doesn't make sense. So…tell me what to do…"

I shake my head and look down again. A few feet from me is a patch of snow. In the center, the snow has partially melted, creating a clear bowl of water with a white-blue bottom. I'm caught by how nice it looks, something so clean and fresh thrown onto a field of ugly, half-frozen dead ferns and mud. Just looking at it fires my thirst up. I don't have any specific thought telling me what to do, but I find myself crawling over to the snow bowl. I put both hands on both sides of the bowl in the snow and lean over to drink. It's the coolest, clearest water I can ever remember drinking. Every sip seems to calm me as much as cool my throat. I didn't realize how thirsty I was.

It's exactly what I need.

Exactly. It's almost as if a water fountain opened right at my feet. Like water in the desert. Yes! Sunday School stories! The children of Israel wander through the desert and what does God do? He gives them water, right out of a rock. They're busy sniping and moaning about their situation and all of a sudden - water for the waterless. Right when they needed it, right where they were.

I remember the stories. I remember believing them. It never crossed my mind to wonder what the people in the desert *felt* like before the water came out of the rock. I grew up thinking the Israelites were a troop of weasels - too busy griping about their situation to remember that God had their back. Suddenly, I'm not so down on them.

"The Lord is my shepherd," I say quietly. "I shall not want. He makes me lie down in green pastures; He leads me beside quiet waters..."

Slowly, I get to my feet. I wipe a drop of water off my chin with the back of my hand and I'm surprised to find stubble scraping my hand. I'd forgotten. I'm only seventeen, going on eighteen, so I probably need to shave twice a week at the most. If I need a shave, it can only mean one thing – I'm not dead yet!

I make myself start walking toward the tree line – back the way I came. I know what I have to do now. I'm not sure how I know or even *what* I know exactly, but I guess that's the mystery in prayer. I asked Him what to do – and now I know.

I don't stand a chance against terrorists with automatic weapons. If they find me, they won't hesitate to kill me on the spot. I've given them way too much headache. Whatever game Mr. Tan Jacket was playing, letting me live is over now. So, I'm careful, as quiet and careful as I know how to be. I creep back to the tree line and find a stick along the way that's about three feet long. It will make a suitable club, but I'm not hunting terrorists. I've already killed one man with my bare hands and another by tossing him into a ravine full of razor sharp rocks and what I've learned is that killing someone isn't easy. This isn't a movie and I'm not a hero. I'm under no daydream I can sneak up on Mr. Tan Jacket and whack his brains out with my stick before he or another terrorist blows me full of holes.

On the other hand, they won't be expecting me. They would never dream I would double back. I figure if I can get close enough to the camp, maybe at night, I can slip back into the tent. Misty should be awake by then. They won't suspect I'm creeping around in the dark, so I think I can get back into the camp! Of course, I don't know

287

how I'm going to get her back out again. I guess I'll cross that bridge when I get there. In the meantime, I know I have to find my way back.

Now that I'm a little calmer, I can think clearer. I've been running and zigzagging away from the camp for at least thirty or forty minutes and I can't see the lake any longer, so I'm effectively lost.

But I'm almost convinced of it now - I don't think they're chasing me at all. I'm more likely to die of hypothermia if they just let me go and they've got at least sixty passengers to guard.

Still, that's just an idea. I could be wrong.

The look in Mr. Tan Jacket's eyes was serial-killer ugly. He may want to find me just so he can have the satisfaction of cutting off my fingers and toes one at a time. It's one thing to be confident they're probably not looking for me – it's another thing to be a moron. I'll have to be incredibly careful.

I also have to find my way back and that could be a challenge. I'm not a hunter decked out in camo with a dozen years experience tracking deer. My training is limited to what George taught me about basic survival when we lived in Alaska. Sure, I can make a fire, catch a fish, and figure out which way is north from the moss on the trees, but other than that, I stick out in the bush like a housecat at a dog rescue.

What I do know is that sudden movements and noise are what give you away in the wild. George was insanely careful and deliberate whenever he walked through the forest. He routinely snuck up on me, scaring the sweat right out of my pores, and then laughing at how much he was able to scare me. So, he didn't spend a lot of time teaching me how to sneak around – it was more fun to keep me forever looking over my shoulder. Besides, he said I was a white kid from the city, which meant I was hopeless from birth as far as he was concerned. He thought that was funny too. Only I know he was just playing with me. I knew in my heart he really cared about me.

So, I tried sneaking up on him – many times. I never got within fifty feet of him before he called my name. I don't suppose the terrorists are bushmen like George so based on what I *do* know, maybe I can creep up on them.

I crouch into the half-stooped position George said worked best for hunting. I set my feet carefully, toe to heel, and use every bit of cover I can find: a boulder here, a tuft of huckleberry bush, then a half-burned stump – anything to conceal me. Carefully and painfully slowly, I work my way back the way I came.

At first, I'm afraid I might not be able to retrace my steps since I only have a general idea which direction I ran. But I recognize a dead tree, charred and split by lightning. Then, I see a boulder I remember because it looks like a sway-backed horse. After about an hour, I'm surprised at how many landmarks I recognize and before long, I know exactly which way to creep along.

I must have been really running, because it takes at least two hours of careful movements from one hiding place to another before I get any sense of the terrorist camp. Dusk is already threatening to fall on the forest, so I won't have long to wait. In fact, I don't see the camp right away in the gathering gloom. Instead, it's a distant voice that tells me I'm getting close and the sound immediately drives me to my knees. Another distant sound of a human voice makes me hold my breath. Everything around me seems to tense up as if the whole forest is listening.

I thread my way carefully and quietly along the length of a fallen log, stooping so low I'm almost crawling on my hands and knees. I find a depression in the ground, like a bowl or a crater behind a huge, rotten old stump. It's a perfect place to crawl closer without being seen. I slip into the crater, crawl forward toward the stump, and then slide down into an elbow-crawl right up to the base of the stump.

I peer around the base of the stump and the sight of three armed terrorists patrolling along the side and the back of the big tent is a little alarming. I don't see Mr. Tan Jacket. What's worse – I don't see any sign of the second tent at all. It's completely gone – the tent, the generator, even the ground has been groomed in some way to hide the fact there was ever a tent there at all.

289

I pull back, bewildered and scared. Why did they get rid of any sign of the second tent? I know they shot up the top of it, but why scrape away everything down to the dirt on the ground? It's almost as if they're trying to hide...

Of course! They're trying to cover their tracks!

It suddenly occurs to me what a monumentally stupid thing I'm doing. I crept back right into the teeth of the monster with nothing more than a stick and the ridiculous idea I can slip in right under Mr. Tan Jacket's nose and somehow steal his prize hostage. He's spent nearly three days trying to find her and somehow, I think he's dumb enough to leave her unguarded! Now that the second tent is gone, she must be planted right in the middle of the rest of the passengers. What am I supposed to do now? Try and slip under the back canvas of the big tent, creep unnoticed past Stan and Mr. Towns and half a dozen terrorist guards and convince Misty to come with me for another wonderful adventure in the woods?

Great move, Kyle! You've proven to be just about as stupid as Stan thinks you are! You escaped with some sort of information that might make sense to somebody about this whole mess, only to wander right back where Mr. Tan Jacket can scoop you up like the dog turd you're proving to be! *Brilliant!*

I squat farther down into a small patch of half-dead ferns to try and think. I guess I wasn't thinking. What was I doing, turning around and going back? Did I honestly think this was God's leading? That's stupid beyond words. What did I have to go on...a puddle of clear water and some sort of "knowing" in my heart of hearts? What did I really know?

Only that I was feeling insanely guilty.

Suddenly, I get the shakes and it's not because it's cold. I've been running on pure adrenaline for days. I never really had a plan – it was just run and slide and hide and go from one idea to the next as soon as the next idea popped into my head. It was like writing a song on three different instruments in a half a dozen keys at the same time – no rhyme, no reason – just a clash of sounds all clanging together in one big ugly mess. Now that the music has stopped, the silence is deafening. And the truth is, I'm more lost in this moment than I've ever been.

I can't figure out any way to get Misty back. Misty's ankle is busted. There's no way to get her back...I've come all this way back here just to figure that out and now I feel like an eight-year-old caught stealing money from his mother's purse.

So why didn't Doctor Paste Face kill me? Obviously, because he wanted me to get whatever he has stashed away in the storage unit in Bellingham. But what good would anything he has in a storage locker do? Everybody already knows the terrorists are guilty. Whatever records he has can only point out the obvious and if a rescue team is on its way, then the terrorists are going to get killed or captured anyway.

And why was the plan to infect Misty, knowing there was a rescue in the works? It just doesn't make any...

Wait a second...

There are at least sixty passengers, but Mr. Tan Jacket said the doctor had "done it thirty times". Infected thirty...not sixty...Why?

Again, to cover their tracks! That's the only explanation. If some of the passengers get sick, but others don't – it will look like any other case of a cold or the flu. No one would suspect anything out of the ordinary if some folks get sick after spending a few cold, wet days in the woods. And anyone who comes into contact with an infected person...will probably get infected too. That means Governor Woods could be their target. So why did the doctor say not to trust...

Oh snap!

Don't trust Woods, he said!

The election is in less than three weeks. It's looking like a landslide for Woods. But he is running for Vice President. And if the new president gets sick and dies...then Woods...

I let out a low, slow curse word. I know I'm not supposed to use bad language, but sometimes...if it looks like poop and smells like poop – it's poop. *Just sayin*!

That's why they knocked her out before they gave her the shot. She won't have any memory of it. And I'm betting whatever other passengers they infected won't have any memory of being injected either. Maybe they jumped them, one at a time, when they went out to the portable toilets. Maybe that's why the doctor was in a whole separate tent – unseen by the passengers.

So, why didn't they try to infect her some other way? Why hijack an airliner, land in a lake, put this whole ruse together instead of just spraying her with a fake can of hairspray to get the virus into her system?

Because a hijacking guarantees sympathy for Governor Woods! It puts the White House in his pocket. No one will suspect the disease was planted because half the passengers won't get it. And if the disease is something sort of normal, like a particularly nasty case of pneumonia or something that's only deadly for a little while and then it disappears, then no one will suspect anything. Even if they had failed, even if we had all died in the lake-landing, there would have been worldwide sorrow and attention for Governor Woods and he would be guaranteed at least the Vice Presidency. And then...

But it didn't fail. Instead, the hijacking guarantees the new President will visit poor Governor Woods' daughter after the rescue so everyone in the fawning media can take his picture at the hospital. That's why Mr. Tan Jacket and the doctor were arguing about timing. The right place, the right time, the right sickness and bingo – you control who is going to be the most powerful man in the world.

But how much of this was planned by Woods? Is the guy so evil he would kill his own daughter just to get to the Presidency? Or is he a pawn too? And who is going to believe me? All I have is a crazy idea, something I overheard. Who is going to believe me? Without the laptop, without the doctor – it's just an insane story made up by a seventeen-year-old kid.

This *is* insane. I don't even know what Doctor Paste Face has in his stupid storage locker. I can't trust anyone either! Who am I supposed to tell? Even if Paste Face has detailed records about the virus, if I tell the wrong person - and that could be anybody – they'll get there first, destroy the evidence, maybe go the extra mile and silence me too. Even detailed evidence probably isn't going to be enough. Any decent lawyer can make that evidence look like the Looney Tunes of a brain-damaged old doctor.

Besides, the terrorists aren't idiots; they wouldn't have let Paste Face keep anything really incriminating. What could he possibly have that would convince anyone the new President conspired to murder his way into the Oval Office? The doctor is dead – and if my connect-the-dots idea is right, then the terrorists have already covered their tracks. No one is ever going to find the doctor's body or his connection to the hijacking. Anything he has in his storage locker is useless.

Except for one thing – me!

I'm a witness, the only witness. I heard what they said, I watched them inject Misty, and if I have whatever evidence the doctor left in his storage locker, it could bring down a President! I'm in more danger right now than I've been since Soda Can Man took a swing at the flight attendant on Day One.

This whole thing is really freaking me out.

I let off another curse word, this one a little nastier than the last. I get to my feet and take a step down into the crater – back the way I crept in. I feel like a complete idiot, running first one way, then the other and now, back the way I came once again.

Just as I step forward a bit more confidently, a furious blizzard of sounds erupts all around me, like a sudden chorus of hissing demons has started to sing. I spin around, trying to find the source of the sound, only to see all three terrorists guarding the camp fall like dominos.

I've heard this sound before, like a fhoosh and a wump. Rifles with silencers! The rescue team! I walked right into them and the assault on the terrorist camp is fully underway.

This is just registering in my brain when some gigantic force literally lifts me off the ground! A hand wraps solidly over my mouth and a second arm wraps right around my waist, lifting me completely off the ground. Someone has grabbed me from behind!

293

I flail and scream, my voice muffled completely by the hand over my mouth. I literally hang two feet off the ground, wrapped up tightly in someone's grip. Then a horrific vision comes to life right in front of me - the ground sort of opens, like the bushes are coming to life and I flip out, throwing every ounce of energy back at whoever is holding me.

But it's not the ground coming to life – it's a soldier, completely covered in camouflage, coming up off the ground. Bits of fern and weeds are stuffed all over his body like he's carrying a piece of the forest floor pasted to his back. He was lying right at my feet, completely hidden. I must have crawled within inches of him as I came up to the base of the stump. My eyes are so wide I'm surprised they don't pop out of my head. Whoever has me wrapped up in his arms is terribly strong. I shake so hard it's a wonder whoever is holding me doesn't lose his grip, but the soldier in front of me slowly points to his left breast. He quickly pulls down a flap of fabric to show me a patch - a Canadian flag. He looks back at me and gives me a thumbs-up.

"You're one of the passengers, right?" he whispers. I nod my head as well as I can, still held tightly from behind. The soldier gestures at whoever is holding me, and I feel myself slowly come back to earth as he lowers me down. The iron grip over my mouth relaxes and I let out a gasp.

"You have to hurry," I say in a rush. My voice cracks a little. "Misty...they gave her...something..."

"Keep your head down," the soldier says in a harsh whisper. Out of the corner of my eye, I see half a dozen or more camouflaged figures rushing in toward the camp.

"There's no time," I hiss. I'm a little angry that he's not getting what I'm saying. "There was another tent. And a laptop, you have to find that laptop..."

I feel the soldier behind me put his hand on my shoulder. I turn to look at him and he has his face so close to my ear, I jump back a little.

"You need to calm down and stay put," he says. "We've got this under control."

"You don't understand," I say a little louder. "They want her to be found alive. They gave her something."

I take a step to back away. I'm shaking again, confused by a Canadian special forces team lying just a few hundred yards from the camp, guilty about Misty, terrified these guys won't get to her and even more afraid that I'm right. No one is going to believe me, and I don't have any time to prove my story. I take another step backward. Something in me just wants to run again. I know these are supposed to be the good guys, but I can't seem to make that register in my brain. I take another step.

"You have to find that laptop," I say, pointing vaguely in the direction of the camp. I'm not making any effort to be quiet now. *They have to understand me!* The first soldier I saw puts up one hand to try and calm me.

"Settle down or we'll have to restrain you," the soldier says firmly.

Around me, several other camouflaged shapes rush forward. In the distance, I hear several shouts.

"There's a laptop," I say again. "You have to get to it before they destroy it." I'm getting a little louder, more insistent, when the soldier I'm looking at gestures at the man standing beside me. Before I know what is happening, both my arms are pulled behind my back, a knee drives forcefully into the back of my legs, I buckle to the ground, and within seconds, my hands and ankles are zip-tied.

It takes a few seconds for me to register the fact that I've been hogtied. I start yelling like an idiot, but the soldier in front of me completely ignores me. He crawls forward to the lip of the crater and I see the boots of the soldier who tied me up pound the dirt a few inches from my nose as he surges forward. The assault is hot and heavy now, hissing shots and a few shouts swirl around me and I'm not even a spectator. All I can do is wait for someone to let me go.

And it turns out to be a long wait.

Shouts and confusing crashes of what sounds like metal on metal ring out for at least an hour, maybe longer. The soldier who first materialized out of the forest floor in front of me eventually slips over the edge of the crater and I lose sight of him. I'm left alone for quite a while, long enough for dusk to finally settle in. Overhead, the clouds have started to break up and a few stars appear, so I try yelling some more, but no one responds. I toss and turn in a wasted attempt to inch worm my way up to the top of the crater to see what's going on. Instead, I only manage to slide to the bottom of the crater. At least there I finally wedge my hogtied ankles against the ground and manage to get into a seated position.

Finally, I hear the distinct sound of a landing helicopter. It must be setting down in the small, cleared area by the lakeshore where we first came ashore. I guess the assault is over and reinforcements have arrived. After about fifteen minutes, I hear more confusing noises, shouts, and then the sound of approaching footsteps. I decide it's time to let loose with a few good yells again.

I have about three minutes to holler before two soldiers descend into the crater. The first thing I say is, "Is Misty okay?" and I don't get an answer. Instead, I get helped to my feet, the zipties get cut, and I find myself rubbing my wrists. One of the men holds a flashlight. He takes a firm hold of my elbow and leads me out of the crater.

The big tent has changed. The canvas sides have been stripped back or flipped up on the roof. Soldiers are everywhere, there's a confusing mass of people, many of them covered in rough green blankets both in the tent and just outside of it. It's the passengers standing shell-shocked in a dream while soldiers weave in and out of them like swordfish darting into a school of mackerel. Some of them are getting onsite medical care and a few are already on stretchers. I don't recognize anyone from this distance. Flashlight beams pierce the darkness and two soldiers work to set up some sort of lighting equipment. Beyond the big tent is the flashing searchlight of the helicopter. From where I stand, I can see at least four bodies on the ground covered in plastic. I wonder if one of them is Mr. Tan Jacket and for some reason, I'm sure he's not there.

296

I'm still at least half a football field away from the other passengers, but I'm not led forward to join the others. Instead, the soldier guides me to a cluster of three men standing apart from everyone else. One of them is dressed in a completely different uniform. It's this man who pulls me aside out of earshot of the others and turns to speak to me.

"Are you Kyle Reynolds?" he asks loudly as he tries to be heard over the sound of the helicopter blades. "I'm Doug Quintan with the American Secret Service. Misty Woods was asking for you."

"She is? Is she okay...?" I answer quickly, but suddenly, I feel hyper-aware. There's something wrong with this situation. I can understand needing to interview everyone, so they can figure out what happened, but why am I not with the rest of the former hostages? Why pick me out so quickly?

"Misty is okay, don't worry – we're already evacuating her. I'm with Governor Woods' secret service detail. I'm here to make sure she's okay. That's why I'm talking to you."

My heart literally skips a beat and then everything in me turns to ice. *Don't trust Woods*...how much did I spout off to the soldier already?

"She's okay?" I ask. "I need to see her. Can I go with her?" I take a step in the direction of the helicopter, but he puts a hand out to stop me.

"She's fine, just fine," he answers. "We'll get you out of here just as soon as we can, but this whole unfortunate incident happened on Canadian soil, so we've got to...you know...interview everyone, get everything sorted out. It's going to be a little while. So...Misty said something about you two being separated from the others."

"Well, I...we got away."

That's a pretty lame explanation, but that little voice, that sixth sense or voice of God, suddenly rings in my ears again. Somehow, I just know I need to be careful. And now I know something about that quiet voice. It was right again! After all, going back to the camp turned out to be the right decision because I nearly stepped on the rescue party. I wonder how long I would have been wandering in the woods if I hadn't gone back.

"But you were with Misty Woods?" he asks. "Right? You escaped into the forest with her at first, right?"

"I...ah...Yes," I say slowly. "I didn't make her follow me...she, she uh...came with me but I didn't, you know, force her to do anything." I can't help giving off a distrustful vibe.

"It's okay. You're not in trouble; I'm just trying to make sure Misty is okay and you said something about them giving her something."

Part of me wants to confess everything. Why should I trust the doctor's warning not to trust Governor Woods? The doctor was a terrorist, an evil man, so why should I believe anything he said?

Then why is a secret service agent connected with Governor Woods already questioning me just minutes after Misty is being evacuated?

Real fear grabs hold of me now. When the silenced rifles started shooting and the terrorists started to fall, I thought it might be all over. Now, the air seems electrified, like there's something hidden around me, something waiting in the dark for me to say or do the wrong thing before it pounces.

"They ah...gave her some protein bars...I was afraid, you know, they might have poisoned them."

"Oh...Okay...you don't have to worry. She's going to get a full medical exam. Nothing to worry about," he says. "And what about this laptop you were so worried about?"

This is the moment. This is when I decide whom to trust – the doctor or Governor Woods. Mr. Tan Jacket wouldn't have driven himself to the edge of death to get Misty for no reason. Paste Face wouldn't have wasted his last breath on a lie either. It only takes me a split second to think about it and decide.

"I'm just...confused...I ah...got hit in the head and I was thinking about my laptop."

"You're sure about that?" he asks. "They said you seemed pretty upset about a laptop."

"Well…it was crazy…you know? They were shooting…and I was, pretty confused."

A huge lump swells up in my throat and my eyes sting with tears. I can spill my guts, tell this guy about the doctor and the virus and everything, and it could make everything worse, not better. If he's part of the plan, he'll just bury whatever I say. Paste Face wasn't lying – and I know it.

I can see that Mr. Secret Service Agent isn't convinced. He hesitates for a second, seems to make up his mind, and then nods at me.

"Okay…I'll pass that on," he says. He turns and walks away, leaving me stranded and alone.

I've spent so long being connected to Misty that without her, I don't know which way to turn. When I first saw her, she took my breath away. She was so far from me, like a celestial being and I was just a mortal. Then the crash brought us together and in the cold and the dark, she opened her heart to me. And now I can say it…

I'm in love with Misty.

But I can't rescue her this time. I can't trust anyone either and I don't even know where they're taking her. There is, however, a storage unit in Bellingham that has answers in it.

So right here…right now…I make up my mind that the gates of hell itself won't keep me from getting there.

End of Book One

Made in the USA
San Bernardino, CA
26 May 2020